Of Polish extraction, Magda Sweetland was born in Edinburgh and educated at George Watson's College and Edinburgh University. As well as having taught for some fifteen years in Britain, she has lived and worked in North America and Europe, and continues to travel widely.

Her first novel, *Eightsome Reel*, was published with the help of a Scottish Arts Council grant and won the Authors' Club First Novel Award for 1985. She has published two further novels, *The Connoisseur* and *The Hermitage*. She now lives in Kent.

Rich Hours

Magda Sweetland

First published in 1995
by HEADLINE BOOK PUBLISHING

First published in paperback in 1996
by HEADLINE BOOK PUBLISHING

A HEADLINE REVIEW paperback

10 9 8 7 6 5 4 3 2 1

ISBN 0 7472 5178 9

Printed and bound in Great Britain by
Cox & Wyman Ltd, Reading, Berks

HEADLINE BOOK PUBLISHING
A division of Hodder Headline PLC
338 Euston Road
London NW1 3BH

In memory of
Robert Millar
in loco parentis

December

Driving to Bury, Morgan thought he'd tried to do too much and set about replanning the schedule of his day. There were three meetings entered in his diary, Bury St Edmunds, then Chelmsford, then Covent Garden, beside the time of each appointment. They covered a logical sweep of countryside but the span of the meetings was less straightforward, or ignored the links between them and the unease that, after all, he might not make it in spite of a precise sense of chronology.

It was a Friday. Lorraine was waiting for him in the entrance hall and, when he walked in, she turned and put the 'Closed' sign up on the outer door for the lunch-hour. He'd rather have slipped in and out without a full-scale marital interview, but she'd changed the locks on the main door, or added to them while he was away, barring easy entry to his own house and his own business. That was final. He was the stranger, no rights, no privileges. Out.

She'd gone as far as washing his clothes, however, and had sorted them into piles on the spare bed to get them out of her way. There was something depressingly name-tagged about these folded belongings, as if he'd been sent away to boarding school and was banished from home for another term. His security, comfort, and a long spell of being attached were suddenly pulled out from under him. Usually when he went away on business trips, Lorraine packed his bags for him, but she wouldn't go as far as that today. She drew the dividing line between a failed marriage and a legal separation. Any volunteering was ruled out.

The house at Bury St Edmunds lay inside the sound of the Cathedral bells and at the right moment they started to peal, alarming the pigeons that had settled, pecking, on the cobbles of the square. The house looked sideways at Dickens's Angel Hotel and

1

the Museum of Horology, and was the fourth point of a compass with the Cathedral. For twenty-five years they'd put up with the bells and the traffic that spilled down the High Street from the marketplace on Saturdays, and the influx of summer visitors who'd stopped off between the cultural highlights of Lavenham and Cambridge – although they didn't know what they were looking for, and never found it. It was cheap to live in a small town like Bury, outside the London commuting radius, and then it became agreeably convenient when the rail link into the capital was upgraded, the M11 motorway opened, and Michael went to the Choir School when he was twelve and subsequently on to Cambridge. Chance turned into foresight, as it rarely did. It had all fitted, a life like ivy growing up the outside of a building which softened its unbecoming angles.

'I've started to hate those bells,' she said. 'They're so dolorous.'

'Why don't you sell up?' The property was worth something, even the rump end of Bury St Edmunds.

'I thought I'd see you settled first.'

He threw more things into a grip. His mother used to speak like that, making him the excuse for not doing something that she had passionately wanted to. I'll wait until you pass your exams. Once you're married, maybe ... Sacrificial women scared him. Did he attract them, or did he make them servile?

'I am making progress. I've got an appointment to see Marise and Boris Fisk later today.'

Lorraine wrinkled up her nose disparagingly. He noticed that she had stopped colouring her hair and, behind the lighter ends, it was predominantly grey. Something else she'd given up on. 'They're such shysters.'

'They're in a spot of bother this time.'

'You mean they said they needed you? Don't you believe it. Just make sure you ... Well—' She shrugged, folding her arms inside the two flaps of her cardigan, like a long and elegant crane folding its wings. 'It's your choice, Morgan. But they've got harder business heads than you. Watch out for their little deals.'

Guardian too, these women. Careful with resources, patching, mending, filling the holes he made in things with quiet stitches.

'Is that all you're going to take with you? I expected you would want to go through it properly, half and half.'

'I've got nowhere to put anything, have I? And besides...'

2

'*Voyageur sans bagages?*'

'For the time being anyway.'

The phone went, nearly as disruptive indoors as the bells were out, and Lorraine moved on to the landing to answer it. Was it on business, he wondered, or pleasure; a friend arranging a concert date, a lover? He would have liked it to be a lover, wouldn't begrudge her that in the way of body comfort.

'Look round,' she called out, with her hand over the mouthpiece. 'You may want to take something after all.'

He browsed, waiting to say a proper goodbye while she went on talking in a murmur. The rooms he walked through revived some of their former selves. They'd never managed to quell the antiquarian habit and had collected a lot of clutter. But then, everything did acquire a story after a quarter of a century. There was a box of cryptic postcards, with messages like 'Having fun and sun' that reminded him of the days when a cheaper postage rate applied if you used not more than five words. Did somebody sit at the GPO and methodically count them? Scenes from the 1950s and 1960s, and already archaic, ruched costumes and box-camera photography. There were a few redundant toys left out on the shelves because they were attractive and well made, his toys and his father's before they were Michael's. And a bookcase full of memorabilia. Rows of Lorraine's paperbacks. She chain-smoked novels, without inhaling. He flicked through, remembering which holidays and journeys they'd accompanied. The inscriptions recorded birthdays gone by, milestone gravestones.

Out of the way, on a top shelf, there were even some of his own books. Publisher's copies of the things he'd slogged over that had failed in spite of his best effort, or had scrabbled together, exciting a quite irritating flurry of critical excitement and success. He'd made money, but spent it more quickly still. Ten years back, he had revamped some of his lecture notes into a television series. The book and the programme turned him into a household name, for a month or two anyway, slotting in between Kenneth Clark and Robert Hughes. It was true, he'd coined a phrase that stuck, a mini motto. It was still widely quoted because it epitomized a change in style, and patterns of ownership, but that wasn't much to build a career on, one slogan for the times. They liked their philosophy neat, the masses. Snappy. They said now that he had triggered something, an art revival, and, in its aftermath, the price war for high-pedigree paintings. That wasn't entirely true. He had just noticed what was happening while it was happening, a rare enough skill, he supposed. Thumbing through, he wondered if he wanted these old books of his enough to filch them from the past. They were here, where he had physically written them, transported from reference book to desk to shelf again, and belonged in place. It was mean-spirited to try and pull them out, wall-crumbling. He wanted to leave a set of memories intact, as if the ideal survived.

'Have you got time to eat? When's your appointment with the Fisks?'

'No, I haven't. At three.'

'Will you have a drink, then?'

'Just coffee would be fine.'

They went downstairs into the kitchen and Morgan put his grip by the door. The business and the house overlapped, with the same entry door for both. People used to say to him, 'Don't you hate it, having strangers downstairs when you're trying to work?' But he was probably a communalist, the product of a big and sprawling family, which meant he felt uncomfortable unless there was a throughput of people. Exclusive marriage, me and thee, didn't suit him. He liked the Saturday afternooners: the men who knew bird's-eye maple from fine walnut by the grain, and the curio-hunting ladies who were filling in a space in their collection, but it provided a mental space that they could share together amicably for an hour. He used to enjoy their conversation. Lorraine didn't know anything technical about the antiques trade, but she did have an instinct for quality; she catered for the careful, local tastes. And did well at it. She kept threading money through the thin spots of his professions, art historian, university lecturer, media man, dealer, critic, down to his most recent stint at being unemployed.

But she was no good at choosing paintings, he thought, as he thumbed through the stacked frames. The two showrooms were their converted living rooms, still homy, with a Victorian sideboard as a counter while its locked drawer, for silver, doubled as the till. She'd got a couple of amateur nineteenth-century watercolours, the equivalent of holiday snapshots of the time, done by Sunday painters in which the Matterhorn looked much the same as Snowdon, or some poor, thin-quality oils dragged down the likeness of grey people in grey suits. Not Richard Wilson, not

4

Augustus John, although he'd laid his hand on both at one time in this room.

'That's the tatty end,' said Lorraine. 'I've got some better stuff over here.'

'Is much coming through?'

'Not at prices I can make a profit on. I had a set of Gustav Doré prints recently, which I sent to auction, and an early Fuseli.'

'Signed?'

'Unfortunately not.'

'I'd like to have seen those.' He'd given her something back, then, in the way of discernment. Not all take.

She poured his coffee. He thumbed through the pile uninterestedly, like a man rummaging through a dull newspaper because it prevents talk. And then, out of the run of mediocre pictures, a face looked up at him which he recognized, the particular shape of the face as much as the handling style. It was a coloured chalk drawing of a young man about twenty years of age, dressed in naval uniform, the eighteenth-century uniform of Nelson and Trafalgar. It was the look in the eyes Morgan remembered, which caught that shift from innocence to boldness, the look of untried youth before it reaches caution.

'What do you reckon this is?'

She glanced at it. 'Norwich school. Thousands floating round.'

'I think it's a Gainsborough.'

'Never,' she said disparagingly, but came to have a second look. 'Near miss. In the style of Gainsborough.'

Morgan knew Gainsborough's portrait of a Dutch sea captain which could easily have been the companion to this picture. There was a long-standing trade route between East Anglia and the Lowlands, wool one way, Delft and spices and wine the other. The drawings would be commissioned as souvenirs to take back home. This strapping lad might even be the captain's midshipman, putting in a sitting before the pair of them dashed off to catch the tide; but why hadn't they come back to collect their portraits? Couldn't they afford the two guineas' fee apiece – which wasn't much even then, but Gainsborough didn't become famous until he went to Bath and painted the fashionable nobility. Had they spent the last of their English money carousing instead, while Thomas the portraitist kicked his heels in his rooms in Sudbury, waiting for payment, not daring to admit it to his wife because she'd say, 'You should always ask for your fee ahead or a deposit down. You can't do anything with those drawings now, can you?' Yes, he knew Mrs Thomas Gainsborough well enough, a stringy woman.

He peered into the details of the drawing, assessing the line, the grainy quality of the paper, the three colours of chalk, and his heart started to pump. A find. Unbelievably, off the square in Bury St Edmunds on a Friday lunch-time, he had found a Gainsborough.

'Take it to the light.'

It was a handsome bit of work, vigorous, fresh, clean, the subject and the style breezy and smacking of the open air. Morgan coveted it more than anything else in the room. The two-hundred-year-old paper had mellowed from grey into a gentle buff, like thinning cloud. He checked that the frame was original, the joints and dowels cut by hand and set with traditional glues. He measured scepticism, he measured wanting, and wanting won. It most emphatically was a Gainsborough.

'How much are you asking for it?'

'Three hundred pounds.'

'It's worth more than that, surely?'

'Probably, but I can't fetch London prices. And I don't think it's genuine.'

'I haven't got three hundred.'

'Oh, I'm not selling it to you. Take it if you want it. It doesn't mean anything to me.'

'Do you know any more about it, where it came from?'

'I know who sold it to me.'

'And?'

'A woman who lives outside town. Her man died last year. He was a bit of a collector and she's had to sell things off to keep the house. I think she's stretched.'

'And this is all you bought from her?'

'It was all I was offered.'

The bareness of the outline whetted his interest. 'Can you remember her name?'

'Naturally, but I'm not at liberty to tell you.'

'Of course not.' But who'd got a house with pictures of this quality left by a casual collector? Constables as well as Gainsboroughs must still be lurking in attics all over Suffolk. He was itching to know more. 'This is going to be bouncing about in the back of the car. I wonder if you've got any padding, some of that plastic, bubbly stuff.'

'Brown paper won't do?'

He shook his head.

'I've some newspapers upstairs that would make a bit of wadding.'

'Great.'

She disappeared. Hurriedly, Morgan ferreted out the ledger that she kept in the sideboard counter. There wouldn't be too many entries in the last year. He ran down the description of the trade items Lorraine had bought, admiring her good order. The picture was filed under October. *White, black and coloured chalk on prepared grey paper. 12 x 10in. Youth in naval dress. Unsigned. 18th C. £175.* Not a bad profit for the two months' care she'd given it. But no name. Only the Initials EP, which he thought meant Express Parcel, and an equally vague address, The Aviary, Odham. He clapped the boards together just in time before she came downstairs with the newsprint, and shoved the ledger back in the cupboard.

This deceit made him uncomfortable, as he watched her meticulously fold the wrapping paper into angles and seal the corners down, not because he'd sneaked a look at the records but because she'd trusted him not to be so callow.

'I hope it's what you think it is,' was Lorraine's judgement. 'Or if it isn't, that you enjoy it all the same.'

He picked up the grip and put the painting under his arm.

Then she leaned forward and pecked him on the cheek. Nearly a kiss.

He drove along the Sudbury road, Gainsborough much in mind. He'd never actually made it to the painter's house in the town, now turned museum. Not today either. He headed in the direction of Odham, thinking he might locate the house of the late collector and the woman who sold his pictures. There were two villages, if he wasn't mistaken, Great and Little Odham, split east and west of the trunk road. But he couldn't remember a house called The Aviary. Couldn't remember a grand house in the district to which it must be attached as a gardener's cottage or a glorified outhouse. The Aviary. What birds did they keep there? Doves? Pigeons? Surely not domestic chickens. The chicken coop wasn't the same thing at all.

Time ran out while he nosed down empty roads. How likely was he to find anyone at home in Odham? And if he did make contact, a fulsome explanation to the occupant would make him late arriving in Chelmsford for the more important interview. Wasn't that the recurring conflict of his priorities? A good painting came before good sense, but once already that day he'd opted for the former, the self-indulgent whim. The minutes rushed by as he idled on the road verge, left or right, deciding between the risk of chasing up an unknown person at an ephemeral address and, ahead of him, the fixed appointment.

He made the wise decision, or the narrow one, closed instead of open-ended, and drove on to the Fisks.

Marise was getting ready for him, tying the neck of her blouse with care. She didn't like her bows floppy but wound the material twice around her neck and looped it in a cravat, then secured the tie under a gold pin. Not mannish. Not feminine. Just right.

'Do you think,' she asked Boris, who strolled about the dressing room, watching the performance, 'that Morgan has got anything left in him?'

'Any work?'

'Any good work?'

Boris gave out opinions reluctantly, a tight man. 'I don't know any more. He used to be sound, but he's had a bad time recently . . .'

Marise wanted very much to engage Morgan, for practical ends, because she really was in a mess with her business outlets, but also because she liked the man with more consistency than she liked other people, liked the way he kept on equally good terms with the egotist who had arrived and the hesitant beginner, gave each person his due and, in thirty years' professional accommodation, hadn't said a single word you could quote in malice. But she was also afraid of him. He had touched fame and came back again with the glow of mission. He believed in a lot of things before he believed in money. He could turn into a champion who ousted her. A period of humility was called for in Morgan and so, although she could have offered him a directorship which would not have been unjustified, she quashed the impulse and was circumspect.

'I can't be sentimental, Boris. You know we said there would be no "old times' sake" for us. I hate losers. And he has lost a lot.'

'Very good. If you have reservations, give him a year's trial. Just one.'

8

She noticed as she fixed her earrings that she was dressing not for a business colleague but to meet a man.

Morgan found his way into the middle of Chelmsford without a hitch and remembered, when he got the hang of the roads again, exactly where their house was. It was a fine period house, Voysey-vintage, rather quaint and chimneyfied for some tastes, but the Fisks had improved its solid points with good grooming over the years and hadn't allowed it to disintegrate into facile prettiness.

A housekeeper let him in and took him to the library. Marise didn't bother to be punctual at home. Nothing harms for waiting, she would say. It was a little offensive, implying her time was more sought after and valuable than his, but it did give Morgan space to order his thoughts. He'd often been a guest here and, in the décor, was most interested in why they changed their pictures round and how. Only one was a constant, an odd picture for the Jewish woman to cherish, always in the same niche, always lit like a shrine. It was a Byzantine icon, sixth century, not much bigger than a postcard, with a later, Cyrillic inscription inside a cartouche: I AM THE WAY. Marise didn't expand on the inconsistency of this image, but rumour had it that she'd hidden with her father in Berlin for the seven years of the purges by selling off the last of their paintings, one by one. And this religious head was the only one she had left in 1945 to bring out of the city. Lost the pictures, and lost her father anyway.

Morgan reviewed the allegation that man and wife were shysters. Yes, their wealth provoked that nasty little spurt of jealousy. He couldn't enter this house or see their personal paintings without thinking peevishly, Why them? He was as able, as hard-working, but something had passed him by. Attack, he didn't really have it, or the lust to possess and make others give up or yield to his grasp. Power or money, he didn't care. But he reminded himself that several people owed their lives and their livelihoods to the Fisks. They'd discovered a couple of dozen artists and put them on the road to something more reliable than glory, a decent working income. That was their true investment capability and why he was here.

Marise came downstairs at last, calm and balanced. 'Boris will be along in a while,' she told him, as she poured the tea.

Boris tended to come at the end of these events, signed but didn't negotiate, couldn't be bothered with preliminary chat. She was the natural haggler but she boosted her partner's power vicariously. Convenient to blame, easy to invoke as the enthusiast she was not, Boris was a good foil for the ambitious wife.

It was hard to believe Marise was nearer seventy than sixty. In the years that Morgan had known her, she hadn't changed her style, a neatly kept figure, an immaculate way of dressing with a hem two inches below the knee which she'd stuck to through mini and maxi vogues, and this inflexible regime made her practically regal, the groomed woman who frankly terrified him with her lacquered perfection. But she was good-looking and natural, not a grim, face-lifted, silicone-injected freak.

'Now we must talk.' Tea taken, she gestured towards the desk placed behind her sofa, where some pieces of paper were spread out, including a contract with his terms of employment, if he agreed. 'Have you had plenty of time to consider? I don't want to rush you into anything. There's no real hurry. Although –' she crumbled a corner of a Viennese pastry – 'I would be pleased to finalize an agreement this afternoon.'

She had tact. Marise worked well alongside men, and was respected in the rather clubbish, donnish enclaves of London's art establishment, because she didn't crowd or berate them. She'd no time for feminism, or used just enough charm to allow her colleagues a degree of hierarchy or status, so that they didn't feel manipulation squeeze their pride. Morgan enjoyed thwarting this now and then.

'I'm not doing you that much of a favour, Marise. You're offering me a job and I'm perceptive enough to know I need it.'

She smiled, because he always was the plain-spoken man, but recognized what a comedown he had suffered. He looked ragged, the seaming round the eyes undone. Lost his son and now, they said, his wife had chosen the moment to shovel him out of doors. Well, well, she knew all about loss and loss of home and, finding her old fondness for him, determined he should have his second start.

'The facts are simple, Morgan. The New Bond Street gallery is holding on to its market share pretty well. The formula has been so successful over the years, I wouldn't want to tamper with it. We should agree it goes on handling the resale end and the big, established names. I wouldn't put anything too new or too *outré* in there. My major sale this year was that Goya I was lucky to get.

Someone in a hurry.' She shrugged. It was good to know the very wealthy had debts and lapses in fortune too. 'A duke.'

She was wary of the pastime of London art circles, clique gossip. Who gave what to whom and why. It reminded Morgan of the parlour game of Consequences, a formula-bound story where the interest lay in how witty or suggestive you could be in fitting name to act. If he'd been indiscreet, he could have asked which duke, although she wouldn't have told him, any more than Lorraine would reveal her sources in case they dried up, even if the story were genuine in the first place.

'But Covent Garden's another matter. I don't know what's gone wrong there. The manager was competent enough. Of course, you'd worked with him before, hadn't you? MacPherson. He'd been good in Glasgow. But Glasgow isn't London. The pace, the pulse is different. I want to give experimental art its chance, but I can't afford to subsidize it. If you think you can take it on, the Covent Garden gallery must break even in the first year.'

She was direct about her terms. He was forewarned, although he'd already put in time sizing up the problem. The gallery in Covent Garden was in a side-street, away from the main area, with a clientele that was either foreign or young, and not likely to buy a framed canvas impulsively in passing. How to convert deficit into profit?

Morgan tried to disguise how anxious he'd become, on the verge of fifty, unemployed for the first time and maybe, if he wasn't careful, for good. Over the summer, slumming it, or outstaying his welcome with friends, he'd had enough disappointments to understand the hardship of the job-hungry young. But that didn't make him young. It made him older. The practical answer for a man in his position was to start his own business, but he'd gone about it the other way round. He'd been self-employed from the start, and had simply run out of credibility or the cash to float new ventures. Besides, his confidence had ebbed in ratio.

'I'm game,' he said, masking the ebb. 'I can't promise you a runaway success in Covent Garden, but I'll see it breaks even.'

'That's excellent,' said Marise. 'But tell me if you've got reservations. Maybe, if we're cautious, cutting the deficit's enough.'

Boris came in on cue. The tailored suits which he wore in New Bond Street were a uniform steely blue, a quite distinctive dye and cloth that marked him off from City gents, a bit lustrous for British tastes, but at home he wore Daks trousers and a polo-necked sweater, outlining the torso that was broad but not heavy. He looked younger than Marise, or was ageless at a cut off point below hers. Bald, tanned, he projected the air of a film director. The word potentate came to mind but, at the same time, he could have been a high-class bouncer.

He ordered fresh tea and they began on another round of cups and the details. Morgan roughed out what he had in mind for Covent Garden.

'The site's got hardly anything going for it. The overheads are high. The passers-by are casual. The shop itself is wrong somehow. It's an 1850s house, isn't it? A bit grand for the work MacPherson's been putting up. It made a clash. There's a basement costing a fortune to heat, and death to anything you want to exhibit. Terrible lighting. And there are no other galleries nearby, so the knock-on effect of a run of galleries doesn't come into play.'

'There is a print shop in Covent Garden.' Marise halted the list of debits.

'And a bookshop opened next to us a few months ago,' Boris added.

Now on the face of it, Boris's remark was adrift. What had a bookshop got to do with an art gallery? More than a print shop five hundred yards away and he'd pre-empted Morgan's line.

'Yes, you've got it. Have you looked closely at that bookshop? It's brightly painted. It's eye-catching. The windows are almost down to the pavement which means you can have huge, bright displays and see right into the interior. It looks cheerful. It looks inviting. I did a survey on that bookshop for the whole of one Monday, not a big selling day, and it was never empty for more than a few minutes. At times it was actually crowded. Office and bank staff were coming in over their lunch-hour. Most people who stopped to look in the window went inside. It's got some sort of drawing power. The salesgirl and I got on good terms and she told me the day's takings. I was impressed, when you consider it's made up of sales under five pounds. That's what we want to catch, a buzz.'

Morgan enjoyed this, not money, but talk of money, making money as a measure of success. Once he'd made it, he couldn't hang on to it, so earning money for other people had a purifying zeal. They'd got the responsibility for investing, securing, gilt-edging it –

even spending it. He didn't care. It was only a game to him, an exercise.

'The bookshop has got the right feel. Nothing but paperbacks. A bright, cheery, chummy staff.'

'What are you saying, Morgan?' Marise asked, impatient with a maze of detail, a doer, while he was mentally labyrinthine, a ruminant thinker. 'Paperback paintings?'

'In a manner of speaking, yes. It could be an interesting trial with no high-cost investment. We need the turnover initially. Open up the frontage, lighten it. Take off the brown varnish. And sell the small. No canvas. No gilt frames. Simple, light work, either watercolour or drawings. Then it would balance the New Bond Street heavyweights properly. You know how hard it is to mix oil and watercolour anyway. And we mustn't be above a bit of gimcrackery. Landscape, street life, small genres. Things that the tourists would buy as an accurate souvenir. Souvenir. Yes, something to remember London by.'

'Morgan, this is heresy.'

'I know. Art under fifty pounds. A carry-out picture gallery. What else do you suggest? MacPherson's stuff, all big and important, didn't go down. I won't sell trash or junk art, I promise you that. But I will sell something.'

Marise shifted. She was impressed by the diagnosis in spite of herself and she trusted the man not to be outlandish or tawdry or in any sense embarrassing. Even worn, he was a gentleman.

'Do you have enough contacts? You'll need a steady supply from a lot of different sources. You've got that under control?'

'I should hope so.'

She side-stepped the accusation that he didn't know his business. 'Of course. Of course. You know more about London and art than anyone. I'm not flattering. You're the expert. That's why we need you to rescue us.'

She played the ingenuous woman, but she never took him in entirely.

'There are some things we ought to clarify,' she went on after the main ground had been covered. 'There are some people I don't choose to work with, for one reason or another. People who represent a spirit that's alien to what we feel. I hope you understand. It's the reason we reserve, Boris and I, the right of veto over the pictures you hang. The artists you hang.'

She smiled and was charming across her cravat and the pin. He was almost beguiled. He'd heard about the vendetta Marise ran against certain painters, usually well-known artists who'd thumbed their nose at her patronage or left her off their party list. He hadn't encountered that ban before, and was shocked to find her small-minded in a business where accounting to popular taste and making a turnover were hard enough masters, without adding prejudice.

'I can't operate with you looking over my shoulder, Marise. If I can't act on my own judgement, then we can't work together.'

'Oh, nothing that serious,' she said airily. 'We would never disagree, in principle. Just occasionally, a feeling about someone's motives – you know, instinct.'

There they left it, and he realized only later that she hadn't retracted a jot of her control. They rose and Morgan took his copy of the contract, extending from 1 January for one year. The Fisks were Teutonically exact and he was glad of the restriction on his tine budget. Last chances shouldn't be infinite. His one year started ticking.

'Where are you going now?' Marise asked. The question showed her sudden power over the disposal of his time.

'To London. I'll go up to Covent Garden. Nick Wylie has asked me to the opening of his new exhibition. I didn't know you'd let him rent the premises for this showing.'

'Sensible to fill it before Christmas,' said Boris. 'Get some rent.'

'I hope he does well. Nick's got some very promising young artists on his list at the moment. We particularly like Petersen's work.'

'Oh? Petersen?' Morgan ran the name through to catch its strangeness. 'A Swede?'

'Swedish extraction. Look out for the name. You could do worse than buy one.'

They shook hands and both came to the door to see him off. It was dark by this time, and he headed the car towards London, turning round to join the M25 at Junction 28 *en route* for Romford, Ilford and the City. He was driving west at the right time of day. The traffic was fast on the urban clearways, but not forbidding, and the winter sunset that geographically was centred on Salisbury Plain was a rosy symbol. The future looked good. He put the grey days behind him.

Elation buoyed him all the way into central London. They'd thrown a cordon round the metropolis in a by-pass motorway. It ought to have severed the city arteries, but instead the heart pumped faster under its tourniquet. He was high on excitement, feeling this was the new beginning he'd hoped for. Not passed over. Not past it. He was coming back into the middle zone again, where he belonged.

But the sheer volume of traffic from late-night shopping, a fortnight before Christmas, slowed him down. He drove along Oxford Street to take in the lights, but any enjoyment he might have had from hexagons, slightly furry under mock flock snow, and stylized bells with their clappers rigid and silent, was spoiled by the snarl of cars. When he was stationary, he noticed the electricity cable that looped from one lamppost to another, and it gave rise to flinty thoughts: what was the annual bill for the Christmas lights and who footed it? Did the shops do more trade because of them and, if so, why? The illuminations came on at dusk when the shops were closing. What was the commercial point of it all? And what was the artistic?

He turned down Regent Street, heading towards Haymarket and Trafalgar Square in his circle back to Covent Garden. The neon lights at Piccadilly Circus flickered overhead. There was more sense in that kind of advertising, the glass alternately empty and refilled, the Coca-Cola trademark synthesized against a city sky, as shifting as the crowds on the pavement. It was pop art of its kind, a memorable image. The electric signwriters were the modern-day fresco painters, their pictures magnified overhead in a simplified colour palette and with a reduced sense of composition, granted, but paintings large on open-air ceilings all the same.

That wasn't a cynical idea. Morgan wasn't vulnerable to the shock of the new and enjoyed the sauciness of technology. He was only scholarly in part and the other side of him – the businessman – was wary of academicians and the coteries that formed round the art establishment. Yes, a monograph on neon culture was called for, punning on neo. He remembered the 1960s vogue for neon statues and located half a dozen mentally. The idea swelled into a book as the engine idled in fits and starts up the Strand. He'd never make it to this opening party. Late for his own show.

Nick Wylie spotted him at once. This was the man for whose arrival you waited, the critic you feared.

'Did you find the car park all right?'

'I found it,' Morgan said, surly at the perfunctory welcome.

'And you closed the door again?'

'I closed the door.'

'Vandals can get in,' Nick explained. 'They're after the car radios and cassette players.'

'I haven't got one. My car's twenty years old and it's identifiable a mile away, even with a respray.'

'As long as you lowered the door,' said Nick, nervous about his own customized Mercedes. He swivelled on his heel. 'What do you think of it, then?'

'I haven't had time to look yet, never mind think.'

Nick changed his tack and propelled Morgan towards some introductions. 'Else,' he called to a long-legged blonde, dressed in something like pyjamas. 'Are there any clean glasses about? Red or white?'

Nick, acknowledged to be edgily brilliant if blurred on the details, was still good at getting a group together. The rooms were full of new people and new pictures, and felt about right for mid-December, a get-together in civilized surroundings but not too formal. A party and a showing weren't dissimilar, something of a fling; you went along hoping you'd find somebody or something, a name, a contact to put on file that would lead in time to somewhere else. Expectations shouldn't be too high when the pay-off might be years away. Morgan looked round him, and suddenly felt tired after the hectic day, wanting home. He saw only the modernist and slick that clashed inside the stately rooms. Voices which were strained to catch a passing notice grated on him. This was a waste of time. About turn. Marise said Nick was handling some promising talent, but Morgan knew that any potential which hadn't fulfilled itself was void, or counterfeit, including his own.

'Is Harriet here?' he asked Nick, hoping to find an old friend.

'No, she's doing her own thing this evening.'

Nick was expert at shedding his wife after business hours.

The girl called Else came forward with a glass of red wine in her hand, smiling at him, while Morgan underwent several spasms of irritation. She was familiar, this girl, Nick's recurring type before Harriet took him out of circulation, the starter secretary at a guess, a classy, well-turned-out girl who was determined to get somewhere, on somebody's arm. She was also sufficiently striking to make him feel peeved. Nick, who was his own age, somehow went on surviving professionally, but why should he be attractive to women

16

into the bargain? He'd got the puffy look of the *enfant terrible*, which had endowed Dylan Thomas and H. G. Wells with their peculiar sex appeal. Was it possible Wells *really* smelled of honey? Morgan thought of poor Harriet, who was doing her own thing, sitting at home in Greenwich moping, if he knew anything about it. The girl, well, this girl must know what she was into and could look after herself.

Nick was good at organizing exhibitions and had had his era of success. Now, he used rather tired tricks, like someone remembering what he used to do better. He'd redeployed two of his standard approaches for this show, a life-sized photograph of each painter and a printed biography that listed awards, exhibitions, grants, residential stint at regional arts centres and so on. For Morgan, this was a bogus exercise. The biography was written in Nick's syncopated prose style, a racy jargon written as big as the photo, all overblown. It didn't tell him much about the painter or help him assess the pictures, never mind like them. Wisely, Mr Petersen had elected to be absent. Neither photograph, nor biography, nor person was supplied.

But when you were as good an artist as Petersen, you didn't need to fall back on the old gimmicks. This was the draughtsmanship the critics despaired of finding at the colleges. Morgan nodded slowly towards Marise's judgement. Yes, you were right. This is it. This is the thing we look for. In the middle of a completely dull evening, he ran into the talent he'd searched for diligently and given up hope of long ago.

For an art historian, Morgan held a strange opinion. He was happy to talk about a painter's sources and methods, or what happened after a picture was finished, its reception or its place in the story of its time, but he thought the picture itself couldn't properly be described. It was an experience and individual. Very good pictures were indescribable and throbbed with a vitality that was almost frightening, off the page.

By that yardstick, Petersen succeeded. Not one of his paintings prepared Morgan for the next. The large alternated with the small canvas, and Morgan browsed round them, unhappy about giving away his admiration like this all at once. The big subjects were done massively with colour, like the history paintings of old masters, the grand theme that had gone out of fashion two hundred years ago. They had an almost classical exaggeration, larger than reality by a seventh, the tone, scale and subject oversize because they were meant to be seen from a distance. They were public pictures, allegorical, symbolic. But at the same time, the business side of Morgan knew they were unsaleable, unhangable and needed church commissions, like Stanley Spencer or Eric Gill, to accommodate the overscale. Trees, landscape, people were caught up in a whirl of creation, like the dream of a fundamentalist or Seventh Day Adventist, and slightly mad. They panted with energy.

The smaller paintings were intimate little patches and had the effect of breaking up the formal work, whisper after shout. In technique, they were different too, with clever compositions, so that his first response was a curiosity. Now let me see. Maybe the two styles were a mistake because they inclined to the feeling that Petersen ought to restrict himself to one or the other, not ride two horses. But more than talent or promise, this was accomplishment.

'Nick says I ought to chat you up.' The girl called Else walked between him and the canvases.

The interruption misfired. Morgan belonged to the age of wooing, not of being wooed. He'd no wish to be chatted up by a trouser-clad independent Ms, however comely. Or maybe he put her attraction to one side, to resist it.

'There are a dozen men here who'd reward your efforts better than I.'

The slanders of the sentence fell like stones into water, each one quiet and plumbed, but with an after-ripple.

Else heard the words and changed her expression. She had waited so long to bring herself and her doings to this man's full notice that anticipation had tired. Like seeing York Minster on a rainy day and thinking, Why did I imagine it would be so special? She removed her approach-me smile and put back common sense. 'I've embarrassed you,' she said without rancour. 'You know, I ought to ignore Nick. He gives you three words as a starter and they're all misleading. I'll begin again. Do you want me to go back to the door, or can I stand here and do it?'

Morgan thawed. Impressions adjusted. He gave her due for more intelligence, while the phrase 'Nick's girlfriend' dissolved on near acquaintance. She wasn't a girl anyway, whatever the word denoted in age, but a woman, and one who was likely to be more proficient than he was in the games of wooing. She was the new type, the woman about town – confident, civilized, completely in

18

control. She had an angular face close up. It was a face you couldn't see into, partly because of the fall of long blonde hair which was its own misleading stereotype. She turned away and talked to one side. Men bent to catch the words that fell. Rooms closed. Other people faded. She was a woman you were always alone with.

'Do you work for Nick and Harriet?' He introduced the wife's name warily to see how she reacted to it.

Indignation! 'No. As far as I know, they work for me.'

The answer hit him like a punch she hadn't pulled, strong and straight. Was Else part of a new partnership Nick hadn't gone public on? This wasn't a secretary after all, but a boardroom executive; for all Morgan knew, a colleague of the Fisks. 'How's that?' he asked, feeling stupid. Being a day behind events denoted him as being out of touch with London life.

She looked at him long and hard. He had the feeling of being known, of old, by repute, and of being measured against the expectation of his fame. This woman knew him all right, or approached him knowingly. As she rose in his esteem, he fell. She was chic and shiny. He watched her eyes taking in the collar of his shirt, which he remembered was slightly old-fashioned, however fine in its two-fold poplin heyday.

'I'm Else Petersen,' she said. 'The painter. Perhaps we should begin again for the third time.'

His haughtiness evaporated; she had every right to be this condescending. 'I do apologize. How was I to know?' He pointed towards the empty space beside the pictures. 'There were no clues.'

The phrase was exact. Morgan had assumed that the strong painting and the strong ideas were masculine. He'd fallen into the sexist trap not once, but twice, thinking that professionally and in her private life she was what she was not. She was neither a man nor a hang-around woman: somewhere in between. The individual making a fresh place for herself, the undefined.

He pursued this new person overzealously. 'Tell me about your work. These are such good paintings. You know they are. They dwarf everything else here, pastiche stuff, though probably I shouldn't say it too loud. Why haven't I heard your name before? I'm not that out of touch. What have you been doing? Where have you been?'

Propelled by his enthusiasm they edged towards the nearest picture and she scanned its surface in much the same way as she had

19

done him, objectively and without indulgence. 'I paint. I don't talk about painting. I leave that to other people.'

The gabble of fifty voices cut across her deliberated silence, like sounds heard over a wall. It was his own point about pictures not needing to be described, but better said.

He persevered, willing her to open up to him. 'What's the tree you've put in this one? I don't recognize it.'

'Isn't it botanically accurate?' She sounded worried.

'No, no, I'm sure it is. I just don't know it. What's its name?'

It was a tall tree with chrome-yellow leaves, painted as if she were looking down on it from the upper storey of a house. It was vividly bright, and she'd managed to light this view of a normal garden from a source she'd somehow put inside the tree. It glowed super-naturally, like a candle that was strong enough to illuminate the open air. A window opened in his perception; subject familiar, style startling, the mark of an original. The picture lived somewhere as a thought and was that rarity, the memorable image. Her tree was the first living thing he'd set eyes on all day.

'It's a robinia.'

'I haven't heard that name.'

'Haven't you? It's a hybrid native to the Frisian islands, or so they tell me. It's quite a popular ornamental tree, but it can be a perfect nuisance and mine's too big for its position. They told me to prune it back into a golden ball, but it didn't want to be a tidy little shrub. It wanted to be a tree and it kept on growing. *Robinia pseudoacacia frisia*.'

'Why *pseudoacacia*?'

'Because it looks like an acacia tree, with the same long leaves, and isn't. It changes all the year round. It's always changing. Late into leaf, early to fall. The leaves change colour all summer until they're this unbelievably brilliant yellow.' She swayed too, describing it.

'You've caught that.'

'I caught that. I didn't exaggerate.'

'It's your own tree, then?'

'It grows in my garden.'

'Where?'

'In the country. In the woods. It shouldn't be there really. It doesn't belong. An implant that probably doesn't work.'

When she spoke, Morgan found himself hypnotized by the omissions. He pressed his questions to the point of rudeness, and she went on deflecting them. She troubled him with the empty, plentiful response, the spaces in her work. What she did and what she said were merged. Her offhand manner caught. Not many people could succeed with understatement. He was propelled by the same longing he felt when he looked at the midshipman drawing, wanted it and wanted her crudely. She was waiting in a dusty corner like the Gainsborough to be discovered, or correctly valued.

He knew he was fantasizing, woman and work, and stood back to reconsider.

'You're too tired,' she intervened, 'to make a sound evaluation. You've had a long day. Look at them tomorrow when you're fresh. They may seem ordinary in daylight. Things often do.'

'I think I could take your small work as a matter of course.'

'Oh, you must talk to Nick about what happens to them after this. He may have other plans for getting rid of them.'

So uninterested! He wanted to block her, seal off her exit, and was clumsy with his invitation. 'Will you have lunch with me one day next week?'

'Next week?' She frowned and looked displeased, as women do to unwelcome propositions. 'No. I'm leaving town until the New Year. I may come by then.'

They were interrupted. His old publisher, Max Edelman, came up and threw his arms round him, Russianesque, long-lost, hail fellow that he genuinely was. 'They said you would be here and that was why I came. How are you doing, my friend? What are you writing? You are writing, I presume?'

'Planning to write.' He was brusque, wanting to get back to Else.

'Nearly as good.' Max was grateful for the success of Morgan's television back-up book which he'd had the vision to publish; it had subsidized a dozen other market leaders and established his own reputation during what had been a lean time for art publishers. 'What are you planning?'

'A book on neon culture.'

'For goodness' sake, I thought you were serious.'

Else had drifted away, flitting in and out of his line of vision as Morgan listened to the news in art books, the cost of colour plates, the paucity of sound academic study, the flood of rubbish. He noticed from a distance that the garment he'd put down at first sight as pyjamas, and Else in it as beddable, was in fact a boilersuit. It amused him now, punning on the house painter, kitted out for the job, except that this was a couturier version, to judge by its colour, not workaday khaki but a pale green, or almond, or something indefinable in dyes. But who was keeping her in these expensive clothes? Unsold paintings didn't.

'What's on your spring list?'

'Else's doing the illustrations to an almanac for me, specialist edition, commissioned sonnets. For the prestige end. No money in it. I've taken a big glossy by Dan Fredericks.'

Morgan groaned. 'You must really be up against it.'

'Better than nothing. The Americans put in the work.'

'I don't agree. Nothing's worse than those mid-ocean art books, especially Dan's. What is it, a critical biography? Dishing the dirt on the long-suffering dead?'

'Roughly. Do you want to come to the launch? Big night.'

The invitation pleased. It put him back in the swim and, after all, he might write something and Max might publish it.

'What do you think of this lot?'

Max twitched. He'd kept to his moustache and used it well. 'It frightens you, doesn't it, to think this is the best around. Petersen's good. It's a shame she started so late.'

'Did she?' Morgan seized on the opinion. Late into leaf, early to fall.

'I'm presuming that she wasted her time. She dropped out of the Slade, you know, after she won their first-year prize. Set her back years.'

'Why did she drop out?'

'I don't know. She's a mystery woman. Ask her and she'll say it wasn't her.'

Morgan looked round the gallery to pin this fact to its owner, but Else Petersen had gone, left town until the New Year, as she promised. He made a mental note to ask a friend who'd lectured at the Slade about this wayward student. The day, crowned with successes, somehow missed its finale.

He got the Gainsborough. He got the job. But did he get the girl? Did he hell.

January

January brought with it some unusually heavy snowfalls.

By early morning, on the first working Monday of the month, the station at Windsor was crowded with city-bound travellers who were reluctantly marooned. Arriving exactly five minutes before his train was due to leave, Adrian Crane found himself jostled on the platform and irritably used the bulk of his briefcase against his fellow passengers to give himself more leg-room.

'Are there no trains running at all?' he asked the ticket collector.

'Oh, some. Cleared the track at six and we had a little rush at seven. But nothing since half-past.'

'What can you guarantee?'

'Can't guarantee nothing. They're using the train on platform two as a waiting room, if you'd care to wait, sir.'

'So the timetable's useless?'

'Time being, sir.'

He turned away in the queue, speechless. He didn't seem to have the words for efficient anger, which led to remedy, seeing in his eyes only the imperative diary on his desk, an appointment at twelve, a committee at two and, at four, a directors' meeting. The first he could cancel by telephone, wasn't wildly important anyway, but the rest would go ahead without him and that marginalized him in future decisions. He'd have to get there. Taxi? No one would take a fare all the way into town, and if he went part-way, he might be more hopelessly stranded up the line.

'Excuse me, sir,' said the man at the barrier. 'There's a train due in eight minutes, signal from Reading. Avoid the stampede.' He winked. An insolence.

Adrian was able to commandeer a corner seat, not too far removed from his habitual place. Twenty-seven minutes late, he checked, but not disastrous. There was a kind of heroism in getting through. He rolled up his coat, lining outermost against soiling,

23

and placed it in the rack, undid his bulwark briefcase and settled down to his reading. The catalogues? The quiet headlines of the quality papers? Adrian's neighbours were often surprised at his paperwork. When he landed the job at Sotheby's, he drew up a list of the books he felt he ought to read, the classics that were missing from his education, varied by the modern greats, Burton, Proust, Joyce, Boswell's *Life of Johnson*, books recommended, books forgotten, no matter if he hated them on opening, they filled the space between Windsor and Paddington with some panache.

By the book. By the book. The phrase intruded into the slowing rhythms of the track, until even the gorgeousness of *Antony and Cleopatra*, Act III, failed to seduce him this morning. He felt it was a touch absurd of him to question the collector about the timetable, or uphold his diary obligations for that matter, in the face of the exempting weather, and he went back over his gestures with hand and briefcase to see if he had made a fool of himself. He knew that he felt an excessive obligation to the printed matter, ignoring that systems knotted and confounded each other in times of stress. But if you gave in to stress, see, the book fell out of your hand, the page went unread, and you achieved absolutely nothing out of your schedule. Really, by the book it had to be.

Morgan looked out and found the weather forecasters had underestimated. It had snowed all through the night in London, not the gentle blanket of clean snow which was laid down in the countryside like somebody's washing spread out to dry on the bushes, or the piste snow of holidays, but that depressing city stuff that only got in the way. He'd an appointment at Sotheby's at midday and thought of cancelling it because of the sheer difficulty of getting over to New Bond Street by any other means than foot, disinclined to risk his car on the roads. He switched on the radio at the bedside for the seven o'clock news, and heard of chaos all over the south of England. Even the railway lines were blocked. Snow ploughs were being sent down from Scotland, where there hadn't been a flake, another example of the irrational geography of the island. Resources were never where they were needed. The commuter network was at a standstill and anyone with sense would stay at home.

He knew these snowdays. Nothing would happen in the city. It would be a day of siege, the stock market reacting to worldwide prices but not actively trading, a run on bread instead of banks, a week long airlock in the arterial system of exchange. Outside, the street that led into Covent Garden was windswept and empty, apart from a dog that nosed round the doorways, turning over the carcass of overnight remains, man or man-eaten something, before it passed on. Bleak as Siberia.

Morgan walked about the apartment, showered and dressed. The luxury of it hadn't palled on him. The gallery had no obvious commercial advantages but, inside, it was a picture-hanger's dream, a little bit of architectural purism with high ceilings and just enough detail to take away the plainness. There were five good-sized rooms, leading off each other round an open arched hallway, and a flight of stairs that led up to Morgan's private flat and offices. It wasn't a showroom but a true town house, which some professional man from the country had used to see his consultancy clients, and accommodate his wife and daughters during the London season. He felt Trollope had strolled through here, and maybe Turner, recording their impressions. Public in front, private behind, it was the fulcrum of real life. In the heart of London, a half-mile radius could supply everything a man needed. That was what made the London Strand one of the world's great street-names; flotsam, cord and landing place, it signified both the accident and the arrival behind movement. The strand surged in him.

The five showrooms were repeated upstairs on a neater scale where, apart from sharing the office with Charlotte, the secretary who'd worked with him before, he could spread himself around. Bedroom, bathroom, a sitting room of lavish proportions. Everything was laid on, as it would be in a hotel suite, luxurious if impersonal. He revelled in the padded curtains, bathmat, hot water – nothing was left out. Cool and white, the rooms had overtones of empire, quite which one he wasn't sure. Blank pages waiting for the stuff of action.

The caretaker arrived at the office by eight promptly, as on every other day, snow notwithstanding. 'Morning, Mr Morgan.'

'It could be a better morning than this, Fred. Have you heard the news? There's a train marooned on the southern line and villages are cut off. Livestock buried in the fields because we've had no proper warning.'

'Ah, don't you worry, sir. Freaks soon pass. Remember '47. It was worse. Perishing long winter that. Late winters don't last.' Fred set to with a snow-shovel to clear the pavements. 'Not many through the doors today, but we'll keep their feet clean.'

Fred had a simple measure of success. Feet through the door. It didn't matter if the people bought nothing and, in a way, he was right. As long as they came in, they might buy, although Morgan was less convinced by turnstile economics. That was the nag behind each innocent snowflake; it made its own slump in turnover.

The pavement was salted and gritted and gleamed like basalt. The postman was cheered up at finding an easy passage and put the mail in Morgan's hands as enthusiastically as a man might who would take three times as long as normal on his round.

Why do you speak to the tradesmen all the time?

I like them. I like what they say. They're funny, and usually right.

How unseemly.

That was Lorraine, drawing the English class distinctions, which put her top of the pile, or somewhere above him.

Morgan threw the envelopes on the bed and went to shave before Charlotte arrived. He disliked shaving and postponed it for as long as possible. Any sensible man got it over with before a shower, but he gave himself an interval of grace, implying that today he might not do it at all. Might rebel. Might break out and be a hippie for a while. He had no wish to be completely regulation in this formal habitat.

He was pleased with his face in the objective mirror. It looked fuller. The lines were cut in it for good, lines of experience, lines of disappointment, but they were filling up with new ambitions. The year fanned out in his hand like a deal at cards, thirteen random values but a challenge for him to play. Accident and arrival. It was almost gratifying to have the future tightly structured like this, and he flicked over the indices of his different projects: how to invest his salary – probably in some decent pictures; a book that came spiralling into the daylight at Max's behest, maybe Max would commission it with money up front; and how his plans for Covent Garden dovetailed into the Fisks' projections, but more amply into his own, leading to an afterwards. A new beginning. A new year. No, he wasn't on the scrapheap yet.

The handwriting on one of the scatter of envelopes took his eye, and the white square confirmed the day's main event, which he'd been trying to dodge as much as the debearding. The envelope contained a greetings card, a safe and tasteful card because this was his birthday and his fiftieth birthday at that. Lorraine had sent his one and only memento of the day; Love L., she signed her name. What was this L.? He'd never seen her use the initial before and felt it was a token of their estrangement. L. in brief. A peck of a name, not love in full. Somehow, the use of the pen-name curtailed her birthday message. She had these infuriating little ploys, like talking under her breath to him, just out of earshot and forcing him to say, 'Excuse me? What was that?' like a dotard.

The truncation made him doubly sorry. Her name was one of the things he'd liked best about her. Morgan and Lorraine went well together, like the characters out of a Celtic Renaissance epic, something Yeatsian, or a forgotten Tudor history play that would have lived if Shakespeare had recut it. But that was his trouble. Nomenclature. You pedantic Welshman, loving sounds that mean nothing. Verbose and windy, his critics said. He'd got the scholar's obsession about naming things, defining and ascribing until he squeezed the life out of them. Don't make it hard about the edges. Let it blur, they told him when he was a student, but he went on drawing lines as hard as the lead fillets separating stained glass. That he chose to drive a Morgan sports car was maybe a sign of the naming weakness. But it was only during his ownership that the car had turned into a cult machine, the world's last handmade engine, so was he wrong to drive one because its name and his happened to coincide? For a while, he'd lived near the original factory in Malvern, and it was satisfying to draw coincidence inside a tight network, saying it was meant to be.

Lorraine resisted naming. I'm not what you think I am, she used to say. I haven't got anything to do with the place-name Lorraine. I don't even know where it is and I don't want to go there. All the same, Morgan firmly believed that she must have a French ancestor, a Huguenot mixed up in her Englishness, and that the name didn't rise spontaneously in someone's consciousness. Attribution. Source. Proof. Everything had a reason. He tracked this reason remorselessly. That might be pedantic of him, but there were worse pedantries around, like laying down a vineyard crop *en primeur* in the hope that it would mature to something drinkable, or high-risk investment in companies that were under threat, or the

27

penny shares. In comparison with these de-personalized commodities, he'd go on thinking the pedigree of paintings and people were interesting and worthwhile.

Deepest Suffolk
Lost track of time

Dear Boris

Thank you for your cheque.

I enjoyed the break – even if I only rediscovered that I'm cross-country, not a downhill skier, no pace, no nerve – and am immensely grateful for the means of having had one, but it's invigorating to be back at work again, maybe because of it. When I walk down to the studio in the morning, the words 'here is my life waiting for me to begin' come into my head. I don't really know what they mean, but I'm working to expand them, or to make them good.

The house is warm and welcoming in spite of my fortnight's neglect and is my best friend, open armed with forgiveness whatever I do. I see my days here as a diagram or design, most significant or perfect when every day is the same. A morning's work before I eat, then a walk to burn off the meal, doubly productive in turning up a bundle of kindling wood for the stove. Its enamel glows and purrs for me like a cosy cat which I've rubbed up the right way. Its spitting is the only noise on these windless evenings when the trees are quiet. It's good feeling this cut off. Accidents bring some walkers through the woods but they keep their distance, sensing mine.

Yesterday the Colonel struggled up from the big house with a new neighbour who's taken on the farm, brave man. He's come to Odham with his wife and two sons, fresh out of the army. Clive Ramage, a good doing name. He may need all the bravery and doing he can lay his hands on to turn that place around. They saw my light was on and came to make sure I wasn't snowbound. Got your firewood? the Colonel says. Got some candles? Get on with it then.

I am getting on with it. I'm working on the illustrations for Max Edelman's almanac. Thirteen. Ten colour drawings, three engravings. Yes, years have thirteen months depending on how you divide them up. The lunar month is much more useful than the calendric cycle, and I can't think why we haven't stuck to it; as I said before, time is model when it falls in equal spans. An hour, a day, a week are precise and measured. Why should we concede to months the privilege of being irregular? I feel like saying, 'Give me back my thirteen months', the way the London mob did when they reformed the Julian calendar. Give us back our eleven days! Except that they thought they'd lost the time in perpetuity. That too. That too.

Seriously, it's a commission for twelve seasonal illustrations and a frontispiece.

Sounds straightforward, doesn't it, but it's so very hard. Everything else gets easier as you become proficient at it. Sex, soufflés. Practice makes near as dammit perfect. Not this. Be real to the activity of the month. Do not be boring. Be a natural progression through to the next plate, without repetition. Be something more than illustrative. Be different from all the other illustrators, Beardsley and Bewick and Robinson ... If only the artist's commandments also stopped at ten, but they go on and on, proliferating into a bibliography that's depressing and inhibiting, because it's huge. I shove it off the desk. All the hints and prohibitions other people give you go crashing to the floor. I'm left alone with the colour and the brush, poring into the lines I paint as myopically as the watchmender with his eyepiece. Mr Beardsley won't altogether go away. It's very difficult not to mimic him because he has the pure and uncompromising line I like. Black and white borrows something from him. Max once told me that Browning was the first English poet who managed to break blank verse out of Shakespeare's rhythm. Think of it, influencing two centuries of your craft. Bad to be so good. It leaves no room for follow-ons.

I am using my own house and the garden and village as a repeated context, not an outside reference but a real framework. Often literally. I've got January as seen through one of the pointed windows of the living room, outside from in. The people down at the pottery have made me a house modelled on this one, correct in every detail, and at night I put a candle inside and leave it on the windowsill. This fills a corner in the January plate. A box within a box within a box. My life.

I suppose I *was* disappointed with Nick's exhibition at Covent Garden. He was careful, the rooms were spacious, the

29

callers were respectful, but it missed. Or rather, the little red stickers went up all round the gallery but not on my pictures. Must I sell to be successful, Boris? Unfortunately, yes. Sale is circulation. I just cannot get over this blockage of people having to part with cash for the experience to be activated. Can you buy experience? Is the life thing enhanced if you pay more for it? Does caviare really taste better than common cod's roe, fried in butter and eaten with granary bread? Not in my canon, it doesn't. Real experience is free.

There was a bonus. I was able to meet Morgan again. He took an instant and overwhelming aversion to me, while genuinely admiring my painting, but that's a nice discrimination I can settle for. I wonder if the man knows he's a legend, or a hero, to my generation. He's the prime example of an idea I've always been a bit of a sucker for: muscled intellect. In those television programmes, he managed to get across what it means to paint, which in the end is a physical activity. He had the verve to talk about the fatigue of the work and make you feel it. Work out? By God, yes, it's the same sweat as a gymnasium, but in your head. Morgan had a way of putting the present into the context of the past and making sense of it. He didn't talk that art jargon that makes you want to squirm, spatial, evaluative, compositional tension. Blah. He always spoke warmly. He didn't lose the common touch in front of the cameras. Do you like it and why? were the only questions he asked and he kept leading back to the painter as an ordinary person who is committed to exploration, an adventurer in ideas and images. Understand him, don't criticize, was what he said. I was greatly struck when he advised against *disliking* a picture. 'A painting you don't like is the same as a person you don't like. You haven't given it enough time. After five years you may have the authority to say I don't like him, or it; not sooner.'

I was therefore dismayed by being abbreviated in his regard. No, if I'm more honest, I behaved like a fool because I was apprehensive about meeting him this time, yuppie, preppie – what other catch word is there for insincere – just phoney, and maybe that's nearer the truth than I care to admit. He made me no better than I am.

Else

* * *

'Your drawing's old,' said Adrian, 'but that doesn't mean it's genuine.'

Adrian was the youngest director at Sotheby's and was one of the formidable young men who'd recently moved into art-dealing. He knew the market, read the trends. His portfolio was in stocks and shares, as much as academic research. Considering the difficult journey from Windsor station that morning, he wasn't very late for his noon appointment with Morgan, but he did walk straight into the office wearing his galoshes, which were fairly elegant wellington boots designed to tie up at the calf, as if they were his demonstrative excuse. He unfastened them on to a mat, where they dropped lumps of Berkshire snow until mid-afternoon, adding a quaint rural touch in the middle of New Bond Street.

'How old?'

'Oh, the right sort of old. Two hundred years. Paper, frame, medium, they all passed the analyst.'

The potential Gainsborough lay face down on Adrian's desk as if the technical innards were more revealing than the face drawn on the front.

'You're doubtful?' Morgan pressed him.

Adrian blew his cheeks out. He was fair-haired and slight and rather faded, with elderly mannerisms for a man in his thirties, aware of his own importance or the weight of his opinion, and could be pretentious if you didn't cut him short. 'Our top Gainsborough expert is abroad. Remember him, Hisslop? He's doing his own research in the States. And anyway, three years ago he was overruled by a senior figure at the Royal Academy, so one man's word is far from incontrovertible.'

'I remember that. Quite a stir.'

'In that instance, the lady owner wrote a book about it and made us all look fools. Which we are. Over and over again, we're discredited. There are two dealers at the moment, one in London, one in New York, who've made their name, as well as a pretty decent percentage at auction, by proving us wrong on old masters. The New York dealer mounted an exhibition of his "rejects" which are now accepted as genuine. They do have the advantage of being able to clean and restore the canvas, of course, before they give their judgement. Whereas we have to evaluate through centuries of dirt, because it's not our picture to tamper with. We're just auctioneers. But, you know, it may well turn out that the authorities they're pleased to cite today, turn round and change their minds tomorrow. New evidence, new techniques. It's a branch of forensic science nowadays, attribution. Look at the Rembrandts.' He shrugged.

Morgan felt he was secure behind his desk, behind his name-plated door, and that the shrug signalled a lack of interest.

'All in a day's work. You say yes. I say no. Which of us is right? What's worse for the credibility of art – or business, come to that – to say it's by a master when it isn't, or to say it isn't when it is? Are we better to be positively or negatively wrong? You answer me that one. We don't know for sure if this is a Gainsborough, any more than we're sure it isn't. Two hundred years ago, the man knocked these out for his keep. Didn't sign them. Didn't catalogue them unless they were exhibition pictures. How on earth do we know if they're authentic, or if his apprentice or his daughters didn't come along and fill in the outline of the master's cartoon? No fraud intended. That was just their work method.'

Morgan was nettled at being told what he already knew. The young man had something smug about him which he found he wanted to shock. 'Yes. Nowadays they sign their droppings in case they're famous later on, but crap wasn't this precious in the old days.'

Adrian laughed a little. Private opinion and off the record. 'Maybe so.'

Morgan was still disappointed that Sotheby's wasn't going to ratify his find. Everybody hated you to stumble accidentally on the real thing. Jealousy was in part why Adrian wouldn't authenticate the picture. And moreover, he was a man who habitually confused the second rate with the first. Morgan had never made that mistake in judgement. 'You're going to err on the side of caution?'

'I'm afraid so. In the style of Gainsborough is our verdict.' Adrian turned the drawing right side up. The face did make its appeal, however unacknowledged. The young man in naval uniform was vital, and as full of his own doings as on the day he sat for it. 'You've never been a collector, Morgan. Why does it matter about this one? Even genuine, a drawing like this isn't worth more than a couple of thousand or so.'

The known face of the drawing nudged Morgan into admitting

more than he wanted to. 'It did remind me of my son. I suppose that was why I took it in the first place.'

Adrian was silent, embarrassed by the reference. It made his commercial assessment sound in poor taste and he felt Morgan shouldn't have gone about mixing attribution and feelings. Not professional. 'Then I hope,' he said, very carefully, in his softest line, 'that you appreciate it for what it is.'

The snow that started as a flurry on Saturday at nightfall lasted for the best part of a week. A polar night had descended on the south of England, gloomy and interminable because it blotted out limits. Every day Else cleared a pathway round the house, but the next morning she found her work had been wiped out by fresh snowfalls. Sometimes, when she'd immured herself beside the stove for comfort and the engraving plate for companionship, she could still be invaded by the loneliness of the season. She leaned over her drawing board and rubbed a windowpane, which changed the condensation to droplets. The woods she framed were grey, eerie, ghosted in light and sound. The rooks rose silently against the snow haze and, although Else put out fresh water every morning, she couldn't be sure the overwintering birds came to drink it. The only robin was the stylized one she had engraved in the corner of her January plate, John Clare's aggressive fellow, beady-eyed.

No walkers broke into the enclosure. The roads were blocked. The railway line to London was snowbound. The conditions at her own back door were multiplied all over the south of England and the only consolation to be had was in news broadcasts, proclaiming it the worst, the longest, the heaviest in living memory. Neither the postman nor the milkman called at her remote address; for five days she saw nobody, but went on labouring over the engraving. Exclusive and intense, it wore her out. She was tired of watching herself living instead of being out and involved. She stretched against the constraint of walls. The house, which was as hot and centred as an igloo, became claustrophobic with the monotonous images of herself and her own breath trapped indoors.

One morning she heard the first train connect down the line in a long loop that broke a vacuum of silence. Go for it, she thought.

She rummaged in a cupboard, bringing dresses to a mirror, different colour, different cloth, trying out techniques against herself. She couldn't decide on a line or a tone because she wasn't sure of her effect.

Flamboyant maybe, a reddish hint and her hair allowed to fall. Or demure blue. Or a touch of severity in an old grey flannel suit, prim to the collar, with her hair tucked up to match. She imagined scenarios for each ensemble, rotating a prism of anticipation. What did she want, and, more significantly, what did she want from him? Go for it, echoed over every junction down the line.

'I am a little late for our appointment,' Else said, 'but the weather held me up.'

They walked round to La Marmite, a restaurant in the main covered area, which Morgan had already picked out from all the watering holes of Covent Garden. It had been put on the map by actors who were appearing nearby at the Adelphi, or the Strand Palace, or the Aldwych, and congregated there as if it were a private club. It survived that vogue, and managed to go on serving unpretentious food round about the stars. Today, because of the snow, it was as good as empty and its noise level, which could be deafening at lunch-time, fell to the acceptable.

It was Saturday and the snow was easing up, with no new falls and the old ones churned to slush by traffic. Saturday had a distinctive feel anyway, relaxed and off duty. At times, Covent Garden could regain its village atmosphere, a few streets behind the Strand pulled under a renovated canopy. The market was like the restaurant, its trendiness hiding some quality things. Inside a month, Morgan had taken out instant citizenship, was known and nodded to by stall-holders, kept informed of local events, just a trader like the rest. He had his favourite buskers, Tam and Linda from the north, who did a routine with the tambourine and flute, and when he went outside the gallery to quiz them about how they came to be so good, they admitted to playing with the London Philharmonic in the evening.

He'd made up his mind not to ask her questions. She was here. She'd come by as she promised. That was enough. Let it blur.

'Are you pleased with things?' Else had to make the opening.

'I'm pleased to be here instead of on my uppers, yes. But I'm not sure touting is my strong point. I have an overcritical reaction to pictures and I unfortunately convey that even when I don't mean to. Too analytical. I just look when I should be enthusing. Some

34

people can say they love a picture when they don't. I've never managed that.'

She hugged the fact close. Art was full of easy lovers, love on and off again, but this man might love with discrimination. 'You need a business manager,' Else said practicably. 'The trouble is, Marise has always tried to run that business on the cheap. If you've got displays on both floors, it stands to reason you need two people besides your secretary. And anyway, you should be out making the contacts, not doing a sales job. She knows that.'

He peeled back the bone from a Dover sole. 'You've worked with Marise before?'

'I don't think she would give it quite that status.'

He wondered about telling her that Petersen came highly recommended but thought he would reserve the compliment.

'I know Boris better,' Else admitted.

'How did you manage that? Nobody knows Boris better.'

She smiled to herself and Morgan thought, My God, they're intimate. That was an insider smile. They were bed friends. The waiter interrupted and gave him time to restrain himself. Else's hair, which was looped up by a couple of grips, moved to one side, and she followed it elusively. Wonderful hair, it was. He was suspicious of blondes in case they were bottle varieties, but this was natural, stranded right down to the root. Nothing had ever happened to it apart from water. No curling, no colouring. Itself. She wore a grey suit with a tidy neckline, giving out a neat impression that was contradicted by the up-down hair. He was sick as a dog, thinking she and Boris might be lovers.

'Boris is good to the people he believes in. Don't be fooled by that bluff. He's got the better judgement of the two and sometimes, you know, he has a conscience. He's the only honest dealer I've met in London's art world. Marise–' she shook her head – 'has no conscience.'

This intrigued him. He had always thought Mr Marise was a cipher, or a financial heavy engaged to see that the lady got her own way. Examining each of the praise words which Else used – good, judgement, honest, conscience – led him round to the questions he was wary of, in case she slammed shut on him. That his instinct about their relationship might be right inhibited him from asking the simple things. After all, Else Petersen was more Boris's type than Nick Wylie's, who dabbled in secretaries. Else

35

moved in the fast crowd. A tan, he couldn't help noticing, acquired over the Christmas break. Did she go skiing in St Moritz with the in-set? Who paid for that, the *après* skier?

'Will you really write something for Max Edelman?' she asked, dragging him back from a dismal, middle-aged jealousy that didn't even have a pretext. Whoever she bedded with, it wasn't likely to be him. 'I heard you say you were thinking of writing something.'

'I'm rusty. I came to words rather late in life. They don't happen easily.'

'It's the right time for you to publish something. An update. That television book was a Bible in its way, you know, unauthorized version. It did slander a lot of the established gods, or do I mean establishment?' She smiled, remembering much fuss and ruffling. 'But people don't know what to believe in any more. They hate modernism and they're afraid to say it. There's been a turn-around in architecture in the last ten years. It needs something like that in painting, don't you think?'

He was gloomy. 'What do you want me to write? A ten-part course in non-ugliness? What's beauty as a measure any more? Aesthetics are obscene in the twentieth century. I can't change a worldwide predilection for the ugly, not single-handed. It's symbolic.' He rolled his eyes and made her laugh. 'And that book only got the exposure it did because of the television series. I said the important things ten years ago. I don't want to be such a bore as to go on saying them. Why do people want pictures anyway, when they can have reality? In the end, I think pictures are pretty dodgy things to set much store by. Market values, insurance policies, protecting your investment. It's gone off. I've lost the burning faith I used to have in truth.'

'I'm working on a project for Max,' she volunteered, to distract him from such abject despair. 'I'm nearly finished. An almanac with the writing by our next poet laureate, or so the man himself keeps telling me. It's a very upmarket limited edition, handmade paper, stitched binding, sold through a folio society. A lovely little anachronism. That's probably why Max chose me to illustrate it.'

'What do you mean?'

'I'd put in all those slavish hours and not expect to be paid. Monk-like. I'll tool away for the sake of doing it well. That's faith, if you like, or truth. And I owed him a favour. I'm always paying back favours.'

'What sort of favours?' Morgan tried to sound light-hearted, but her connection with his world and the people in it, which he'd thought were exclusive and personal to him, was beginning to erode his resistance to her. She invaded a secret place of self.

'He found me some old paper that I wanted – old type, you know, guaranteed all rag, not available on the market any more.'

'You're that perfectionist?'

'About some things.'

Then they relaxed, pushing away their plates, professionals who knew the shape of each other's skill and could take the rest for granted.

'I've something to confess to you,' he said. 'It's been on my conscience, especially when I took steps to cover it up.'

'Oh?' she asked, intrigued.

'I bought one of your paintings from Nick at the December showing.'

'Is that all? It's a pity you didn't wait and buy it from me direct. That would have saved his fee.'

Lord, she was unpleasable! Then he stopped and thought, What do I want her to say? Prink and curtsy and say thank you. Though she might at least be curious about which painting.

'It was the robinia,' she supplied. 'Easy. It was the only one that sold. I wouldn't be surprised if Marise put you up to it. It's just the sort of thing she would do. Be charming about me, and vile to my face.'

She pre-empted him on that as well. He had saved the compliment to souring point.

'I bought it because I admired it, not because Marise recommended your work. It was something I hadn't seen before, that tree specimen, and I had a notion I might be allowed to see your robinia in reality.'

'In reality? You place a hell of a lot of emphasis on reality.'

He felt he was going badly wrong in being open or inquisitive about her life, but he pressed ahead with the actual site of this tree to try and locate her permanently, pin her down. 'Where is it that you came from?'

'Came from?'

The buskers reassembled at the end of the street. They must be cold, he thought. They were in shade as the winter sun dropped below the building. Cold outside without cover. Chapped hands when you were going on to the Festival Hall at eight. What was this country doing with its talent? Making ten-year-trained musicians into street beggars.

'I came from nowhere.'

'I didn't mean, Where did you come from originally. I meant, Where do you live?'

No answer, because it was an impertinent question. It struck him that what he'd said to her at Nick's exhibition was increasingly true. There were no clues. Her sex had wrong-footed him at first and then her age. Married? Unmarried? Divorced? Good-time girl? He'd no idea about her background, couldn't even put a circle round her accent and say 'here'. Of Swedish extraction, Marise said, but the only hint was the pale hair. Nothing else. She's a mystery woman, Max confirmed, and he presumably knew a smattering about her, if he commissioned her work. Her past had died somewhere, or she had deliberately killed it.

'Today I came from Suffolk. On the train,' she gave out awkwardly, following the noise of the flute like distant wood-smoke. 'I live in a village you won't have heard of. Backwoods. It's so small it's not on the road maps. Odham.'

Gears meshed in his mind. As he paid the bill, his head lurched. Oh no, oh no. Not that one.

'A cottage *orné*, gingerbread sort of place called The Aviary.'

Morgan was immobilized at the cash desk, trying to remember what it was Lorraine had told him. A story about a man who was something of a collector and she'd had to sell off paintings to keep the house. EP. Express Parcel, fool that he was. The letters stood for Else Petersen and she was known well enough for Lorraine to use the abbreviation in the ledger. Had hers been the Gustav Doré prints and the unsigned Fuseli? A second confession formed in his head, admitting to her that she'd passed over a likely Gainsborough and that he was the gainer. Two pictures of hers he had bought, not one.

'Have you lived there long?' he stalled.

He encountered a third man in her life, not Nick or Boris, whom he now scored off a lengthening list, but the connoisseur she'd lived with. That was where the holidays and the couture clothes came from. She was selling off his pictures one by one. What else had she got hidden down at The Aviary, Odham? Should he tell her straight off about the coincidence of his finding the Gainsborough in Lorraine's second-hand shop or wait? Better do it now, he thought, before it gets too complicated.

'I must get back to work,' he said. 'Will you come for a little while? There's something I feel I ought to show you.'

It had gone two thirty. Marise had called in at the gallery and rung at the front door until Charlotte let her in. The woman pointedly looked at her watch when Morgan and Else arrived back, suggesting that her manager had overshot his lunch-hour by five minutes. He felt he was meant to be reproved by this glance, which she'd have kept to herself if he'd been entertaining an official client. Only Else? That was a leisure pursuit and not legitimate business. Morgan ran into the restrictions of being a hired man after the free space of self-employment. He realized Marise could make a pastime of checking up on him like this and bringing him to heel. Besides, his attitude had shifted over lunch. She had no conscience, while Boris came uneasily into focus as the other man he'd like to have along to square the numbers up or to amplify.

Morgan went on to the offensive. 'Were you just passing, Marise?'

'I thought I hadn't been in to see you for some time.'

'Then you're quiet at New Bond Street too with all this snow?'

The woman turned on her heel away from explanations. 'We did have a little rush. Extraordinary, isn't it? You have a picture in the racks for ten years with nobody interested and then, for no reason at all, several buyers are competing. A Scottish Impressionist painting. Ducks. Rather large and plain.'

Marise wore a raincoat with an ocelot lining, a bit of status-dressing in which she looked what she was, a powerhouse. Else thought it was a token gesture to the Anti-blood Sports League, to wear her fur inside.

The three walked together down to the basement, where the beige sisal cording underfoot and quiet lights made a cell, a haven below ground level that enclosed you like a rock cave, out of the main wash. This place would soothe the wildest nerves. Morgan was proud of the drawings and watercolours he'd chosen, well displayed and well lit, although he wasn't likely to forget this was the politest form of consumerism. Not vulgar, not brash, but, by heavens, money.

Marise made an inspection, walking up and down the ranks

with hardly a glance. A click maybe of recognition, know that, know him, that one's out of line. New face. She gave him a run-down as she went. Morgan had to grant her some astuteness. There weren't many unknowns in her sphere. Photographic memory, was it, encyclopedic knowledge or just her sound commercial graft.

Else's small pieces were well represented downstairs. She lagged behind them, grey on beige, bored with her old work.

'Sold any?' Marise asked, tapping a Petersen glass like a barometer to watch it fall.

'Not yet.' Morgan was forced into defending them and his choice. 'It's early days.'

'They're overpriced.'

Else moved up closer to see what someone overvalued. She'd forgotten the drawing and hadn't set its price. Nick had done that. A memory of other times, a waterside, a sunny day, the shape of an elusive idea, came back to her. A nugget of her personal experience went on sale for fifty pounds, from which the gallery and Nick's percentage might leave her a fiver. A pound an hour? The caretaker earned more sweeping pavements.

'I don't think you should persevere with anything for too long, Morgan. A shelf-life of six months for this sort of stuff is enough. In and out.'

He was appalled at the insensitivity, felt Marise was deliberately sharp in her economics to score against the painter. Was she angry because Else had come out to lunch with him, angry at some sideline of Boris's or simply sexist angry at the talent she didn't possess, including youth. He couldn't fathom this dis-missiveness when Marise had already singled out the work as exceptional.

Else walked off, aloof. She wasn't going to justify herself. The Scottish Impressionist which Marise had sold in the New Bond Street gallery was granted a shelf-life of ten years or more, but she and her contemporaries had less lasting power than a packet of cornflakes. Paint differently was the drive behind Marise's words. Be a norm of non-excellence, or give the punter what he wants and, for goodness' sake, no challenges. Either safe or conventionally subversive, but not the personal view. That doesn't fit the bill.

As they split away, Marise was angry with herself for saying so much. Yes, she was annoyed that Morgan was out when she called, was out with Else, that the pair of them returning made a sound in the echoing hallway of liking, of being alike, that wound its way upstairs in a burst of vitality against cool white walls. She told herself she wasn't jealous in any practical way. She simply distrusted human preference as a steady guide. Both these people had flawed pasts; she didn't want them to make a bungled future at her expense. Talent, which they each had in abundance, must be trained and restrained before it was useful. She was employing one to promote the other and her matchmaking stopped there. A curtailment was in their own interests.

Morgan stepped in, thinking it might soften this abrasive tone if he showed Else the robinia, which he'd hung between the two windows in his office, shedding its welcome yellow light out of season. At the same time, he wanted to avoid Marise's intrusion into his own quarters up above. But she was unstoppable on the tour of her property. The three of them sat round the desk in his office, while the woman scanned the sales ledger and Charlotte discreetly moved her paperwork downstairs.

'As you can see –' Morgan staked his ground – 'it's too much for one person to patrol. I need a business manager, a trainee possibly who could go on with you in time. I can't leave Charlotte in charge for long stretches. I should be out and about more, going to the provincial art colleges, going to auctions. Seeing the scene.'

Marise considered the suggestion reasonably, listening to the wisp of flute and tambourine through the sash windows which broke her concentration. 'Boris said as much. I've already got someone in mind and I'll make an appointment for him to see you next week. His name's John Camperdown. But perhaps,' she qualified, in case he thought he was getting it all his own way, 'you'd better have a car phone if you're going to be away from the gallery for any length of time. I might need to get you in a hurry. Can you see to that?'

Mess up his period car with modernist technology? He thought not. The three of them stood on the landing, looking down the white balustrade with the lantern light switched on to counteract the dark January afternoon. The women hovered, each of them wanting to be the last to leave, to see the other off. A terrible long moment of suspense that he couldn't abbreviate. He could cope with either of them alone, but together they were an impossible strain.

'What was it that you were going to show me?' Else asked the question he'd been dreading.

He was in for it and no mistake. The last person he wanted to explain the Gainsborough acquisition to was Marise, cynical about both of the delicate sentiments he attached to the picture, its source in Else, its subject his son. He'd have to make light of it. He backtracked to a wall on the landing outside the upstairs sitting room where he'd hung the drawing of the head.

'What's this?' Marise grasped the event at once and made it hers.

Else's face turned away. She was aghast that he'd shown her the picture in this casual way and in front of Marise, as if he had set out to monitor her reactions to its reappearance cold-bloodedly. She worked out the train of events that had brought the head into his possession, but was less happy at being dragged into any form of collusion herself. Exposing the picture meant showing her up as well and she looked terrified in case he implicated her, removed her cover, gave out information on her whereabouts that she guarded as an intensely private secret.

'Something like Gainsborough, isn't it?'

'Have you had it authenticated?' Marise checked such facts on reflex.

'I took it to Sotheby's. They said it could be, but won't swear to it. The style of –'

'But you think it is the real thing?'

'I'm eighty per cent sure.'

'It's not a Gainsborough,' objected Else. 'I don't believe it.'

'I found it in the right place,' he teased her. 'And it's old. Sotheby's confirmed that. The frame's original.' He told them about the companion drawing in the Royal Scottish Academy, elaborating on the similarities. Angle of the head, handling and colour tones. It was a see-saw game with them, Marise willing it to be genuine, Else refuting each item of his evidence. Morgan thought he was simply boasting, puffing it up before he let the story collapse again. He wanted to prompt the older woman into saying, You lucky devil, and the younger, Why didn't I spot that? Then both get up and go home.

Marise capped these normal responses by saying, 'I've a client who's on the look-out for just this. He wants to fill a gap in an eighteenth-century collection. I'll give you three thousand pounds for it.'

'It's not worth that,' said Else, feeling more drained by the minute. Her quiet objections were weak and overruled by Marise's strident confidence.

'What's anything worth? He'll pay it, I'm sure.'

Morgan was foiled. He'd thought it was genuine and here was a genuine buyer. Grab it, but some shreds of integrity made him hesitate. The picture had acquired a sentimental value, and he could not give its pedigree. 'It's not for sale, Marise.'

'Three and a half.'

'At any price.'

'Why not?'

'I can't guarantee it.'

'Let me worry about that.'

She moved back to the office to write a cheque on the spot, while he and Else followed impassively behind. 'I'm as surprised as you are,' he admitted to her, sideways in the door.

Marise took the picture away with her there and then, motivated to be off. Morgan saw her out, checked that Charlotte was supervising things below and retreated upstairs again to explain his doings to Else.

She had moved from the office and was sitting on the edge of his bed. When he walked in, she rolled over on her side and curled her legs up on the white coverlet. There wasn't anything provocative about the move and, going up to her, he saw that she was crumpled up in crying. Long years of marriage had taught him a bit about women's tears, at least that the immediate occasion wasn't the cause at all but had set off a regret or a memory that had to be released. He thought that these tears of Else's weren't for a lost picture but for a lost companion, the man she'd lived with, and that her loss was as human as his own, now that the face of his son had been carried away out of his knowledge.

'That picture meant something to you,' she said perceptively, in gasps through her crying. 'You shouldn't have sold it.'

Had she guessed his own association with the face? 'What makes you say that?' He sat down on the bed edge. She didn't hide the mess she was in. Tears were smeared all down her face. The sudden collapse of her cool alarmed him, an urbane woman just letting go of her poise.

'Because you wouldn't buy anything without good reason. That's proper buying. It means nothing to her except money. She'll sell it for twice what she gave you. She doesn't give a damn about pictures, that one or any other.'

She sobbed out loud, touching on a deeper woe. Oh, over-valued, quick in and out. He put his hand on her face. She submitted to his caress. He rubbed the tears out, thumb round the eye, palm on her cheeks. 'Buck up, love. It's only a ruddy piece of paper.'

'Oh, well.' She lay on her back and the tears poured unabashed over her hair, into her ears, until she smeared them. Her body, flattened out like this on top of the bed, was shamelessly accessible.

'I'll give you half.'

'Half the money? Why? Why would you do that?' She looked over in surprise but didn't doubt his word.

'Because you need it and, besides, we both know that the drawing was yours in the first place.'

'I'll give up my half if you will. Give her back the cheque.'

He hummed, wanting to do what she wanted. 'I could do with a cash input, but I'll try. Knowing Marise, she may not be open to persuasion.'

Else sat up, more composed. She looked like a child with big dark eyes and he was afraid about her fallen defences in front of men who might be less scrupulous than he was. Or was she, in a round-about way, inviting seduction. His pulse rate shot up and the desire which had been quashed by her helpless, unresponsive state came back.

'Did the dealer I sold it to give you my name?'

He avoided mention of Lorraine. Time later for that. 'No. I sneaked a look at your address from the ledger. When you repeated it over lunch, I nearly fell off my chair and thought I'd got to explain things straight away.'

'Will you come to Odham, even though the tree's bare?'

'I'll come.'

She stood up. 'Marise will blame you for this, you know. Say you were an accomplice.'

'Why? An accomplice to what?'

'You're too innocent, you know. You haven't got a clue about the real evil in people.'

In her, he thought, or in Marise?

February

'Forget it,' said Marise over the telephone. 'It's gone. Out of my hands. And anyway, Morgan, even if my client hadn't taken it so promptly, I wouldn't go back on my initial agreement with you. Bad business practice. What's the matter? I would have thought three and a half thousand was welcome news in your position.'

Why was she so sharp with him? She could hear the saw edge of her own notes and, after he rang off, the woman sat for a long time smoothing over them like unsightly creases on a dress. She justified her acrimonious tone by reiterating that there would be no 'old time's sake' excuses for being unprofessional, that Morgan and Else needed a strict regime of supervision to keep them up to the mark, that she mustn't pamper them to the point where they failed her or their own substantial gifts.

The street below was audibly busy, with the sudden bustle of a dry, crisp day. She went over to the window to take it in. Smartly dressed people were wending their way towards the Burlington Arcade, where the boutiques offered silver, cashmere, gentleman's outfitting, all so good and solid, or to the Friend's Room at the Royal Academy, and then on to Fortnum and Mason's for some delicacies that would be served up for afternoon tea. How she relished it! Success was simply being here in New Bond Street. Every precise detail of the building, the curved show windows, the unchanging Gothic script of their letterhead, the border pattern of the custom-woven carpet, which had been expertly mitred into the angles of the doorways, all proclaimed the triumph of her achievement.

But she couldn't rest easy, thinking that success would go on like this for ever. She had stood in the same position once before, different city, different times, and fallen. The gallery that her father ran in Heilegestrasse was more distinguished than the one in New

45

Bond Street, and older. It was a third-generation business – was business the best word for an institution anyway? – built on impeccable standards of taste and authority. We have sold paintings to the crowned heads of Europe was a credential that time had brutally eroded when it started to redefine the shape of Europe in 1939, as well as the shape of crowns and heads. In those days, they handled the very greatest works, because Berlin was the actual cultural centre of Europe between the wars, placed at the crossroads of a route that ran from Petersburg to Paris, and from Stockholm to Rome, *Metteleuropa*. What was London in comparison? London was only safe for pictures, never exciting. The English were principally collectors for their museums and public galleries, staring, acquisitive and inglorious people, she admitted, a nation of shoppers. But they had no private sense of taste, lacking finesse or visual training, and were too willingly impressed by fashion.

Berlin, well, people knew what they were looking at in Berlin. The Krupp Foundation had acquired a fine collection through their good offices, and Hindenburg too. Maybe it was those personal contacts that militated against her and her father in the event, the jealousy of influence, rather than the half of half of Jewish blood. Who knew it? Who sold them? Or was a name, a look, a merest suspicion all it took to put them on a wanted list. Anyway, a fire bomb through a plate-glass window in the dead of night was a summary conclusion to all boasts.

Hiding, hunger, fear, she could hardly catch the feel of it after more than forty years, when the London crowds carried on undisturbed. Never overrun or physically invaded, the memory of these people was shorter, or was curtailed by their insular securities. Mainland Europeans didn't forget the look of fugitives, and the apology that transmits itself into a stance, a voice.

That girl she was had perfected apology and invisibility. Walk beside an unleashed Alsatian dog, part killer wolf, and will it not to attack you, will it with every hair down your back, control your body's smell of fear, will your muscles not to betray you into hurrying too fast. Three or four times a year, she had to come up for air, emerged from hiding to sell another picture, broke cover, caught the tram from whatever apartment or cellar they had taken refuge in, and went to call on some of the dealers her father had done business with before 1938. Any one of them could have betrayed her, but they didn't, hoping there would be more from the same source. Kill her and they killed profit.

Why did she expose herself to danger? Hunger. Pictures eked out like grain in famine were enough, great works undersold to men who haggled on the strength of fear, debased into the valuation of so many bushels of bread and so many litres of milk. She used to see fat women in the street and wonder, where do they get the food from? They must feel so warm, wrapped up in all that fat.

After the war, she discovered that she was one of hundreds of U-boat people who were hiding out in Berlin, submerged like submarines and only rarely daring to put up periscope. But I was not a machine, she recalled. I was not waterproof. I was not naturally adapted to survive in those conditions. She remembered bombings like terrible storms raging overhead, wondering what the damage would be when she emerged, the unlooked-for kindness from strangers, the bitterness and anger of friends, and the difficulty of telling one from the other. To this day, she could recall her own frail shape as a girl walking through gunfire, haloed with terror. It was Anne Frank's life, except that she did survive. Die and you are a martyr, survive and you are hard.

So maybe she was hard. She would have put it as tenacious, or ambitious, not ruthless as such. And she didn't lose her respect for the thing she traded in. There were fifty pictures in their private collection at the outbreak of war; one at the end: I AM THE WAY. She could never part with that, her passport, her motto, her actual proof of tenacity.

Although it was Lorraine's idea to hold the memorial service, one year on, Morgan couldn't refuse to go. He was still trying to do the honourable thing. And anyway, if she'd already arranged it, giving it a miss made him look heartless or even more of an outsider to their common past than he already felt. All the same, he shied away from publicity for such a private grief. He couldn't grieve, couldn't externalize, while Lorraine made a ritual of her feelings in a way that made him embarrassed. It had driven him away, because without their son as a nucleus, there was nothing more than an empty house and an empty convention to keep them together.

Lorraine had busied herself in the right things in Bury St

Edmunds; worked for the Cathedral conservation society, the extra-mural committee of the University of East Anglia, was a patron of the Sainsbury art centre, made friends with the prestigious people in Suffolk – architects and professors, deans and industrialists – had a huge fund of contacts and was actually a very well-liked woman. She was looking better without him, he conceded, as he met her on the Cathedral steps. A handsome woman who could turn herself out for the big occasion. Dark grey, not black. Enough. He was still proud of her and that she'd cared about him once.

'What's the form?'

'It's a very simple service. A reading and a hymn. I endowed the Choir School with a prize in Michael's name and the headmaster asked if he could give a short blessing by way of thanks.'

'And afterwards?'

'You don't need to come back to the house, if you'd rather not.'

'You know I wouldn't let you down.'

How civil they were to each other! He remembered Else writhing on his bed from some inexplicable sense of loss; he'd never come across Lorraine behaving without self-restraint like that. If they had rolled on the floor and punched each other, they might have broken through the constraints, but theirs had been such an English marriage. Portrait of Mr and Mrs Andrews, placed slightly off-centre. The interest is in the landscape. The human beings are props. This serves as an illustration of ownership. He often felt an extra to this marriage, a male figure filling the corner who had certain advantages salary-wise, handy at the bar, reliable chauffeur and a contained sex drive. He had all but turned into the functionary husband she wanted, the right dark suit, the formal Melton topcoat, respectability incarnate.

A lusty green boy from the valleys, he'd not met convention until Lorraine embodied it, or presented her own intellectual seam of society as an attractive way of being received into it. She and her family had cut adroit steps across the class system, using taste, correctness, good manners, like safe second-rate pictures on your walls. There was a bishop, a title some way back, and a Georgian grade II listed house in Buckinghamshire, most English of the shires. These were impressive holdings when your grandfather was a miner and your mother a schoolmistress, and you were that terrible, unacceptable person, the scholarship boy and too clever for anybody's liking.

Morgan was rougher-cast than these English moulds, or newer, took risks, plunged in, not to destroy but to learn by living dangerously. It was unfair to blame her for the lack of spontaneity in their relationship. Inside marriage, the small-town precepts of being known, and being permanent, wore him down and he fretted at the collar of good works. He travelled. He escaped. He went to remote places to write articles for remote publications. He laid up the material for ten books in note form, raw firsthand experience, hurting, squeezing, storing the retentive capacity for his own future like a coil he'd unwind in time, but he didn't settle long enough to write more than half of them. Morgan is away, said repeatedly, became more than an excuse or a proof of his absence, but a systematic withdrawal from the joint state, mind and body. And really, he thought, a missing husband suited Lorraine better than the burdens of his presence, made up of washing, food and bed. He blamed himself for not being with her more often, an accusation that weighed more heavily because she never made it.

Lorraine went ahead of him into the dark vaults of the Cathedral. Behind her, men fell in. Morgan kept in step, unsure about his exact place in this ceremony, and feeling the pressure of hundreds behind him, watching as if he were being recorded on a screen for posterity, or judgement.

The Cathedral choir filtered slowly into their stalls from left to right, or bass round to soprano. The anthems they sang were High Episcopal, a long way from the chapel plainsong of the Welsh Methodist, like gilding over limewash. They arched and vaulted into descants and rounds he wasn't familiar with, resonances more emotive to his senses because they weren't everyday. They soared overhead. They invoked deity or the son of God in person, Baroque music and architecture together bridging the gulf between the lower and upper spheres, actually touching the unknown space and making it definite, or credible, in Gothic tracery and spires.

The first hymn which the congregation joined in singing, 'Nearer my God to thee', crystallized that sense of reaching out in words. He interpreted the line as meaning God the agent rather than God the objective – nearer, through god, to thee – because the thee in his own tablets of iconography, human or divine, was still unfocused. Although he had a secular mind, Morgan recognized the power of many presences in the Cathedral stalls. The words were very moving, although he tried to distance himself from their effect and not give in, or be swamped by the surges of feeling they gave off, like a man damping down a fire he knows will rage out of control if he lets it get a hold.

The commemorative speech was given by Michael's Cambridge tutor, who'd known him since his teens. He spoke prosaically about the boy-cum-man who fell short of his final manhood, listing his sporting interests, the cups he'd won at school and college, and his academic achievements. This comprised the standard public record, the outward show which everyone present at the service could share. But all the time, images flashed in front of Morgan's eyes of more intimate and fatherly moments, squalling birth, a sturdy-legged child running up a garden with a football, falling down then picking himself up courageously, without a sound, determined to get to the goalpost before his father. Sculls in the Cam, a picnic one isolated Sunday when Morgan joined the rest of his crew on the bank, pints of cooling beer drunk while they hung their feet in the river, trousers rolled; these pictures recorded the progressive stages of his maturity. In this litany, the name Michael was repeated several times and carried, on the cold February morning, into the tower until it was lost in the echo. Michael, Michael, Michael, like a peal of bells, the swell of sound was a congested pain. It prodded Morgan's memory unbearably with its surging refrain. Memorial service? Oh, God, give him the grace to not remember. He began to sweat in the effort of not weeping, or even shaking visibly, and held himself to attention. His head had gone to sponge, full of empty space.

The hardest moments to bear were the nearest ones, a home-coming that was cut short ten miles outside Bury St Edmunds, when a heavy-goods lorry skidded in rain and ploughed into the car that was driven by Michael's friend from Cambridge. He also failed to come back for the weekend. Or ever. They wait. He is late. Maybe held up leaving College. He should think to telephone. Don't fret, he'll be here soon. Just twenty. Vigorous and sensible, not his son or Lorraine's son, but the bypass of their weakness and fusion of their strength. At times he hurt for himself, with the incalculable bafflement of his emptiness, like a man moving round the vacancy of his heart, but more often he hurt for a world that couldn't spare young men like these.

Michael, my son, my friend, my hopes, myself, and all wiped out. Gone. There was nothing more final than the going out. 'Do not go gentle into that good-night.' That would have been his hymn or his reading, if he had been asked to choose. But he was not. He stood at one side, isolated in the intense and now unsharable sorrow of his lost fatherhood.

Blinding rain. A sharp corner. A waiting ditch and not a mark on him. How he wept at the cruel perfection of his son's body, chaffing the hands into life. He lay in a hospital bed for days, not even flat, but curling embryonically as if something would start in him and grow again. Twenty. The pointless waste.

The crash had broken everything for him, including his willpower. For months he sleepwalked. The future had come to an end. There was no point in ambition or striving, and he went through the daily routine like an automaton, without a human spark. All his old griefs were focused in this one, and his other failures. Each day was a new beginning, not in any adventurous sense but in fear, crawling out over ice, growing sensitive skin over a scar. Press him too hard and he would start to bleed all over again.

Summer. Some time.

The lawnmower was playing up and he and Michael had stripped the machine down and laid the parts out on the grass. Michael was the instigator, being more confident of his engineering skills. Only a tappet missing. Only a dirty spark plug. But when they were cleaned or replaced, the tappet and the plug didn't make any difference. The infernal machine still wouldn't fire. Two hours on, with the sun high and hot and scratchy, parts of the motor were lying around uncooperatively. They'd started to become pieces of a jigsaw puzzle to which they'd lost the illustration. How *did* it all fit together again? Michael fiddled without energy, thinking about a rowing practice in the afternoon, Morgan looking on.

'Just lump it along to the service agents. They'll stick it back together in no time,' was Michael's happy solution.

'I can't take a bag of bits into them.'

'Why not?'

'I know the manager.'

'You mean he might laugh at you?'

'You'd need to be a damn fool to dismantle a machine and forget where the screws go.'

Lunch was prepared off. Lorraine appeared with periodic admonitions. There were people coming for drinks at seven, remember. An evening on the terrace had been planned and the grass looked awful. Whose lawnmower could they borrow in the meantime?

'Why does it matter? It really doesn't matter.'

Michael was languid. Maddening to his father, who tugged at an unresponsive cord. 'Oh, leave it out, Dad.'

Morgan went into a silent rage. The incident reminded him of repeated bicycle punctures when the boy was young. Everything went well until the tyre was off, the limp inner tube lay snaked in a bowl of water and the trace of bubbles pinpointed a hole – at which point the boy gave up on the mending. He went out to play. He fell into a book. It rained. The bicycle rusted. Or Morgan had to set to with the repair kit and finish it off himself. He just couldn't leave it negligently to rust outdoors. It was disrespectful to his own work, to his paid time, to a childhood which wasn't deprived exactly, but had never been crowned with a new three-gear bicycle, and all waste was a sin against someone's labour. You didn't forget that upbringing. Michael was so casual, it drove him wild. This boy procrastinates, he had complained to Lorraine, which sent her into fits of laughter and afterwards was the standard family quip on his own half-done jobs, a manuscript past deadline or an unpaid, red-remindered bill.

'Well, what are we going to do?' He nudged the lawnmower problem forward.

Michael winked into the sun. The grass was warm inside the high-walled garden, and its flatness was tempting. 'I think I'll have a kip.' He rolled over on his side, knees curled up and shut his eyes in ostensible sleep.

Morgan flung some of the loose bits of machinery into a plastic bag and heaved the lawnmower towards the back of the car. It probably wouldn't fit inside the boot anyway. Even if they managed to borrow somebody's machine, how would they transport it home in a sports car?

52

As he passed his dozing son, his temper got the better of him. He lifted his foot and kicked him. Kicked him in the small of the back. Kicked his sleeping son. Not viciously, but hard enough to show he meant it.

Why? He'd had plenty of time to dwell on the offence afterwards. Why youth is carefree. Why it doesn't care much about counter-stripes on lawns. It was Lorraine's party and Michael was resolute enough to treat the event more lightly than his father. He'd serve the drinks, be entertaining, make the running in the laughter. To pot with stripes. He drew his own definitions.

Morgan should have knelt down and cradled his boy in his arms for love. So fragile and so fleeting a carcass.

Morgan spotted Derek Hisslop ahead of him when they got back to the house. 'I'm surprised to see you here. I heard you were in America.'

'I was.'

'Researching Gainsborough?'

'Well, they've got half the work over there. You can't study anything these days without going to the Paul Getty and the Metropolitan.'

Derek was a crinkly man, with hair that rose up from his forehead in crenellated waves and a wheezy voice. His students thought he was pedantic when he was at the Slade and maybe he was, for their needs, overly precise and professorial. He took to books. Books didn't argue back. People were jostling them as they stood in the hallway of the shop house across the square, as busy as if it were the first day of a sale, and they moved upstairs with the crowd.

Morgan could hear Lorraine in one corner of the room saying, No, he finds commuting into town isn't nearly as tedious as it used to be. The trains are half-hourly on the link. Is that me who is commuting? he wondered. Then she wasn't making their separation public. She was suggesting to her friends that it was just a temporary removal. When he looked round the drawing room, he could see she'd left a few of his belongings on show, as if he still lived there. But it was her idea to split up; she'd given him the final push – I really can't go on sharing my space with you – so what was she playing at, pretending?

'How long ago was it that you stopped lecturing at the Slade?'

'Fifteen years. Never looked back.'

'That's maybe too long. You won't remember a student called Petersen?'

Derek pushed up his forehead into wrinkles, thinking hard, and Morgan knew his memory was accurate enough to be relied on after fifty years, not fifteen. 'No. I never taught a Petersen. Ever.'

'Else Petersen. She won the first-year prize apparently.'

Morgan had never seen anybody's face change the way Hisslop's did then. Faces were normally masked in a conventional response but, for a second, the man's was stark-naked. Bare emotions. Amazement, anger, pain. He'd known the girl all right. 'Else Petersen. Is that what she's calling herself nowadays? She must be on to her ninth life by this time, I should think, or her ninth man. It's the same thing.'

Derek wasn't a nasty individual. Morgan hadn't heard this kind of bitterness from him before. Sackings, disappointments, he'd stayed equable through them all. 'Why did she drop out of the Slade when she was doing so well?'

'We never knew that. I was supposed to be her academic tutor and I never found out a thing about her. Not one. Nothing. I couldn't tell you anything about her to this day, where she came from, her family background, who she was friendly with. An absolute blank.'

'She wasn't called Else Petersen at that time?'

Derek drew back cautiously at the too definite question. 'Look, you must have met her, to be asking me all this. If she's tinkered with her name, that's her business. She's the one to explain it to you. But I can tell you one thing about her. There isn't a man alive who doesn't think to himself, If only I'd got to her first.' He'd had a shock, but gradually the teacher in him revived. 'So, she's painting again, is she? That's the main thing. She had the most versatile talent I came across at the Slade. Most students have got something, or enough of something to be going on with. She had the everything talent, still life, landscape, figure drawing, she could do it all. I couldn't forgive her for throwing that away. Just walking out on us over the first summer. Never showed again. Girls go and bugger up their private lives. That's why they don't make it.'

Lorraine came to find him with the headmaster of the Choir

School, but as Morgan left him, Derek said, 'I'd love to hear her version of events. It would be plausible anyway.'

All he could think about was getting away from here. Else was at the end of that day's journey. Else and her birdhouse waiting for him to pay his visit to Odham, even though the tree was bare. Hurry to catch it before it changes.

When everyone had gone, and he did the respectable thing and waited to the end, keeping up the make-believe that he was living there, Lorraine said to him, 'You've met somebody new, haven't you?'

They were familiar, man and wife, and likely to stay on reasonable terms. He didn't see fit to lie. 'Yes. A painter whose work I've been handling. I've got her on exhibition at the moment.' He thought of saying, You bought her Gainsborough, the one you gave me the last time I was here, but balked at it. She might know more about Else than he did, but on Derek's cue he didn't want to hear anything from Lorraine's lips first. 'Why did you think I'd met someone?'

'You don't look like a man who's looking for a woman any more.'

'How long did I look like that?'

'A year or two.'

'How maddening for you.'

'Are you in love with her?'

This felt disloyal and he dodged it. 'I don't know her that well. There's a long way to go.'

'How old is she?'

'Again, I don't know. Probably about thirty-five.'

'I wonder how much damage there's been.' She got up and put on the lamps, a moment she valued because it marked time. 'You can't get to thirty-five without a bit of damage. You won't expect too much, will you?'

He stood to go. The phone rang behind them but before she lifted the receiver, Lorraine said, 'You picked up some baggage after all.'

He didn't like this county any more than he liked this time of year; they went together, flatness and February and fens. Else said the village wasn't on the road maps and she was right. All he had to go on were her directions, a crossroads, a big house on the left behind a wall, a footpath and half a mile of winding B road before you reached the turn-off. It could have been anywhere. The hills lifted a little towards what would have been a Saxon encampment years ago, but a history-laden past was the only event in unrelieved dullness. He found the turning, with some misgivings. It headed off left under a hedge and straight into a gloomy clump of trees. Dismal. Blue woodsmoke hung in the air but, from a distance, there was no sign of a chimney as its source, or a bonfire. After a few hundred yards he came across a faded notice: PRIVATE. NO ACCESS. He thought he must be off-course but nosed on, intending to reverse and go back when he reached a side lane.

The trees opened suddenly. There was a clearing after all and Else's house sat in the middle of it, just visible over a boundary stone wall. What had she said about it? Cottage orné, gingerbread sort of place. It was just that. Gothic windows, crone, boy and girl, where you expected a cat with an arched back on the roof and stacked wood piles, and, in fact, some rooks started to caw in the bare-leaf trees as Morgan walked over the gravel. A folly. A fancy. Somebody's idea of a summerhouse at the far end of the estate, then gone tatty, out of fashion and later on restored, possibly by the man who left the house to Else.

Else came to answer the door while Morgan heard voices behind her, proving that she wasn't alone in the house. There were two cars parked on the drive apart from his. He was disappointed at finding other company.

'I'm sorry,' she said. 'I couldn't put them off. I won't be much longer. Look round, or make yourself some tea in the kitchen.' She was quite dismissive and went back to her other guests, who were a couple of tweedy, solid-looking women he could see through a glass door in a sitting room. Why couldn't he go in and join them? What was wrong with a few sociable, hand-me-round introductions?

He wandered, a bit disgruntled at being shuffled to one side, or not made much of, but you couldn't be bad-tempered in this house for long. Everything in it was interesting, not necessarily old or valuable, but the objects raised a question, often: What on earth can this be for? It reminded him of the royal accolade to a famous interior designer: How clever of you to make it so shabby. The house didn't pretend at all but it hid its secrets with some charm: stairs in a cupboard, a landing that had been opened out and fitted with library shelves from top to bottom, while a curtain was hung in one corner round a dormer window, to make a bachelor bedroom if needed. There was a crop of surprises, spaces you wouldn't guess at and false fronts. The layout had become complicated to the point where you couldn't work out the original design.

He leaned out of the landing window and encountered the view that was hanging in his office. The robinia was planted in the well of the sloping garden, surging up in the middle of it like a fountain, although it wasn't an impressive tree out of season. Prompted by Else's résumé, he'd looked up its strange name in a horticultural dictionary. Beautiful foliage but much flawed as a garden specimen, was the professional verdict. Even at this distance, he could make out the spikes underneath each bract which would scratch the unwary. The wood was brittle and probably susceptible to wind damage; this one had suffered in a couple of storms and grew in a lopsided way. But it filled the space of the window and the garden pleasingly, as if it had taken all the air it needed: a full tree. He looked forward to a fuller spring. Behind it was a view of the plain lands of Suffolk that would take your breath away, and the sea lay just over the horizon, rolling, hilltop, treetop prospects that tantalized you with what you couldn't see. Morgan was taken by the place, a close enough identity to what he liked that it actually shocked and stimulated, like a facsimile of his own choices, meeting himself unknown.

He saw that Else had been working at a large table on the landing and had pulled out books to consult some reference or other. These were unusual, specialist books, he thought, running down the shelves. He quickly located a rare sixteenth-century Bible, and portfolio books such as a Toulouse-Lautrec with art reproductions at full-size – he remembered when that one was being issued, because he'd wanted to buy a copy and it was way beyond his means – and some examples of Victorian printing, which routinely employed up to a dozen separate colour plates, before the introduction of trichromatics made run-offs bland and safe. This was a bibliophile's paradise. He found a few that were inscribed to someone called Ralph Pennington. It looked as if he'd been a friend of Allen Lane's and other publishers Morgan had known through Max. They even shared a few of the same limited editions and special print runs. He found one that was imprinted on the frontispiece:

Colophon of this book. 1,500 copies were printed at Christmas 1958, at the Westerham Press and bound at the Dorshel Press, Harlow, Essex. Monotype Van Dyck was used for the text. The paper is Hosho-Shi from Berrick Bros., who also supplied wood veneer for the cover.

When he picked up one of these books at random, newspaper cuttings would fall out of it, old reviews, articles about the writer or the subject, the book being used as a handy file index. This was a real, working library and, to an extraordinary degree, the collection overlapped with the personal books he'd left behind at Bury, including well-thumbed copies of his work. So Ralph Pennington had been a fan of his. He felt he'd come into his own.

He kept on flicking through the inscriptions, piecing together the man's circle of acquaintance, but at the same time he was laying the ghost of Else's other persona. He hoped that he might come across the birth name she had tinkered with. Inside a couple of hours, he'd rationalized Derek Hisslop's outburst about her being on to her ninth life or her ninth man. He couldn't literally mean nine name changes. People sometimes did revert to a middle name later in life and, for all either of them knew, Else had been married or chose to use a professional name that was different from her maiden one. What was wrong with that? There was nothing sinister in using a pseudonym.

'Who were they?' Morgan asked as he turned around and saw Else coming up the open-rail stairs to find him. The windows were wide on the latch in a lustreless February, although she was wearing nothing but a pair of loose trousers and a denim shirt with turned-back cuffs. The faded blue colour went well with her hair. Bare legs and slip-on shoes. She kept her tan and looked too young to be seeing men like him.

'They were from the Friend's of Sudbury Hospital. We're fund-raising. They were good to Ralph when he was dying. And good to me. I do what I can to repay.'

'Why couldn't I meet them?'

Her back was towards him as she turned to go down the stairs again, but he sensed her stiffen along the spine. 'I keep my lives separate. It doesn't do to mix the on-duty with the off.' Her tone was light; her meaning was unarguable.

But which was he?

They were crossing the hall and, as he walked in front of it, a painting forced an acknowledgement out of him. 'Don't tell me this is a Picasso?'

She smiled. 'OK. I won't tell you it's a Picasso. That one was Ralph's.'

An uncatalogued painting. One of the escapees. 'Do you get many people here?' He was thinking about security, and if she vetted her hospital committee.

'Invited or uninvited?'

Derek said she kept her friends close. But did she have any in the first place? 'Either. You should have a burglar alarm installed with these pictures about.'

'The trees are good security, as well as a ten-foot wall. Nobody knows I'm here and I don't advertise it. A total hideaway. And if the pictures go, they go. I'm not going to get into a frenzy about insuring them or locking them up.'

Two Constables, a Modigliani and a Chagall at a quick stocktake, apart from the Picasso. And as yet he hadn't gone into a single room. These were on the stairwell or the hall. The place was a treasure trove. He valued the pictures one way, she another, and her downbeat attitudes reminded him of no one more than Michael. Human ease or enjoyment was more important than the fuss of ownership. Leave it out.

They had tea in the kitchen. She was quick and casual with things. Not much matched. No sets of things. No conscious collecting. A teapot and a pair of hand-thrown mugs plonked down on an oak gateleg. No ceremony either. Morgan didn't know what Else had in mind when she extended the invitation. Call in on the way back from Bury was all she'd said. For afternoon tea, for supper, or would the invitation be extended to staying overnight? Her place, her conditions.

'Ralph was...?' He started to explore hesitantly round the first personal name she'd given him after her own.

She looked tentative, someone private or preternaturally shy. 'The man I lived with. For a long time. Much older. He found me when I was ill and sent me down here to convalesce. He was married, of course.'

'His wife's still alive?'

'Oh yes. They had a house in Belgravia, but it was a tomb of a place and she sold it when he died. She's moved away to Salisbury.'

'He left you this cottage?'

'The birdcage. Yes, he left me the birdcage. Not everyone was overwhelmingly pleased. His son still tries to make life difficult for me.'

'Ralph was living here at the end?'

'He hated London latterly. He wanted to be in the country all the time, just listen to the birds and look out over the woods. This was his retreat for years and I could hardly stop him coming even when he was very ill.'

'Ralph's other name was?' he asked, innocent of the library browsing.

'Pennington. You've maybe heard of him. He was a well-known printer in his day. They said he was the best fine-art printer in England. He was the one who introduced me to Max Edelman and the illustrated book people. He sold his business interest to Max when he retired ten years ago. He probably could have been an illustrator himself, or a designer. He was a fine draughtsman. Studied in Paris in the 1930s. I mean he was a personal friend of Dufy and Picasso and Chagall.' She confirmed the route of the pictures into his collection, as gifts not purchases. That's right, the Picasso was early period. 'But he was too sociable, or too impatient. He didn't stick at it.'

'Tell me more about Ralph. I feel I'd have liked him, from the way he did things and the friends he made.'

Else put her cup down. When her eyes caught fire and she looked straight at you, she was irresistible. She lost the rather passive sexiness of herself in repose, a looker, and turned dynamic, a doer, drawing you inside her interests, forcing you to share ideas. 'He did so like and admire you. We had to have the phone off the hook when your series was being broadcast. It was compulsory viewing. Or compulsive.'

'I'm flattered.'

'We made the journeys you suggested, like pilgrimages. We did the new cathedrals and the recent collections. We even went to the States especially to retrace programme six, and kept tripping over other addicts while we were there.'

Morgan approached her praise cautiously. Did she mean it? Why was he on the look-out for an ulterior motive with her? Curse

Max and Derek for sowing these doubts. He'd found no evidence whatsoever of insincerity in her but was still tentative. She didn't overexpand on her background, but neither was she the mystery woman of repute. Take her for what she was.

'Ralph was a strange man, multiple. Could have been almost anything: which meant he ended up dabbling and felt unfulfilled. But he taught me more than anyone else about colour and precision and harmony on the page. He was very strict about sloppy lines. About all sloppiness and sentiment.'

'How lucky you were to know him.'

'And unlucky.'

'Why?'

'Oh, standards of excellence you can't match.'

The passing remark had one meaning, that she couldn't live up to Ralph's expectations, but it went on to imply that neither could he, or any man afterwards. He could have left her a more accommodating legacy.

'We'll go out now and walk. That's enough indoors for one day.'

He continued moment by moment.

Great Odham had been a sizeable estate at one time, starting with a Tudor farmhouse and eighteenth-century outbuildings that were solidly built, and spread out with the generations to a Victorian stableblock and a line of tied cottages for the outworkers. The Aviary was where gamebirds were raised for the shoots in the wood, and there was an inappropriate Doric temple two hundred yards away from it, built to commemorate the victory against Napoleon. Else had converted it into a studio, with windows on each side and a glass cupola. It got all the light that was going, although the studio was without electricity and that meant she couldn't carry on working after dark, which was probably as well.

The plot of land attached to The Aviary was a thin cross-section of the original grounds, bounded by estate walls on three sides, while the narrowest verge was sectioned off by a running stream, and it was virtually open beyond this lower level of the garden, which gave a view on to fields and more distant woods. The garden was totally secluded on three sides and unprotected on the last, which did, as they walked down it a little before sunset, give uninhibited vistas to the west.

Magda Sweetland

The First World War brought hardship and a chronic labour shortage to small country estates like this one. Taking the carriage or the horses over to have tea at The Aviary, where the ladies could feed the caged birds, wasn't a fit occupation for serious-minded people who'd lost their fortune and their sons in the war anyway. Bits of land were parcelled out here and there until the thing disintegrated. The village dwindled from a census count of five hundred in 1871 to nearer two hundred a century later. Half a dozen different groups shared the original estate, including a pottery commune in the stableblock, the new farmer and his wife struggling to make a start on the smallholding, Colonel Eversley in the main house, which he inherited from his father, and Else perched at the top of the hill, looking down on the rest of them through the trees.

An hour saw it all as they toured inside the perimeter. Change, decay and the native woods re-establishing themselves as walkers became discouraged over time. It was tough going in the dark, with not a light for miles, the real, impenetrable night of countryside. Morgan carried the haversack which she filled with kindling wood. Why were woods prohibited places after dark? They snared the foot and deceived the eye, providing cover for evildoers. And yet Else walked through here every day, frequently at nightfall, and was unafraid. He would have thought twice about doing this shady circuit alone and was impressed by her lack of fear.

'What have I got to lose?' she asked dismissively, just as when he expressed caution about her valuables. 'You've a terribly safe mind. This much danger is exhilarating.'

She wore no jacket either. A sweater mid-February and frost threatened. Dampness settled on her hair.

'Danger.' In the dark, she took his hand and put it on her face underneath her own hand. 'See. You're cold in spite of all those clothes and I'm warm. You just need to say to yourself, I will not be cold. I will not be afraid. And you won't be.' She peeled back the layers of him until she found the shirt.

He put his free hand round her and held the clasp steady so that she was three times trapped and couldn't move out of the embrace. They kissed for a long time with feeling, cold-lipped, warm-mouthed, remembering the fire indoors. She leaned on him and moved inside him, sparing nothing.

'Warmer, that,' she said. 'Now let's get back for supper.'

* * *

This woman had long phases when she was quiet. It wasn't a surly, non-communicative silence, he decided, but the preoccupation of people who had spent a lot of time alone. He felt there was a monologue going on inside her head if he could only break into that wavelength and get her to transmit. Her face was changing in expression all the time, pouring or beating, as she went about the kitchen. It was satisfying, that peaceable companionship, a talking without words.

He set places at the kitchen table in the meantime, filled the stove in the living room and hung about to enjoy the heat it gave out. He found her tapes and played some motets by Monteverdi. But all the time the question burned in his head, What about tonight? I'm no good at this, he thought, the transitional relationship. It was a long, lonely time when a marriage disintegrated, and he wasn't at all macho or bullish about the thought of getting into bed with a stranger, or what was expected of a man nowadays under the covers – or on top. He tried to quell anxiety. Kindness, comfort first.

Else called him for supper. She served English food, pie, potato and no pretence. The only concession she made to twoness was dimming the lights over the work surface, and pulling a weighted lampshade down lower over the table. And she had changed into a different and more stylish blouse from the afternoon, with short sleeves. As she served him, her wrist turned over and, for the first time, he noticed two unparallel scars on it. They were deep, deliberate cuts that had silvered over with age.

Morgan sat stunned with the implications and wondered about ignoring them, but he couldn't turn away. When she finally took her place opposite him at the kitchen table, he took her left hand and deliberately opened it outwards. There wasn't any doubt about the cause of the double incision.

She looked down, remembering a mental pain so severe it made the pain of cutting her own artery trivial. 'Tin-opener job,' she said.

He was shocked by the words as much as by the act. He needed more of a cushion. He needed the story, or the softening of circumstance which she'd probably never divulge voluntarily. 'Do you regret doing it?'

'I regret not succeeding, yes. But I didn't hurt anyone except myself.'

'That's not true. It hurts me now.' It did. What could have driven the lovely and talented have-everything young woman to make an attempt on her own life? It did involve him retrospectively, at least in the effort to understand her.

She took up her fork to eat. A rift opened between them and Morgan could see that he'd been taken in by attraction, by wanting to connect with another person so much that he'd overlooked the disparities. They might be alike, in taste, in interests, in the people they worked with, but they hadn't lived alike. Start again. Be patient.

'Do you want to tell me how it happened or why?'

'I was twenty and I didn't want to go on living. People had let me down and I expect I'd disappointed them too.'

She was unemotional, just milling salt on to her food. The words demoralized him because Michael's memorial service was still to the fore, an unhappy and self-reproachful corner in the mind. He put these words she spoke into his son's mouth and they hurt twice as much, as if early death must encompass a willingness to die. In an illogical way, he was aggrieved that she didn't know about Michael's dreadful accidental death, or didn't care enough to ask him the questions that he was asking her. What have you been doing in Bury until three in the afternoon? He would have answered the prompt honestly. That was the trouble second time around. He wanted a new relationship, wanted desperately to succeed with another person, and so must she. But they came carrying the old trappings of failure or prejudice. There was no such thing as a fresh start. Just as he wanted exposition, she wanted quiet. Average that one out. The burst of tears about the Gainsborough came back to him, and he felt out of his depth in unravelling her responses. The big and the little style cancelled each other out, or were too complicated for him to put into an easy focus.

Maybe he should have left well alone.

'Was that while you were at the Slade?'

She went on eating for a second, then actually choked with her own tension. He'd done that himself before now. The rise of feeling cut off air to the oesophagus and made you gasp for air. She got up, roughing back her chair against the quarry tiles, and poured herself a glass of water, coughing harshly all the while, the nervous, breathless cough of fear. 'You have no right to quiz me about the things I've done.'

'I'm not quizzing you,' Morgan said peaceably, worried at how she was overreacting.

'Who told you I was at the Slade, then? I didn't tell you that. I know exactly what I've said to you and I never told you that.'

They were standing together at the sink and he tried to soothe her shoulders. She knocked his hands off, tipping a little undrunk water on to the floor.

'It was Max Edelman, I think, the first time I met you. Remember, he came up while we were talking. And then I saw Derek Hisslop this afternoon when I was in Bury. He remembered you, very kindly. What harm's in that?'

Her features were written in dark distaste, and the more powerful for it, like black enamelling. 'You've been checking up on me, Morgan. I don't like that one bit. They say women gossip, but it's the men who are really unscrupulous. London's a whispering gallery. There's no privacy and no honour in those people. What did Derek say about me?' she demanded. 'It would be personal and probably sexist. It wasn't about my painting.'

'That's not true. He said you had the most versatile talent he'd come across at the Slade.'

'Versatile for what?' She wasn't mollified. 'You were swapping notes about me.'

Morgan started to get heated in return. 'You're exaggerating about what's been said. These men admire your work, Max and Derek. And besides, if you behave in this secretive way, people will invent secrets for you.'

She picked up a dish from the table and put it back down in the same place, roughly, blind with rage. 'Why should I have to explain myself? I'm not public property. I have every right to protect myself against these people. They mean no good. They're vicious and small-minded. Would you confide anything to Nick Wylie? He'd tell it all over town, and inaccurately too.'

I paint, I don't talk about painting, could be converted into I live, I don't talk about life.

'I do respect that. You don't have to explain yourself to me or to anyone else. But I can't change human nature. You're talented,

65

you're an attractive woman and you're elusive. That's a high-profile combination, whether you like it or not.' Even as he was trying to reassure her, Morgan thought, What is it that this woman doesn't want me to find out? She was afraid of nothing, not night, not solitude, nothing except the fragile reputation, of words in other people's mouths.

She groaned and, leaning on the work top, dropped her head below her shoulders, turned inside herself. He could see that being exposed or talked about was a source of very real distress to her. 'There's nothing more that I can say to you. You've let me down. As I am or not at all. Go away. I think you should go away and leave me alone now.'

The food congealed on the plates. Morgan couldn't find anything to do to redeem the day. The pleasures of firelight, music, staying into Sunday lost their appeal. She meant it and he didn't have the brute strength of bullying to argue it out with her, or the seduction confidence to take her in his arms and persuade her otherwise. 'Will you be all right on your own?' The scar lines haunted him.

'Never better.'

She turned round without any warning and caught her place setting with the back of her hand and swept it dramatically on to the floor. Glass, plate, half-eaten food, the lot went crashing down on the quarry tiles. Morgan had never broken anything wantonly in his life and felt this wasn't typical of her either. The house was careful and well tended. No, he had to admire the genius of her malice; this was the waste most likely to offend him. Innocent objects, innocent labour. It made her the spoiled rich kid and him the doddering mender, down on his hands and knees picking up pieces. But it'll be me next, he thought, and did as she suggested. Vamoose. I've not been into this long enough to hang around.

He wasn't minded to wait for an apology or her explanation, or more of the same. There was a violent streak in her he hadn't bargained for, irrational weeping, irrational temper. Damn her and damn deception. He hadn't brought anything inside except himself, so it was easy to walk out. He revved the car engine, angry too, as he skidded on the gravel lanes towards the village lights.

March

Most of the art establishment in London was to be found along a golden mile that ran from Harrods in Knightsbridge as far as Simpsons in Piccadilly. Any other position was an alloy. The mile didn't run true. It dipped down to Belgravia and the back streets of embassies, it moved up New Bond Street, but by and large everything worth selling was sold along that axis.

Nick Wylie was feeling irritable, while the gravitational curve of the floorboards in his office, behind the behind of Piccadilly, added to the mood of misalignment. He was tired of operating from this backwater and wanted to move up to the main street and the mainstream, somehow. But no matter how hard he and Harriet worked, however many clients they represented and exhibited, they managed only to squeeze by. Three years into it, he had to conclude that marriage was of itself an expensive occupation, or a drain on the personal resource. And women had a way of ganging up on you. The bank clerk at the corner branch was actually in the habit of telling Harriet when he'd been in to cash a cheque. The nerve of it, the sheer insensitivity. Harriet had spent half an hour that morning nagging him about his claim for expenses against the business, and produced a bank statement to prove that their deficits were larger than credits last month. Where were they going wrong? Where were their savings?

Savings? The word had a hollow, hypothetical ring to it, implying some grim economies which they'd have to make in the future, rather than money already put aside. They could cut down on employing a personal secretary each and double up with one. Bit cosy that. Bit lacking in ... the desirable confidentiality. He'd come to rely a lot on Lindsay. She was a bright girl, he thought, as he watched her through the open doorway of his office, really too sharp for the filing or typing jobs he gave her. She was nice to have around, amusing, fuzzy-haired and a good trim figure. He liked the way she walked, pushing her legs out in front of her, pushing her thighs. And breasts not insignificant, as he cupped them in his mind. Couldn't cut down on that. If the truth were told, Harriet had a rather hard, straight body, not sensuous anyway, and he'd overheard someone of late apply the deadening word matronly to her looks. Her real asset, her wonderful bronze hair, had started to look messy rather than bohemian, and unsuitable about the office. You shouldn't work with your marriage partner, he sighed, day in, day out.

Their desks said everything. At the start, he'd claimed the larger room of right, had more theoretical space but, all the same, things spilled over. There were always piles of pending. He liked a sense of busyness and filled the walls of his room with colour, old posters from his favourite exhibitions, signed artists' photographs, some leftover blow-ups, the handsomely bound catalogues printed for the showings he was proud of: all of these memorabilia were pinned on to the peg-board cladding of the walls and their loose edges flapped at him gently as he paced. Harriet was bandbox. Cream Regency stripes, wipe-clean desk, not a stray dossier in sight. That depressed him mightily, as if, among her attributes, she were even more efficient with blank space than he was.

Going out for his lunch appointment with Morgan, he put his head round the door of her office and her quiet precision screamed at him.

The woman hadn't meant to nag, only warn. Debt frightened her. Solo, she'd never been in debt, and she felt, like Nick, it was the duo act that was threatening to run them out of control. What if they went down, he and she? Bankrupt or divorced, the shame of it. 'Do you think you'll be at home this evening?' she asked tentatively, hoping for a smile from him or something gentle, a bit of simple kindness.

He could hardly bring himself to answer. 'I doubt that very much. The management committee could go on with this agenda pretty late and if they suggest adjournment to the bar I, for one, will not be saying no.' His voice thinned dangerously to a whetted knife. 'I've got to make progress where I can, Harriet. You know that.'

She looked away, stung by the hostility in his voice. Made her tearful now, he thought, without a pang beyond dreading the length of the reconciliation period. The huffs. Oh, God, the marital huffs that nobody had warned him would take the oxygen out of his air. He'd just about worked himself into a position where he could have an evening out alone, old friends, a drink, so what, only to find Harriet sitting alone, in the dark, in tears when he got back home to Greenwich. He had thought he'd either get marriage right straight away or not at all. It looked like the latter.

The most recent tiff was complex and had started at the weekend, when they were asked for dinner by some old friends of his. The day before the dinner party, their hostess had rung him up: I just wanted to clarify that Harriet knows about us; I wouldn't want to say something wildly tactless that dropped you in it. No problem, he assured her, pre-marital water under the bridge. Ten minutes later, the second lady guest rang up and said, As far as Harriet's concerned, are there any snags about you and me? No problem, all forgotten and forgiven. Clean-slate stuff. When they arrived, there was his first fiancée he hadn't known was going to be invited, plus her new husband, and when they sat round the dinner table, he thought to himself, Nick, you old scoundrel, you've slept with all of these women at one time. It was very polite, though, giving rise to discreet inner mirth. During bored moments of the meal, he toyed with the various characters in the piece, casting them in a scene for a television play. It could come off. *Tranche de vie.*

He repeated the whole episode to his sisters the next day at Sunday lunch, much amused. Harriet had interposed, 'I've heard this story before. I'll blush for you, dear.' He didn't take the hint. He thought it was a genuinely funny incident and he'd been faithful since his marriage, sort of. What more did she want? If you married at over forty, the chances were you'd knocked around a bit. They were neither of them in the first flush. Just as she had much to overlook, so did he. Her affair with Martin Price, London's last impresario publisher, had been a byword. Harriet was the official mistress and hung around for ten years, waiting for him to shed his wife. Which in time he did, but not for her. He cast off wife and mistress in one go, in favour of a catching assistant, twenty years his junior and pregnant to boot. Nick saw that Harriet lacked a certain life wisdom he couldn't now implant. He'd always been a quick-turnover man and couldn't change either.

Even more to his regret, the business wasn't gelling. Harriet's clients weren't good exhibition material. She tended to handle the commercial side of things, those poor toilers who drew landscapes on a wine-bottle label for a living and put 'Artist' proudly on their passport. He had to spend too much non-constructive time with them, and wasn't getting his hands on the big names he used to work with when he was an exhibition organizer full-time. He'd given up too much of his own talent for spotting, to suit Harriet's bent and her established, rather run of the mill clientele. Covent Garden had served to remind him of his real vocation, putting on a live show, making it fuse there and then as ringmaster, not the hack drudgery of agency work, all paper and negotiations. He felt he'd dropped a notch. What he needed was a star.

'Dry your eyes before your chappy comes, there's a good girl.'

The kind word did cheer her. Harriet had truly believed that if she persevered with Nick, was patient, loving and understanding, he would in time become the same. When they were courting, and it was a whirlwind courtship, she reminded herself, blazing, a meteoric passion in their sphere, bright enough to put out other lights, she had found herself saying to him, Your trouble is, you've never been loved properly. Implying? That she could sustain him through a slower turnover, could compensate for other lacks, could be the all-in-all. This was her last-chance marriage and when he left her alone in the evening for male carouses – or whatever – he demoralized the ethic of industry which she believed she could apply to men. In time that phrase, spoken in the sots of passion, had amended itself more meaningfully to, You've never been loved improperly, because she started to suspect that what Nick wanted was adultery, or the thrill of mental philandering, and he needed a wife only to make his scenarios tense or wicked. What did he do between seven and eleven in the evening, most days of the week? It implied a vacuum she couldn't fill. Admonishing him about his expense account was a token complaint about the unknown side of these indulgences. A bottle of champagne was who he shared it with. A hotel suite for entertaining in the Cotswolds, likewise.

And the lies he told! The evasive answers! She had pushed and cornered him with every means she knew into telling her the truth, not so that she absolutely knew but to share whatever he had been doing in the interim, but he wouldn't yield. She began to hope the lies were truth, and knew herself the bigger schemer by complicity. She had no pure standards left.

'Who is it you've got coming in this afternoon?'

Harriet named an American painter who'd had a vogue ten years before, then faded away. 'He thinks he may do better on this side. Taste's not so brittle. The Tate are doing a 1970s retrospective and he'll be featured in it. It might be timely to take him on.'

'Ah, well. I'm sure you've done the spadework.'

Harriet shifted. She knew several things about this forthcoming meeting of hers were unscrupulous. The passed-over American already had an agent in the UK, although she was attempting to part them. She was not so different from Nick after all, promiscuous with partnerships. She'd been chagrined to discover recently that the two of them were nicknamed 'The Pinchers' among their circle. Bottoms and other people's clients. Harriet had had a degree of success with the disaffected: artists whose recent exhibitions hadn't met their expected sales targets, old hands looking for new outlets or those, like the American, hoping to be remodelled into the latest fashion. She didn't see the need to apologize for her methods when she'd revitalized a dozen slack careers and handled some prestigious painters, for all Nick's scoffing. From a thousand to ten thousand pounds a canvas was the all-important step. Get on or get out was the motto on the golden mile.

'I must go or I'll be late. Morgan won't come more than half-way to meet me. He says he's seeing someone at the Royal Academy this afternoon. I wonder who that can be, and what he's up to. Isn't it odious how quickly he's got back in the swim? Oh, and don't wait up for me, darling.'

As he went out, Nick paused to check the copy typing he'd given his secretary. 'Have you finished that already, Lindsay? You clever little thing. You'll be wanting a bonus next.'

She had a ravishing smile too.

Harriet heard the door close behind him enviously. He could do that. Walk out. Farewell to you, farewell to her. Farewell. Envious too because she'd rather be lunching with Morgan than doing an ego massage on the American. She had a sense of time in hand with Morgan, or an old friendship pending renewal. Maybe not yet. If they sat over a table in Piccadilly, she couldn't avoid confiding her fears on Nick's sincerity, and she feared most of all that Morgan was too honest not to confirm them.

* * *

Over lunch, Morgan was dour. What was it about Welshmen? All the Celts, really, temperamentally dour and cheerless.

He was annoyed at being kept waiting, at Nick swinging in without an apology. It was one fifteen by now and his next appointment was two prompt. 'I'll settle for an omelette. Ham. That'll be quick.'

'So things are picking up at Covent Garden?'

'I don't think they were ever particularly down during my tenure. Quiet in the snow, but who wasn't? Painting that house green marble was an affront, but it did work. Good colour, green. Restful. A park in the city. We're thinking of putting up racks in one room of the basement and selling art books. It's a bit tacky, but who can afford to be élitist nowadays?'

'Max Edelman will be pleased if you shift some of his back list for him. He's got enough unsold stock to keep you going for years. Bad chooser, Max.'

Morgan ignored the slur against their mutual friend and ordered drinks. 'Perrier for me.'

That was a bloodless Welsh drink. 'I hear you've got John Camperdown as your trainee manager.'

'Yes. Have you met him?' John was no highbrow but he had a sympathetic manner and didn't put off the younger clients who strolled through the doors in Covent Garden. When he said, Can I help you? he sounded as though he meant it.

'Marise introduced us once. He was doing a couple of months' work experience at New Bond Street. He'll never be as good as he thinks.'

Morgan had heard this phrase so often from Nick over the years that he'd started to turn it round and fix it to the speaker. It was a facile judgement, the opinion that was hard to prove but impossible to refute, and defined Nick himself as attuned to the inferior. The acute mind would have been able to say why, in more specific terms: you know that he dropped a clanger once, he failed to spot a major talent, has self-indulgent taste. Nick had said it of most people at some time, including the artists he routinely exhibited, which the other man thought was disingenuous. This game was energy. Success was strident or assertive, not taking swipes at the folk you were meant to represent.

'I came because I wanted to ask you if you had anything in mind

72

for Else Petersen later this year.' Three weeks after his summary departure from Odham, the name was still congested with pain for him. She hadn't been in touch, and Morgan wasn't going to crack first. But their kisses waited for more.

'No, not really. Max is publishing the almanac in June and she put her flag out last December at Covent Garden. That's not too bad.'

'How long is it since she had a one-man show?'

'Let me think. Three years, or more. You don't mind if I smoke?'

Nick rummaged in the scatters of his memory for her card file and couldn't actually remember how long it was. Prickly in case the man implied he hadn't been looking after Else's interests properly, he covered himself with a comment that was only incidentally disparaging. 'I did like the early work. That dense style. She'll be very lucky if she ever reaches that pitch again. How are you doing with her?' deflected any residual guilt that he had not done well with her either.

'She's selling steadily. But, of course, it's small and not very valuable work.'

'Oh, she doesn't need the money. She's well provided for. Rich sugar daddy. And still owes me some fees,' he mused.

I'll throttle you, thought Morgan. What is Else doing hanging round with this fellow? He was almost grotesque, a scavenger of ideas and not a legitimate scout. 'I've got to come clean, Nick.'

'I know, I know. It's wonderful stuff, but you can't do a thing with it. Much the same as Else herself. We've all said the same about her at one time. You've tried, given it a fling. So. She'll have to settle for immortality. It pays better.'

Nick was glib partly from his own disappointment. This painter, on whom he'd pinned considerable hope, hadn't turned into the star he had projected. He'd been patient, fifteen years patient with her. Encouraged, talked up, lent her money when she needed it, gave her space, a room in his own house in one of her runaway moods, before the Harriet days, in fact had done more for her than any other woman ... any other woman he hadn't slept with, but she didn't deliver the alternative goods either and every philanthropy needed its return to go on being given. Some agents had a single artist who paid for all the overheads. But Else wouldn't capitalize on her talent. Wouldn't play the game. Dozens of worse artists were better self-publicists because, whatever opportunities you made for Else, she'd quit on them. I am going away on those dates. No photographs. No biographical details. It was like trying to hype a ghost. In the vacuum she created round herself, it was easier to blame her for a lack of marketable talent, or of energy for paint, rather than blame himself for not promoting her effectively.

Morgan watched the second double vodka disappear, innocuous on the breath. Was that the alcohol talking? It certainly wasn't caution. Didn't Nick realize people remembered what he said? He grimaced to himself, and plodded on regardless. If he wanted to do Else a favour, he'd have to go through the proper channels in dealing with her representative, however distasteful. 'There's an empty church in Cambridge where I thought we could organize something for her.'

'A wake? No, right, sorry. It's about time for a benefit performance.'

'It'll be vacant in October, which isn't a bad time in Cambridge. Students back. It's a good site. Good venue. I have several contacts at the university and the arts centre, and they can guide things along.' Morgan doubted Else but he had never doubted her ability and, whatever the state of play between them, was determined to use his influence to give her work more prominence. It was a gesture, love of sorts.

Nick began to get edgy at the suggestion. Was Morgan going to oust him? He might actually make a success of the proposed exhibition and take over the handling of Else's portfolio. You never knew, she might come good after all, and if she did, he wanted his fifteen-year return. 'Have you spoken to her about this?' Nick ordered another refill.

Morgan wondered who was paying for the lunch as the multiple vodka arrived. Not him, anyway. He'd give Nick the chance of earning commission on this show if it came off. He paid his own bill in ideas. 'No. I'm approaching you, in the first instance, as her agent. I'm passing you a tip and have done your groundwork for you. Be good enough to acknowledge it.'

Nick caught the tone, which was far from aloof. He pulled out a pad of paper from his breast pocket and scribbled down some notes on time and place. 'I'll see to that. Splendid idea. Wonderful,' he said, as if he had alighted on it himself. 'Wonderful. Confab to follow.'

Rising to leave, Morgan watched the paper disappear back into the pocket, curious about where that scrap of information would be filed, if at all, in the chaotic office behind Piccadilly. Everyone put up with the random methods and the gossip for the same reason: five per cent of it might find the target. He was bull's-eye or miss.

Alone in the thinning restaurant, Nick realized he had five hours still unaccounted for before the management committee meeting. He had wangled himself a whole afternoon out of the office. Pity there was no one he could ring to come and spend it with him. Lindsay perhaps? Harriet wouldn't know anything about it, out to lunch herself with this American painter. Harriet's own secretary would provide cover at the office. Time for one more. You've changed my life, he heard himself say in preparation as he went to make the call. I couldn't do without you.

Morgan telephoned the Chairman of the Friends of Sudbury Hospital and a made an appointment to see her the next time he was driving to Bury, *en route* for Cambridge this time and the church of St Martin. He told her he was an old colleague of Ralph Pennington and would like to make a donation to their current appeal fund on his behalf.

She was a pleasant woman, guileless in spite of being diary-organized and let him lead her. She was probably one of the tweedy team visiting The Aviary at the same time he was there. Ralph had died on 14 August last year, of cancer, she said without concealment. He gently introduced the name of Miss Petersen into the conversation. The woman changed tempo at once, saying Miss Petersen was a most generous benefactor of the hospital and an untiring worker. She visited their hospice every other week and had done so for the last two years. 'She's a saint,' the Chairman said, 'the woman is a saint. She's there all day sometimes, talking it out with patients or their families. Thoughtful, and kindness itself. We often find that it's the people who've lost someone close who can listen that way, with endless patience, and help them to cope with terminal illness. They've lived through it themselves. They know. It's a tremendous strain, giving that back-up, and not everyone can take it. She's pulled the unit together in a way I wouldn't have believed. We've raised almost enough for a second scanner.'

Not a bad rate for canonization, Morgan thought, as he passed over a cheque for a hundred pounds.

18 March

Maybe you've seen this already, but I was taken aback by lot 27. Can we retrieve it before it goes any further? I've entered five paintings for the Royal Academy Summer Exhibition. Hard at work but I am missing you.

Else

Enclosed in the envelope was a copy of a Sotheby's catalogue for a sale the following week, offering fine-quality English paintings of the seventeenth and eighteenth centuries. Lot 27 was down as:

A recent discovery, presented at auction for the first time. White, black and coloured chalk on prepared grey paper. 12 x 10in. Head of a young Dutchman in naval dress. 18th century. Unsigned but attribution to Gainsborough. Uncatalogued.

Straight away, Morgan got on the telephone to Adrian Crane for an explanation.

'I'm sorry if you think I boobed over that one. It looks like a bit of self-interest, doesn't it, feeding our own commission? But you know we checked it out as best we could, at the time. I said it could change any minute, but I do agree the minutes seem to be getting closer together than they used to.'

'Who authenticated it?'

'Hisslop. He's back from the States.'

'I know. I ran into him last month. Did he have any corroboration?'

'He went and looked at a similar drawing in the Royal Scottish Academy before he pronounced on it. And he consulted someone else besides their curator. I'll look it up if you want. All three were for it.'

Morgan's instinct was vindicated, if not his staying power. 'It's been a pretty quick turnaround for the vendor. Marise sold it to a private collector only last month.'

Adrian stalled because he wasn't supposed to reveal the owners' names. 'It's Marise herself who's selling it.'

Morgan was disconcerted by that bit of news and, coming off the phone, started to worry at something more deep-seated than his own stupidity in not hanging on to the thing. He found that he was drawing triangles on his blotting pad. The auction houses took ten per cent of the selling price. Their resident consultant – Derek Hisslop in this case – gave a previously unknown work his official blessing. Fair enough. The vendor was delighted to own a substantiated picture which now fetched a much higher price at auction. After all, like the companion drawing in Edinburgh, it was public-gallery collectable and moved into a different league. The snare in all this was that a percentage was normally paid by the vendor to the expert, in much the same way that an insurance assessor took a proportion of the value of the jewellery or furniture he'd priced. There was nothing to prevent this 'fee' being subject to private negotiation – that is, the more you as art historian say it's worth, the more I as auctioneer will give you from my commission on the auction price. In whose interest was it to undervalue a piece that had no other pedigree than a man's opinion? The higher the estimated value, the higher the premium paid to everyone concerned if the picture reached that pitch at auction. The triangles interlocked and got bigger. And all done by gentleman's agreement.

He'd started to pick up odd and troubling rumours about the way the auction houses were operating. They'd lend their own clients the money to pay these artificial prices; they earned interest from the loan, plus a commission from the original sale, and went on inflating the art market and their own stock-market quotation, all in one go. Or they planted 'bidders' who would step in and make a simulated bid if things were sluggish, with the picture occasionally being marked down as sold when it was nothing of the sort but was returned to sender after the dealings closed. Auction hysteria was what they were whipping up. Record prices made good headlines. Mysterious telephone bids, undisclosed sources, the frisson of getting rich quick in a sedate, dress-suited milieu, all very enticing but it was ephemeral in the end, creating false markets and false hopes. The last person to benefit was the painter. The condition for wanton fashion to operate successfully was that he'd already parted with his work and would not touch a penny of the profit.

As an art historian, Morgan had been outside that triangle hitherto, a commentator, a free agent. Now he was in there wrangling. Twenty per cent to you. Twenty per cent to me. Twenty-five per cent to the tax man. Let's see if we can take the artist out to lunch and keep him alive a little bit longer. Don't want him to peg out exactly.

He phoned the New Bond Street gallery with the intention of tackling Marise about it. She wasn't in. He left a message with her assistant, and got the answering machine when he redialled impatiently at lunch-time. All that tiresome business of getting a straight reply in London offices where people were hiding down the electricity cables. Eventually at four o'clock she got back to him. 'You rang?'

Did telephones emphasize the Teutonic notes? Marise had a powerful and pleasant voice, but the receiver took out the more subtle inflections and made it monotonous and cold, like a mechanical music box, lacking the quartertones. Was that his subjective opinion? No, he started to notice the brittle accent like a drill of sound, which was masked by her personal charm when he was with her.

'What's the background on the Gainsborough drawing that's in the Sotheby's catalogue?'

'My client turned it down. It wasn't what he wanted after all. Simple.' At least she wasn't covering up the fact that she had put it into the auction personally, and he wouldn't have to implicate Crane for breaking their professional code.

'I had asked to repossess it, if you recall.'

There was a steely silence. 'Repossess, Morgan? A slip of the tongue, surely. It implies non-payment. My bank has not defaulted on honouring my cheque. In fact, I have the statement in front of me. It has been cleared – 23 January. Prompt. You drew on my account quite promptly.'

'Repurchase then.'

'But you are perfectly free to repurchase it at auction. What are you complaining about?'

'I'm complaining about being stitched up, Marise.'

The silence grew and breathed. 'Your wish to reacquire the drawing could be misinterpreted as sour grapes. On the other hand, if you're accusing me of double-dealing, that's a charge you might find it hard to substantiate. Be careful.' Marise was very used to this, people complaining about misevaluations, and she had her arguments prepared ahead. It made no difference that the man was her employee; he must be shown that her methods were inflexible.

Something clicked on the line. Morgan thought she probably recorded her phone calls. Yes, she was the type to sue for an unwary word or force a public retraction that wouldn't do his credibility any good.

'What I'm trying to clarify, Marise, is that I sold you a drawing on the understanding that it hadn't been authenticated by Sotheby's experts or anyone else. I said so in front of an independent third party. I only want to establish that it was a spontaneous, voluntary purchase on your part. I reiterated several times that I couldn't guarantee its history, and cannot now.'

She laughed and was jolly once she felt he was backing off. 'Let Sotheby's worry about that. You had their informal opinion. I have their formal one. The difference is a bit of paper.'

'Hisslop put his signature to a certificate?'

'Yes.'

'Then I wash my hands of it.'

Morgan turned up at the auction for the hell of it. It had attracted more than its fair share of interest among buyers and the press. The art market had been matching the stock market that spring. Every auction set new record prices and this in itself made him uneasy. The sententious old moralist in him thought people were buying paintings who didn't know the first thing about them, and didn't care. Oh, they'd look after them. Temperature controls, humidifiers, darkened rooms against fading from sunlight, but they were guarding an investment, not a love affair. Art markets hadn't worked like that until recently. The Medicis had bought a craft or a skill and looked after their artisans as highly valued men. Admittedly, those traditional patrons took some reflected glory from the artist, by way of power or grandeur or illusion, something non-ascertainable or uncertificated, but there was never this gilt-edging of works of art to hedge against inflation. Using art as bonds, unique but tradable. It upset him somehow. It was a life's work, after all.

He'd been to enough auctions to find them repetitive. Normally, he could read a novel through the early lots or do some paperwork. This one was different. It crackled from the start. Boris was there, standing in for Marise, blue-suited, glittering. The auctioneer was one of the senior men at Sotheby's and knew most of the bidders by name. Twenty major London galleries were represented and another twenty institutions world-wide. There were Japanese and American scouts, poker-faced men bidding on behalf of anonymous clients, while the busy telephone lines were more discreet still. Morgan folded up his book and put it in his raincoat pocket.

The Gainsborough drawing was small beer. There was a full-sized Joshua Reynolds portrait in oils further down the list which was going to attract heavy competition, but these introductory pieces set the tone. They made more than respectable prices. The auctioneer gave a brief run down of lot 27, stressing its newness on the market, so that the opening bids were slow, or possibly nervous. Marise hadn't put a reserve price on it. Two, two and a half thousand, it straggled upwards. Morgan wasn't going to go above the three and a half thousand he'd been paid for it and put in his bids at two and a half upwards, alternating with a variety of others, but then had to drop out. He wasn't going to pauperize himself for the sake of proving that he'd been right all along.

It rocked about ten. A new bidder put up another five hundred and the room looked round to see who'd come late into the dealings. It was Else at the back of the room, grey-suited and tidy again, still a stunning woman in the crowd. Just her appearance created the right excitement of glamour. It would be assumed by the house she wasn't bidding with her own money, so whose front was she? She started questions flying. She was bidding strongly, determined to recover her drawing. Morgan wondered where she was going to get ten and a half grand, for a picture she'd sold for under two hundred pounds and which she'd consistently averred was not authentic. Sell a Picasso to buy a dubious Gainsborough? Strange economics, those.

There was a lull, a small shock of reappraisal, before things gathered momentum. Two bidders went neck and neck, dropping the hundreds and leap-frogging over each other a thousand at a time. The auctioneer stumbled catching their figures. Morgan had never been privy to such a piece of lunacy in his life. The heat in the room, the mood of bull markets, the plush hunting pink of Sotheby's above austere panelling, gave the lie to common sense. Something broke out and paid up seventeen and a half thousand pounds for a paltry drawing in a frame. Madness.

It was cooler outside, one of spring's deceits.

Through the glass entrance doors, Morgan watched Else and

Boris as they met in the hallway. They embraced, talked, touched the other's arm and were visibly fond of each other. He sensed it would have been a different encounter had Marise been about and that there was something private in their regard. He bent over her. She listened carefully. Let it go. Morgan hadn't acknowledged Else's note, thinking it a ploy. He'd never run after a woman in his life and was too old to start. He turned about and waited forlornly in the taxi rank.

A minute later, Else walked through the swing doors and came to stand beside him on the pavement under the green and gold canopy, as if she'd seen him all along and was following him on purpose. 'Made a mess of that one, didn't we?'

'And some,' he agreed.

This must be the modern way of doing things. You travelled into a relationship, changed your mind and moved on. Met in the light of day and it meant nothing in particular, the warm cold kiss in Odham woods or a mental giving, not much more than a handshake, yours in mine and mine in yours, body camaraderie. It was an adult form of Pass-the-parcel, unwrapping a layer as you went. Hand it on round when the music starts, to find who's paying for the next meal and the next holiday.

Was he being cool enough? He didn't feel it. There was that draining into the loins, not even a wholehearted passion, but an emptying of the rational functions into the instinctive ones, and not dignified. He'd thought more about her in the interval than if he'd gone on seeing her. The empty space pulsed. Things she said went on enlarging; that she was a perfectionist over some things, which included people at a guess and mostly herself. She couldn't bear to fail or be reminded of the fact of failure, because Ralph had left standards of excellence you couldn't match. Or was her passionate outburst that evening simply an inability to come to terms with what was real, and really boring? She'd said she missed him in her note, but he suspected she could say whatever was expedient. She'd wanted him to get the Gainsborough back and, by her precepts, he had tried. A quick cab ride was her gratitude.

A taxi drew up as it came to his turn in the queue. Else opened the door ahead of him and got in first.

'I presume that you're coming my way?' he asked, joining her.

'You can always open the door and throw me out.'

'Need I remind you that that's the lady's privilege?'

Her eyes were chastened but a touch amused. 'I didn't mean to throw you out that Saturday. I really didn't. I was quite surprised when you drove away. I thought you'd go upstairs and leave me alone until I got myself together. Anyway, I do apologize most sincerely for being a nuisance. My problems have piled up lately and I haven't been myself.'

'Whatever that pronoun entails.' His wit was edged. A little dip in caustic.

'You're used to sharing your life with someone. I'm not. I'm no good at communicating. It's the thing I've failed at.'

'And so have I, it seems. But you've just proved you know more about my private life than I have personally told you. What am I supposed to do? Rant because Nick Wylie handed you a bit of uncensored gossip?'

'I won't rant again, ever. My second and my last chance, if you'll give it me.'

'I'll take an option on that, without penalties.'

Before he left Sotheby's, Boris looked round for Adrian Crane to thank him for speeding the Gainsborough through the sale, but couldn't locate the young director. Not in the auction room. Not in his office either. He buttoned up his jacket and took to the blusters of the street in March. He crossed behind Morgan and Else on the pavement edge and plied the road at an angle through parked cars to stay out of their sight. He came to a halt outside Asprey's for a few seconds, eying a pair of Georgian silver fighting cocks which they had on display. He thought he'd buy them, then applied the corrective of asking if he needed them and concluded that silver was a time-consuming product, with endless polishing.

'Seventeen and a half,' he said on one side to Marise, who was entertaining two foreign customers. Like the great public galleries, they kept the majority of their stock in the storeroom and not on display. Paintings were racked with rows of cardboard in between, which made recognizing them more difficult. Marise was working with one of their assistants, who would lift pictures out and put them on a stand for the client's perusal, a long and tiring process. This was an old client of theirs who had moved on to his third wife. She didn't like the last wife's pictures and would replace them from top to bottom. Marise was skilled at fitting pictures to people as seamlessly as a couturier.

'Seventeen and a half!' Not the amount but the mark-up pleased her, four hundred per cent. She clapped. Just once. It was an irritating gesture, part command, part approval, and it reverberated after him upstairs. Thunder, cannon, the one-note peal caught at his heels like a dog-bark. He moved quickly ahead of it, a little afraid of being caught.

So Else was seeing Morgan in earnest. The other's abbreviation of regard was short-lived since Else's letter, at the turn of the year, implied they hadn't hit it off. Marise had passed on to him that they were together at the Covent Garden gallery in January, but he had presumed it was a working reference. Now a taxi ride was taken as a double fare. A development.

He was upset by seeing Else, always upset. He could view her objectively, or with less affiliation, than at one time. It hadn't escaped his notice that on the golden mile they were all childless people, he and Marise, Nick, Max, Morgan – who tragically lost his only son – Else herself. Different reasons, different accidents of alliance. The dynasties ran sideways, husband and wife, siblings, uncle and nephew, but children did not seem to be in the order of things, as if their world were a dead end, or a self-absorbing one. He had heard Nick Wylie pass a facile comment once: 'Harriet and I are adopting our family gradually, lots of young talent.' That smarminess had sickened him, glib and insincere, making a joke out of the largest vacuum of a life. What did they value? What was there left to value once you had lost your future, or the people who might inherit your workload?

Looking at the silver birds in Asprey's window, he had thought to himself, Money no object. It was the shorthand gloat of Midas but once he tried to write the sentence out in full, the elided words asserted themselves as powerful and complex, beyond parsing. Money wasn't an object in itself. Money had no objective. I don't object to money when it can buy anything. The possible declensions of the idea sobered. The phrase had as little roundness as one of Nick's; they had worshipped simulacra too long and it had made them counterfeit in turn.

Boris didn't boast that he'd survived a year in Buchenwald, knowing it was not intact. Or that Marise survived her own kind of house arrest in Berlin, when she was not unscathed. In 1945, they were the old young who made the roll call of their dead, among whom they counted, although they didn't know it, their own unborn. They met each other after liberation, when they were sent for some months of convalescence at one of the United Nations rehabilitation camps in Sweden. They had tried to pull themselves back together into human shape from being monsterized, with advice that was medical but more often psychological. Don't overeat, don't overrun, don't expect too much of your system because the post-traumatic shock will take years to work itself out. They met in a spring like this, cruel alternating with balmy days. Recovery. Growth. Finding the capacity to share with other human beings without going through the round of suspicion, withdrawal, reprisal and cunning. England had no memories. They went to England afterwards.

Else put a battered cotton raincoat on top of her grey suit and walked through the lanes behind Covent Garden, turning men's heads. John Camperdown and Charlotte had already left the gallery, which reverted to being a house again, a private place where they would return together after an evening out. A date. Yes, a date. Morgan got the old buzz from city streets and walking beside a woman he knew only half well, wondering what the all of her entailed. Her shoes made the right noise through the sound of his, and sometimes she swayed towards him on her heels, emanating promise.

On Thursdays, the shops stayed open late. There was enough light from the windows for a theatre workshop group to put on a pantomime show outside the Punch and Judy bar. Else hung about on the edge of the crowd, frowning. 'What is it that they're laughing at?'

'Topical jokes. It's a kind of calypso about current affairs. That's the Prime Minister's nickname they're playing on.'

'No wonder I'm not with it. I don't think I've read a paper for a year. Oh, don't you start to scold me about all that up-to-dateness. It just gets in the way, being informed. How pretentious. I am formed, not informed. Right?'

'Tiresome woman. Are you hungry?'

'Well, you obviously are. That's a good enough excuse for eating.'

'Full fig?'

'Half fig. I'm not dressed up for a lah-de-dah dinner.'

They paused in front of the pub. Her breath came warm through a chilly evening, suggesting openness. I want to kiss you in one of these doorways, he thought. This is my patch, I'm known, but I don't care who sees me. I've lost track of what anybody else thinks because I want to hold you in my arms so badly.

'I know,' she said, reading the look. 'But it'll wait well. It always does'

They drifted back in front of the shops again, looking at the clothes they couldn't afford. She twisted a silk-screen scarf round her shoulders and declined it; he thought of all the times he wouldn't wear a Harris tweed jacket.

'So Germanic. So macho.'

'Do you mean it?'

'Hm. Sandringham and shoots and leather patches when it comes of age. I'll go for that. I like functional clothes, hard-wearing outdoor clothes built like houses, to last.'

'I'd rather buy you something.'

'All right. Buy me a hamburger and a pint.'

They sat outside. Her breath thickened against the colder air. She curled her legs for warmth, legs so long that she could twist them round twice. She wore an angora sweater under her suit. He remembered how girls wore these to birthday parties when he was young, soft and shedding. Every so often she blew into the rollneck collar of her sweater and burrowed into the heat it gave back.

'Why don't we go inside? You must be cold.'

'It's full of smoke inside. And people. Out here, look.' She put her head back on her chair. 'Even in the middle of London, the stars can shine.'

They did too.

'There's a blackbird in one of those gardens. Can you hear it? And somewhere near, a very healthy specimen of viburnum. Smells like lilac. Can't you pick it up? Well, you're too citified a gent. We should have got you that country jacket after all. Or maybe I've got an old one somewhere that would fit.' Under her suggestion, the garden reasserted itself in Covent, maybe a prosaic market garden in the first instance, but one air pocket of the open organic spaces that ensured London was able to breathe.

The other hardy souls moved away after a time, shrugging off the cold like a dew on their shoulders. They were left alone on the piazza. The music and laughter at the far end of the avenue receded into the archways. There was no hurry, nothing to catch. Their own door was round the corner. Living in the middle of the city was like being the last partygoer. The chairs sat out all night and they could too if they wanted, talk the stars round the orbit, wait for the blackbird and the sun to come up, as they laid out his plans and hers, side by side. Had Nick broached the Cambridge exhibition to her and attributed the idea back to its source? Or they could go through the zodiac of her book illustrations, some of which he'd put on sale as limited-edition prints. He liked them very much, but mostly because he liked her. There were a lot of seductions in talking about the self. He could kiss her into compliance, not the cold outside kiss of woods and doorways, the brushing stuff of youth, but the warm inner one of fulfilment and maturity, and make it impossible for her to leave.

His place, his conditions.

The flat was lit on a time switch and always warm. Once she was inside the door, she shed her jacket, and underneath that, she shed her sweater too. She was wearing only an all-in-one body stocking and was surprisingly warm and insulated. Hers was a scooped-out shape that could hide its femininity, strong joints, a shield of hair and shoulderblades as flat as a boy's. It was how she moved that was provocative, something unusual in his experience. He felt, in their first uncovered embrace, that he was touching on areas of anatomy he'd not encountered before – or was touched by them. Women could love you with their hands. She felt his head, drew to a point, shaping flesh intimately as if she had to feel him to see him. What put that line there? her kisses asked. A meeting of lips wasn't that simple. She tested his mouth, was sceptical and went back again, back and forth, to prove it. She made other incidental meetings, a shoulder burrowed into his arm, a knee lifted the back of his, taking up all of the floor space; it made for total and on-going envelopment. In this mood, at least, she hid nothing or was completely truthful. She was the everything lover, strong, compliant, modest, demanding. His first reaction to what she was offering was simply carnal, lusty after so long.

'Else, I—'

'I know. I am too, but we might as well try to make it to the bedroom.'

They didn't.

Rich Hours

The second lovemaking was more emotional and more thought-ful. She made things easy for him, moving ahead, drawing back the coverlet, undressing down finally without shame or prudery, hidden in her hair. You didn't need to know a lot of men to know a lot about men. It was the calibre of intensity that held him. She had a wide berth of forgiveness and acceptance, so that he felt in her arms not absolutely loved – who would dare to make such a boast – but absolutely known, not necessarily in time but in essence. The moments she created with him were new and unanticipated. Some women could say or do things in the privacy of sex that you never forgot. They redeemed ordinariness, where the self was seen vivid and most alive.

She lay back, done.

The walls of the room, as pale as screens, threw up the lights from the late-night traffic on the Strand.

'I used to lie like this in Islington and watch the cars. I was stuck. They were on the move. The whole city was going somewhere, except me. I hated London then. London isn't for the young, or only for the rich young.' She moved her elbow on an angle and looked at him in the intermittent neon dark. 'What would have happened to us fifteen years ago?'

'I'd probably have treated you very badly.'

She sighed. 'Who says that you won't now?' She flattened herself, arms under her head. 'We did meet, you know. You came to give a lecture at the Slade while I was there.'

He slewed round, disbelieving. 'I don't remember that.' And yet he did, in the chink of recollection she opened. Just one lecture, on his speciality at the time, and it was Derek Hisslop who had invited him at short notice because a guest speaker had cancelled. The smell of art institutions, turps mixed with disinfectant, over-whelmed his memory.

'I do. You talked on postmodernism. I showed you where the staff room was. You stopped to ask me the way. I wonder what would have happened if I'd bitten. I knew who you were. Was mad about you in that kind of cerebral crush. Were you into adultery? Well, I'd have made you choose. You wouldn't have got off lightly. You should have known me at nineteen. Think of that, what you could have spared me. I'm sometimes sick with jealousy about what I hung back from. All I needed was a bit more courage, a bit of the flirt in me. When I hear you say you're taking on students' work, I am sick, not about them, but about me and what might have been different. I don't suppose it would have been this, but you'd have given me something.'

'That's foolish talk.'

'I know. But I'm not given to it. Indulge me once.' She ran her hand down his torso, making him bristle. 'I like you. I like this. I was lovesick for months afterwards, the way girls are. But then I did what men do and took up with someone else instead, poor substitute. At least I did concentrate all my mistakes in one year. It was after that I dropped out of the college.'

'Why?' He asked the leaden question. Didn't show after the summer. No excuses given.

'Free love, well, I'd like to see it. Nothing's free for me.'

'What did you do?'

'Went to live with a man. It seemed more important at the time.'

'Who was he?'

'Who? Now, why would you ask that? Does it matter?'

'Only if you think so.'

'It doesn't. Oh, let's not dwell on that. I have been mad, but I am not mad any more.'

'Can you sleep now?'

'With a little help.'

April

A month of honey followed.
 They took a break from both places, his and hers, and set off for Binham in Norfolk, where Morgan borrowed a friend's house for the long Easter weekend. The foreground of the journey to the sea, the London to Odham stretch, was mutual or held in both memories, but taken in a rush with the hood down and Else's hair flapping with a noise like sail, blowing sometimes across her face, sometimes across his until she tied it back, it was untravelled country. She knew the woods at Thetford well and told him she'd scrambled along the prehistoric shafts of Grimes Graves, taking the fifty-foot drop down a steel ladder in dodgy shoes. She'd collected pine cones for Christmas decorations from the Forestry Commission woods at Thetford, although she found cartridges from the army firing ranges in among the pine needles. He knew the salt flats at Walberswick better, the reedy beds and strange half-world of that foreshore like a moonscape, weird with chemical distortions in the pools which turned them bright pink or yellow, neither sea nor land. On their trek north, Swaffham market on Saturday morning slowed them down with wares put out on street stalls. Things to turn, things to hold and want. She liked a tub chair, but turned it down because they'd nowhere to stow it now, or in the foreseeable future.
 The hinterland of north Norfolk came as a surprise to both of them, one of the unexplored kingdoms. Tidy little villages were connected by roads that either went sturdily on from church to church or dived off under hedgerows of thorn intercut with umbrella plant, quite prettily green, a bit like hellebore. So you tell me, he said, and I believe you, for I'm no plantsman. It was rich growing land, the soil pink and friable. There was a fair bit of rapeseed upsetting the balance of the landscape, and cereals too young to identify, but otherwise these were almost prairie lands in

richness and immensity to the horizon. The farms were hearty places, with red-brick houses and red-brick barns, no lesser shelter for the livestock, joined up to each other with solid walls, and well kept almost without exception. These farms were the wealth behind the wool churches.

And the churches were like the farms, in continuous cultivation. Built of flint, or flint plus dressed stone, they were a striking testament to affluence, good design, the initial homage to religion and then its stewardship by later generations. The best were more like ships than land buildings, battered, storm-tossed, grey odysseys of survival riding high on the plains.

This was Else's commentary while he was driving her round the places she wanted to visit, Norwich Cathedral and Our Lady of Walsingham. When she arrived, she fell silent again, focused into seeing and drawing, spilling out dozens of quick thumbnail sketches to help her remember the shape of each outline. I'm sorry, she said, there are no real holidays. Everything's a research trip.

They meandered along the slow, flat country, riddled with waterways and double-barrelled names which sounded more like people than villages, and arrived at Binham by the easterly of its five-point-star approach. They drove up and down the High Street looking for the address, admiring the good, the plain, the solid artisanry of the place, until they found a sizeable house where a caretaker neighbour let them in. The good woman was already dressed in her coat, hurrying off to a concert in the Priory, and, intrigued, they dropped their bags in ready-warmed rooms and set off after her along the High Street on foot.

Morgan thought there were few unknowns left for him in buildings. He'd never seen Binham Priory, or heard of it, like a famous book that had completely passed him by, and was unprepared for the hulk of the west face, so that the size of the discovery was doubled. The remains of the Priory lay at the north end of the village, stark on a flat, sea-reflecting sky. A Benedictine foundation, it had had a glorious heyday, cousin to Westminster and Rheims, until it was suppressed in the Dissolution of the Monasteries and largely decayed, although it wasn't a broken or forlorn place. The shell was saved, with three rows of arches re-enclosed, Norman through to Early English, with the stone scoured and bleached of its limewash from exposure to the wild salt air. Externally, the guidebook said, the church is a reduced structure within its own greater ruin. Many meanings and many resonances that gave off.

A quartet was performing the Requiem by Bartók. The four musicians in sombre evening dress were past youth. The cellist in particular had a passion for his instrument, lived this piece of music in his mind as well as in his hands and face, until Morgan was wrung and stretched by the sympathies of the narration. There was a pervasive loneliness in the notes, written by a European exiled in America, but exiled from a war that would have victimized him if he'd stayed. The stress of that was in every phrase, as graves opened and spirits flew. The terrors of Treblinka rose again in the English air. The modern war of Holocaust echoed the centuries-old sacrilege against the brotherhood of monks in Binham, the particular bound into the general. This audience was quiet, attentive, musically alert, the people of the local congregation who came by weekly habit to pray. It was closer to what Morgan understood than the high cathedral services in Bury, or maybe the secular application of the sacred place had a special appeal.

When they walked outside at the end of the recital, the sun had gone, but the last of the strong rays highlighted the ribcage of the ruined arches, and again he was reminded of the caulks of a stranded vessel, hauled on to land and salvaged into a watertight condition. Not beautiful, not whole, but a relic of the staunch remained. Himself.

Else did that for him. She gave him a rush of new ideas about himself, stimulating his own interest in the way he walked, dressed, spoke, arranged his day and hair. Sometimes it was stunningly mundane. They were a good-looking couple, or conformed to certain prototypes of male and female: grey and blonde, solid and slender. When Else bothered to groom herself, she had those shimmering film-star looks that brought every restaurant they entered to a hush, while diners racked their brains for where they'd seen her, which film, which play. Maybe he did look like her business manager, cruising her round sets. He didn't care. At fifty, he had all his hair and all his teeth. That was the power of survival. He had never felt so good. It was a time of superlatives fixed in his own memory. He noticed what was happening while it was happening. These were the heady days. They only came once. He made the most of them.

She was a practical woman, a grafter. Citified to look at, she was a countrywoman by habit. She could navigate by divination across those five-way intersections laid over the farmland tracks, where the wobbly white signposts pointed them into fields and it was anybody's guess. With an instinct for ground, a memory for maps and contours, she guessed right every time. Her cooking was paranormal. She banged about the kitchen in their borrowed house, hurrying with bacon and eggs. She could be in three places at once, kick the door of the fridge shut, retrieve a bottle, stir a pan all in the synchronization of one moment. This gave off high voltage, as if she exploited time to the limit, making it yield double. What she could accomplish in one hour was extravagant, ear- and blood-vessel-bursting energy to get the business of the day cleared and on to better things. Manic, these moods.

In company, he saw her in a different light. He'd imagined her to be a recluse at Odham, like a songbird in a gilded cage. No such thing. At dinner, in those worthy, uninspired, middle-of-the-range hotels and pubs where they ate, she drew naturally into groups. Or rather, she was drawn. People were fascinated by her glamour, but not distanced. It wasn't a cold, made-up front she presented. Accurate and knowledgeable about what she'd seen that day, she could share it, making the other people round the bar see it too. Why is Holkham Bay a bird sanctuary? All we saw were black and white spooners. There was a skipper fishing inshore, using two square nets on winches. Have you seen those? The yew hedges at Blickling Hall are big enough for human beings to nest in. It was a recitative in its own way, small chords, small passes of conversation. She wasn't awkward or out of tune with strangers, only those she knew.

Driving around in the car, she invented a game of picture quizzes to pass the time. They had to say which painting a house or landscape reminded them of. She was faster than he was by a mile, until he felt his reputation was quite dented. He was overly academic, thought to himself, Not Constable, we're too far north, not Van de Velde, it isn't Holland after all. Ruisdael, she cried triumphantly in recognition before he got a syllable out. Three paths converge. Let's call it 'Wood in Spring'. She didn't forget what she'd seen, gallery or reproduction, and had a well-stocked mind and a well-trained eye. She provided him with such cleverness and fun that he wanted the circular coast-bound road never to end, the days never to run to their sand-emptying term.

The moments of the long weekend weren't simple or temporary. They were locked into two important sequences. The past ran in parallel lines in Else's experience. Younger, she'd still been in the same places at the same time and they glimpsed each other down the past through many open doors. He was haunted by the missing fifteen years of their acquaintance. There weren't many more intriguing possibilities than, What if ... the might-have-beens of mistimed encounter. He'd started to slot her into a mutual past, as a presence not a vacuum, and worked out they'd nearly met half a dozen times after the Slade, through Max, through Marise, at a party he'd ducked at the last minute although she went along, accompanied by Ralph. Imagine if he'd come face to face with Ralph! No, it was impossible to meet him, like a drama where two parts were played by the same man, the requirement was that the actors never appeared physically on the stage together. That Else had been obsessed with him wasn't totally improbable. Hadn't Dickens modelled a dozen fictional heroines on a woman he met just once? Intense, projective, the power of her imaginary affair with him or the man whose shape he filled had stunned him when she admitted it. Now he turned the interregnum to advantage, so that even though they hadn't met, they knew something jointly and talked from a common pool of experience.

But the moments also had a future. All his working life, Morgan had been around creative people, without having one spark of originality himself beyond the ability to organize the present well. The most exciting woman for him was always likely to be the one who could create images. He picked up her fallen sketches with awe. How marvellous to see this way! How to make moments last! She gave him much, but he did give her this, the certainty of going on. When she projected a vast allegorical painting about the spring, its pagan and its Christian symbolism, enabling him to see it in his mind exactly the way she saw it in hers, he came as near as he could to the fusion point of inspiration. The black and white spooners, the fishing smack, the human hedges would all re-appear in another guise when she had bodied them into the durables of paint. Time compacted into a new density, or made an impression of long and short that was almost painful, as if he ran uphill.

* * *

Adrian got on the telephone to Covent Garden. 'I know it's a small detail, but the client who bought the Gainsborough last month wondered how it came into the auction. Nothing official, you understand. Off the record. He's trying to piece together its background, that's all.'

'I sold it to Marise. Full stop.'

'I wondered if you'd like to reveal your sources?'

No, Morgan would not. Bought in good faith, sold in good faith. Leave it at that. 'It was part of a job lot I came across in Suffolk. Someone who was selling up house contents after a death.'

'No improvement on that?'

'I can't help you much, I'm afraid. If you remember, Sotheby's put the Gainsborough tag on it, not me.'

As he put the phone down, something nagged at Morgan. The two women merging at the source of this picture disturbed him, partly because he hadn't admitted the connection to either of them. He wasn't quite ready for that. For wife and lover to have met was enough of a coincidence, without putting in a painting as the unlikely means of introduction. And what was a buyer doing, anyway, checking up on the previous owners if he was satisfied with his purchase?

It nagged equally at the Sotheby's director. He didn't blame Morgan for being brusque about the reattribution and, in truth, it wasn't the purchaser but Adrian himself who was anxious to follow up the pre-auction sources. Part of a job lot in Suffolk? He didn't like the sound of that any better. An expert relied on pedigree, the written lineage of a picture handed down with it like a formal letter of recommendation. I am what I am. Didn't like little bastard pictures popping all over the place to weaken heritage. Provenance: it was a sturdy, first-born word. Maybe Adrian was oversensitive about that, having to give way to intruders over title. Eton had bred in him a sobering respect for the traditions. A master once said to him, 'It's not quite the thing, Crane, is it?' when the schoolboy disagreed with the official policy on some house rule or other and registered his protest. Not quite what thing? As if he had no innate right to question or even test authority. Adrian had started to go into hiding from whatever he was not, quite. Eton, Bristol and the Courtauld Institute, two years at the V and A before a baptism of fire as a ring dealer on the commodities market, each of the big City institutions relied on the unwritten codes – gentleman's agreement, taken at face value – against which he measured his private standards in some trepidation. Morgan, much lauded as an art critic, Marise and the in-house experts at Sotheby's all thought this portrait was genuine, but he did not. He still did not. But just how far was it incumbent on him to disturb their good opinion with a niggly, queasy little phrase like, 'No, this picture is not quite the thing'?

During the Easter weekend at Odham, which was dry and bright, Jane and Clive Ramage walked to the top of the hill behind the farm and looked down at the cluster of houses round the criss-cross at the centre of the village, with angled roofs, barnyards, a mucky duck pond and scattered outhouses that made random patches of light and shade on the green of the new year's growth.

It wasn't an idle, rambling walk, man and wife taking an evening stroll at leisure. They both felt it was a real accomplishment. Three months back, they couldn't have walked to the edge of the farm. It was a morass after the snows and, when Clive toiled round the perimeter boundaries in a Land Rover at the end of the thaw in January, he was appalled at what he'd let himself in for. Sunk his savings and his wife's and the whole of his army pension into a mudbath. And probably sunk them for good. The fields were running wet. There was no drainage system and no feeding in the soil, no tilth, just waterlogged and sticky clay. How on earth could he pull it round and make it profitable?

Ignorance was his best ally, or the feeling that each of the mammoth tasks ahead of him would only need one doing. First, he had to clear the fields of debris. That took a month by itself, heaving the rusting junkyard of machinery and neglected equipment, troughs, barrows, binders, into the back of a contractor's truck that rolled and lolloped in the mud. The barn was overflowing with rain-split furniture abandoned by the previous occupants. Trip after trip they made to the municipal rubbish dump, or burned the rotted and unusable wood, until a smoke pall tainted with old varnish hung heavy and offensive over the village.

Even the hedges had been desecrated by a series of incompetent owners, hacked, part-burned when cutting didn't work, and had resprouted into full-sized trees: wiry hawthorn, impenetrable beech. The roots had to be grubbed out with the tractor, using metal clamps and lines. It was work as laborious as dragging anchors, and smeared yet more mud over the bedraggled fields, where the tyres and broken stumps mangled the squish of soil all over again. They fell into a kind of static anguish, man and woman, as they watched the mess of disrepair accumulate.

Next, the paths went in. The bricks and stones heaved out of the soil in the early stages, were broken up to make foundations, strict pebble lines like a causeway on a beach, and on top of these Clive spread his mix inside two parallel sets of wooden shuttering. He hired an electric cement mixer and shovelled in grit and sand and turned it and laid the aggregate until, over the sixty-acre site, he put down a gridded network. It was sweet labour. He roughened the smooth surface of the concrete with the edge of a plank to give better adhesion underfoot, every yard textured by his own hand, and to finish, he flat-trowelled a neat edge before he left the green concrete to dry and harden, like logic over chaos. Not up to Roman standards, but a roadway of sorts.

On this sanity, they walked in the morning and hugged themselves with a happiness warm in self-congratulation, although this stage of the work was only a clearance before productivity could start.

When Else came back from Norfolk, she was impressed by the progress they'd made and hurried to get their developments down on paper, a before and after transformation, the mud bath being turned into a networking of paths, as symmetrical as knot gardens, tied up tidy. It made for powerful images when chaos was marshalled into order over the farmyard battlefield. The paths were figurative to her, stretched canvas, primed paper, a clean start before the real work began.

24 April

My dear Boris

Thank you for your cheque. I feel the quantum is growing faster than my ability to repay, or even thank you adequately, but I do thank you by compound rates all the same.

My finances aren't healthy. I sold Nick Wylie one of the pictures from the house to pay off my debts. 'Sold' is a euphemism. It's a bit like the Inland Revenue accepting works of art in lieu of death duties. I didn't actually get cash for it, just the cancellation of a minus sum. He was pleased enough to get it.

Several things are coming off this year, the book which is a new venture for me, Covent Garden are shifting bits and pieces, I have five paintings ready for the Royal Academy hanging committee and am hopeful they will take at least one of them. Then there's the Cambridge exhibition I'm working hard for. It's such a big responsibility, having all that space to fill. How can you take one voice and make it expand to fill the Albert Hall? Before, I've had the excuse at mixed showings that I didn't sit well with the style of others, that I needed more space to myself, or that I don't hang well in galleries ... Such a massive opportunity precludes excuses: it's do or die time. I'm excited and terrified by it. All that exposure! The word says everything. Some lap publicity up. I don't.

And Nick is exerting himself this time, although he's a great promiser without being a great deliverer. The trouble with Nick is, when he talks he's thinking out loud and the suggestions he makes are stray ideas he eradicates in the act of airing them. That's all they are, air. Experiments with sound. Afterwards, he doesn't remember what he's said, whereas I do, every word in detail, in sequence, when and why locked into a pattern, and it infuriates him if I draw him up short, or remind him of what he hasn't done that he categorically said he'd do. But in a way, this is his chance too and I don't begrudge him it. He likes the fibre of exhibitions, the drama of it, and I'm not blind to the fact that this could incidentally be the making of him.

I'm glad to be finished with the almanac. I'm not a miniaturist by nature, or an illustrator. Working parallel to a text and to the set page size was a curb I fretted on, like doing gymnastics in a sleeping bag. I kept kicking the corners. It's back to bigger work and primed canvas where, if I'm so moved, I can tack on another yard and go on left. Out of bounds. That always was me.

We had an interesting day last week. Max Edelman invited us to see the first run-offs of the book. I hadn't been to his new Rotherhithe print works before – have you been there? – and was amazed at the clean efficiency of modern printing, more like a laboratory. My memory of print shops has got something to do with inking up by hand, the plates a giant lino cut, and piles of oily rag cloths and Guttenberg presses with hefty mangles you have to wind down on a screw. That's all gone. Technology's hit. The scanning and the proof-making are done by computers. It was bewildering to see my pictures broken down into a series of dots, like newsprint, no more mysterious than that and quite deflating to the ego. In dot matrix, I suppose anyone could do this, even a machine. What did they tell me that I didn't know? Watercolours are especially difficult in fine art printing because they're subtle. Max says modern inks are too harsh and modern paper, not all rag, can throw up batch variations because of the chemical reaction to ink, or creates too big a dot spread, and the inconsistency has to be corrected by eye. Thank heavens for that. The eye has some para-excellence over the accuracy of computers. Black and white is the hardest of all to reproduce well, he tells me, ending up indeterminate or grey.

These printing machines are marvellous beasts, the best part of a million pounds spent on a colour roller-coaster that looks first cousin to a Chinese dragon, heaving up and down and puffing as it goes. Sheets fly through end to end, picking up a colour at a time. The blue is hanging out, says Max. Do you like that? Lovely phrase. It means the blue has printed fractionally over the edge of magenta red and yellow giving a faint shadow line. We adjust. We wait. Perfection is elusive at every stage.

I'm rather childish about the process, and want them to give me a copy to take home right now, all neat and bound and jacketed. The binding, perfect not saddle stitch, is done elsewhere and the jacket is out-work. The various stages won't come together for another week or two. Ten thousand by subscription, not bad going. The verse isn't as good as John Clare's, which we imitated. 'Annuals and Almanacks all the rage, with their gilt edges and luscious illustrations.' I've been looking again at that much-neglected author. The hedgerow talent is inspiring, the seed that won't be stifled by falling on stony ground. I was heartbroken when I read his life story, because of the struggle he went through first to be a published, and then an independent writer, making no deference to popularity. I liked his insights into people. This on his publisher and one-time friend –

Taylor is a man of very pleasant address, and works himself into the good opinion of people in a moment; but it is not lasting for he grows into a studied carelessness and neglect that he carries into a system, till the purpose for doing it becomes transparent and reflects its own picture while he would hide it. He is a very pleasant talker and is excessive fluent on paper currency and such politics ... He never asks a direct question or gives a direct reply, but continually saps your information by a secret passage, coming at it as it were by working a mine – like a lawyer examining a witness.

Do we know dozens of such parvenus in London, apart from Nick? He is describing the modern publicist, the PR, media man, press secretary a hundred and fifty years before the type was invented. They're the ones who frighten me most because they manipulate response, having none themselves. I like John Clare a great deal, and understand how he felt abused by the ploys of the city. If anyone cried out for a welfare state, it was that man. Just a meal and a weekly Giro cheque, my God, let's not forget the sufferers for our security. But, on the other hand, those last poems wouldn't have been written if he'd been a prosperous landowner with a fat annuity. They were born of beauty and daily dying, both.

Did I say we?

Yes, twice. Morgan and I are we. Somewhat to my surprise. Somewhat to my happiness. Happy. The skill is to be content with moments, not expecting days. I look at John Clare's schizophrenia and cling to little things. Don't go mad about the past; it will madden if you let it. Can I succeed with this man at long last? He's easy, genial, probably a really good man in the simple sense, or simple in the good. Not a pushover and is often on his guard in a cogitative way, you know, wary, not believing. I have had the old problems of divesting myself of that fabrication which they call the truth. What I am trying to say is that he's so normal he's no idea of how wide of normality I am and that makes me afraid for both of us, because we use terms differently in negotiation. By committed he means wholeheartedly endorsed; I mean imprisoned or, at best, on trial.

Max is all charm, deft and witty, showing off colour calibration machines as if I were an *ingénue*. I know all there is to know about traditional printing techniques from Ralph but don't spoil Max's show. Why has it come about that my good friends are gentlemen of a certain age? Is that the safest interaction of the sexes, a mental rapport for me, a personal one for them, while the disparities of generation or place or temperament neutralize danger? Good word, neutralize. It defines that I've given up with women or have a horrible capacity to become genderless with my own sex. I am only a woman with men. In female company, well, we're not akin. They provoke me and, in mixed groups, I have a tendency to turn into a vamp or a bully so that I won't atrophy from contact with inestimable niceness. If ever I turn nice will you please assassinate me. I'm unladylike – hooray. But I still find it hard to take any of these real, interpersonal events seriously or as final; they're preparatory sketches for a tableau which I go on adjusting and amending in my head, or in my hand, until they're right.

Apologia for being awful.

John Camperdown walked so fast on the way to work, he almost broke into a run.

Why was the working day fun? Where were the deadlines and depressions he'd feared? We'll take you on a three-month trial, said Mrs Fisk, to be reviewed on both sides. I like your work and disposition but you don't defer to me any more. You're accountable to someone else, and his standards are notoriously high. John was so anxious to please this cult man-god who was his boss that he'd looked out his college notebooks on spread sheets and double entry book-keeping, in case the impossible was asked of him. He smiled now. Morgan did set him an examination of sorts, like a friend who went to a publishing house and was given a book to read, stripped of cover, title, author and left to read it cold. A stringent test. Morgan walked him round the rooms and made him give a spontaneous testimonial for a dozen pictures, and seemed satisfied. There are only two contractual things I would ask of you, he added, good health and good manners. Everything else follows.

It did. It had. After they painted the frontage at Covent Garden in fairly radical marbling, they called it the Green Gallery and for no good reason it became a swift success. It hit the sort of vogue that wine bars and nightclubs had under a new management, word circulating among the young and mobile and ready spenders that this was the place to go. Some unlikely paintings flew off the walls and their sales rocketed. Why was hard to say. Morgan had managed to capture the paperback-painting ethos after all, without downgrading either concept. The shop catered for the compromise choice, showing modern classics or the quality popular – which might be impossible conjunctions, or a myth – but was a leader in one of the more reliable forms of novelty all the same. Their critics said they were too middle of the road, their competitors too cheap, but that didn't matter. A sold painting was better than an unsold one and receipts silenced the sceptic.

Who were their clients? In spare moments, John tried to do a demographic breakdown. Men mostly, young single men or the retired. People paying a mortgage or school fees didn't buy wall hangings, although the polarization didn't restrict their range. Morgan used his own framer so that he established a harmonious look. A lot of painters went adrift on the framing and the mounting, getting the weights all wrong, which unbalanced the work. Surrounds were pine or matt rubbed steel. Nothing else. By controlling every aspect of the input they found, as ever, that what was consistent with one emphatic set of standards matched. This mattered in rooms where pictures were close hung and dense, and Morgan was meticulous about eye-lines and symmetry. At times the layout of the walls was soothingly beautiful. That was what they had for sale. Repose. Good taste. And everyone who came through the green door knew they were in touch with charisma.

That might seem solemn. It wasn't. The Green Gallery did the heretical and brought the sound of laughter into the composed atmosphere of art galleries. It was enjoyable. People arranged to meet each other there, dropping off their belongings at the counter, before going in to join the party, as if Nick Wylie had left a residue of good cheer behind. Their rooms were never empty, never quiet, only had lulls to draw breath before the next wave came. And there was a thrill in introducing people to the paintings they would like, two that would go on together for a long time afterwards, each enriched. Friends came by and linked up with other friends. Rare in London, strangers talked to each other without suspicion as if being here was recommendation enough. The Saturday afternooners came again, the amateurs who knew, whose fathers were specialists in something esoteric and to whom a single name set off enlarging ripples of coincidence or scholarship.

And between them, they'd struck up a successful partnership. Sometimes John asked himself if it was cynical or manipulative, the way they divided their customers, although it wasn't pre-planned but evolved from instinct. He took the older customers, the retired, the managers, the men of settled view, while Morgan broached the young. Inverting the prescribed order worked brilliantly. Neither of them pushed or hurried, because you couldn't hard-sell pictures anyway, but talked about the artist's work the way they felt it, and carried their conviction. The older men left feeling they'd bought something modern and significant, an inspired impulse, the younger that they touched a tradition and keyed into bigger trends than the transitory.

They could hardly keep pace with themselves. A second assistant was appointed and Fred was upgraded from caretaker to doorman, mostly for security. They thought about hiring a researcher for pre-war paintings, as they dipped into resale. The place hummed. John hurried towards work, for it was more like play.

On the last Friday of the month he worked alone in the gallery while Morgan was away at the fortnightly directors' meeting in New Bond Street. He went upstairs to the office to check the previous day's entries were correctly logged. You see to the nuts and bolts, said Morgan, I never seem to get them turning on the right thread.

This was how John spent the first hour of the day, tallying invoices against takings and bringing the vast stock register up to date. This morning it didn't balance. He checked and checked again, disbelieving that there could be such a huge discrepancy on the stock sheet. Morgan himself had brought four of Else Petersen's paintings back from Suffolk and for a long time they'd admired them in a hush, for they were funny and serious things, a farmer working in the fields and she'd put him in uniform to emphasize his war against a land enemy, with his medals and decorations flapping, heroic and superfluous. Touching. Strange. They argued about how much they were worth and eventually decided, against their normal pricing policy, to ask four figures each.

And on the first day of showing, all four had sold. All four to one buyer and even while he was writing out his cheque, two other purchasers were queuing up in case he changed his mind. The scenes had hit the brio of the season. Neither of them had seen anything like it.

But search as he might, John couldn't find an entry for them in the stock ledger, or a receipt, or a bank paying-in slip for the night deposit box. Morgan must have put the cheque aside and not credited it. John chewed his thumbnail down to the quick worrying for an answer, took a turn about the office and had another cup of coffee, thinking anxious thoughts.

Morgan had asked if he could stand in again on Saturday while he went back to Odham, so John was up to date with matters as they stood. But if the man intended using the gallery as a private showroom for Else Petersen's works, without authorizing them through the business, then it was no longer a personal matter. Why would he do such a thing? To save her paying the gallery's percentage or her agent's? John sympathized with the motive, but it was still irregular behaviour, and unethical. He was troubled as he reassessed his senior.

There were practical considerations too. The stock record was a form of certificate for insurance purposes against fire or theft, so had some legal standing. And Mrs Fisk? She might say largely, You don't defer to me, but it would be different if she dropped in unexpectedly and found marked discrepancies. For a start, she might implicate John himself. He gnawed on in doubt. What to say? How to clear the air without accusing.

Morgan came back before one, showing all the signs of having been trapped in a boardroom chair for too long, restless and irritable, while John considered postponing his query. But he steeled himself to say, with the books open as corroboration, 'I think I must have made a mistake here, mislaid something. I can't get this to add up.'

Morgan frowned, following the finger down to the date entry. He'd had enough small print for one day. Marise's meetings were the worst aspect of the job, with a myopic attention to detail that made him blind. She'd suggested he spend one week a month travelling round the provincial cities, Manchester, Birmingham, Leeds, Glasgow, because Boris was tired of the routine. And then his expression cleared.

'That's my fault. I didn't put the Petersens in because, quite honestly, I wasn't sure they'd go. They're outside our normal currency. I wanted to brief Mrs Fisk when I saw her this morning, before they went through the books. But she's impressed by the sale, and the size of one cheque. We've been given *carte blanche*. People are beginning to imitate us.' Morgan grimaced. Annoying that, to set trends and see them overtaken by something trendier. 'So we'll move ahead of them. Hardbacks we'll stock, and some limited editions.'

John hesitated to ask for mundane details.

'Go upmarket. Weave a few expensive pieces through and see what happens. More scope. Experiment, size, the next step up. I'm sorry I forgot to tell you what I'd done before I went out this morning. That must have made you feel uncomfortable. It may happen more and more if things move fast. Our book-keeping will have to be postdated.'

The trainee didn't disagree, turning back to make the entries good. The explanation was fair, but he sensed a lack of real commercial nous in Morgan, however sympathetic in handling people and the spaces they described. Built on the big side, even his gestures had largesse and he would always tend to magnificence of scale. Was it really sensible to change their image so soon after establishing it, the younger man asked, feeling he might have to be wise for both of them.

The fire from Clive's split logs burned well, beech and knotty oak, although every now and then a spark flew loose, lighting the room and the table more vividly for a second, until it landed on the further reaches of the carpet, from where it sent up a smell of singeing wool.

Now they were in the country, Clive and Jane took to inviting their friends to supper instead of dinner. They served it on a long oak refectory table, patinated by old mutton as well as candle grease, and strange dark stains, black with time and absorption, the rims of goblets or spilt wine, until it was almost as marked and indented as the carpet. Their low light scheme was practical before it was stage-managed. The farm had no usable electricity supply and they fell back on candlelight, which glossed over empty corners, or clothed with the enhancing shadows of a good photograph. Sconces, black wrought-iron firedogs, simple roasted food, faces in high, flamelit relief: so minimal it was strong.

The women round the table took on a historical radiance too. Jane's boat-neck sweater took the lines of a medieval stomacher, flat and straight, while Maud Eversley, the Colonel's wife, had a resplendent top-table glitter in jet and bombazine, brightly black. Else wore a red velvet redingote, although, typically enough, her magnificence stopped short at the waist. Underneath she wore jeans and a pair of mudproof walking shoes, like an actress in a budget-made spectacular.

'We ought to drink a toast, you know,' said the Colonel, 'in congratulations to our host. A splendid meal and an achievement in the circumstances. Only three months in the making. Not long at all.'

They rose in a small show of formality, although Jack Eversley raised his glass to several things that went unsaid. He was pleased to have new neighbours this congenial, pleased to see the local folly being turned to good purpose. Drained marshes fired the imagination with the spirit of renewal, usable land from waste. He was pleased, too, that Else had made new moves and felt easy enough to bring Morgan with her this evening. Perhaps her professional upturn was attributable to him. He listened to news of her pending exhibition and her London sales in relief, tinged with incomprehension at an esoteric genre. Principally, he wanted these developments to bond, farm and people to revitalize the countryside nearby. He'd no official position in the village beyond longevity, taking on the squire's house from his father, along with his debts and a weed-choked lake, but felt a pride in the community. However disadvantaged at the start, his young neighbours could change circumstances the way he'd done it, by careful investment, hard work and studious planning. He could boast that the big house would be handed down unencumbered to his son. The past wasn't an irreversible drain on the present. You could get clear.

Clive thought through their congratulations, warm and welcome. 'Yes, we've done a lot. We've put in three months at the groundwork and it was tiresome, but it never daunted us.

Callouses don't last. It was easy because we didn't have to think about what to do next.'

'Only fall sleep exhausted and postpone the worry until the next day,' his wife reminded him 'The strain's cumulative.'

'But now we're having to make decisions which may well turn out to be ill-thought. When you're starting on this sort of project, the choice and the variety of advice you get about it are overwhelming. I've no experience of land work, so one idea sounds as good as another to me. I've got this gnawing feeling I'll have to make all my mistakes firsthand.'

'Sugar beet's done well in this soil,' the Colonel reminded him.

'Well, yes, I've put in a crop to see me into the autumn, but sugar beet's got no soul. It's got to be livestock. Something controllable, or outside freaks of weather, and more responsive to handling than turnip tops. You can't coax crops along.'

'I have a friend who would help you buy your herds at the Norwich auctions. He's a stock breeder himself.'

'Beef or dairy?' asked the Colonel's wife. 'We've got other friends who zero-graze, take the fodder to the stalls, and they're very efficient at it. You get high yields and spend less time shifting herds from field to field.'

'But intensive farming is so ugly,' Else groaned. 'Don't the creatures get to run around and see the sunlight any more?' The rest laughed but she challenged them. 'All right, I'm sentimental and my idea of agriculture's on the biblical side. It owes a lot to Noah's Ark and children's farm sets, two of each. But beasts of the field just sounds better than beasts of the battery. That may be my problem. It doesn't make good pictures, heads poking through grids and looking baleful.'

'Else's my best labourer,' said Clive aside to Morgan, trying to avoid a discussion of vegan values as he carved their roast rib, 'so I'm obliged to consult her about what I decide to stock.'

'Don't pay any attention. I'm an incompetent navvy. I'm only on the scrounge for ideas.'

'No bad thing, is it, if the perspiration provides the inspiration?'

Morgan felt this increasingly, that Else was a physical painter needing an acreage of canvas and that she'd found her ideal subject and frame of reference in the earthworks at Odham. She tended to rely on the domestic motif that came to hand, the Gothic window arch, the *pseudoacacia*, the pattern of the local fields as the emblem of something larger. He was therefore unprepared for the turn Maud Eversley introduced into the conversation.

'Tell me, my dear, have you found the piece of paper you were looking for?'

'Not yet. I haven't looked very hard,' Else answered nonchalantly.

'Well, shouldn't you? Surely this is serious. We'll all rally round if we can.'

'Oh, it's probably bluff. I shan't pay too much attention.'

Maud, believing that the most intractable problem was only bindweed that needed patient unravelling, coped badly with this show of negligence. The set of her shoulders signalled a challenge to the rest of them.

'What piece of paper?' Jane asked in all innocence.

Else shied away from public comment even among friends. She didn't want anyone's handy hints on how to pasture out her life, but when she'd already consulted the Colonel as the local magistrate, she knew evasion would look bizarre. 'I've been hunting for a will,' she said, 'or something like a will. A paper. I thought the house had been secured as mine a long time back, but it appears I've no actual title. I'm allowed to stay on under sufferance, and Ralph's son is making moves to evict me. Or says he is. I think it's only threat.'

Morgan found himself too hot at the fire end of the table and got up to walk about. The group had shifted round all evening, women at plates, men at wine and logs, a sort of all-hands meal. He went to cool by the uncurtained window. Darkness still fell early in April. The lights of Odham shone like messages in code across the rise. He could pick out the high gable and dormer of her roof from here. The idea of being evicted made him fearful for her in a situation that ran parallel to his own. Someone changing the locks on what you thought was memory and the ties of association, being barred access to the source of your own life, or home, wasn't easy to take. She told him the first time he visited Odham that not everyone was overwhelmingly pleased, but the turn of events still came too sharp for him to accept; her inheritance was the first fact Lorraine passed on about her, and Else hadn't taken time to discuss her predicament with him privately, the moment not right this evening before they set out. They hurried, or tried to safeguard their leisure time together with happiness as if they still separated the on and off duty. There was only time to change and for him to catch sight in passing, of the words, *My dear Boris, Thank you for your cheque*, which started off a series of new fears and revived several old ones. Morgan had to compel himself not to read further into her correspondence.

'Did you ever see a will?' He pinned her down.

'No, I wasn't that – specific.'

That greedy, he thought. That grasping. He looked objectively at Else's situation, a woman who'd spent fifteen years with a married man twice her age who was also wealthy, without gaining any material advantage. It was almost calculatedly naïve of her. Absurd, absurd, the incaution he most admired, to take no thought for the morrow.

'I don't care about owning the house,' she said as if to corroborate what he was thinking. 'It doesn't matter who it belongs to. I only want to live there because I like it and I've been there a long time.'

'But it's quite despicable that you've got this hanging over you,' said Maud heatedly in her defence. 'You made that place, built it up out of nothing. Do you remember–' she appealed for the Colonel's nod – 'it was covered with mould inside. Walls blown. Not a drop of paint. And the garden gone to seed. Else did what Clive's done on the farm. Resurrected the place out of a mud bath and done it single-handed. All right, Ralph owned it, but you made it. Maybe every woman feels that. His money but my effort. Doesn't effort count for anything?'

Else sat silently, thinking, Yes, it was derelict and I brought it back to life. But what you don't know is Ralph did that for me too, rebuilt me stone by stone, gave me back an interest and the peace of mind to pursue it. She saw that the prejudice of his family against her was no greater than her friends' against him, that the slightest irregularity brought out extreme responses, where decent people resorted to vulgar gossip and hostility. That had not been the way it was at all.

'Was there a formal will?' Clive insisted on the basics.

'Yes. Passed probate. No mention of me or The Aviary.'

'But he did speak about it?' Clive had difficulty addressing this 'he', Pennington being a man he knew only by rumour and posthumously. Referring to him in front of Morgan made statements seem all the more pointed and intrusive.

'Broadly to me, yes. I didn't discuss it with anyone else.'

Morgan recalled that she'd sold the midshipman in the first place because she was in financial straits, and felt his own inability to underwrite her because he made the same improvidential mistakes. What could he offer her as security apart from sharing a shaky professional platform? He felt all the more unsettled because the cottage had begun to feel his by assimilation. Who could dismantle that library? There was something sacred about the collection of working, illustrative volumes on the open landing which ought to be inalienable by a process Morgan couldn't even define, unless it was entitlement or context – the belonging terms themselves were book-endowed.

'And you didn't challenge probate?'

'Well, no,' she answered, 'I didn't agitate. I thought fairness would assert itself – as of right.'

The Colonel recalled how little of the legal mind she had. It wasn't enough to operate on a broad sweep of fairness. The wife had a house, the son had a house, why shouldn't she have a house? was Else's line. It had pained him that she was only a crisis thinker, or lacked wiles and strategy for the planning game. Securing written affidavits from her friends, demanding palimony were concepts Else shunned. He had suggested, when she came to him for advice some weeks earlier, that she bought the place outright. What with, she replied. Cash in my life insurance policies? As I stand, I'm worth about a hundred pounds.

On one side, Jane listened to these exchanges. When she first met Else Petersen, she looked at the self-regulated, glamorous lifestyle with transparent envy. A woman who saw in the New Year at a ski resort, disappeared to London haunts, was effortless with men, had a standing in Odham that was due to nothing more energetic than being an unknown quantity or mentally reclusive. Gradually, the empty spaces began to fill. She realized that Else's recent successes were discontinuous, or added the note of poignancy to a fallow decade. In comparison, Jane downgraded her own talents because Else as an amateur shared them too, the farm labourer, counsellor, child-minder. The wife knew she'd boxed herself into the serviceable mode of life. Her whole life had been service: following a husband to the Ruhr, Belfast and Hong Kong to attend to his career, then raising two boys, with sixty acres of derelict farmland and thirty weaners to follow shortly. There wasn't much glamour in that.

But now she thought Else's enlarging freedoms came at too high a price. She'd chosen to live at the edge of a cliff. The risk of slippage was unreasonably high. They were under an element of threat at the farm, from financial loss but not from outright ruin. Nobody could evict them, not even the bank. Else was trading in the most volatile commodity, her own reputation. She relied on nothing more substantial than a man happening to cross a threshold one day and buy a picture, or a man putting his name to another form of money transfer and willing her a property which, God knows, she'd fashioned with her own hands and will-power. She stood outside the normal contracts of exchange, and was one of those foolish or inspired people who left too much to chance.

May

Max and Sybil Edelman drove out of London to open up their house in Southwold for the summer season. With the upturn in light levels, they veered towards the sea and the open countryside, like plants turning to observe the sun. They always tried to complete the cumbersome transit in one go and always failed. Their car was stuffed to danger point with bedding and kitchen gadgets without which Sybil, who vacated London from May Day to the August Bank Holiday, couldn't entertain the flocks of migratory friends who drifted after her up the coast.

Today, the journey was complicated by a stop at Chelmsford to see the Fisks. Marise had said, 'Do come in for lunch', although she was in the habit of adding a practical rider: 'And bring the proofs with you.'

Dry sherry went with a burst of hot sunshine on the stones outdoors, all the more welcome for being the first harbingers of summer. Overlooking the Chelmer, the Fisks had made a terraced garden in different sections to which Boris invited their guests when he saw how distracted Marise was, avid to look at the bundle of galley proofs. Max stayed behind with her. He might as well get this over with, here or at Rotherhithe. He watched her as she scanned the print minutely. This woman had the most accurate eye in London. She frowned, looking down to concentrate on details below the level of the early sun.

'This blue you've used on the border is too garish. Duck egg, we agreed. This is way off. You've got a bright turquoise. Gaudy. Vulgar.'

And it was. She was quite right. Blues were notoriously fugitive. In her head, the pupil of her seeing, Marise could remember what she'd specified three months ago, and compare it with the inescapable flaws of colour printing. Every time, they went through the same tussle, evoking in him part admiration, part despair. Twice a year, she sent out a catalogue to her established buyers. She'd fallen for the easy returns of computer mailing: if the auction houses and public galleries kept their clientele informed in this way, then there was nothing amiss with the ethics of the postbag. She put together a small brochure of the best of her recent acquisitions which, it must be said, could have been handled by most printshops in the High Street. But no, she would have it done properly, full colour, impeccably researched and laid out according to her in-house rules, which were so strict they were imperial.

That was what Max admired. Compared with a lot of what floated round the London art salons, shoddy and makeshift masquerading as inspired, the exact science thrilled. But Marise overdid it. She found so many faults, on the width of a margin or the placing of a caption, so many loopholes in their initial consensus that, out of the dozen brochures he'd printed for her, he'd lost money on ten. That was an unacceptable loss and, moreover, he resented that work was carried over to friendship and to holiday.

And for what? For a thousand paltry copies, not one of which might directly influence a sale. It was her version of vanity publishing, for which he met the bill.

While John Camperdown was in training with her at New Bond Street, the young man had confided to him that Marise ran her business like a cottage industry. She wouldn't delegate and didn't have the skill in harnessing nearby talents. The whole masterplan was in her head, built up over irreplaceable years. He said her management meetings were a farce. Invariably in the chair, she presented no formal agenda to committee and their decisions went unminuted. Because instructions were fixed in her memory – finance to Boris, PR to her assistant, export to a reliable director, Covent Garden to Morgan – there was no arguing with her. Nor any need. She could go round a roomful of colleagues and pick up their workload at the second where the last meeting broke off and, without notes, probe into their speciality, of contracts or expertise, and push them out to a wider exploration, because she'd done it all herself at one time. It was a one-woman show, her passion, her hobby. She was daunting. No stray names. No misrelated facts. And her energy! She didn't sit down, didn't rest but ricocheted from shop to boardroom to committee without let-up. I have learned an enormous amount, said the trainee, on how not to do things.

'A shade lighter, then?'

'Two shades lighter. And delicate. Marled not blotchy.' She winked again into the colour bands, while Max reflected on a further run-off, a further set of proofs to be submitted for her disapproval. Futile fastidiousness.

Above the curvature of the lawn and the formal close of hedges, Boris and Sybil reappeared, distracting Max from the sharp reply that was forming in his head. Why did he persevere with her and Boris? Because Chelmsford was *en route* for Southwold and that lie of the land wouldn't alter now. Because there were more pluses than minuses in the association. And an unspoken bond. There was a family here, of sorts, not genetic although it might be as strong as the blood tie. Going inside to the shaded dining room for lunch, Max passed the famous icon she'd brought out of the bombed ruins of Berlin. I AM THE WAY suggested several devious routes by which a Byzantine image might be carried to an Essex market town.

Their working family was made up of exiles, from somewhere. He Lvov, they Berlin, Morgan not English, or MacPherson either, while Else came from other extremities, human flotsam washed up by the Thames and silted there along the embankment. There weren't many natives in this business. Books, pictures, the printing of one into the format of the other was a natural profession for drifters, or people drawn to the permanently insecure. They had no pedigree and no papers. None was needed. Nobody asked Nick for his qualifications to represent other talents, and really they were self-appointed experts who wrapped themselves in jargon and mystique, in which it helped to be untraceable. The most professional among them found it hard to be self-monitoring and keep out the charlatans and cheats.

'You've upset him,' Boris observed, as they waved goodbye to the packed car at five o'clock, through the rear window of which their gestures couldn't be seen.

'Upset him? Why should I do that?'

'You bully him. And he's a nice man. Let him be.'

'I only told him he was wrong and he must redo it.'

'He's not a schoolboy writing homework.' As a rule, Boris didn't interfere with her, and kept his tone light, thinking it was too late to criticize the methods which were implicit in her nature.

'But it *is* work,' she emphasized, 'at home or not. And I am paying him to do it properly. We are not amateurs.'

Boris closed the series of outer doors, methodically removing the key from each one in turn and placing it in a handy drawer or under a vase. No more callers today. The rest alone. 'It's May Day,' he remembered. 'Or Labour Day.'

'Red flag day,' she supplied.

'I'd quite like to stop, you know. Stop labouring,' he amplified.

'You mean retire? But surely that's for old people.'

He half smiled at the pejorative word, which excluded them at any age. 'But I am old, Marise. I'll be seventy next year.'

He sat down under the plate-glass window in the living room, among the clutter of coffee cups and liqueur glasses left over from their lunch. The sight irritated her, like last week's sheet left on the office calendar. Move on and tidy up. Don't let things slump. Slowing circulation, that was what aged. You got oxygen into the brain only by moving it around and using it.

'Nonsense. You've got years to go.'

'At any rate, I'm going to come off the boards on my birthday, or at each AGM as it falls. Nobody should go on for ever. It's bad for company policy. I've declared that as my intention openly.'

'But what will you do?' To Marise, life was work and without it she died. She didn't have leisure time.

'I'd like to travel.'

'But we already do. We go on holiday. Greece and the States last year.'

'Not business trips. Travel slowly, I mean. Dwell. I'd like to go back, to Berlin and Sweden and maybe Israel.' The names were so provocative, he shrank from introducing them.

'Go backwards, you mean! What do we want with those places any more? We've finished with all that.'

'Oh, you know, cousins. Contacts. We carry something forward.'

She saw that he was serious and that if she didn't go with him, he would go alone. In the early years, when he was scout and buyer for the business, peripatetic while she stayed put in London to consolidate, he was away for long periods of time. Not ideal, but necessary. She could think of several marriages that had foundered under the strain of enforced separation. When her friends asked her, How do you do it – work and live together, incredible? she had been known to reply, You could call it one of the great love affairs. For her and Boris to sever at this stage emptied her boast. Although they had stayed technically together, she sensed the man had many groups of friends in many cities from which she was removed by choice as well as evolution. 'You know I'm nothing like ready to retire.'

'I would agree. It's so well organized, the business, you wouldn't need me all the time. Make Morgan a director. Give him shares. He can do all that I can and more. He's got a way to go.'

She saw how far his projects had been finalized without consulting her, in that he'd tendered his resignation from the City boardroom committees he sat on and worked out his trans-Europe itinerary towards Haifa and Tel Aviv, his own Star of David shrines! Absurd regression.

He confirmed this sense by adding, 'I'd like to make the time to read. I missed my classics. They may be waiting for me somewhere.'

So he was overtaken by sentiment at last, the old man's weakness. *Das ist der alt Herren Weg.* The lower slopes, the worn path, easy on weak hearts. She looked at the man she imagined was a bulwark with unutterable scorn and disappointment that his last adventure should be as tame as reminiscence. They had an empire waiting for them to enjoy, of power and wealth and influence, having their opinion and their presence sought, the absolute leaders of their age. How could the London markets possibly operate without them. Resign? Retire? These notions did not apply to empires. You were either overthrown or died and there was no alternative. 'I cannot give up my place voluntarily.'

'Nor would I ask it of you.' He didn't want to antagonize her, knowing how cruelly she whiplashed her opponents. In time, she might be able to phrase a more tender translation of godspeed.

The long manila envelope came into Morgan's hand without sparking much curiosity. On Her Majesty's Service and no stamp. This was official business. A tax return. And then, looking more closely, he saw that it was addressed in his own handwriting. He'd scrawled the words hurriedly a fortnight before at Somerset House.

Other things were more pressing that morning before he left for Odham, a difficult client full of imagined wrongs, complaining he was hung too high in some rooms, hung too low in others, didn't like his neighbours in either spot, plus a showing in one of the galleries at the National Theatre which he wanted to supervise in person – illustrations to the Roman plays which were about to open – and an hour with John discussing sales and moves, a slot he guarded carefully, thinking it was a training session for both of them. Rates of exchange, your know-how versus mine, were all-important. It was the end of Friday before he had time to himself to pick through the personal envelopes again.

He'd gone to Somerset House on an impulse one lunch-hour. It was only three minutes' walk across the Strand. Anxious that Else might lose the cottage through a mere oversight or bungling, he thought that Ralph Pennington's recorded will was the best starting point. Getting a photocopy proved to be less direct than the route. The Civil Service provided no list of instructions round the Wills and Probate Department on the procedure he ought to follow, while the desk clerks were busy with other callers making enquiries, so he stood and watched.

It was a wide hallway, leading off to corridors and courts in the Family Division, draughty and silently congested. Bookcases and reading lecterns filled the space where lawyers' runners and family burrowers made pencil jottings from the red-bound ledgers, stacked wall to wall. He quickly found Ralph's entry in last year's register. Died 14 August. Probate granted Norwich in December. Half a million as the balance of the estate, property excluded, not an immense sum but enough to see Else as well as his wife out of need, if the man had been thoughtful enough to do it. He filled in a form for recall of the will which turned out to be three sheets long. A paltry fee secured him a postal copy.

The contents of the envelope, when they did arrive, surprised him none the less. I, Ralph Edward Pennington, of The Aviary, Odham, do hereby will and bequeath ... Morgan took in the pedantic rigmarole of a last testament and skipped impatiently to the end. It had been drawn up by a Sudbury solicitor and witnessed by a company secretary and the Chairman of the Friends of Sudbury only two years ago. No update, no codicils, no unforeseen change of plan. Revoking no other, it stood alone.

The narrative it contained made a sort of story, like headstones, bald and touching because the feelings that bound its component parts and moved the man to do these things were completely missing, mere fleshing that had melted away, leaving the durable facts. Feelings were insignificant compared to wills. Morgan discovered that there were three women in this story, not two as he'd supposed, and rather more than three houses. The one in Belgravia went to Sheila Pennington, even if she'd since sold it lock, stock and barrel, and gone back to Salisbury. There was a flat in Paris, district of Montmartre, a beach house in Cornwall and, surprisingly, a house in Windsor, which he left without condition to his son. There was no mention of The Aviary in the list of properties, apart from its being quoted as his address, and none of Else. It therefore felt like a deliberate omission, or a thought that was still pending.

Three women, not two. Sheila Pennington and Else and a third. It appeared that the wife in Belgravia was not the mother of the son. That was a woman called Martha Crane, now married to someone else, whom he endowed with a small annuity. The son who inherited the house at Windsor, the son who pursued Else Petersen for restoration of the final property in the estate, was Adrian Crane, the Sotheby's director. Morgan ran into a familiar face, but one so wildly out of its normal context it felt improbable that the features should turn up here, folded in three inside manila.

Morgan put the sheets down on his office desk, shaken but only half mystified. No, he hadn't thought to ask Else for a name when they talked about her imminent loss of the cottage round the Ramages' dinner table, or he'd felt it was irrelevant, for neither of them could reconstruct the significance of Adrian Crane to the other. It was more than a coincidence; it was inevitable in the small circle of their acquaintance that roles should overlap. He respected her discretion. She'd never slandered anyone in his hearing and he started to understand why. She'd been too often pilloried herself. She left Ralph his dignity and his secrets, incidentally conceding the same to his son, although all of this intrigue, which must have made a considerable scandal in its day and milieu, could become public knowledge on down-payment of a pound.

He felt a wave of pity for the dependants this man had left unwillingly manacled to each other. Yes, he could understand Adrian's overcautious ways when he realized he was the son of a very careless one. The wife; the abandoned woman together with her son; the current woman. Nobody in that cast list was enviable. But the largest share of pity went to Ralph, who'd led a life disabled by its compound fracture.

What should he do with this information? Speak directly to Else? Tackle Adrian in person? He wasn't sure. There was something covert in the attitude of both which made a reconciliation or even open dealings improbable. At the same time, he felt he ought to do something. The pages testified to Ralph's broad intention. A house apiece. Like Else, he saw it as simply just. Why hadn't the man added the final clause? Maybe Ralph wanted to keep it as a lever, a hold over Else, a bargaining counter, but ran out of time to close.

It was an uncomfortable privilege knowing this much. Morgan felt a constriction, like a man in a maze he thought he'd mastered who discovered he was still going round and round, tighter and tighter in decreasing circles. Most of all, he didn't want to disturb the flow of Else's work, her actual concentration towards the exhibition in the autumn. It called for special tact. He couldn't act on her behalf without her consent, although he knew it was going to be hard to look young Crane in the face again and carry on normal dealings with the auction house.

Marise went back to her study to finish off some paperwork, leaving Boris alone in the long shadowed room while the housekeeper apologetically cleared the last of the lunch things, ahead of serving tea. 'Ignore me,' he said, 'and carry on.'

As she put each individual item on her tray, he noticed it minutely, as if he'd never seen it before but surprised himself by finding in his inventory mind some fact about its origin. Those wine glasses were Venetian, coloured the most precious garnet red. The coffee cups were turn-of-the-century Limoges, bought in a Burgundy farmhouse where they'd stayed one Easter. The farmer's wife needed the cash more than the family heirloom cups, although the gold on them was thicker than a fingernail. The room was filled, layer on layer, with the plunders of Europe but he found that the displacement was sad, or jarred on his eye, because the effect wasn't comfortable in this dowdy, plain-walled English house that asked for pewter and coffers and simple unturned angles on the wood. Things shouldn't shift, any more than people.

He hadn't managed that scene well with Marise. He shirked dredging up the unpleasant memories, just as he dodged correcting her stridencies. See, when he mentioned Berlin and Sweden and Israel, she'd dismissed any continuum in their own history. What do we want with those places any more? We've finished with all that. But he hadn't. He hadn't been able to lay his memories to rest.

In the concentration camps, the doctors had experimented grotesquely with the human body. After the war men and women, called to give witness at the trial of Nazi officers for crimes against humanity, broke down and wept in telling the court how their bodies had been used to prove ... to prove what could be performed at the limits of human endurance, while still allowing the victims to survive. Among other things, they experimented with genetics. Genocide could involve killing the second generation as well as the first. With castration or ovarian removal, control of the demographic shape of a future population, the Nazis had carried out the first systematic form of genetic engineering.

Their own cases weren't even that simple. They'd been spared the ghoulish. Marise, well, some natural flower had withered in the thin, ill-nourished soil of the walls she hid behind in Berlin. Something had been crushed in her. Too little food. Too much fear. They said a plant instinctively stifled its own seed production when survival of the parent was threatened. Over the years he watched her change with this knowledge, harden as a different form of cell production took over, drive or ambition, into which she poured her effort. The woman didn't develop roundly in the way he'd anticipated. In Sweden, she was more yielding, and softhearted, open to other suggestions, other minds.

And his own history was further complicated. He knew he had a child somewhere, conceived in haste, repented at leisure. He'd only tenuous reports and rumours to go on, and one letter that arrived in the middle of his displacement and found its way to him in hiding. For three years he'd lived the way Marise had done, in cellars and attics, rat holes, even hid down a farmer's dry well for a month before the rains started and it puddled up. His girlfriend in Weimar wrote in her letter that she had given birth to their child, a daughter, but at the outbreak of hostilities, she went back to her parents in Helsingborg, in Sweden. After he was released by the Allies, he went to the United Nations rehabilitation camp in Sweden principally to find them. But he failed. The family were displaced themselves. Their neighbours shrugged. England, Israel, they didn't know where the family had gone. Maybe he hadn't persevered long enough, or Marise came along and the idea fell into limbo, as if his time to make amends were malleable or endless, or his energies were not.

Now the desire to look for her again was all-consuming. Meeting Else through his friend Ralph Pennington, he'd had a momentary surge of belief that this might be his child who'd chased a name over the North Sea and missed him in crossing. The Swedish surname, the Nordic looks, the right age bracket. What wouldn't he have given for the lovely and clever young woman to be his blood family? She'd fulfil all of his parental wishes, which he heaped on her vicariously. It's not me, she said, absolutely not me, and disabused him of certain notions, kindly cruel.

When he had said to Marise, Cousins. Contacts. We carry something forward, he wanted her to give him a painless opening so that he could share the burden of the facts with his wife. To say it baldly after all this time was like a recrimination, shifting the blame for what they'd accepted as the mutual failure of their childlessness on to her. Look, I'm a father after all, but you are not a mother. He couldn't do that, while without proof the claim was void, but he went on suffering alone and longing for a sight of the face he felt he'd recognize in the thick of a crowd. Some one person. No other. He often played with these features that shadowed the imprint of his own, wondering and reconstructing. He'd go to Europe first. Records were plentiful and he knew better how to follow up enquiries. Then on to Israel. He'd a cousin in Tel Aviv. It wasn't an impossible search, or an unbridgeable lapse of time.

What then? He wasn't sure. If the hunt was fruitless, he could at least live with the quietus of having tried. And if it were successful, he would wait for Marise to speak the words he'd found tucked in the corner of a humble English book, which moved him unbearably because, in asking no questions, they summed up humanity as he saw it in simple greatness. A husband, hearing his wife of many years' standing had had a child before their marriage, now fallen sick, found it in his heart to say to her, You go and fetch her home and look after her. Your child's my child and your home's her home.

Because the alternative, sitting in the shadow-lengthening room among museum pieces, was intolerable and he must move before the darkness overtook him.

Each weekend at Odham followed the same unexceptional curve, tied to natural light and the simple, outdoor tasks. Morgan arrived after dark on Friday, left before dawn on Monday. The year began to stretch out to accommodate more usage and for the first time in May he made both journeys in a hopeful half-light.

There was still an unavoidable strain on meeting, or the clash of lifestyles. He felt he was hurtling along a conveyor belt of traffic out of London, and went on jotting down ideas for hours after entering the different specific density of Suffolk. Else was so bemused by her monophasic working days that she had lost track of time completely. Was it one week since he was last here or two? They both resented the interruption to their trains of thought, while admitting the coming together was the driving climax of the week.

With the change of air, Morgan tried to slow down and to esteem the inconsequent. The house and garden at The Aviary were often silent. A whole weekend could pass without sight of any human being, an antithesis so marked to Covent Garden and the Strand that he was startled at the reverberation of his own thoughts ringing in quiet space. But on the other hand, the Odham minutes were filled to bursting point by infinitesimal detail. The tractor plied the hillside in a steady drone. The pottery clattered within earshot on the days when they were emptying the kiln after a batch-firing. Dogs barked off, while inside the garden Else laid out a prearranged set of tasks that kept her busy, ticking over, whereby in tired or dull or frustrated moments she could walk out of the claustrophobic studio and mow the lawn, chop an onion or play with the ever-fascinating stream that purled across her boundary lines, clearing sticks or debris from the bank.

She grew nervous if Morgan watched her when she was painting, so he tended to wander into the studio very early or at the end of a day's work to monitor her progress. She'd started a large

121

canvas, experimentally large for her, and it filled the back wall of the studio. He already knew the subject. They'd discussed it prior to the tour round Norfolk churches which sourced it, and on his last weekend visit he'd come across some of her preliminary notes around the theme. He found these rough-ups especially evocative, simply because they were unfinished and had a mental hugeness about them as she conjured open space into a shape. The word rough-up wasn't accurate. There was a delicate, undefined quality about each page, a line from Chaucer written out in Gothic script, Whanne that Aprille with his shoures sote, on top of a sketch of the traditional three-panel altar, and her self-prompts enumerated underneath. The notes tailed off, or were finalized in drawings with the pen hardly lifted between word and concrete form, random, stuttering first impulses as fixed in his mind as a finished poem and so beautiful in long and elegant lettering that he wanted to lift and frame them there and then.

The actual canvas was solid and compacted, with the infill of experience. The cartoon outline was complete and she put in colour at the top left corner and would continue downwards with implacable logic to the bottom right. She'd put the village people in her processional pilgrimage, the Colonel stiff on duty, Clive scouring out his stables, heads real, faces as seen. Over the hills, the sea yielded a square-rig smack as her Norfolk sketches were applied, a Galilee to hand. Morgan was so intimately involved with every line of her imagination that the forms might have sprouted from his own eyes.

The bond between the place and her activity in it was powerful and convincing. It was what he understood by symbiosis, that Odham provided the conditions for ideal growth, not easily replicated. She'd cast off so much, been shiftless and rootless hitherto, that tenacity took over from the affectionate pulses of sentiment which most people attached to the word home. He was afraid of upheaval for her sake, which led him to ignore his first instinct to keep silent. When he went outside and found her tidying up a border in the semidark, he broached his find.

'You didn't tell me that Ralph's son was Adrian Crane.'

'I didn't think it mattered. Do you know him?'

'Only in a professional way. Our conversation wouldn't stretch to fill a dinner.'

'Who told you?'

Ah, her obsessive sourcing! 'Well, I'm afraid I meddled. I didn't want you to be put out of here without some intervention, and asked for a copy of Ralph's will from Somerset House.'

Strangely, Else didn't seem to mind that but went on tidying a flowerbed, dead-heading and weeding with a quick neatness. She favoured annuals, an instant show of colour and begin again next year. Intermittently, she straightened up and looked over the unaccomplished area. Why ever did one do it, the never-finished toil? Because otherwise something grew up and stopped her passageways. Clumsy at this manual work, Morgan was often reduced to watching her, or being barrow boy.

No, she didn't mind the unarguable facts; it was the lazy or gossip motivated repetition of them that she detested, either malicicious or inaccurate.

'Do you like Adrian?'

'Like him? I hardly know him. He's overly correct.'

She smiled. 'Yes, he relies on forms of address. He wrote to Ralph as Esquire, and now I'm M/s, as if some central section is omitted.'

'Why is he trying to get you out?'

'Oh, he's unhappy, or dissatisfied with his lot. It's good to blame someone for that. He thinks I suggested various things to Ralph which aren't true. Such as? Such as making his study allowance modest rather than handsome. Such as travelling abroad with me and not with him. Adrian wanted to come on that trip to America, but Ralph said no. It was none of my doing. I never set any conditions, as you can see.' She gestured helplessly at the long season of work with no return.

'How is Adrian attacking you? Does he come here?'

'Oh no. He's made an image of me and decided to hate that instead. Sometimes he remembers things that belong to him and writes and demands them back. I always send them. At other times, he gets his solicitor to write vaguely threatening letters.'

'That's an expensive form of amusement.' He recalled Adrian, so dry, so old in his presumptuousness, saying, Are we better to be positively or negatively wrong? To say it's genuine when it isn't, or it isn't when it is. He ought to test his own infallibility on another question. Was it better for Else to own the house when Ralph had let its surety slip, or for her to be ejected against the run of his intentions? But he was convinced Adrian was sincere in his dislike, just as Marise was, and pondered why people had violent reactions to this woman. She provoked the exceptional response because of distortions in her own perception of herself. He'd been fooled time and again by the mismatch between inner and outer, and still she kept him guessing.

'I'd rather have an open strike than all this harrying. It wears you down, the worry. I can't be bothered arguing. But I haven't got a jot of title if it really comes to a showdown.'

'What a hopeless pair we are. Living on your wits is a meagre portion. Why have we never been able to soak the rich, Else? I've had so many chances to cash in and so must you. Why didn't you marry Ralph and see them all off?'

She looked at him curiously, dusting the fine earth powder from her hands. 'Soak the rich? As a premeditated course of action, it's hardly ethical. I suppose I wanted my independence.'

'What'll you do if he turns nasty?'

'You ask too many questions. Take each day as it comes.'

'I know some good people if you land in trouble. That's all I wanted to say.'

'I may need them.'

Lorraine had invited him to lunch on Sunday, sending out cards with RSVP added in the corner. If numbers were important, she must be planning some sort of a do. Morgan went along semi-reluctantly, thinking that the time had come to formalize divisions and, however much of a wrench, the final break was imminent. Even if he and Else hedged on the final suggestion of space-sharing, in effect they were alternating London and Odham, week about, more intimately than many recognized couples. He wanted his options uncomplicated, and no third parties.

Lorraine had asked twenty other friends and decided to hold her lunch party in the garden, as if that would compel the summer to arrive.

'Would you mind doing a stint on the bar?' she asked him. 'It's been set up outside. I thought we'd have a buffet and then people can mingle.'

I hate cold food, he thought, and salady stuff.

There were a lot of things he'd rather do than socialize with Lorraine's friends. They were either county hearties, the sort of men who had joined the Young Farmers in their youth and hadn't grown out of it, or civic dignitaries who talked aggressive local politics. Besides, the last time he was in Bury was for Michael's memorial service. He thought it was tactless of her to imitate that gathering, or repeat it as hastily as May with the same faces and the same venue. Perhaps standing behind the bar was the best spot for him, having a function that didn't depend on being affable.

She was a good hostess, all the same, and had thought through the sequence of things carefully, folding tables, crockery, bowls of salad, cooked meat. She left nothing to chance, but the day defeated her in the form of sullen weather. The afternoon was too raw for standing about outside. Even through a six-foot wall, the wind found chinks. And the bells tolled round the hours remorselessly.

'How's the Smoke?' asked a dapper man he didn't think he'd met before who lived outside Cambridge but didn't declare at once what he did for a living. 'This and that' usually implied nothing. 'Are you glad to be back in it?'

'London's not so smoky now,' said Morgan, irritated with the *passé* jargon of peasoupers. 'The gallery I operate from is on a rise.'

'You shouldn't be in trade, you know.'

'I don't know that I am. Talent-scouting is more like it.'

'Talent, yes, that's always an attractive proposition.'

The sentence had enough sail to slow him down, or was he wearing adultery so high it caught every breeze. He felt the man must be in Lorraine's confidence, or guessed that they were in the throes of separation. Was this more than a friend? Morgan couldn't help noticing that he was urging his wife towards another man with unseemly enthusiasm, because that would let him off the hook.

'What good stuff have you seen of late?'

Morgan was wary of confidential note-takers. Something of Else's secrecy had rubbed off on him. He'd found poaching was widespread in the art business, like Nick and Harriet's, a jackal interest in picking over other people's kill. The problem was how to answer without being rude, or how to encourage reciprocal information without in fact giving anything away. A little sleight of tongue.

'The London colleges have gone downhill. The principals I meet keep on telling me the same thing. Lack of government funding through to the local authorities has meant a real downturn.

Students get a discretionary not a mandatory grant, depending on how their county council views art training. Very depressing. The provincial colleges I've been to are more vigorous. There's a chap in his last year at Manchester who's worth tracking.'

'Oh?'

'But there's a lot of wordy painting going on. I went to the Royal College retrospective. Did you see that? You know where you are up to 1950. Drawing, structure, something you'd recognize as workmanship. Then a chasm. They've gone cerebral, all the symbols right, technically tremendous and no heartache. What's anybody painting *about* these days? How, not why. The isms have taken over. It's a completely mechanical way of looking at things, with the idea stifling its own device. It's this pressure to pass exams. I just hope there's a little man painting in Bradford or Sheffield or Leeds, without a qualification to his name, who'll make us look fools in twenty-five years' time. Make us look the poseurs we are.'

'I thought you were an academician?' said the other narrowly.

'Not always. A bit of me likes to spite the system.'

'You don't really admire Lowry?' he pressed finally for a name.

'Well, maybe it's a style you tire of, like pointillism. Missing shadows. Missing an ultimate depth. But I admire the man, oh yes. He said a lot of the elusive things. "If they didn't want my paintings when they were cheap, why do they want them when they're expensive?" Could you give him an answer that wouldn't break his heart?' Or Else's for that matter, balancing at the top of a ladder in the sub-zero outhouse to reach the top corner of a vast allegorical narrative. 'Precisely because they're expensive and for no other reason.'

'Are you selling much?'

'Oh, pretty tidy.'

Why's he being cagey, thought the other, trying to cut a piece of meat with his one free hand.

Lorraine paid a lot of attention to her husband, as if he were a very special guest. 'You've been fantastic, doing that boring job all afternoon. You must be perished by now. Come and eat. I've kept something special for you. Secret hoard.' She drew her arm through his and led him uxoriously down the path to salad bowls. 'Will you stay?' she asked, watching him eat.

Being touched by his wife was disconcerting, like being pressed in a numb spot. All it triggered was unfeeling and the dreaded passionless routine of their contact, that art which he'd been speaking of just now, cerebral, mechanical and dull. 'Yes, I will hang on if you don't mind. There's something I wanted to clear up with you before I go.'

He could see his answer didn't please her. She moved away to talk to someone else. Fondly absent, was he? Less fond in presence.

'I think we met a few weeks ago,' said a lady in a summer dress inappropriate to the day. 'You came to see me.'

'Oh yes, indeed. In Sudbury. Thank you for your note.'

'You'll be glad to hear we've made it for the second scanner now. Every little helps.'

She was the hospital friend who'd witnessed Ralph Pennington's will. That information burned in Morgan's skull. It was interference, but he'd try a bit of a prompt to test her memory.

'I didn't know Mr Pennington all that well, more by reputation, but Miss Petersen is a good friend. She may have told you already, but she's having trouble over her ownership of The Aviary. She might have to give it up.'

'Oh, surely not,' said the chairwoman, deeply concerned, 'when she could buy it outright. She told me herself that if she sold all Mr Pennington's paintings, she'd be a millionaire.'

The estimate was conveyed without mischief between two impartials. This woman wouldn't know a Brueghel from a Braque, so it must have been Else herself who made the remark. And it was true. At auction, those pictures in the house would probably go towards the million mark, or more. Put with such clarion simplicity, why was Else worried about inheriting her cottage or pleading poverty? Why was Adrian not putting pressure on her for the return of those paintings, when he'd apparently visited The Aviary many times and must know what they were worth? If one area of Ralph's estate was in dispute, why not the other and much more valuable portion? And why was Else footling around getting rid of things to small-time provincial dealers like Lorraine when she could make a major entry at Sotheby's or Christie's?

He hoped the woman wasn't, in her naïvety, suggesting as much to outsiders. 'I think that's on the inflated side. You know the way people exaggerate. They're not significant works.'

'Oh, I see. Not so valuable. I should have brought a cardigan but we live in hope. I didn't realize you were Lorraine's husband until today.' And in no particular order, but no mention of papers she had signed. Well, she was a scatterbrained type.

It was late afternoon by the time the last guest went and left them to their walls. He and Lorraine tidied the garden, folding up tables, wiping down until it was almost dark. It felt odd, like going camping, being outdoors for hours until they could feel the chill coming over the grass. Stiffness on the trestle joints. Rheumatism next.

'Have you made any sort of decision?' he asked when they moved inside.

'About?

'You vaguely talked of selling up before Christmas.'

'No, that was you.'

'Well, you said the place got you down.'

'It was the bells,' she specified. 'And I think you probably hear those wherever you go.'

They observed a minute's silence, working quietly together, then he spoke.

'I think we ought to regularize things.'

'That's a strange way to put it. Are they irregular?'

'Separation's not a very satisfactory state, I find. It's a postpone-ment of decision. We're either married or we're divorced.'

She scraped bowls of food into smaller bowls to fit inside the fridge.

'Your girlfriend's serious then? You want to remarry?'

She had noted a discernible change in him as he came though the door today. He wasn't her husband any more. The angle of his look had shifted, upwards, roaming, not downcast, while his face had both thinned and filled. The suit he was wearing was a different cut from the ones favoured in Bury, and it fitted him with the small details of hand-tailoring. Was that the only thing that made him look younger? The prospect of a second marriage might be the best rejuvenator. Lorraine touched a spot of jealousy, near her own sensitivity. She found she wanted to know their intimate passions, to prove to herself that they were unseemly after all.

He was surprised at the bitterness of her tone. Didn't want him before, damn well wanted him now. 'We've not got near to discussing that. I wouldn't think so.'

'Then why?'

'Oh, to be clear.'

'Clear of me?'

'No, clear-headed.'

'You'd like me to sell the business and the house and divide the proceeds between us?' She made the facts of the matter sound like an accusation.

'Again, that seemed your disposition when I came to collect my clothes before Christmas.'

'I think we spoke about sentimental items, not splitting the value of the property.'

Morgan didn't enjoy this wrangling any more than Else and got the worst of deals because he wouldn't haggle. Leave it intact, an old past like a civilised wall of memory, crumbling, antique, but in the name of decency, let there be no further pillage. Walk away with nothing in your pockets was his attitude, but his balance sheet wasn't so healthy that he could indulge his more gentlemanly habits. The woman's efforts should have their reward, but not at the expense of his. 'It may come to that.'

'I've taken advice on this,' she said rapidly. 'It might be difficult for you to press a claim on the property since you did actually desert the marital home.'

'Pushed, Lorraine. You pushed, remember.'

Yes, she had eased him out, to relieve the unbearable intensity of their grief, which multiplied when they were too much alone together. What she'd envisaged last December was that his new outlook would regenerate their relationship, not put an end to it. Or was she being dishonest about that? Was she finding that nothing enhanced her own view of his possibilities so much as another woman finding him attractive too? Yes, she was intrigued by the shape of their sex, wondering if it were learnable. Would he be different now in her arms? Would she? 'But if we leave it as it is, then money doesn't really enter into it.'

What was he? Some sort of parti-coloured husband, half and half, useful as a social adjunct when she wanted him behind the bar. He stepped into the invidiousness of Else's situation, the person with no fixed status. He found that letting someone get a tether round your neck was offensive. It made you buck.

'Thank you for being so exact.' Would he stay? No way. In a minute she'd point out that he was living in sin, legally reducing the slice of his incumbency still further.

* * *

Counselling was a terrible business.

Else had had no formal training in it. She'd started to talk to other in-patients at the hospice while Ralph was being treated and turned out to have a gift for it. But it was like giving blood for transfusions; you couldn't do it too often. The body needed time to restore its own fluid, the mind its equilibrium.

She was very careful to look good when she went to Sudbury, by way of a compliment to the people she'd be meeting, skirt and sweater tidy, hair tied, no make-up, raincoat on top. The last thing they wanted was to see someone turning up bedraggled or depressed. The head-on strain of the encounters kept her cheerful, like adrenalin; if she'd been in a dismal frame of mind she'd have collapsed.

The patients weren't the problem on the whole. She could play Scrabble with them, wind balls of knitting wool or fetch things from other wards. Read and write their letters. Sometimes they wanted to be drawn, recorded for a friend, and she was able to work so fast that a likeness could be done in half an hour without a wearisome sitting, something as fleeting as a smile, and they were pleased. That was a real service she could do them; their face made special, permanent, often the one and only time they sat for a portrait. She was able to gloss over any unhappy lines, catch their very best angle.

Or they wanted advice, an objective opinion. Illness itself had prepared them for the end and she was unshockable about the practicalities of death. She was positive. This is the next stage, and the next. The patients worried most about their personal dignity. Will I be incontinent? How will I look? What is dying really? Is it soft or hard, like being pressed or hit? It was a dreadful form of expiation, resubmitting herself to Ralph's last few months, but she had strong nerves and, when triggered, found she had infinite patience, going over the same ground again and again. She felt no task was too small, no act too menial. And she was pleased that the staff had come to trust her as someone both able-bodied and shrewd. The men and women in the hospice stayed human, after all, and tried to hoard their pills, skip naps and otherwise infringe the system. You had to be alert to all their tricks.

It was the relatives who were unbearable.

That day, Sunday, a boy died from leukaemia. He'd arrived at the spectral beauty of sick children, too blue, too veined, and over the months she'd become quite attached to him because he liked to spend his time drawing. Latterly, he'd become so weak he couldn't sit upright and she'd rigged a tilting board at the bedside for him to use, and found a pen that was chunky enough for him to grasp easily. He enjoyed her comments and would go back over his work persistently, with an adult care. They did age. Even his outlines suggested prematurity, something hard and seized before the shading went in, like the drawings by autistic children, something absolutely known but not with subtlety. Seen, not lived. Eye drawings, not heart. She kept one or two of them.

It was the parents who were heart-breaking, weeping and inconsolable by any normal means, looking into their innermost mind and saying, If this hadn't happened, we might have had a good life. It was hard to make them rally, but she still tried, with the false arguments of life going on.

A day spent like this was an antidote to the frivolity, the sheer self-indulgence of art. As if what happened in your head had any final significance. One picture more or less in the world, so what? She would trade off all her paintings for an extension of that boy's life to normal term, had made the equation time and time again between inner and outer existence, and concluded that the images of life were second best. A lived life came first.

But in that was the irony. Life short, art long. The people went on dying and the pictures went on accumulating, in total and in value. The canvas tacked on to stretchers in the studio was a substitute for death as well as living, compulsive, inevitable, draining, just like the real thing.

Sometimes she came home ready to collapse from her own emotional exhaustion and sometimes she came home to paint. There was no difference.

June

'Just a thought,' said Max, calling Else early in the month. 'In a fortnight's time we have a party. Do you want to come to a party?'

'What sort of party is this? A publishing party? No, thanks.'

'An arty party.'

'That's worse still. The suits are more old-fashioned.'

'Serious big-shot art. Somebody puts up some money for a prize and we all sit round and eat and clap. That kind of a do. A banquet they call it.'

'I haven't got a frock.'

'Sure you've got a frock. Or somebody's got a frock they'll lend you. It doesn't need to be Balmain with you in it.'

'You persuaded me.'

'And do I ask that nice man you've been seen around town with?'

'What nice man is this?'

'Kind of older man. Famous. I forgot his name.'

Nick didn't own a dinner suit which he felt was wearable and had to hire one. He left the office at half four to pick it up from Moss Bros. before they closed, although he didn't use their fitting rooms to put it on. He waited at the end of Bolton Street for Lindsay, a manoeuvre they'd repeated so often they could do it tacitly on the passing of a time for assignation, even a hand signal would do, five fingers on the right hand for the hour, quarters on the left. He drove south instead of going north to Portman Square, where Max Edelman had invited the entourage of his guests to his flat for drinks before the banquet: 6 p.m. for carriages at 7.15 said the printed card. Nick thought he'd never make it down the Fulham Road to Lindsay's flat and back again in time for the drinks hour.

* * *

Their chauffeur waited in the street below the gallery, while the Fisks changed for the evening's appointment. Marise had fitted a small dressing room into the back wall of her office and kept a rack of clothes pressed and ready for these after-hours engagements plus a little jewellery, which saved her crossing London to the flat. She'd have liked to juggle a corner for a proper bathroom. More pleasant to go out fresh and showered.

'You say we're Max's guests?' Boris clarified, since he let Marise arrange their social calendar.

'Unfortunately, we'd accepted his invitation by the time the Sporting Art people asked us. That would have been better really.'

The Trust was getting up a subscription to buy a major Stubbs for the nation, a transaction she hoped she would be entrusted with. She knew an owner in straits who might be persuaded to part with it for such a prestigious cause.

'And who will be at Max's?'

'I'm not quite sure. Sybil's come down from Suffolk for the weekend to oversee things. He tells me he's taken three tables, so there will be a crowd at Portman Square. Some of the people he's publishing this year. An American professor who writes rather manufactured biography. Morgan is going. And I suspect the girl he's taken up with.'

Boris, knotting his own bow tie expertly without the aid of a mirror, was glad of the forewarning. 'The painter?'

'Oh? Had you heard too? Wrong type, wrong age. What good can come of it?'

'And what harm?'

'That we await.'

Dan Fredericks landed at Heathrow from Kennedy Airport only to discover that the publisher's publicity girl hadn't booked him into the Astoria as promised. Great outlook for the trip if she couldn't even get that right. He had to settle his own taxi fare into central London and use his personal credit card to guarantee the hotel booking. Would Edelman refund it? Should have got a written agreement about the payment of expenses before he left. Thought UK publishers would have been more reliable.

He got out the typescript of his schedule again. Looked

professional enough. Plenty of action. The interviews were quality. The broadsheet press. The last publicity tour he was on, the girl kept getting lost and missing deadlines. The two of them drove round for days to bookshops that were closed, half-day, on holiday, to signing sessions where the people had gone home and he drank about two gallons of coffee waiting around with staff. Nobody had caffeine-free here either. Bad for the thyroid. This one, well, she'd have to come up with something better. Hadn't reminded him to bring a DJ, come to that. It was his wife who had made him pack it. Sure was going to be useful.

Else pulled a zip and let it hang.

Underneath, her body reacted to the chemistry of evening. A little cold, a little ridged with anticipation, a shell she might move into for a while like the hermit crab, or reject for something fitter. She moved free under its covering.

London reinstated the lost glamour of her early youth. Covent Garden with its large neutral spaces, open to potential, provided a second summer. The days stretched out, days into evenings which she hadn't maximized for a long time. There was an interregnum of mood as the capital turned from earning to spending with an hour's turn-around in between. How to fill it? Washing, changing, getting ready to go out and put the next show on the road. She liked walking the streets at the changeover, business to pleasure, city into dinner suits, and would stroll up to Leicester Square to get the feel of the crowds under the cinema hoardings. Someone tried to pick her up. She played along with him, enjoying the frisson of danger and sexual adventure, as much an eye flirt as any man.

Max shook Dan Fredericks heartily by the hand and tried to make him feel welcome. He held the chair in fine art at a Midwest university, not true to type, not at all effete, but built on the burly side with a neck like a bull. He wrote rather scurrilous chat biographies and had specialized in English painters, preferring, in the main, ones with literary connections who might have been given to letter-writing. He'd made his mark a few years earlier by discovering a cache of Bloomsbury letters which underlined how savagely the Bell–Woolf clique had anathematized each other's work. A spiteful collection he edited. This was the first of Dan's books which Max had bought, in a cooperative venture with a New

York publisher who was already sick to death of Mr Fredericks, it transpired heatedly across the transatlantic telephone. The man wouldn't compile his own index, do the research for his illustrations or acknowledge primary sources. They'd run into trouble over the current book with some unlicensed quotation, permission now refused, and had to rebind it at the last minute. Not a good prognosis. They were trying to limit the damage before he went off on his publicity tour. Max kept smiling.

The butler who ushered guests up the internal lift at Portman Square doubled as a waiter on the cocktails and canapés. It was a smaller flat than Max would have liked to entertain in, having a decent drawing room and not much else, but since Sybil preferred the house in Southwold, they kept their best furniture by the sea and the city flat was relegated to second place.

'Marise, you're looking like a queen. This is not a dress. It is a gown. Royalty couldn't be more gracious. You do me proud.' It was the cloth called lamé, generously cut. He forgave her everything for being imperturbable. The summer catalogue had been printed and delivered without more ado, and they were friends till next time. 'You know Marise Fisk, don't you, Else? But have you met her husband, Boris?'

Else and the man shook hands on the exchange of names like perfect strangers. The gesture implied that no, they hadn't met, although they'd greeted each other in the foyer of Sotheby's with more than formal coolness. An embrace and warmth withal. Unblinking, Morgan watched one of the side-shows of the evening, transfixed by turns with jealousy and curiosity. Marise, he surmised, was ignorant of whatever had passed between these two, whatever made the bond, as she turned away without a hint of interest to commandeer her host.

'You have all these beautiful books on your shelves, Max, but why have you taken the covers off?'

'Oh, I do keep the jackets, I promise you, but separately. In drawers. Pristine, like paintings lying flat. I don't want them dog-eared by being thumbed.' The muted colour of the binding boards glowed in the firelight, their titles tooled uniformly in gold lettering. 'And it's a philistine thing to say, Marise, but they fit better with the décor when they're undressed.'

'But how interesting. What an interesting idea! I never thought of it like that, although it does seem a shame to hide the covers away after all the trouble you go to to design them.' The idea claimed her attention. Within seconds, Marise had envisaged an exhibition of historic jacket designs, of books both famous and infamous, in different print media. That was a possible exhibition for Covent Garden. She looked round for Morgan to convert the idea into actuality.

'To sell what?' was his objection. 'That would be a museum piece. Static. Nothing to sell.'

'Prints of jackets, I'm thinking of. We could buy the rights. Old editions, half of them remaindered. The plates will be going for nothing. I heard about a publisher who was moving premises and came across some early woodcuts in a filing cabinet. Now, who was that? Was it for Graham Greene? Bodley Head?'

Clever, prehensile woman. It wasn't an improbable idea at that, the Cockerell Press, the Chaucer Press, Eric Gill had cut some impressive letter heads ... Morgan quickly ran through a list of diverse sources he could collate. The Pre-Raphaelite bindings could be copied. They'd make a handsome set of prints. Old maps from atlases, and illustrations separated from their binder did well enough, so why not the actual covers as a subject? Somebody had designed them in the first place, to be aesthetic and to sell. Nothing wrong with the illustrative. Max warmed to the idea too. He thought book designs were undervalued and could think of at least one jacket in the last year which had been issued separately as a limited-edition print.

'You will put this in hand, Morgan? And better still if they are out of copyright.' Marise found she was increasingly pleased with her new manager. Once again, he'd shown an aptitude for timing. The Green Gallery was succeeding beyond her wildest hopes, but he'd sharpened New Bond Street too. He was right about the Gainsborough, but not so right as to deny her profit. Dealers had been interested in that acquisition. It did her good. He had the wider cull, as she had anticipated, scholarly and experienced, and filtered it through her. It was time, perhaps, to up his status before someone else poached his talents. The directorship resuggested itself as something she must broach before too long.

But Morgan knew at the outset he wouldn't jump at this book-cover project. It was neat and packageable, but it smacked of dwarfism. It wasn't new art, and that was his brief and his personal self-justification, that he was intent on promoting the raw or rougher theme. No prints, said the wise collector, even limited edition.

Nick lay on his back and smoked. Bad habit and all that, but it did relax. Lindsay was a good girl. He enjoyed being with her: the breasts were not disappointing and it tuned life up no end. He tried to squeeze out a trace of guilt and heard himself saying to someone who was often Else – You must know what it's like when you're very fond of *two* people at once – but the problem with his particular two women, wife and lover, partner and secretary, tended to reduce itself to logistics, not ethics. He wanted to stay here, talk, smoke, laugh, but in half an hour he'd have to get up and drive to Portman Square and be Harriet's husband, take his share in the business of it all, which made these out-of-hours demands. When was he free? When did his off-duty period arrive? The office was turning claustrophobic, he in one room, Harriet next door and Lindsay typing up his notes through a partition wall, visible, audible, fracturing his peace of mind because she was all the lovely and light-hearted and youthful things he'd given up for a lifetime on the mile. An hour at a time with her wasn't good enough. She deserved a lot more of his attention.

Else didn't often wear a dress and the one she'd borrowed for the evening was probably like Morgan's own dinner suit, mothballed. Black, grosgrain trimmed, it was the universal little number that was meant to make women uniform. Hers didn't. It wasn't particularly revealing but did give scope for being uninhibited, which she exploited to the full. Morgan genuflected to every worthwhile feminist principle, as he thought it, but there were some women who put clothes on, for clothes' sake. Street-cred, snappy dressers, elegance in skirts. She wasn't one of them. Else's clothes had a tendency to suggest the nude. You drew the lines of underwear and under that, the body. Kept you guessing. Was she or wasn't she? It might not be nice, and was calculated to annoy every decent, self-respecting matron in the room, but those were the facts of life. Sex and sin were absorbing pastimes and, without ostensible effort, she embodied them.

'Where can he be?' asked Harriet. 'The last I saw of him, he was off to pick his suit up. Half past four. I had a client with me and came on by myself. Do you suppose they forgot it, or put the wrong size aside?'

She was genuinely upset that the poor man should have had all this trouble to fulfil his professional obligations. He hadn't wanted to come this evening and she had made him. Was being late a subtle revenge?

'Do you want to phone the outfitter's? No, that's no good, they'll have closed by now.'

'The traffic's been impossible across town,' Morgan tried to console her, 'and we were in a taxi.'

'But it isn't across town. It's a direct route.'

Else found a sceptical corner of her mouth. Maybe undressing was taking Nick longer these days. Not as nimble as he used to be.

Nick arrived last among the guests at seven, fully apparelled. 'I'm so sorry, darling. Terrible jams all over and then I couldn't park the car. I should have taken a cab. Friday getaway, of course.'

He smiled, cherubic innocent.

This is a badly behaved young man, thought Max. He upsets his wife, he annoys me by being late. This is my show. He could try. But we go on forgiving him. Why do we forgive him? Because he has the best eye in London for the unpredictable. Then the publisher pulled himself up short, realizing Nick didn't qualify as a young man any more. They forgave him because they had lost track of time and had failed to elicit the dues of his coming of age, which was responsibility.

Left alone, Lindsay reconsidered. When she was with Nick, she felt charmed out of her common sense. Yes, he was a charmer, talker, lover flattery fluent. Her body just said yes. She couldn't resist him because he seemed perfectly harmless. But she knew this couldn't go on. Here she was spending another evening at home by herself, with no escort and no plans, the cocoa hairwash evening too familiarly repeated.

And sometimes she felt that Harriet knew quite well what was happening, could read their secret code and hand signals as if she'd worked them out herself. She looked at Nick's secretary with patient, ancient eyes, thinking, I can't criticize you because I did exactly this myself with a married man. Sneaked out of the office early, pretended to work late. She had an impulse to talk it out with

139

Harriet; Nick was no good for that, wouldn't concentrate to the end of any idea or face unpleasantness. She rather liked Harriet's ways, preferring the tidy desk, the balanced account. She even shared the woman's frustration that Nick was able to walk out on both of them, begging a prior appointment, while they stayed behind and picked up the tag end of his emergencies.

She lay on in the darkening rooms, surrounded by the disorder their hurried hour gave rise to, and teased her hair distractedly. She pulled a strand to its full length and watched it bounce back into corkscrew curls again. Nick did that to her, admiring its long springiness. Spring, spring, he said, that's what you are. My second spring.

Was he genuine? And if he wasn't, did it matter? She was happily deceived. How could she give it up? She felt she made a difference to him, organized his papers, loved the work, the hum, the wonky floorboards and the traffic roar throwing dust into the cracks of the ill-fitting windows. He would occasionally turn to her and ask, How does this man's work look to you? You've got younger eyes. Is it any good? They took scouting jaunts to country auctions and more than once he acted on her opinion. Not seeing Nick any more would mean giving up her job as well, and possibly her flat, the contacts she was forging incidentally that might lead on somewhere, because one thing was certain in the Piccadilly mayhem – she could do what they were doing, given time. Learn from them, she concluded, taking good notes while you are about it.

Eight hundred people had congregated in the banqueting suite of the Dorchester Hotel in Park Lane. Eighty tables, each laid for ten, at forty pounds a head. Wine inclusive. Deductable as a legitimate entertainment expense.

It wasn't going to be a comfortable evening, Max could see when he walked into the overcrowded foyer, and anyway he had misgivings about these big-bout occasions. He started out by thinking it was a good way to repay hospitality, look after his book people, and half an hour into it repented of the impulse. It was about as intimate as holding a party for your friends in an airport lounge. The noise was antisocial for a start. However high the ceiling, any sound multiplied by eight hundred rose with the energy of a water hydrant when you uncapped it, hit the top and fell back down with a roar. Up and down it went, recycling itself. More words, more volume. Talking to anyone apart from your immediate neighbour was a strain, and neighbours were a lottery at public dinners. The ten he'd put at his own table were an ill-assorted group, three couples, himself and Sybil plus the American critic and the poet whose work Else had illustrated in the almanac. But, after all, he reasoned, you were only asking them to be civil to each other for two hours, not spend the rest of their lives together. Give it a chance.

Morgan drew Dan, the short conversational straw. He wished he'd been rude enough to ask Max to juggle him next to Else or Harriet. They were low on ladies. Ladies were a dilute to the men only, bar-room dialogue of the book trade, which could end up as raw on the back palate as high-percentage proof. Money, names, successes, who'd come a cropper this season, it was an indigestible aperitif.

Dan was late settling into his place for dinner because he'd stopped to buttonhole the guest speaker, the President of the Royal Academy, as he came down the stairs into the banqueting hall.

'He did say he was too pressed to speak to me just then, but I think maybe I can fit it in to see him later this week. I don't know when. I'm going to be pushed on my schedule. Manchester Monday, Glasgow Tuesday. I was very surprised when he said he didn't know about my new book. A man in his position needs to keep himself topped up. It's had about fifty reviews in the States already.' He did pause to recount them. 'I wanted his help too about a piece on Sickert and his circle. Maybe I'll write to him when I get back home, now I can say I've met him. I do not say this egotistically,' Dan said, 'but I am most surprised the President hadn't heard of my book about Whistler.'

'Whistler? Oh, you're not giving us another one!'

'But it's been six years since the last major biography appeared. Besides, I had access to some of the papers that have been undisclosed to date. You get hold of people,' he said lowering his voice confidentially, while Morgan sensed he wouldn't like bovine Dan to get hold of him, 'give them a few drinks and they tell you about the private life.'

Morgan's antipathy grew but he went on being polite for Max's sake.

'I was disappointed in the President's latest book, weren't you? It was really too personal a look at Lutyens. I suppose you have to broaden the readership, but I was disappointed. You know the great biographies of the 1950s. It didn't come close.'

Morgan flunked duels, especially literary ones. 'I've always agreed with Philip Larkin on that score. Writers shouldn't read too much.'

'That's a rather naïve attitude,' Dan began, but spotted the useful side-issue, eager to meet the man who met the man. 'Did you know Larkin?'

'On paper.'

'Oh, you wrote to him? Did you keep his letters?'

Morgan didn't answer, pretending to be busy eating, although in fact it was Else's nearby conversation with Nick he'd hoisted an antenna to. He realized that the American hadn't recognized him or paid proper attention to his name during the introductions and, if he turned round to ask for it again, Morgan would pull out a pseudonym. Dan Fredericks was ready to take him for a minor friend of Philip Larkin's, someone whose value lay in a series of private letters which the American might have the task of editing in twenty years' time. Dan's interest was in the posthumous. If Morgan admitted to being the author of several books which the other academic had certainly read, and possibly even taught on his syllabus in the last ten years, he'd be discountenanced. The critic had no time for a man as a living person, although he'd probably boast of having met him once he was dead. The biographer wanted that safe perspective on the past. The deceased were the OK people. Roll on famous death.

What Morgan had heard Else say to Nick was, 'Have you managed to sell that picture yet? I don't know what it's worth, not much, but even if it doesn't wipe out my bill, it may go part way.'

What picture and what bill? Was her debt for the husband and wife professional fees Nick had mentioned, or one of her long-standing pay-back favours? The Wylies should be taking a percentage of her earnings as they came in. Why were their dealings underhand like this, paid in kind, horrible phrase usually implying something unkind?

The Dorchester served them spinach and an indeterminate meat which some swore was chicken, others pork, while a third backed escalope of veal. Nick shoved his food around the plate as if to sample whether it tasted better from each of the different quadrants. He didn't eat starch. Carb gave him the gripes. He gave up on the food, ordering another brandy to wash away the flavour. He didn't drink wine either, having acidified his stomach irreversibly on cheap plonk. Or so he said. Penalty of early poverty. Spirits only now. Pure alcohol. When he'd emptied that glass, he fumbled with the printed guest list. 'Where are the big names? There aren't many big boys here tonight. They could have shipped us in some greats.'

Boris was distant, speaking little. The meal was poor, the wine inferior, the company not of his choosing and all for the sake of a bogus ceremony. He was lucky to have Else sitting on his left, but sensible comment was constrained by the noise and by Marise, three places to his right. He guarded his eyes and his expression unbendingly. He could sit comatose for quite long periods like this, sit through committees and financial statements in the boardroom in a trance, absorbing everything, saying nothing until the end, when he would point out the flaw *vis-à-vis* the tax implications, or whatever it was they'd overlooked in their keenness to come to a decision, any decision, quality apart. He liked to confound a premature show of hands like that. He listened to them in turn and would sum up. I am stolid and stolid I will stay. He'd built his reputation as a hard man by never entering into the idle discussion of preamble but ramming down on the motion or action which they thought they had word-perfected for the minutes.

He was in no hurry himself, had no planned objectives. If someone round the table had put down an item on the agenda, Why do you send a regular quarterly cheque to the artist left, he would have twenty unflurried answers. It is a charitable gift. It is a retainer against future work in which I deem myself to have a stake. It is better than an Arts Council grant, subject to the whim of government. It is a levy from the indecently rich to the indecently poor. It is a concession to the inequity of our positions and I write the debt off against conscience. It is a subscription to Jehovah's fund, not to strike me dead tomorrow for my sins.

Beyond these parrying replies, he made no offer of information, even to himself. He was a noticer. He noticed how fragile were the egos of the American and the poet, on the look-out for praise. But they were parasites. It didn't escape his notice that each and every one of them round that table made their living out of Else, or the other Else counterparts scattered round the room, and Nick's complaint, which carried down the table, about there being no famous names in the assembly was two-edged. Outnumbered nine to one, fame was under-represented from the start. Morgan, and even the American, had more clout writing about pictures, while agent and publisher and himself as vendor, for that matter, had a more secure income handling aspects of the work, than the painter was likely to achieve in merely doing it.

A quarterly cheque went some way to counter-balance that.

Slowly a frenzy had overtaken Else. It started when she shook hands with Boris, which, outrageously, had made her want to dissolve in laughter or come clean, and then she realized that repression was going to be the keynote of her evening. Here she was wearing the conformist dress, going through the civilized rote of menu, guest list, invited speakers with some annotated hand-clapping to come, and she felt she'd been too easily persuaded into attending. Wedged at a table for more than two hours, listening to public speeches! Who could sit with their elbows demurely tucked in for that long? The boredom of physical inertia got to her.

She winked down the table at Morgan during the pre-speech lull and he thought, Fireworks. She's quite capable of standing up on the table and giving us a show.

The room hushed attentively for the speeches and prize-giving. The great man, the President of the Royal Academy, was getting to his feet. 'What we celebrate this evening is the widespread importance of—'

'Pictorial art,' Else helped him along under her breath.

'Pictorial art.'

Nick sniggered.

'That art is alive and well,' she prompted.

'That art is alive and well is evidenced by the presence of so many art lovers here, patrons, societies whose concern is to promote good exhibitions and good ownership, and painters themselves.'

'Evidenced?' she queried to the table at large. 'Has this become standard usage?'

'God, I could do with a smoke,' said Nick.

'Sh,' she admonished him.

'Are you listening or something?'

'Yes, he may tell me why my five pictures were rejected.'

The room could accommodate a certain level of distraction. Waiters hovered at the kitchen exits, mouthing instructions to each other, and trays clattered in a distant percussion across the gravy-thickened air. But when someone began a campaign of systematic sabotage of the speech, there was no element in the room that could contain it. The formal quickly succumbed to sedition, even if it was done in the guise of approval. Else clapped solemnly at the clichés, hear-heared his labouring quotations and, before the President had reached half-way, the rest of the audience had picked up the derisory tone she had imperceptibly introduced. They simultaneously remembered, all eight hundred, that he was a boring placeman who hadn't made an interesting decision in his life and, seeing him defenceless, they were cruel, groaning at his jokes, jeering at his precious *mots*. They bayed 'Surprise, surprise' when he formally awarded the put-up prize to the man who was sitting next to him – What is it for anyway? Oh, relatively major contribution to art this year, calculated from 1 April. They'd had a scrappy dinner, suspected this sort of pageant came down to self-flattery and were going to take it out on someone. The loudest applause of the evening went to the prizewinner, in whom all infelicities were overlooked for saying so, on behalf of the rest of the paying guests. The banter could have been good-humoured; or it could not.

Else leaned sideways and said something irreverent. Morgan didn't hear it, although Nick laughed, but there was the sound of a small scrunch which carried out loud. She'd come close enough to catch a strand of his hair between her teeth. She didn't think about why she encouraged Nick to flirt like this. He was handy and he was game for most mischief. There was a certain fun in irritating po-faced Harriet. And the other men were just too old or too far away, while the poet didn't have a frolic in him. Nick would serve.

Marise watched them disapprovingly. Yes, it had been a dull speech and the man deserved to be baited for it, underpitching his remarks below the intellect of his audience. Guest speakers ran many risks, among them being buttonholed by bores or barracked from the floor. Else had just caught that hint of sham and broadcast it ... and Marise had joined quietly in the pack when no one would notice. But Else herself, oh, Else Petersen. What to do about the person. She wanted Morgan in her team, but didn't want the extras. She remembered hearing a phrase applied to Zelda

Fitzgerald, that tiresome woman who was so pathologically jealous of her husband's success that she tried to write her own novels to outdo his, then gave it up to train as a professional ballet dancer, when she was getting on for forty. Died insane. The stress of her made Scott Fitzgerald into an alcoholic. 'Zelda is a very deleterious woman.' The word fitted. Destructive, negative and untrustworthy. She and Morgan came together to Portman Square, having left Covent Garden, which was her apartment, and while her manager was entitled to some private life, it ought to be seemly and publicly acceptable. These things rebounded. Sidetrack Else, she thought, and then we have a simple negotiation.

'I hear that New York prices at auction are dipping,' Nick said to their visitor. 'It hasn't happened here yet, but it'll come.'

'Nobody would disagree with a bit of moderation in the markets,' said Morgan.

'Who told you that, Nick, or have you been cutting your opinions out of the *Sunday Times* again?'

'I was in New York recently.'

'Five years ago recently,' Else scoffed genially, and turned to the biographer. 'Who *is* your New York publisher, by the way?'

At this question, Dan puffed up like an adder full of his venom. 'They've had the last book they're getting out of me. I finished a monograph on Lawrence on schedule, thirty thousand words. They should have been damned glad to get it, it was very good, though I say it myself. I have thirty or forty publishers world-wide, Japan, Europe, Australia, South America, so I can pick and choose. But my home publishers won't commit themselves to terms. Mess me about. And they didn't promote the Whistler the way they said they would. Sure slow to pay. I would say, as of this moment, various publishers round the world owe me around eighteen hundred dollars. And that's not peanuts.'

'I know, that man's a crook,' Nick sympathized about Dan's commissioning editor. 'And his boss is an absolute wimp. No stamina. No go.'

'Another good friend of yours, Nick?'

Across the table, Harriet gave up the struggle to support her intermittent conversation with the poet. She felt bedraggled in misery, like a wet red setter with her lustre gone. She wanted someone to pay attention to her and the easiest route was to blame her escort for being inattentive, which was pointless eight feet

146

away. Her reproving looks fell short. The evening's equilibrium had been upset. At another table, she had noticed Martin Price with his second wife, newly emerged from her third confinement. Three children in as many years. Such prolific output! The sorrow of all that misbegotten time had almost passed, but she wanted to look as sleek and comfortable with herself as Martin did. Be blithe with the same cheerful wave of the hand, saying in code, See, I did survive.

Morgan, watching her mood fall, felt sorry for her, another elder partner out of her depth with the current modes. Harriet looked over at him and he sensed the impermanence of today in her glance that had no focus. Others lovers impinged, or other standards by which they were inadequate. Possibly he or Max should have done the gallant thing and started some badinage with her, but it was too far and they were too involved in the intricacies at the other side of the table. Nick and Else weren't exactly misbehaving, no physical and not much verbal, but they were the dangerous types where anything might happen. Else was the instigator, vital, blasé, exciting and simply man-aware. Hers was the centrifugal force that flung them against each other.

'You know,' said Max, 'you'll all shout at me when I say this, but we ought to put on this sort of event with more style. A banquet, fine, you like a banquet. But not one prize, not two prizes. You want to run it like the Oscar ceremony, with nominations and sealed envelopes, different committees in on it. Prizes for the best exhibition, best catalogue. Yes, a prize for art criticism, for the best new talent. Make it more glamorous, more fun. Televised. Speeches. It is so visual. Why is nobody doing this already?'

'What an appalling idea.'

Max's table was placed near the centre. Squashed in at the top edge of the suite, at the furthermost corner from the action, interest, involvement with any ambience or mood, sat Adrian Crane and his wife, as guests of Sotheby's. This alone displeased him, as if he'd suffered an intentional slight, although every now and then a clearing opened up in sound and view, down which he could witness the events that were taking place in the middle.

He saw Else clearly, saw the antics going on around her in which she was provocative. He had a concentrated look, like a man wearing blinkers, and could focus on essentials: Morgan and Else.

They didn't touch. They didn't need to. Couples engendered their own helix. Body-language was the current phrase for it; they melted the space between them. Adrian was stunned with surprise and sat in a state of recovery for most of the evening. He convinced himself he was proud that he didn't know about the pairing, because it meant he didn't dabble in low-life gossip, but he felt snubbed by the passage of events all the same, because he had no part in them.

Antony and Cleopatra: during his reading on the train, he hadn't found it in himself to admire the famous lovers in the famous play, and wondered why it and they were praised. Odious he found them both, libertine and untidy in their shapes. Why squander so much energy on passion, even losing fortunes and their ruling dignity? They wasted their greatness. Rather, it was the character of Augustus he admired, the just pauses, the cool head. When Cleopatra, captured after Actium and required to submit her treasury, withheld some private jewels for her own use, Caesar didn't upbraid her but stayed magisterial and remote. He liked that distant power, although the caprice and the charm of the couple might be more eye-catching and dramatic on the stage. Wrong, unjust, that steadiness had no praise. Maybe Augustus was jealous for his father, who was so readily replaced.

Else had taken possession of a house, Morgan a picture. The two facts hadn't been connected until this moment but now they moved in parallel. A job lot I came across in Suffolk. In Adrian's head, inner avenues opened, long lines of logic that connected dissimilar happenings. A house clearance after a death. Wouldn't reveal his sources about the Gainsborough. The miasma of doubt which surrounded a missing clause from Ralph Pennington's last will and testament made a dramatic leap to this particular picture, for no other reason than that man and woman walked down a staircase talking as if they often talked. He would make further enquiries. Just ascription.

The Wylies, who were going on to Greenwich, gave Else and Morgan a lift back to Covent Garden. They dropped them in the Strand with only a couple of hundred yards to go but refused the invitation to come up to Morgan's apartment for a drink. 'We've had enough for one evening,' said Harriet icily, drink and stress. The streets were empty after midnight, when the last train ended the night shift in the city. Two people in evening clothes were conspicuous, and Morgan took Else's arm for closeness as much as warmth across the final stretch of cobbled roadway.

A noise grew under the streetlamps. Tinkling. A pair of youths came down an alleyway kicking a beer can to each other. The sound was louder under the metal edge of hobnail boots. Threat came their way, side to side, bashed against walls. The hand under Else's arm grew tense as Morgan hurried his pace to reach the green door of the gallery before the lads reached them.

'Hold it there, mate.'

One of the men pulled a knife out of his back pocket and flicked it open. The other glanced in both directions. Behind a screen of buildings, out of sight of the main thoroughfare, a man and a woman were an easy target. 'You're gonna be nicked,' laughed the knife carrier. 'Just a little nick.'

Morgan and Else hadn't quite made it to the gallery. His mind was racing about how much money he'd gone on him. Too much, in preparation for the evening. Two hundred pounds, a calf wallet, his cufflinks and a gold watch which was his father's retirement present. Not a bad little haul, quite apart from any jewellery Else might be wearing. Should he make a show of bravado or give in to the knife? They were an unsavoury pair, stank, dirt mixed with beer, and were dressed in leather and studs. You'd cross over if you could.

Under her breath, Else said to him, 'Walk on. Don't stop anywhere near our door.'

Then turning aside, she said to the two louts, 'Over 'ere. I've got something for you.' Her walk changed as Morgan looked back. She slouched her hips, became low. The group separated, with the two muggers following Else to the corner of the precinct. She dropped her own accent and picked up the East End one effortlessly. 'This is my punter, see, and nobody's screwing him for money except me. Piss off out of it.'

'What about our fares home?'

Her voice went shrill. 'Don't you give me none of that sauce. I'm a working girl. I don't steal and nobody's stealing from me. Get out of it or I'll scream fit to burst your eardrums.'

They hesitated, swaggering in doubt. They hadn't been bullied by anybody except their sisters. Sisters fought dirty. Went for your tabs. They turned away.

'See if I don't. There's people all round here.' Her bright hair gleamed in the passageways. She used it tartily, with flicks.

The knife went up and into the pocket. They cantered off, laughing into the dark.

Morgan breathed again but, unlocking the main door, his hand shook. The ruse had worked but wasn't he supposed to be protecting her?

'Aren't you afraid?' he asked, putting the lantern light on gratefully. The woods at Odham were one thing, city roughnecks quite another.

'Why afraid? You only die once.'

'But they had knives.'

'Tell them you've got AIDS. They won't be quite so keen to shed your blood.'

Morgan was shocked again at the callousness in her words, maybe hardy rather than hard. Lift a manhole cover and there was stench, dirt, a real-life rat run under the floorboards of your house. They said the sewer vermin were out of control. He shuddered with apprehension now that the moment of danger had passed, although the knife kept flashing between his ribs.

She sloughed her shoes against the white carpet and took the coffee he was offering.

'How did you know to do that? Have you had to do that before?' Her reflex action reminded him of a simple children's game, where you passed a hand in front of your face, grinning up, gruesome down. It was the instant change of her expression, turning from sophisticate to tramp in the muscle that was impressive. Frightening too, that versatility which they called presence of mind.

'I'd worked it out before. Don't forget I lived in Islington for a year. I had to walk home every evening from University College in those days. I didn't have the fare and I had to look out for myself. You don't forget the gutter. Little tricks. Trousers are a first defence against night prowlers. They're not so easy to get off.'

Men postured with bravery; women had the courage. 'Have you been molested?' The thought of her having to put up with even being pestered in the streets was nauseous. The beautiful head, the composed Nordic features having to dodge brawls. He hadn't thought of himself as especially protected or privileged before. Just being a man exempted him from routine annoyance.

'A few skirmishes. You learn combat techniques. Camouflage is better than karate. I always kept an old knitted hat in my pocket. If you pull it down over your hair, you look sixty and mad. That's pretty rape-proof. Walk fast. Don't look round. Don't look bold. Don't look anybody in the eye. I heard someone say the only way to avoid muggers in New York is to behave like a drug addict, out of your brain.' She spoke normally again, in the well-bred neutral accent which was at odds with the survival wisdom she propounded.

'Didn't you expect me to do something?' She'd put herself at risk to protect him but it might not have worked. They might have slit her throat instead. He grafted Lorraine, or any one of the other women round the table at Max's party that evening, into the situation and it came out differently.

'What? A bit of old-world chivalry? Let's do a deal, chaps?' She mimicked him, fine-vowelled. 'Don't be stupid. Any man's fair game for mugging, especially one who talks like you. Let's face it, Morgan, you're a gentleman and I am not a lady. I like it that way, being anonymous. I always wanted to spit further than the boys at school.'

Wonder woman. She made him wonder while he laughed. Else in gymslip, Else in pigtails that unwound themselves from the restraints. He was eager for the variants he would never know.

Harriet put the lamps on and illuminated nothing. The tension of the evening didn't recede at home. They should have accepted Morgan's invitation after all. Any company was easier than each other's. Nick went to pour himself a drink without offering her one, knowing she'd refuse or say, Must you? so he avoided giving her the chance. No, the room they constructed together didn't soothe her nerves. They'd tried to merge two ready-made house-holds and two styles into one at Greenwich, she classical, he modern. The effect – which others managed to fuse into one eclectic whole, with witticisms where some African tribal masks carved in wood were hung underneath a plaster cast of Apollo – was disastrous in their combination.

She abhorred his paintings, abhorred his choice of paintings, brightly daubed primitives that broke in on her restrained walls. Nick hoarded pictures the way Max hoarded books, not for their content but for their brazen effect, or something sentimental to do with their production and, hung edge to edge, they were so copious you couldn't see them for multiplicity. She felt crowded by the congestion he made. There was no visual peace to be found in the indiscriminate.

'What a tedious evening!' he said at last, sitting far away from her. 'Let's not do that again.'

'I thought you were rather enjoying it. You seemed to be.'

'I can put on a convincing act.'

'I'll say. Else was on good form.'

'Oh, Else's always in good form.'

The shift in preposition wounded her, and he knew it. Following Harriet up the staircase at the Dorchester, he noticed the hang of the moiré skirt about her hips was wide, a wide trapeze, not the tight tube or rectangle he admired. The awkward geometry of her shape irritated him. In the old days, they'd been able to laugh about it ... Oh, the Venus de Milo was quite well endowed, forty-three-inch lustworthy, you metre-lover, you, and then go on to argue about the gradations implied in the different euphemisms, statuesque, Junoesque, Rubenesque. There were no more laughs left. She broadened, he narrowed.

Harriet locked and unlocked her fingers, wondering how to come to the point. Why do you insist on shaming me in public? Why are you late? We never arrive together. It looks bad. But she lacked the courage, or the experience, to manipulate him. With Martin Price, she'd pushed and harangued, and still lost him to the prolific secretary. People made only one mistake in the course of their lives, and that was the recurring one. She saw herself a sedate woman who made a fool of herself over a man, not once but twice, and was mortified by the pity in other men's eyes at having chosen the disreputable from among them. Like wearing a stained dress, everybody could see the fault but her. Clean-minded, crisp, she hated to be so marked.

Nick wouldn't have mentioned Else by choice. He was afraid that if they quarrelled that evening, he and Harriet, it would be because she'd overheard the remark about the painting Else had given him to sell. Had he been underhand about that transfer of dues? Not really, he rationalized. Else owed him a lot of money, dating from before his marriage. The proceeds from the sale were heading towards a separate account he hadn't declared. He had to have a bit of independence, and it stopped Harriet worrying about how much his expenses cost. He didn't want to quarrel with his wife at all, but she made a leaden atmosphere he could break out of only by resorting to abuse, or walking out.

Harriet's eyes strayed over the jangling walls and came to rest in a far corner. Her single contribution to the décor. It was a photograph Nick took of her before they were married. It had made a small scandal when they framed and put it on the wall, because she was taken in the bath, although even her mother, swallowing hard, had said, That is a good picture. She was smiling in it. She smiled at him, the taker, behind his camera with such a trusting and adoring expression that she was tormented now by the sight of her former happiness, when it measured the openness to its abuse. The simple image, starkly black and white, sat oddly among the hectic paraphernalia of their massed belongings, or was their only personal note.

And now, for the first time, it changed before her eyes into a severe and restrained composition, like the almost monochrome history painting of David, as the helpless hand trailed over the edge. Marat murdered in the bath. Not stabbed, but drowning.

Afterwards, Morgan reconsidered.

The vagaries of Else's behaviour had reassured him at the time. She grew strong again. She took her old emotional risks. Coming out was the modish phrase for homosexuals who publicly declared themselves, but it had been in use for débutantes long before that, as well as widows when they shed their weeds. The period of mourning for Ralph, and for the retiring lifestyle she'd been locked into through him, had come to an end. It might be stressful, this coming out, but it was a more realistic and positive stance in the wider world. She emerged from a long trance of hibernation. She socialized. She went public. And she was painting for some part of each day, which was the best proof that her therapy was complete.

On the mend, was she really? The mood swings, the dramatic variants of her personality, unsettled a constant view. Warming to the passionate, Morgan was still wary of the hysterical, or didn't know where he should draw the line. The flirt and the tramp, whose physique she had dropped into that evening without effort, were new Elses to him. For the first time, the name flitted across his mind as more than a stray collocation of sounds. It had a meaning. What else? Who else? Elsewhere. At once he warned himself against that old predilection for making the name fit, but that was the power of an apt metaphor, and a name was a metaphor of sorts; sometimes it did fit all the way and was insightful. Else had a stock of personalities she could rotate, always disguising from herself and others who she was at base. Did this matter if it kept her interested in her own potential? Yes, it alarmed him, like the process of cleaning an oil painting and finding layer upon layer of change under the surface, shadows of interpretation you discovered only by destroying them. Rub too hard and he would rub her out. He didn't want to be that forensic with her, submitting a palimpsest to the scrutiny of X-rays. Psychoanalysis was the least exact science or the least constructive. He suspected both the analyst and his subject, however cooperative, feeling deep down that survival people were self-healers.

Did he even like the peripheral notation of her character? She formed an evening partnership with Nick that made them both disreputable, and brought a frown to older foreheads. The art establishment, if that was what the soirée represented, deserved to be sent up as much as any other entrenched group which made private and unarguable decisions that ensured its own grasp on things but, in doing so, she encouraged antagonism from powerful factions who wouldn't tolerate too much ridicule of their self-esteem.

July

Jane Ramage came back from the sties where she'd been putting out the last feed of the day and locked the door afterwards, for even live piglets were game for the scrubland foxes, whether hungry or simply malicious. She spotted Else coming up over the brow of the hill that hid them from the lower half of the village, walking slowly, with two awkward bundles under her arm, and waited for her to catch up before they went into the kitchen together. Clive was finalizing the family supper, which he looked on as his recreation after a day in the open.

The first parcel Else undid was a dry-cleaner's. She shook out the black dress that had had an outing to the Dorchester a couple of weeks before and put the hanger on a door knob, ready to go back upstairs. 'It was perfect,' she said. 'Did the trick.' She unfastened the cleaner's safety pins, like someone meticulous with her belongings, or trained not to presume on those of others.

'No trouble. I didn't exactly miss it.' Jane noticed that Else never said the bald words 'thank you'. She'd had the good manners to have the thing cleaned, however, while her real effusions were in the second parcel, payment for supper at their table and the gown hire in one go.

It was a box of food she'd bought at the delicatessen in Sudbury, French cheese and coffee, assorted teas in foil-lined packs, blocks of Italian cooking chocolate and Parmesan. Jane's boys fell on it with whoops. And Jane too lifted and smelled the distant aroma of self-indulgence, relishing the thick glossy paper of the packaging and the quality printing, with a surge of long ago. Like the black dress which had graced several mess functions in Frankfurt and Hong Kong, these luxuries were superfluous enough to seem peculiar. Nowadays, their meals consisted of such humble ingredients that they could have broken husks with the swine, although she didn't think there was any real slight in that.

'What goodies. Such extravagance! I'd forgotten all about Earl Grey.'

'I've had a bit of a break,' said Else, who felt she had to apologize for the expense, or prove it was abnormal.

'Did you sell more?'

'No, but I came across the piece of paper I was looking for.'

'The amended will? That's cause for celebration, isn't it? You don't look as if you're thrilled about it.'

'Puzzled, really. I found it in a book on the landing, but I could have sworn I used that book fairly recently. Spenser, *The Shepheardes Calendar*. Maybe not. Half a million volumes, you get confused.'

'You're not quibbling. This is the end of the road, surely.'

Else nodded. Ostensibly so, but it brought decision or action closer, which meant lawyer's meetings, more eye-to-eye disagreement with Adrian, for the paper was unwitnessed, undated, and he would contest it. Inertia was simpler.

The meal with the boys relaxed them all at the end of the day. They cleared their homework from the table and laid it while Jane went to change from her pigswill outfit, as she called it. Bread was set to prove at one side of the stove, adding another layer to the warm smells that blew through the room.

'I weighed the pigs yesterday,' said Clive. 'Fifty per cent increase in body-weight in six weeks. They'll be a good herd.'

'So, what's that in conversion rates?'

'Profit. That's what. It converts to profit.'

The two women laughed, while the boys looked up from the floor, where they pushed motor cars along the cracks of flagstones as simulated roadways. Clive, seeing he'd released a tension in the group, joined in.

They got to the last course, opening up a ripened Brie and a round of Stilton, to which the best accompaniment was a bottle of vintage port. They leaned back in their chairs and let the day unwind.

'How wonderful it would be,' breathed Jane, as the cork came clean, 'to be able to buy all your groceries from Sudbury.'

'Why wonderful?' the other two asked together, and she realized that, overcome with end-of-day fatigue, she'd been tactless enough to imply several things that were offensive: that Else could afford expensive titbits like this on a daily basis, undercutting the kindness of her sharing the windfall from whatever source with them, that she herself resented the financial stringency they lived under on the farm, with every penny counted and ploughed back into future production.

The truth was simpler and could hurt neither of the others. 'I mean, then I wouldn't have to go into the village stores any more.'

'What's wrong with them?' asked Clive, who never set foot inside the grocer's shop. 'They carry all the basics, don't they?'

'Oh, it's silly, really. They do gossip, and I think we're their favourite topic. I went in yesterday and heard the shopkeeper say to the woman in front of me, Do you know what they're thinking of doing next up there? And I knew it was us he meant.'

'No harm in that. A favourite country pursuit. And I don't remember the regimental wives being much different, come to think of it. Camp gossip used to be internecine.'

'I know, but they don't wish us well. Have you noticed, they've stopped calling in now that we look as if we'll make a go of it. They've never reared pigs on this farm before and they don't think we should. I just can't grasp the small-mindedness of it. It's not done! What does that phrase mean, It's not done?'

The boys fell silent, hearing the rising note of their mother's annoyance, wondering if it was directed at them, as they lay and played on the floor again. 'Half-past nine,' said their father. 'That's zero hour. Off you go. And take your stuff with you or we'll be tripping over it in the dark.'

They scampered off, quickly obedient, one fair, one dark. Jane got up to oversee their bedtime, afraid they might play with candles on their own.

While she was out of the room, Else asked, 'Have *you* noticed if they do that? That the people in the village want you to fail?'

'Well, it's true they were very supportive to begin with, lots of visits and advice. Too much, really, dropping in when we were hurrying to get things in hand. They'd lend us machinery to get started and even help us themselves. Some still do. I wouldn't have bought my herd of weaners without the Colonel's advice, or his stockbreeder friend's. But it didn't take me long to realize the locals were only coming round so they could see what we were up to, get a foot inside the door. Not admirable, but human enough. And then I felt they did want the farm to come good, and prove Suffolk was the best land in the whole country, although Odham

157

Farm had been badly managed, but they wanted us to fail while we were about it.'

'But why? That's not logical.'

'Because we're different. We're not tenth-generation farmers. We've no right to learn farming from a book, or just by doing it. That makes it less special, because they want it to be in the blood. That's the way they think. The skill's got to be inherited, an apprenticeship handed down father to son like the land. Buying's not good enough. You've got to pass it on.'

'And will you make it work?'

'Only the natural disasters will stop me.'

Although he sounded confident, Clive did have his misgivings. Mixed arable was the most gruelling form of farming because it involved a non-stop cycle of tasks as well as having several intensive, seasonal highs. There was no slack period in the year, no fallow. Each new day and each month was a treadmill he raced round, turning the wheels faster. But he reconciled himself to the enforced learning, however many mistakes he made, because he was still thrilled with the regimentation of it. Maybe that was the clue. Army men were drawn to farming. They liked the land work and being responsible for their own decisions, while being alone in the fields for long parts of the day didn't make them dismal. Soldiers were often loners, paradoxically, especially the regulars, the peace-time men, used to hardship and danger without cushioning. If he fell, it was a crash from which nobody would save him.

He was beginning to foresee new problem areas. The boys went to the village primary school, barely viable with eighteen children on the register. There was convenience in it, a basic rural charm and intimacy, but no challenge. The only other child with similar potential was the potter's son, another incomer. Next year, his older boy would move on to Sudbury secondary school. Part of the appeal of resigning his commission was having the boys at home for their education, instead of shipping them off to boarding school. But he felt quality control was slipping. The local children, Odham or Sudbury, were keyed in to the practical, good adders and subtracters, as if their birthright preselected what was usable in knowledge. Clive struggled with the notion that he might have to meet fees after all, if his sons were to have a chance of scholarships and university places. The village tittle-tattle and its implied narrowness didn't affect him directly, but became the communal air and was stifling.

Else could still find it in herself to envy him. The work he'd taken on was back-breaking but not heart-breaking. It lacked the cerebral cruelty of art, and was active enough to inspire her with a small sense of fulfilment if she could only weigh six weeks' work as poundage! When Clive got out his entry book after supper, excusing himself that if he didn't do this every Tuesday evening he'd get woefully out of step, she saw there were no intangibles in his headed columns. Capital outlay. Feed stuffs. Petrol. It was reassuring and added up to some conclusion. She knew she idealized it because it wasn't her own fight, because it was leisure to her to come over the hill and help, memory-inducing about an old happiness in her childhood, like the tins and bowl in which Jane made her bread. To her the chips were redolent of an honoured age and use, but to the cook they were annoying splits that gathered dirt and rust, ever to be scoured out.

When she came back downstairs, Jane found the two of them sitting together without a word in the shadowy kitchen, he writing at one end, she sketching him at the other. She didn't experience resentment. In one way or another, Else worked for her keep, and it was good for Clive to have a bit of company, while the pair of them were too alike to strike the physical spark. There was nothing to choose between the lean arms on the table, his or hers, skin brown from outdoors, the work-flexed hands holding the pen or pencil with a concentration so total it was rude. They hardly noticed her as she carried on with kneading the bread, long overproved next to the stove. It would taste of yeast now and be full of air holes.

Else mulled over her dismay that the incomers had found the local people hostile, or even wary. Had she been too self-absorbed to notice such an attitude? No, the villagers were pleasant with her, curious and maybe proud of her in an obtuse way. Her big picture of the pilgrims had assumed the importance of an Odham village passion play, the majority involved, however small a part, and not to be in it was an omission. Her life drawing was pinpoint accurate and they took a primitive delight in seeing their faces first drawn, then coloured, like Third World villagers when shown a photograph who nudged and glowed at their own image. 'Don't I get to be in it?' the butcher's brother had asked plaintively when she ran out of space. The Colonel had no more real notion of her oblique slants but thought, all in all, it was a well-done thing. 'What fun!' he said, but with less conviction than he would greet a new litter of hounds. 'We'll come to Cambridge for that.'

True to Marise's directives, Morgan had started talent-hunting in the major art colleges. He was on the road again, making contacts, and liked it, even if it made him not much better than a high-class rep who was out touting talent instead of bootlaces. For the first time in his life, he went north of the border. He began with Glasgow and discovered he liked it. It had a zing to it, the most American of British cities, with a raw edge that excited, rough and jagged, like living under the flyover. It scratched torment into his eardrums and often into his eyes, as the flight paths of cars and planes intercut each other across an urban freeway, hammering the surface overhead down into the ground. It was the place where, ten yards from the lounge suite of his plush downtown hotel, prostitutes and pushers came up and offered their wares in broad daylight, but they were canny and canty and couthy, not like the two London muggers, suggesting that their own lives were just round the corner too. They didn't actually pester him, or could take no for an answer. This was where his pulse raced with the adrenalin of the heavy, and the running into other shocks unprepared, a dazzling pinnacled church that had been built with sugar baron money, suitably confectioned, some throwaway genius in the wrought ironwork of restful squares, skewed like a doodle in the corner of the city's margin. The grace of trade had been put into the skyrise of its day. This was where the city council had the courage to charge a tax if you didn't clean up the stonework on your Georgian façade. He was impressed by how negligently the city carried its own greatness.

The taxi drivers were as sharp as New Yorkers too, but less rude, having the advantage of polysyllables. Are you a delegate? asked one, knowing there was a dentists' conference being held in town. Naw, he reconsidered, you've no got that drilling look. Are you in films? said another, scanning Morgan carefully in the driver's mirror, while he wondered if he'd begun to emanate some sort of traduceable glamour, or displayed his ostensible difference from anything native. Is that in the imperative? asked a third when his street directions were too brusque. Lord, the man in the street still knew what the imperative mood was up here. In the backstreets, something of the best survived.

Glasgow smiles better, or miles better than solemn Edinburgh across the lowland gap, was the point of the city's advertising slogan. Like one of Shakespeare's endlines, Hark the Trojans' trumpet to announce the stage entry of Cressida, it was all in the elision.

On the first afternoon, Morgan almost had an American encounter. Browsing harmlessly in one of the city's central bookshops for a copy of Burns, he discovered the place was on Dan Fredericks' publicity tour. It was one of those embarrassing occasions when the manager had asked a hundred librarians, the most likely people to order Dan's hefty tome, but alas, there was a Civil Servants' strike and not one of the hundred came. It was reduced to a party of one. Bored, Dan looked up and caught his eye twenty feet away, over the top of racks. The professor came bearing down on him with recognition stamped on his face. Was he going to claim belated friendship? Say, when I met you the other night, you didn't tell me you were the one and only ... or ask him for a reference to some other usable contact. Duck, he thought, as he stood paralysed with indecision about how to escape out of the maze of shelving. Why can't you duck like normal people? Fold up and disappear. Too tall for that.

Mercifully, a woman came up to him and asked for his advice, thinking he had stood still so long he must be a shop assistant and, at the same moment, the PR girl recollared Dan to sign a book, so he was spared.

He spent the next two days doing the round of exhibitions currently on offer in the city, from the art college leavers to the formal municipal shows. He found the fashion for the large had travelled north ahead of him, although width often went with quality in paint, and there was a taking brio in the very young and very unafraid. They were honest, the Glasgow school, depicting what they saw in social change, and didn't give a damn about hangability as yet, or how the clanks of human machinery and the raw style would sit above the sideboards of Kelvinside and Bearsden. The style was too big for him as well. Ten by twelve, as feet not inches. He blasted the pocket-size curbs of Covent Garden and the portable, but wrote down names and took addresses into the larger future.

Magda Sweetland

He came across a few idiocies. A child's all-metal tricycle, bought at a junk shop before being painted in primary colours, one wheel red, another blue. Then a collection of yellow plastic from the kitchen sink, up-marketed from a tenement habitat. He sat down on a bench, to try and assimilate it and the rationale which held non-biodegradable flotsam in such high esteem. He pushed at that idea, trying to accept it, then threw it out. Piffle logic. Make something silly to prove the silliness of things. He was starting to suffer from pictorial indigestion. Meanwhile, a sharp object poked into his back, the corner of another exhibit. It was a 1930s radiator, brought here from a hospital, to judge by its bulk, a fat hobby-horse of a radiator, painted lovingly evenly brown like a moulded chocolate bar. So. It made a statement, or a surreal link, waiting for a Dali meltdown. And then he noticed another one at the opposite end of the gallery – ah, a pair of statements. And then a third. They were just the old-fashioned central heating system of the gallery, painted out to minimize.

He took a break from this and did the same again, going out to the landscaped park around the Burrell and was lucky in hitting on a quiet, off-peak day. There was much to admire. That one man from his private income could find the wealth and the taste and the time to put together a collection of the best. That was always impressive and Morgan enjoyed walking round, making acquaintance with another man's mind in such intimate detail. He liked the tapestries, warm and honest, the work of women, woven backwards in mirrors at the Gobelin factory or Mortlake or Bruges. The expression stitched on the face of a camel made him laugh out loud, full of its own surprise, until other people looked round at his irreverent praise.

But deep down, he wasn't at all sure about the purpose of the gallery. It did have something Americanized and theme-parked about it, like the Cloisters in New York, where a haul of Benedictine stones were transposed to the top of a Manhattan hill from Nîmes, with the missing gaps made by time, wear and tear, desuetude, made good. A sort of perfected Disney version of the past. He thought Binham Priory should stay exactly where it was built, architecture and history locked into the place where it had happened. He suspected the urge to museumize every stick and stone of antiquity. Strange, that old was a commendation for everything except people.

* * *

Meanwhile, Marise took the opportunity to go through the sales book at Covent Garden, looking for something invisible.

She didn't find it because she hadn't precisely defined for herself what an irregularity might be. A slip of entry, an overvaluation, something to hang something on. She wanted only barter power over Morgan when it came to signing their next agreement.

'Tell me,' she asked, turning to John Camperdown, who stood carefully in attendance to the right of the windows, so as not to block her light, 'what have you learned while you've been here?'

'Oh,' said the new deputy, 'how to manage people better.'

She turned her head quickly to see if he was mocking her, and he added, with a pause so brief it was merely periodic, 'Better than I used to.'

Marise closed the books with a persuasive smile. 'Now why is that?'

'New Bond Street is for the old masters. Covent Garden's for the new, and they're dreadfully temperamental.'

She laughed in spite of herself. 'And *how* have you learned it?'

'Well, Morgan's brilliantly patient with them. They come here themselves looking for him.'

'With paintings for sale?'

'Not always. Photographs or sketches. He's quite exact about what we can take here, but he's good at putting no tactfully.'

'Ah, now how does he manage that?'

'I've heard him look at a piece of work and say, This has got something, but I don't know what it is. Can you go on from here? Take it a stage further. Then I'll look at it again.'

'You mean he can make no sound like yes?'

'I never thought of it like that.'

'And do you get several of these casual callers?'

'Oh, every day. A lot of the time they're our good sellers, coming in to see how things are going, because it's a good drop-in place, but we get new arrivals too. Word of mouth. Word has got around that he's good. That's why we do well.'

Marise noticed the lack of envy in this disciple. 'Do you think he should have stayed a teacher? Or been an agent?'

'No. He hasn't got such a classifiable talent. His is vision.'

So Morgan was running a club at Covent Garden, with the

163

membership registered in his name, not in hers. Marise ransacked her memory to see if some clause in their contract had allowed for the free disbursement of advice. He should be operating a business, not a salon. What kind of people called in? Would she want to know them? Famous or only famous in the making? But her main reaction was that the greater reputation he cultivated was his own, and that he was starting to overshadow her. He resisted her advice. She hadn't overlooked the fact that he hadn't installed a phone in his car, or developed her suggestion of selling prints of book jackets. His innovations were his own. That the mainspring of his personal power was as nebulous as vision was troubling. She could outbid him or outbuy him, but not outshine. The notion of her employee as a guru, an actual taste-maker, was repellent because she couldn't trace the origin of those terms. She knew what it was her New Bond Street customers wanted to own, and could influence their choice even by her presence and example, because her looks embodied what they aspired to, measurable success, tailored, trim, impeccable, lacking the dangerous or intrusive edge, but she couldn't influence anyone's creativity. She had no yardstick for genius and knew only the known.

She looked round the apartment she had lent him. The restrained classicism, executed in white and black, she chose deliberately as anonymous, because that would suit anyone she might engage. But something had happened to the walls. They were no longer neutral. They were studded with Morgan's private collection of pictures, one great golden tree looming out at her, lit against logic by its inner source, and some strange images of slanting people she couldn't drag her eyes away from, entranced in horror. In twenty years would he be proved right? Was this the best, tomorrow's leaders? She wasn't sure. Modernity was written in a language she hadn't had time to learn. Oh, to know what had survival in its genes! But she noticed, whatever his own personal paintings were worth, that he had taken advantage of the in-built security alarms to safeguard them, and insurance on property and contents, but quelled a pointless sense of being used.

'And tell me, what would *you* do differently here?'

'In this actual location? I never thought about it.' John faltered under the negative drift of her question. It implied something in Morgan's arrangements could be bettered, and that he thought so too. He was frigid with the idea that he'd been disloyal to one or other of his masters, to him or to her, because their aims were disparate. Flustered, he tried to remember what it was he'd said. Surely he'd spoken only the truth. When could the truth sound like disloyalty, he asked himself. When it was wilfully misinterpreted.

'Well,' she said smoothly, 'give it some consideration. I would like to be privy to your thoughts. You are on the ground, and I may be a little out of touch. We'll talk again like this, when you are free. Perhaps at lunch one day.'

After she had closed the shop for the lunch-hour, the door bell jangled and Lorraine hurriedly put down her cup and went to meet it, slightly annoyed. It was a wicked day, with slashing rain, not at all like the July they should be having, and the bell was likely to announce nothing more than a browser coming in out of the wet to shelter. Umbrellas, damp feet, but someone who traversed the possibilities of being a shoplifter or a serious buyer. And she would have to stand and wait for twenty minutes before she found out which.

It was neither. It was EP, the young woman with the Gainsborough head. She came at these erratic intervals.

'What have you come to sell?' The question wasn't inviting.

Else put a package down on the table. She felt self-conscious in her dripping mac that shed puddles. Both women watched them soak into the carpet.

'Shall we hang that up?' Lorraine whisked away the folded umbrella and dropped it in the stand.

Else was tense. In years gone by, she'd met Sheila Pennington just once, she a girl in her early twenties facing up to a woman over fifty. Hope and disillusion side by side. It was hard to think they had a man in common. What they resented wasn't each other but that the man encompassed their differences. It made them limited, or singular, where he was plural. They didn't row or become abusive. The accidental meeting had passed off politely but the endurance of the older woman haunted her. She'd no doubt Ralph had made his wife very unhappy – what was the difference between a passionate, important affair and philandering except a point of view – giving his love, his house, his son to other women. His wife could have cast him off ten times over but clung on and found death was the most satisfactory form of divorce. It called for no public explanations.

'I'm not sure that you will want this,' Else said defensively about her picture.

'Neither am I. People won't pay a few hundred pounds for anything nowadays. They'll pay ten thousand at Christie's or a fiver at a jumble sale. But there's no middle market any more. The people who used to collect in a small way are the new poor. Or they've gone over to CD players and refitting their kitchen with hand-painted units. Poor fools. They have fallen for the transient.'

Well, thought Else smiling, if I were to be immured in this shop for forty nights and forty days until the rain let up, there are worse inmates than you. She sifted the attitudes for hints of her husband. What rubbed off on whom after a quarter of a century? Morgan was softer in all senses, kinder, more impressionable, less sharp. Sweet-sour, they maybe had complemented each other.

She undid a small landscape in a gilt frame, both the worse for wear.

'It's rather insignificant,' complained Lorraine.

But delicate. Foliage like feathers, like lace. A Suffolk snatch by Constable.

'Why don't you try sending it to auction?' said Lorraine slyly.

'Do you think it's worth it?' Else was as quick.

'I don't know. If it really is a Constable, it's out of my league. I can give you the name of a London dealer who specializes in English landscape.' The wife paused. 'Or maybe you know one already?'

Derek Hisslop came into view, Adrian Crane, the common pool of their acquaintance. The husband might say nothing to the wife, but others could. Else had avoided admitting the connections to herself when she set out for Bury in the rain. She realized that everything was known, that she was bare of deceit. She pulled her coat close, a Burberry so old it was porous.

'I don't choose to broadcast my source.'

'Why's that? You didn't steal them, did you? Or are they not quite yours to sell? Or too much yours?'

The rain drummed on the window, falling in sheets not drops. Midsummer gone and many wasted days.

Lorraine folded her arms around her body, hands in pockets. EP. An artist Morgan handled. Unfortunate phrase really. Derek Hisslop was so smitten by the reappearance, he couldn't help passing the facts on to her and she was thankful for the revelation.

She wasn't going to sell her house to line their love nest down in Odham.

'Elsie Paterson. That's not quite so glamorous, is it? Somebody very uninspired must have christened you with that, but we can't help what others call us. You have come a long way in your time, I can tell. The Garbo turn of phrase suits you better. You are very impressive. I can see – that Morgan would be impressed.'

Else waited for a deliberate cut. Wives could turn shrill. You're not his usual type. Is he off with the old love already? Maybe he's overlapping. It's his age, an attempt at the last flower of manhood. Make the most of it. It could be short-lived. He will fall down, you know, he will fall down.

But the nastiness didn't come.

'I'm having some lunch. Have you eaten yet?'

'No, I don't usually eat at midday.'

'You should. You are too thin. And you look very tired.'

Else passed a hand over her forehead, finding her hair quite wet. 'I was in Sudbury all this morning.' Two hours with her solicitor, two at the hospice. A draining day.

'Ah, were you? And you have come straight on.' Without fuss, the older woman took her coat and led her unresisting down a long corridor to a simple kitchen where blue china hung on a dresser. It had a fuggy, unstirred atmosphere made by closed windows and the unadventurous mind. Deftly, she set another place.

Else was overcome by lethargy. She was very tired and very wet and suddenly ravenous. This woman was the remedy, noiselessly bustling over a sandwich and hot tea. Morgan's home, not the showrooms where she had come more than once with pictures to sell, but the behind. It was endearingly cluttered, not like his sparse apartment now, as if he had rejected ownership entirely after the communal days. This was the wife's place in marriage, not his. Else re-evaluated Morgan, not as dispossessed but as a transitory man weighted with nothing more ponderous than the knowledge in his head.

'Morgan never lived here as such,' his wife confirmed. 'Just kept his things. I didn't realize how little he belonged until he came to move out. I thought he'd take trunks of stuff away with him, and I wouldn't have resisted it at that point. I was more hurt than if he'd fought over his rights, his chattels. He really didn't care.'

'Wasn't it a more generous impulse, to leave the house intact? And memories.'

'Ah,' said Lorraine, 'you think like him.'

As she ate, Else had time to draw another conclusion than Morgan wanting to start his new life unencumbered: the old one was inviolate, and waited for him to return. Fail-safe. Nothing had happened between these people that would make resumption impossible. This grey, cardigan-clad woman was insidious, imbued with the self-control to give her husband a long and unconstricting line, but she could gently, gently reel him in with a memorial service and a Sunday lunch. For the first time in her life, Else wanted passionately not to lose this man, or sensed she might. Her eyes widened to take in his wife. The woman had more wisdom than Sheila Pennington or Harriet, tearful and abject at marital neglect. Lorraine would carry on, whatever happened. The kitchen mantelpiece housed a run of invitations, followed by thank-you cards for the hospitality she had extended in return. They bespoke a methodical lifestyle. She would run a full diary, never be without a companion for an event at short notice. Her easy sociability was the inverse of Else's own life, walled up at Odham, and the integrated pattern of its give-and-take wholeness demoralized her because it wasn't, at root, incompatible with her own private and exclusive modes. Worse than losing Morgan, she fell prey to the fear of sharing him.

'When did Michael die?'

The question arrested. Lorraine took stock of its ignorance. If Else knew the name, why did she not know the date? 'Last March. A year past. The spring term of his second year at Clare. In a car crash as a friend was driving him home for the weekend. I think it was very quick.'

'Thank you.'

Lorraine was braced to tell the outline. So strong. She had the personal resources for quiet coping that Else was the first to acknowledge and admire. The pulse rate dropped in some people, a form of paralysis or numbness which was the body's own anaesthesia. There would have been no collapse here into prostration, no sedatives or hysteria, but a steady on-going competence, the door kept open for business, the files kept up to date in sequence day after day. Else didn't think this was the sign of a cold person but a deep one.

'I have never been able to talk to him about this.' They both thought it.

'You should, you know. However difficult. It's so important, the talking out.'

Two o'clock came but no customers. She'd stretch the rest-hour. 'What else have you not told him?'

'Nothing that he would want to know.'

Lorraine considered. She was under no obligation to make the course of their events less painful but, taking no material advantage, Morgan still might benefit from the empirical of her advice. 'Let me warn you about him. He is a know-all. He must know everything. He is ruthless with facts, and uses them to supplant feelings. It's wearing to live under close scrutiny, to have nothing taken for granted or to be quizzed about where you are in relation to an idea. You may already have discovered for yourself how he makes people fit theories.' She thought back to stories of the old man down the mines; what Morgan was proudest of was that his grandfather had come by a used copy of the *Encyclopaedia Britannica* and read it every day, until it turned into the Bible substitute of the agnostic. An old man sitting in a room full of disarray, if not actual squalor, turning the tissue pages with reverence. The miner had educated himself from its archives and had a prodigious recall of stray facts he came across. The only time Lorraine had met him, he lectured her on the height of the Aswan Dam and its engineering problems. Maybe it did have a glint of a connection with deep-shaft mining, but he was a lamp man anyway. He and his schoolmistress daughter had passed on an avenging regard for learning, the weapon of the minority, underprivileged nations, through which they prospered over their neighbours. 'Of course, for all I know, you may have that in common too. People who came from nowhere.'

The phrase went home. They circled each other warily. Else felt the power of the other's personality bearing down on her, willing her to expand on her natal name, on her relation to this minority status or which specific nowhere she had come from, and thought, If she pushes me hard, I must give way. There's no resisting her because she's infallibly right.

At the last minute, Lorraine deflected. 'This picture then, your Constable look-alike. Is it also on offer under an assumed name, or is it genuine?'

'It is not a Constable.'

'Then it would be as well to obtain a correct evaluation. I am not an expert. I take in what I like, on a restricted scale. Bury–' she smiled – 'has few knowledgeable collectors.'

It was the most plausible put-off Else could imagine.

They straggled back down the passageway. The coat, thoughtfully placed beside a heater, had dried out and the umbrella was crisp as Else rolled it up.

'What does intrigue me is, did you bring those pictures to me deliberately, knowing that Morgan would be here? Forgive my asking. Did you hope to run into him in the shop instead of me?'

Else turned on the level of the entry steps. 'Were there so many visitors with crushes on him?'

'Dozens. Very tiresome how a television programme can make a star of quite a modest man.' Lorraine relented, feeling the phrase was too dismissive. She came forward, grasped Else's hands among the umbrella and the package with the painting, and kissed her on the cheek with warmth. 'Treat him kindly.'

The Aviary
Rainy days

Dear Boris

Thank you for your latest cheque. I wonder what you do with these letters that I write you, and what I would do with yours – if I were lucky enough to get one. That's not to be judged as a reproof, but your silence makes me think you may want me to be silent in return and not crowd you with my thanks. They may even be an embarrassment, something we should let slip. Dear me, that you and I should have to sit side by side at a dinner table, without acknowledging each other. My oldest friend, my patron, my first and best supporter, how really can I thank you for the patient ear, the open purse. If I bow to public constraints, be assured it isn't from ingratitude.

I made an unscheduled visit yesterday afternoon, to see Morgan's wife. I've no idea why I did it, when I half knew that she would half know me. It endorsed my view that there are only two kinds of women, married and other, wedding rings apart. I am the other woman. I don't seem to want to move into the middle ground of a relationship, or bear its full weight, but am mentally conditioned to being a supplement.

170

This is akin to a certain painterly shyness. I could go out and grab a quick style, centre-stage, but I keep holding back from the exposure of publicity, success, the full declaration. Even with this exhibition in Cambridge, I go on and then off the idea alarmingly, until Nick and Morgan are quite weary with me. Now, how is a man or a promoter to deal with someone who blows hot and cold as variously as I do?

It may be the combination that's static: woman painter, like two horses that won't yoke. Add subtract, and end up getting nowhere. I want you to name me three women artists, any century. Very good, you got to two, and you are in the business. But tell me this, is Angelica Kauffmann fetching the same prices as Tiepolo or Turner in the auction rooms? Why is this? Is it because men are predominantly the buyers and buy men's pictures? That's one of the reasons I won't be photographed beside my work. You may well say this implies that I'm disowning them. But it's my face, over which I have no power of command, that I disown. The face and the sex of it should be irrelevant, but it isn't in short-term marketing. Else Petersen, the blonde-haired painter. It would make you scream. Music's the same. There are thousands of proficient female instrumentalists boosting professional standards in the world's orchestras, but no composers of international repute.

An amateur lady watercolourist seeks agreeable, non-demanding companion to share expenses on trip to Lake District.

Post this for me, will you?

We women just don't rise above the level of the doodler. It's easy for feminists to say it's lack of training opportunity, or that a lot of established artists have made a practice of using their female relations as hacks and background fillers, so underpaid they were the next best thing to slaves. That implies there's some great and glorious future in the next millennium. Doubt it. They've had women at the Slade since – well, let's say for the best part of a hundred years, when here is Dora Carrington sitting along the row from Stanley Spencer in 1912. Yes, Dora Who, remembered because she was a famous man's three-way lover, when he wasn't into men. Where's the yield from that invested training? We women have the mind that fails at chess, that builds hospitals instead of churches, worthily competent and practical but uninspired. I am disillusioned by my own sex's lack of stamina, vision, balls or whatever it is that's missing. Not having it makes us unhappy, like the great personal accord we call love and will not find. It is men who love greatly and do greatly: women are too circumspect for either leap into the unknown.

Or maybe it's something altogether different, that my lifetime lover is this bastard art and I only have a little spare for men who must necessarily be spoken for themselves to be content with the halves I'm offering them. I don't want to be this person I was born, and have no means of changing it except to pretend that I am otherwise. Maybe this is my entire character, the flaw, that I believe I may be a better painter by pulling over myself a shroud of anonymity, may become trousered, cold or enigmatic, man.

She sussed me anyway, did Mrs Morgan, name and number. Known from afar. Mercilessly exact and fair. I liked her a great deal, those greys you do not weary of but can build up, shade on shade.

Afterwards, I went next door into the Museum of Horology to calm down. They keep all the clocks on display fully wound, so the striking hour is a cacophony, where you have to strain to separate the mechanical from the musical. Several little objects I lusted after, ivory sundials that can be folded into your pocket and are calibrated for different latitudes, as neatly done as scrimshaw work by sailors. Men can be so dainty! And a silver casement called 'Almanach Universel et Perpétuel'. I'm not smitten by workmanship that's there just for decoration or utility, table chair stuff, but *intelligent* craft is so very exciting. Mechanism is the thing. Is this the nub of a painting? Chronometry by hourglass, candle, moon face painted in a sky. Time could be my motif, you know, like sad cypresses.

I came back to Odham at the end of a troubled day to find the sun had been shining for hours – or as long as it takes to evaporate the rain. This is the real place for me, my Cookham out of Jerusalem, the village where things are mystical by association, by continuous habitation from the Saxons, the

Romans and the back of that. The pottery, the forge, the farm, it's that folded sundial, everything in pocket-size. Apply its calibrations and you have the world.

This simile is just: I am the dial's gnomon, casting shadows long or short according to an outward power. It can be sun-power, work-power, but just as often man-power. When the power is at its height, or when I am most under the influence of that sphere, my own magnitude is least. I disappear. That is the state of passion, to be nul. Heat. Burn out. All imply the same melting point. I am slowly working myself towards this terrifying position of annihilation as the planets in me collide. What I must do and what I must be are incompatible. Cross-starred, who would be that?

I walked down the garden, spirited. The stream was running fast and fields behind were hazed with a high summer sun. So difficult to catch that feeling of looking into the centre, bluish bright. Some trees on the boundary were fully massed, the flowering chestnut perpendicular, the oak broad-lying, a spinney of mixed plane and elm as a bridge between the clumps. Take from life. It is the only way. If I lose this place then I am done for. I am hurrying to catch the light.

Goodbye for now. I feel a note of change in our dealings, as if seeing you a few weeks back made you remote, or defined how the turnings of time distance. But I am – always – your,

Else

A man of moderate years saw Morgan checking in at Glasgow airport, and was dismayed at the second's inhibition about going up and speaking to him. He shouldn't have had misgivings. When he approached, Morgan shook his hand warmly. Tall, mid-thirties, red-headed with the shock of Celtic hair, this man would have been distinctive on the rugby terraces.

'MacPherson. Good heavens. Are you booked on this flight?'

'The midday to Heathrow, yes. Have you got your seat number? I'll try to get the one next to you.' The airport was crowded. The Glasgow trades fortnight started with a mass exodus and the two men had no quiet time until they were boarded. 'Have you been up long?'

'Three days non-stop.'

'I wish I'd known. I'd have shown you round. Though I've been buried in scripts.'

'You did take that lectureship then?'

'Glad to get it, even a two-year contract. I was confident the Senate would adhere to their terms honestly.'

A silence fell round the putative dishonesty of other signers. At length, Morgan broke the vacuum. 'Didn't Marise?'

'She paid me as stipulated, but she made sure I was unemployable in London.'

'You can't be sure of that.'

'Nobody will tell you that she's passed the poison reference, no. But I put in for half a dozen jobs last September when it was clear she was going to give me the push. I could have done them with my eyes shut, and I didn't get a single interview. Quick phone call. That's all it takes to keep somebody out.'

'Did you tackle her?'

'What's the point? The next call's more vitriolic. Systems of confidentiality are the most open to abuse.'

Morgan wavered. How likely was this to be true? Disappointment resolved itself in spite, or other self-excusing. But he'd worked with MacPherson on an early television programme, about the Scottish Impressionists, Charles Rennie Mackintosh and the Glasgow School, and found him not just academically sound but opinion-solid too. Marise's version of exclusivity rested on cutting people out, but he hadn't thought she'd stoop to wilfully blighting a man's career. He doubted anyway if one person's word could be that influential, although he recalled he hadn't contradicted her when she said MacPherson hadn't got London right and felt a pang of conscience.

'But I hear that you're the miracle worker,' said the younger man more generously. 'That the water's turned to wine.'

'A different vintage. I've been lucky. No wands. Tell me, are you enjoying the lecturing?'

'What's familiar is gratifying. But having made the move, I'd have liked to stay south. I seem to spend a disproportionate amount of time zooming up and down on this plane.'

Morgan noticed that he paused in extending a similar invitation to his junior, of hospitality, of company. But then, MacPherson had known where to find him in London if he'd really wanted to. During this pause, Morgan arranged the reading material which turned out to be superfluous on the sixty-minute flight. Two newspapers and two small books, one of which the other spotted.

'John Clare? He's come a long way from Northamptonshire, surely.'

'He's still my local version of Robbie Burns. I've been catching up on them together.'

'Oh, that's stretching it. If I remember rightly, Clare's on the lugubrious side. Burns knew how to sing a song.'

'But the cheerless can be quite tuneful too.'

MacPherson picked the book up, turning its pages thoughtfully, back to front. There were similarities, he conceded. Poems short enough to be called lyrics, another Mary invoked, dates that overlapped – what did thirty years matter in the country – the life parallel too, the ploughboy who struck a measure of success in the capital, be that London or Edinburgh, and then fell into a larger, disappointing lapse. Insanity followed in one case, alcoholism in the other, with both poets having to rely on their old friends and benefactors. He came at last to the fly leaf, where Else had inscribed her name in her own copy, as she always did in pale, erasable pencil.

'So you brought our Else on this trip with you after all?'

Morgan looked up at familiar knowledge. That intrusive our, why our?

'She doesn't often come back in person now.'

'Back? To Glasgow?'

'Didn't you know she was from Glasgow?'

Morgan was winded as if he'd been struck, for yes, he did bring Else with him everywhere, past or present, and he'd been thinking about her rather misplaced enthusiasm for this minor poet, apart from one memorable sonnet. I am – yet what I am none cares or knows. That stood as everyman's elegy. Perhaps the life was greater than the work. He had to control himself from asking more, but was still dying to know. What happened to the Swedish extraction? Her nationality was like her ownership of The Aviary, a condition he accepted on hearsay without too much probing. Why didn't she come north in person? Why was north never mentioned? But he only nodded slowly as if he were conversant with the facts.

'Yes. Was it in Glasgow that you met her?'

'Indeed. The local school. Not the fee-paying, public school, you

175

understand. A bit lowlier than that. Corporation school in the scheme.'

The words weren't Morgan's dialect but struck a chord, in the epicentre of the truth. Spoiled rich kid? He readjusted. Got it wrong again. She was that rare creature, the self-made woman.

Before his next visit to Odham, Morgan had time to place the episode. He admitted he was in the grip of the obsessional and didn't like it. It was his mid-life crisis, or the last life one. He was convinced that MacPherson was the man Else took up with after their own chance meeting at the Slade, the man she called her second best, because Morgan knew the young man well enough to know he'd been a contemporary student. The two talents must have drifted south together. There had been something awkward and regretful in the other's stance when he said she never came north in person. Our Else, indeed.

Morgan resented the emotional intrusion. On one side, he rebuilt his professional strength, but the weakness of the other, feeling side undermined any achieved sense of well-being. He was lopsided or holed. The problem was, Else had become central. Every renewed work contact in the last six months had thrown some sidelight on to her, until he was becoming paranoic with a possessiveness, a total knowing of her, that wasn't possible because it was retrospective. The meeting in December was as disruptive in the current of his feelings as the Slade meeting fifteen years ago must have been in hers. The irony wasn't simply that the same two people ran into each other again, but that circumstances encouraged a rapport which common sense ought to have discounted.

He was disappointed that she'd not come clean with him in the first place, or chose to lay a minefield with her secrecy. He was afraid of his mental outbursts against her, lapses into irrational dismay where he berated her, because of her stubborn refusal to be ample and explain herself. But why should she? And what right had he to expect it? When had he been so forthcoming with Lorraine? Cause and effect. He would despise other men for being this vulnerable, and thought that was the real meaning behind the change of life: to need more than he was needed.

As calm sanity prevailed again, he saw the weakness of the connection was its strength. He'd made the same mistake again and worked alongside the woman he was involved with. He'd never stop living above the shop. It must be in his nature to mix work and home and, of the two, work was the more important issue, not just his. Else's was the larger capacity and on that he wouldn't flinch. Throughout all this personal turmoil, he owed it to her to absorb the self-inflicted stress. Arguably, that was how she'd coped with her own upheavals, in silence, a kind of swallowing. If he provoked her, she could throw those plate-throwing tantrums that were destructive to their joint peace of mind. He must say nothing.

August

A well-made catalogue was more than a functional map to the layout of one particular exhibition. It was a concordance of the artist's entire output. It listed in chronological order where the paintings had appeared on exhibition, illustrated the more important ones, and gave some insight into the training or the theory behind the work, all of which made it more than a passing introduction. It could be a complete text. A book and not a guide. Max flicked back through several of the compendia he'd printed for the Tate and the Royal Academy, massive tomes buried under footnotes and cross-references. Such comprehensive treatment was beyond the means of most living artists but, observing a strict regard for quality, Max decided he would do Else's Cambridge catalogue in style. Morgan's scholarship he would combine with Marise's perfectionism over printing styles and layout.

'I don't want to make a profit from it. What's profit? You lose it in next month's inflation figures. But don't say a word to Else. She would go into contortions. All that scruple. I'm too old for scruple. I hate to be thanked. Tell her Nick's paying me top book.' Max laughed a little grimly. The reference grounded him. 'Nick should have all the information we need on his files. But make sure, will you, that I don't have to speak to him in person about it. Can you deal with the Nick end of the thing?'

Morgan wondered why, as he parcelled up the details Else had to hand at Odham and sent them on to the Wylies' office premises in Bolton Street, with a covering note about the need for urgency. And waited.

Julius and Augustus, the Roman months were meant for basking in. Fixated by the character of Augustus Caesar, Adrian had abandoned his prescribed reading list in favour of Suetonius, *The*

179

Twelve Caesars, and then went on to read Tacitus, *The Annals of Imperial Rome.*

He admired the stately measure of the sentences, even in translation, and regretted Eton hadn't given him quite enough Latin to take the originals on board. Of the twelve emperors, Adrian thought Augustus the greatest, perhaps because he was the least debauched. Patron of the arts, general, enlightened ruler, justicer, he lacked only the prose record of his deeds for posterity, although it was admirable in its way, that failure to self-proclaim. Adrian was proud to celebrate his birthday in this month and, being Leo by a day, to be coupled with the other great Caesar in July.

He considered it remarkable that the phrase 'august personage' had been handed down as a commendation after nearly two thousand years and sometimes he would examine himself in the mirrors of the word – until his wife told him that it was also a French word for clown.

'Have you found those references yet, Nick?'

'Haven't had a minute. I'm getting Lindsay on to it.'

'Who's Lindsay? Your research assistant?'

'Something like that.'

'I'd rather you checked them in person.'

'No sweat. I'll tick that off this afternoon. I've got a function at seven, so I'll be in the office till then. I'll ring you beforehand.'

'I thought I saw you leaving half an hour ago,' Harriet said when she walked in on Lindsay in the cloakroom at the end of the day.

'Taking time to get myself together,' said the girl, flustered over her comb.

Harriet observed the more elegant hairstyle and the freshly ironed blouse hanging in a carrier. 'Are you going out this evening?'

'Yes.' Lindsay beamed at the ease of it.

'Anything interesting?'

'Some friends got tickets for the theatre.' But the moment she said it, Lindsay realized she'd launched herself on the irredeemable lie.

'Which play?'

'Oh – Shakespeare.'

'It must be the Roman plays. They're doing a new version at the National. It's the only Shakespeare on in London this season. Very strange, usually several productions at once. Nick and I saw *Julius Caesar* a fortnight ago. I'd love to hear what you think about it.'

Oh, damn, thought Lindsay. Shakespeare was just the first name that came to mind. Now she'd have to ask Nick what to say about it, and he'd be cross that she was getting clumsy about making their exits. Maybe at the end of the evening she'd ask him, maybe afterwards.

A minor painter had won a minor prize and, to underscore its insignificance, the committee were awarding it in August, when most people were on holiday. Harriet had her own reception lined up, a Royal Command evening at the Academy, which freed Nick to ask his standby guest. 'I'm bringing one of our trainees,' he'd said to the secretary at the Arts Club. 'It does them good at the outset to see how things are done properly. I'm looking forward to it. It'll be wonderful.' All the same, he knew it was risky taking Lindsay, too close to home. The Club was five minutes' walk from the Royal Academy, and five minutes from the office, shaving it fine.

It turned out to be the usual do, seen through columns. Black tie, dinner, speeches. His winning client gave a heavy, self-important speech which lay on the humid August air like a layer of fog. Nick sat at the outer end of the head table, away from the line of notice until he was called on to make a few final and rather well-chosen remarks, he thought, about how important the Club's support was for young artists in the face of hostile economics and hostile reviews. The audience lapped that up. Clapped like fury. They always enjoyed hearing how beastly it was being a freelance, free-choice, creative individual. But there wasn't a pretty woman in the place to break the boredom.

So he entertained himself as best he could, with a view of Lindsay at one of the lower tables. She conversed with her fellow guests, was really a good girl, behaving perfectly on her first big night out. Smiling to this side, chatting to that. She wore a blouse he was particularly fond of, plain white linen with a square neck which was charmingly girlish, like the thing they wore under gymslips or on the hockey pitch. Quite a thought.

He'd banked on it being over quickly and at nine thirty Lindsay said to the briefly noticed painter, 'I'm so sorry, I must rush.'

'Yes, I must rush too,' Nick added and they proceeded to rush off together. Last seen walking hand in hand down Piccadilly.

By mischance, Harriet's reception finished at the same time. Her taxi was pulling out of the inner courtyard at the Royal Academy when a couple crossed the street in front of her. She saw them clearly, with a seizure that was more instinct than optical recognition. Just the shape of duplicity, something wrapped up between angles of the two of them, sloped in, something exclusive.

Anxious as she was, Harriet hadn't doubted Lindsay's story for a second, any more than she'd finalized the thought of Nick as being unfaithful, or this insultingly undemanding in his choice. The girl, well, she was an absurd companion for him. She dripped lower every day, until she positively slunk about the office. She couldn't even spell. Dinning room in her last letter, like instead of as, didn't know collective nouns took the singular form of the verb. And this hash of English went out in their advertising material, Nick too lazy to proofread it beforehand, sending off letters unsigned. But Harriet noticed that she was moving into the zone of outrage rather than hurt, shifting her focus from the axis of marriage, back to the centre of herself. Passing the lighted globes of Covent Garden, she thought she would call in on Morgan. He'd been a solid ally over Martin Price, reassuring her the man always was a scoundrel and she was well shot of him, but she'd not helped him much through his own troubles. Was he in London, or in the country? Later on she'd call.

What do I do to stop this? she asked herself all the way through the dreary streets round the Elephant and Castle and on to Lewisham, mean all the way until they sped into the open areas of Blackheath, without an answer surfacing. An eminent libel lawyer had talked to her once about what constituted defamation, or stopped short at the point at which most people confused it, identification or invasion of privacy. How do you defend yourself from slander? she asked. You can't, he replied. There's no invasion of privacy bill, as yet, and whatever action you take as the complainant must ensure that the irritating behaviour stops. Otherwise you risk exacerbating it. Half-measures are worse than none. By that token, his philanders might be endless.

When Nick did come in after midnight, she asked from her cream-upholstered chair, 'Did it go on a bit, this evening?'

'Oh, it dragged. The main thing was over by nine thirty but then it was shop talk at the bar. Some of them are quite useful old codgers, it does to be seen, but lots of bores.'

And to Lindsay in the morning, 'Did you enjoy the play?'

'I loved it. I thought it was a brilliant idea, doing it in modern dress. Stabbing in pinstripe suits seemed more wicked, somehow, so the senators looked like members of the Mafia.'

Harriet nodded. She and Nick had thought so too. The phrase was her own originally. Stupid that Nick couldn't even recall who had said what. But yesterday evening, the National had shown *Antony and Cleopatra*, not the earlier play. Careless that slip, like uncorrected grammar when it was so easy to check your references. Harriet wasn't sure if it was good manners that restrained her from pointing it out or the impulse to work a more subtle revenge on them.

Although Nick, flitting tra-la about the office, hadn't made any approach last night, he would, soon. How would she respond then? Would she take him back into her arms, uncomplaining? There were some awful sexual truths still to discover, because she wasn't sure she could repel his advances even if they were merely dutiful, and shuddered at how she was drawn inside their complicity to be three a-bed.

'What happened to that phone call, Nick? I waited. Seven o'clock, just as you promised.'

'Oh, Lord, we've been snowed under. Lindsay didn't stop all day.'

'Snow in August? That's something of the paranormal, surely?'

Nick laughed emptily. 'Look, I'll bring the sheets round this afternoon in person. Promise, promise. Are you staying put?'

'If you're not here by six, I'm coming round there myself. You can give me the keys and I'll sit and go through your files. Understood? And don't forget you're coming to Cambridge, two on Saturday. Prompt.'

'No problem.' They hadn't even started on the job of sifting Else's records. Where were they? Were they even in the office, or at Greenwich? Nick's eyes flew over the flapping posters in a panic that was driven by irritation. How dare Morgan put him under pressure like this over some tuppenny show in the backwoods. If the worst came to the worst, he'd have to do it from memory. He glanced down at his diary entry for the rest of the day. But when?

Before Nick had a chance to extricate himself, however, the line went dead. Blast. The Welshman had hung up on him. Nerve.

Morgan jarred as he woke up at The Aviary, not sure which room he was in or which town. A habitual dawn riser, Else had got up ahead of him. Sometimes she heard him pad about upstairs and joined him, but this morning she'd gone out, possibly down to the village. He went outside, tempted by a pure and brilliant day, already hot. It pulled him to the woods, light-shod, dressing-gowned, but half-way along the path he thought Else might be at work in the studio and cut back to look for her.

She wasn't there. The place was still cold, the windows misted with overnight condensation. He turned up the paraffin heater a degree too high, making it reek. Her big canvas was still tacked up on the back wall and he sat down to consider its progress. He and Nick were the official hanging committee, but Else had been astonishingly coy about letting them see the body of work which she wanted to include. She said she'd sorted through all of the paintings that she'd held on to over the years but on two weekends now, when he was back at Odham, she'd been evasive about submitting them to his second opinion.

He noticed a stack of frames which she'd brought out of storage and sat down in the corner of the studio to do his own review. Morgan thought he wasn't really prying since she'd agreed in principle that he would need to oversee the rest. He'd donate his robinia back, there was the Odham procession, the dozen or so pieces which she'd shown at Covent Garden, locally owned work that would come back for an exhibition, the almanac prints and some copies of the finished book, together with what she had selected from a hundred or so pieces in different media that she'd retained over the years. That was a good core of work. When they talked it through, it felt like a substantial exhibition, but if they were printing catalogues by the end of the month to give Max six weeks' lead time, they needed to make final decisions soon. There was no point in his hounding Nick if she didn't motivate herself either.

He was careful not to change her order but the deeper he went into her pile, the more troubled he became. He'd come to the point of having almost no correct value judgement about this work. Aesthetics were suspended. These images were bruisingly real because he'd started to share their source. Knowing her in person stripped away the overlay of allegory she cloaked her ideas in, leaving the meaning raw and bruising. Looking at them, he wasn't an art critic any more but a social worker analysing the mental working of a patient, or unravelling a disturbance which the paintings had helped her work out. Some of these old pictures were the output of an individual in trauma and reminded him of Sylvia Plath's poems or the tensions in Oskar Kokoschka. Screams came from them, maybe not to the casual onlooker but to the interpretist, screams of pain. What did they call this kind of work? Confessional.

Faces drawn from the known. Dürer did it that way, and sometimes Leonardo, so dispassionately cruel and seeing that you felt the breath of their victims, or their visions, was curling the page. Hell's people. There was a beaten gold shield of a face that was both man and woman, seamed down the middle where the two halves joined, and she called it 'Midas and Medusa'. The connection between the two mythological stories, the turning to gold and turning to stone, hadn't occurred to him before. The paired ideas and the paired faces were fused into a mask, mouths agape, like a male and female unit of parenting, but it wasn't kind or caring, this face. The couple she imagined were as violent as some of Goya's black images, 'Zeus devouring his own children'. It was a terrible head, slit eyes and wolfish mouth, a dehumanized face that would have struck terror when it went into battle against its enemies.

Not many paintings shocked you by their impact, but that one did. He found he was shaking. Maybe he was only cold, and he moved the smoking heater closer. August. Why was it so cold?

An overweight woman sat at a kitchen table between a full ashtray and an empty teapot. Drags and dregs lay scattered among a setting which, when you looked closely, was wallpapered in the background with delicate green pound notes. The woman wore the same features of the Medusa female, recast, and was entitled 'Evil Indoors'. It was unmistakable and awful and he had to laugh at the accuracy of the domestic detail. The truth had that frisson about it. Drawn from life. Whose features were they? Any middle-class, middle-aged woman would do, maybe Marise, or some

185

woman in Glasgow whose address he didn't ask for in the middle of the scheme, or even Lorraine, according to which of the type you knew best, gone grey and greedy.

Erotica. Not pornography, which incited to an imitation of the act. This drew a kind of studied distaste. Not even that, distance, as if Else watched herself watching. Pseudo-voyeurism. This was worse than descending to reading her letters; he was reading her mind.

No wonder she was dubious about letting him and Nick vet the paintings; if they were reproduced in photographs, these images would contravene the Obscene Publications Act. Calling them artistic was the thinnest edge of language. They were indecent, not because of anything they showed, no crotch, no close-ups, but from the power of the metaphors she used for the connection. Ballfight out of bull. Plumbing, complete with the provocative turn of the screw threads, male and female ends, sealed bonding. Pant, sock, belt, where in portraying the innocent garment she discovered acts which winded him with blows. New sex always shocked. Invention probed your own body potential and made it feel uncomfortable.

Or was it in his eye beholding? Surely the naked human body couldn't present any more surprises towards the end of the twentieth century? Maybe these were harmless mounds and hillocks, not a body map. She left the options open. Take it as you will.

Then there were new paintings she'd finished in the time she'd known him, calmer, more collected groups, not two figures in an empty unsupportive landscape. A cinema queue in Leicester Square which they'd shared, more village portraits. The figure painting had got bigger of late, and was as distinctive as El Greco's or Stanley Spencer's. Figurative. What did that word mean? The body was bent aside and implied something as well as holding its own shape. Metaphysical. He remembered once writing that style was the sugar that made raw ideas palatable. This was a comely style, so that you just kept looking even when you knew that it was difficult. Busy interest on the surface, detail heaped on detail.

He rested the series back against the wall. That was an uncompromising power and it shook its fist at him. He sat numbed. He hadn't been this flattened since he read a sex manual which his parents had failed to hide from him. The excitement that he might do these things, that this was what his body was for, was overtaken by dismay that they'd discovered the secrets long before him. They did it too. He had felt his adolescent prudery and shame mixed with tumescence, as when he'd masturbated and couldn't look his own eye straight in the mirror afterwards.

Was he going to support this work, irrespective of its content, of its likely reception and the effect it might have on the reputation she was trying to build? The problems of censorship became urgent. Should he carry the responsibility alone, for he was in no doubt that it was good work and deserved its showing. Total immersion in the round of galleries in Glasgow hadn't confused his view; this was the best he'd seen. It still stood up, carried and convinced him. Or should he confide in Nick and let him into these hesitations? The public still carped at nudes, got up and walked out of the theatre when the grunts were loud or overly suggestive. Maybe not. Maybe they were passable. He might be exaggerating. He'd look at them again when the shock had worn off.

It was the full range. Subtle through to strong. Not dwarfism at any rate. What did he want? The notion expanded that this collection should come to London and that, if they pulled it off, he would transfer it to the rooms at Covent Garden, whatever opposition Marise put up, for a fortnight at the beginning of November. If this was it, dangerous living, dangerous painting, what was he complaining about? Exhibit and be damned.

Adrian emerged from the side alley that led to the offices of Allander and Furness and joined the main thoroughfare of Cheapside, discovering that it was a hot midday and that he'd been closeted with his solicitor for nearly two hours.

As there were no taxis to hand, he struck out in the direction of Bond Street on foot, refusing to descend to using tubes or buses. Every so often, he held an imperious arm aloft but the cabs zoomed past, full of tourists. He kept on walking west, although he noticed unhappily that his shoes were picking up the dust of pavements.

Mr Allander himself had come in on the meeting. Else Petersen's solicitor in Sudbury had sent him a copy of a hand-written will, purporting to be Ralph's, as well as a letter from a local man, a Colonel Eversley, citing his standing in the community, a Justice of the Peace, military background, long-term friend, et cetera, and his belief that such a disposition of the assets at Odham in favour of Miss Petersen had always been Mr Pennington's intention. Verbal undertaking in front of another.

Unimpeachable, said Mr Allander. Give it up.

Unimpeachable! The very word invited an attack, so solidly walled, with the Colonel waving medals on its battlements. Adrian wanted to see an original document, not some meagre photocopy and this word-of-mouth business. He wanted to submit that original to handwriting experts and prove its authenticity.

He got as far as Fleet Street before a taxi stopped for him. ''Ot work, in'it?'

Adrian thought he might be looking rather pink with the heat and dabbed at his face with his handkerchief. 'Sotheby's,' he said, but, speeding round the congested lanes of Trafalgar Square, had second thoughts and tapped on the glass partition. 'Drop me a few doors down, will you, at the Fisk Gallery.' Twelve forty. With a bit of luck, he'd catch Marise before she went to lunch. A letter or telephone call wouldn't do. For her ear only.

'Adrian Crane?' She was perturbed by the impromptu request for an interview. 'Of course I'll see him. In the small boardroom. But give me ten minutes to get ready.' She spent it in mulling over several files and carried them with her to the cooler of the office suites. These London buildings had an inherent problem; they needed air-conditioning on only ten days in the average year, which didn't justify the cost of installing it.

'I've ordered some coffee and sandwiches. I do hope you can stay and join me.' She offered her hand, cool as herself, exquisitely dressed in ice blue.

'How thoughtful. Yes, I'd like to stay.'

She noticed that he was perspiring freely and was embarrassed for him. 'There's nothing wrong with the Stubbs transaction, I hope?' Adrian was on the Sporting Art Trust committee and had dealt speedily with the purchase from their side.

'Far from it. The Trust is delighted with the quality of the painting you secured. I do congratulate you.'

Marise bowed, stately dues. 'So what can I do for you?'

Adrian grimaced involuntarily. 'A sticky one. Doubts that have been forming and which I'd like to talk over with someone – unimpeachable.' He unrolled the word like a red carpet and she stepped on it.

A girl came in with a tray on which were laid linen napkins, Wedgwood china and a Cona jug of fresh coffee on its spirit burner. 'If this is something problematical, would you mind if Boris joined us? He has a much better head for detail than I. Husband and wife, you know, discreet. Is that sun troubling you? I'll close the blind.'

Adrian nodded, and they handed round sandwiches while the girl fetched Boris. A contract, he thought as he received the summons, needing to be sieved for flaws, and was therefore not prepared for the Sotheby's director saying, 'I know I'm treading on dangerous ground. I've no evidence apart from the thing we all have to rely on from time to time in this business, the gut reaction. That Gainsborough head we sold for you in March, I had already turned it down in January.'

'Morgan told me that much when I bought it from him.'

'Well and good. I'm sure his intentions weren't fraudulent.' The sentence, smoothly affirmative, snagged on their attention with an invisible barb.

'After Easter,' Adrian went on, 'Nick Wylie offered me a small landscape which he felt was also a Gainsborough. I turned it down. Nick has since sold it privately through a London auction house whose eighteenth-century expert had given it the all clear. Two completely new, uncatalogued Gainsboroughs turning up in so many months? I am much mistaken if there isn't an element of mischief here.'

'You think it was wrongful attribution?'

'Yes, in both cases.'

Marise fretted. She was on good terms with the Japanese dealer who had bought the midshipman at Sotheby's in March, and had done more than a little boasting on its account. She looked over at Boris to solidify their position. Public hand-washing was needed.

'What can we do?' he rejoined. 'Mistakes are endemic when the dealers and the auctioneers are too greedy for their mark-up.' That was not at all what she would have wanted him to say.

Adrian moved on to the edge of his chair. 'It is the source that troubles me. Morgan in one instance, although he refuses to declare where he obtained it, and Nick was given his landscape by Else Petersen in payment of an outstanding debt.'

Marise couldn't contain a burst of dismay at the juxtaposition of the two names. 'What are you saying to us?'

'In short, that Else may be faking English paintings and Morgan may be inadvertently handling them for her.'

The woman had no resistance to prejudice, disposed as she already was to thinking ill. She recalled Morgan's reluctance for the sale, which had the primary effect of boosting her offer, and his attempt to regain the picture with the curious disclaimer about its authenticity in front of an impartial third party. It was very strange to want a picture back you thought wasn't genuine. In a second, Else was impugned, Morgan a dupe like herself, as well as Nick and the Japanese dealer and the entire self-respecting circle of art connoisseurs, honesty foiled by cunning. Rumour was proof. Hereafter, she would see to it that certain people were alerted and the doors they operated remained closed.

Boris moved more cautiously. 'This is a slanderous statement, Adrian.'

'I know. I only say may. I say it privately to you and to no one else. I am not normally given, as you appreciate, to intemperate language. I am here to ask for your advice.'

Marise was distracted for a second. 'How much did Nick get for his landscape?'

'Fifty thousand plus,' he replied deviously.

'How can she owe her agent so much?' Marise was irate to be outdone by such a margin. Why couldn't the order of the pictures have been reversed? She deserved the oils. Let Nick have the paltry drawing.

Boris grieved silently for an old standard which had operated without computation. The true was the true. 'Do you want to report this matter to the police? If not, then you must be quiet. You must be quiet because these rumours do none of us service. We trade in good faith. Reputation takes fifty years to build and five minutes to demolish.'

Adrian felt he had been unjustly reprimanded. 'I wanted to warn you about being caught out by more dubious paintings. It seems a rather neat triangle they've set up to front fakes through legitimate contacts in the auction houses, or reputable galleries.'

Boris read this as a warning in itself; be more vigilant, be an accessory to hunt out the people against whom this young man had a grudge, or be implicated by him in turn. I did warn them, your Lordship, and they paid no heed. The net trawled everyone. He paused to wonder how the dialogue would have evolved without Marise present. Almost certainly, he would have mentioned Ralph and The Aviary, and his old association with Else, man to man. 'Yes, we are all suspect. We have all made errors of judgement in our day which we would not wish broadcast. We sold a picture to the New York Metropolitan ten years ago which isn't ... isn't kosher. It came from a palace but what does that mean? Princes can be impostors too.'

Marise listened astonished as her husband made a gratuitous confession. The man was warm. Such lack of caution was foolhardy. 'We are digressing, although Boris is right to say we must not be rash in making accusations. It stops here, for the moment, but I do thank you for your warning. I will be more alert about what comes my way.' She fussed over Adrian on the way out, taking him on a detour to see a Renoir she had for sale, only the second by this painter she had offered in her entire career.

'Nice thing,' he agreed, at the dapples of sunny light. 'Such happy pictures.'

Ah, well, there may be hope for you yet, she thought.

Boris was picking over the remains of lunch when she went back upstairs, the blind tilted, the glare removed. 'He is very angry,' was his verdict, 'and that impairs his common sense.'

She brushed some crumbs away. 'Why do you say that? I thought he showed real foresight.'

'It's easy to be malicious without proof.'

He sat. Marise stood, unsettled. For several minutes her mind agonized over the problem of Else while she revisited herself at twenty years of age, and the handful of fine art dealers who were left trading in Berlin after 1939, down the streets that ran away from the Tiergarten. They had knocked her down, mark by mark, because she was visibly desperate. She knew the pictures she sold would almost certainly find their way into the hands of Nazi officers; they were the only people who could be sure they wouldn't be confiscated. She paid off her persecutors in instalments. She tasted that old hunger, she tasted fear, stringencies that blurred the edge of provenance. She would have fabricated anything to offload her Dürer for twice its black-market price. Would have faked it, would have enjoyed faking it to make a fool of them, and lacked only the skill. Two dealers had refused that Dürer on the same day, saying it was a forgery, or that she'd stolen it, and she walked on down Viktoria Strasse, conspicuous with a parcel under her arm, dogged by risk. Was that Marise very different from this Else? At knife point, principles wore thin. A painting could be measured in how many days' grace it bought. Beauty for shelter, culture for food: it was a base equation. What had she been paid for the Dürer? It made her sick to think how little. And where was it lodged now? The others which she sold out of need had turned up again in public collections, private mansions, loaded with the guilt of their unspecified route, maybe traded against torture in a dungeon, but not that one. Possibly the Dürer was lost, burned by accident among a pile of incriminating papers while the Allied tanks drew nearer to Berlin. It was the drawing of a horse's head, maybe a preparation for 'The Four Horsemen of the Apocalypse'. Well enough.

That process coarsened; skin often beaten turned tough. The older woman reasoned that if Else were made of the necessary stuff, she would survive a test, a small test of veracity. She drew out some sheets of paper from one of the folders and passed them to Boris, still pensive under the filtered light.

'I'm sorry about the way this happened. You were in Bath. Your secretary was on holiday. Mine opened all the correspondence and put it in one pile for me to read.'

He took the letter that Else had written to him in July. His wife watched keenly while he sat and read it through, not hurrying, but pausing to weigh the phrases, assimilating as if it were Scripture. Ten, fifteen minutes he spent, then folded it and handed it back. 'Thank you for letting me read that.'

His calm incited her. The ice blue crackled. What was natural and pressed flat creased in the wearing, after all. 'Why is this neurotic young woman writing to you?'

'To thank me, it appears.'

'And why? What are these cheques you send her?'

'A levy, on talent. We profit when we sell her work and it is sensible to see that she goes on producing it. A rental system, if you like. Lease lend on people. Not impossible.' His sardonic tone chilled. She knew she had made a mistake in prodding him open, which he would never forgive.

Marise ground on although her nerves were too steady for the dramatic outburst. 'You can advance no explanation?'

'I owe none, not with Else.'

She did not tear the letter up or throw it away in a tantrum, remembering that, in afterlife, men collected letters and put them into print. She inserted it into the file on her desk.

He watched it go. He shed his last fear of his wife. He had been the hard man for so long at her behest, avoiding sentimental lapses, that now he had turned into the stone figure that she wanted.

Nick resented being press-ganged into turning out on a Saturday, and refused to wear a deferential collar and tie, but came sporting his cords and a much distressed leather jacket instead. Sometimes his rebellion creaked.

It was good to be out of London. Increasingly, the summer heat stifled him, the office-recycled humidity unbearable, a street sauna that made jackets wilt and tempers fray. He couldn't decide if using British Rail or the car was worse, or, in essence, he balanced the tics of his fellow passengers against the parking hassles. The week before, his car had been broken into in broad daylight on the street. He'd only just picked it up from the garage and was enjoying the free-wheel out of the fug, as he sauntered north through the Blackwall Tunnel and up the M11, breathing the softer air, letting his eye lap over the roll of unassuming countryside.

Morgan and Else were punctual at the Cambridge church, ahead of him, sizing up mechanically with tape and pad.

'So this is what we've got?' Nick cast his eyes upwards to a run of exposed beams, plain plaster walls without trim, a faint odour of cinnamon and pepper that emanated from the fitments and might be half-way to woodworm. The church had been stripped out ten years earlier and sold privately, when it lost its congregation as a diocesan boundary was redrawn. Even the Church of England sold off its glebe fields and vicarages. It was headed for conversion to a private dwelling, but a stubborn council had refused planning permission. It hung on in the western suburbs of the city, facing fields in a limbotic trance, hired out for the occasional concert when its five-hundred-stop organ was reused, and other cultural events.

That was the better news. There was none good. Nick heaved. Your clients always expected magic, the conversion of raw space into the stuff of dreams, and he felt he arrived in the same guise as an architect whose contract was to design the model house. What was attainable on a compromise of cost, site, his taste versus theirs, inevitably disappointed all of them. He'd two options, to gloss over the problems he foresaw and be positive, or prepare them honestly for the end result, and grumble all the way. He chose the former.

He prowled, sniffing. He'd been asked to fill some unlikely venues in his time, theatres, once a barn, ordinary houses like Covent Garden. He wasn't chastened by this, found the purpose-built gallery a bit dull and stereotyped anyway, or hard to rejig. The impossible site demanded more. But, good Lord, sixty-foot arches, great blank walls to break down to scale. How and with what? he wondered, as he dug into himself to find some answering response.

Morgan had got as far as typing out a list of projective inclusions which Nick glanced down, but really that was the next stage, the fine tuning. He needed a theme or a bit of inspiration to backdrop frames.

'When we went round Norfolk, church-visiting, I thought they were more like ships along the coast than buildings. This nearly gets there.' Else was dreamy, contemplative, the remark floating upwards untrapped.

'Why ships?' Nick caught the comment on a rise.

'Oh, journeys, spiritual voyage, something about stem and stern and maybe the height of ceiling to take a set of sails. A pulpit's always looked like a crow's-nest to me.'

The idea went home and Nick fired on it. They watched him change, become quick and light and excited. An exhibition was a new woman to him, something to be captivated, and his eyes and skin changed at the prospect, in a cross between soft and keen. He started to laugh. 'This could work, you know. It really could. Two levels.'

'How can you make two levels?'

'Scaffolding. Builders' stuff. Costs nothing to rent. Or they'll give it free if we offer them some advertising. It's good stuff, not heavy, like big Meccano and adaptable. We can use it to break up the height. Upper and lower deck.' He filled the empty, uninviting space with the three-dimensional, pictures in the round, pliable canvas. The harder he thought, the faster he talked, clipped and snappy as he arrived at click decisions. 'Your pilgrims triptych here, the tree thing at the other side. Four of the big works could be laid out to make a cruciform, like Stations of the Cross. Have you held on to that Crucifixion? Good. Altarpieces. We'll separate the landscape from the figure drawing, make different rooms with moods. Hang them back to back. We need something else to break it up, make walls, make distinctions. Banners, posters?' He glanced into the roof space, remembering that regimental flags were often hung in churches and could simulate the movement of sails on his scaffold rigging. 'We'll find something. Now, you said you knew people in Cambridge who might be useful. And we've got to decide how much we're going to commit to advertising.'

Nick pulled the notebook from his inside pocket and scribbled words. Free from Harriet, he had a bubbly humour like an unstoppered bottle. He was good at laughter, Else remembered, and should use it more. Nick lost years and inhibitions when he did what he was best at, or became more simply likeable.

Morgan was less indulgent with Nick's spasms of effort. All right, he was gifted at this. Not everybody could package A inside B, frame in the round or achieve the enhancement of the portrait photographer, manipulating harmonies and lighting until the plain was made interesting and the interesting beautiful.

He still found him peevish. Nick had a rudimentary face which recorded only two expressions, bravura or pique, and even then the cast of his features was monotonous behind the mood, pushed-out, pulled-in sameness. He thought he was endemically immature, wanting the accoutrements of success without the slog. Nick set great store by the Mercedes, the status house, the status marriage, but still confused facts with states of being. He'd no understanding of the means, that what others in the business admired was the day-in, day-out solidity and not the spasmodic flourish. Morgan found him too easily led and impressionable. Working with him once on a major exhibition, he was dismayed at his closet secrecy. He couldn't let anyone see the layout until it was finished, by which time faults were ineradicable. Was this egotism, or immunity to the second opinion? Rather the reverse. Nick was easily swayed and deterred, unable to hold his position in the face of argument because he possessed only a faltering vision, and reversed his opinion on a whim. 'I didn't love it' he would say of something failed, for which he'd previously expressed much liking. He was given to tantrums too, resigning petulantly at least twice in his career. Like a child, he wouldn't play the game by any rules but his own. Boris Fisk had once broken his laconic cover about Nick and said publicly at the second flounce out of the professional door, 'Anyone over thirty-five is a busted flush.' The saying flew with the truth of an arrow and Nick, hearing it repeated, knew he'd never escape its accurate aim.

But this was what you worked with, this is all there was, human second-bests. Who would Morgan have chosen voluntarily out of this cadre of talents? Not many. The better they were at their job, the more limited in personality, and intolerable. The inspired were rude and lazy, the careful were dullards. You had to forgive twice over in this business, man and machinations. Besides, Nick had known Else a long time and actually grasped how it was she thought, could pick up sails as a metaphor and apply it, could say, Have you still hung on to that big Crucifixion? and outdistance him on memory. He was content to stand aside and let them rediscover jointly what they could.

Max broke one of his invariable rules of politeness and called unannounced at Odham on his way to the coast. He nosed along the tree-heavy lanes, wondering why he'd never called at The Aviary in Ralph's time but felt a greater licence to drop in now. Knew Morgan better than the other man. Had more contact with Else of late, was curious, was passing, although none of these reasons conveyed the impulse in full.

He didn't make it as far as the house. Driving along the top track, near the PRIVATE. NO ACCESS notice, he caught sight of the shirt-sleeved Morgan heading off into a field and caught up with him on foot.

'Well, here you are. Come and join us. We're in the upper field. Only chicken and white wine for lunch. Picnics,' he said, 'the bane of summer. We eat outside, if we eat at all. Else's feasts are always removable. On the lap or on the hoof, we eat in transit.'

'It slims.'

'It does that. I'm shedding everything excess. No pretensions left. I came down for a holiday but we go and work for the local farmer every day.'

They shook hands at last and realized this was absurd in the middle of the countryside. 'You don't mind that I called?'

Morgan slapped him on the arm. 'Definition of a friend. Someone you're glad to have drop in.'

'What are you working at?'

'A bit of general farmhand work. Like those postwar holidays for city kids when they were shipped out to the country. I hadn't handled a pig in the round before, but I'm getting quite good at swilling.'

'Feeding pigs?' In his blazer, bow tie, striped shirt, the trimmings of a city summer, Max found this improbable. 'Surely not.'

'Surely yes. Come and meet Clive and Jane. They'll have knocked off by now. We're plum-picking today.'

Max slipped off his blazer and bow tie when he thought Morgan wasn't looking and undid his top button. Quite jaunty at that.

At the end of the eight-acre field, where the plum trees made a cool spot, Else was sitting with the Ramages. The Colonel had strolled up from the manor house to commend their progress and stood hesitating. There were some jugs of cider going round and he thought he'd stop for those. Max had misgivings as he drew near, because the group was constructed as it was. The impromptu was an imposition really, requiring so much explanation.

He had to give none. They accepted him as readily as one of the seasonal workers, camped out in tents and caravans at the end of the lane, job-hopping to different harvests. Else found him another plate and glass, while she coerced the Colonel to take the eighth place. The imperatives of London and business slipped away as corks were pulled, and the chicken and bread were broken and given out. Else organized them swiftly. Max was unprepared for her briskness and realized he'd not seen her outside London before, or in anything but city-slicker clothes, like his own. The rolled-up trousers made her look younger, and free. Morgan was right. She looked like one of the Land Army girls who could tackle anything.

Short wooden ladders reached into the plum trees, the wide-bottomed, narrow-topped kind that were stable and easy to wield in among the boughs. Crates of the yellow-egg plums were stacked in the shade, waiting for the lorry at the end of the day to take them to the fruit and vegetable auction held twice a week in Sudbury. And from there to the kitchens of housewives who would jam and purée and freeze and bottle in eloquent ordinariness, golden globes preserved to light the winter months. The profit to the farmer would be negligible. Next year, Clive was determined to grub them out and plant more beet. Imbued with the slow rhythms of growth, Max succumbed. There was no hurrying them. A lolling lunch would be followed by a snooze, two hours up the tree and a long straggle down the hill before he could talk to Morgan and Else alone.

'You stay in Southwold?' asked the Colonel. 'Poor you. It must be swamped with holidaymakers. I like the place, but I never got the hang of it. Lighthouse in the middle of the town. Those big verges round the green. Funny mixture, though I still run up to Adnam's twice a year for my wine. Might as well clutter up their cellars as my own.'

'Now, their Beaujolais last year...' began Max, brushing the edges of his moustache in savour.

'I like Dunwich the best of those coastal towns,' said Clive.

'But didn't it all fall in the sea?' Jane objected.

'Only half of it. And that's what I like. The stories about submerged bells ringing in the night.'

'But that's what I can't abide,' said the Colonel. 'All those settlements are half and half. Did I go to Aldeburgh on the wrong day? It had no charm. The beaches have no quality along the east coast, nothing intrinsic, just stretches of sand. Give me the Cornish inlets every time. A bit of indentation.'

'Walberswick's on an inlet.'

'Still got that Dutch lowlands feel, like polder, and it has the windmills.'

'Do you know,' said Max, 'Charles Rennie Mackintosh went there during the First World War. He took his notebook and sketched things. Of course, he spoke in Lowland Scots and the good local people thought he was a German and reported him to the constabulary as a spy. He was arrested on suspicion but discharged.'

'Was it the accent or the notebook, do you think?'

'The place,' said the Colonel. 'Endemic ignorance.'

The two boys ran off under the low-hanging trees and Else made a third with them, arms outstretched and laughing as she joined in the game of tig. The trees were bays of immunity she chased them round. Morgan closed his eyes for a moment, head back on the tussocks of long meadow grass, and drifted, listening to snatches of uninhibited laughter. The boys pulled an arm each, dragging Else off in different directions. That woman has lost her real vocation, he thought. She should have been the mother of six children and damn the pictures.

When he came to again, Max was asking, 'And why was it called The Aviary in the first place?'

'Game birds were raised there, for stocking the grounds with pheasant and woodcock for their shoots,' Morgan replied, as if he were the knowing native.

'I'll tell you an awful thing, though,' the Colonel capped his information. 'At the outbreak of the war, the first, all the men from the estate went up to Ipswich to enlist. Head gardener, game-keeper, the lot. Very patriotic of them, signed on, did their duty, but they forgot about the birds tied up in their cages in the birdhouse. And when they came back from the recruiting office, they found they were all dead. Every last chick. Not good enough, forgetting about the livestock.'

And they laughed in a hollow way, as they got to their feet again, searching for a panier among the higgled stack.

Else knew why Max had dropped in and delayed the trouble-some moment as long as possible, just as she had delayed going through the old pictures with Morgan, and for the same reason. As she turned the pages of the printer's proofs, which Max had conveyed with utter pride at his workmanship, encapsulating hers, her courage to face the consequences ebbed. Faced with the indelibles of what she'd done and the images that had ridden her for fifteen years, she knew there was no escape. A catalogue to fill, with dates and names and places, the specifics she had let blur because time rounded was less painful than time counted out to minutes. To lie or to be silent over what she hadn't achieved: which was the lesser evasion?

Since the visit to Cambridge and its absolute, concrete finalities, she'd had the old relapse of confidence. She could foresee only failure, but failure on a larger and more public scale. Of course, she was frazzled with pent-up energy, wondering what impossible feats they'd ask of her. It would be the usual battle about holding on to her privacy. She watched her own control dwindle as Nick invented round about her – fascinating, it was like watching an embalming, but terrifying too, because it was hers. She watched herself being anatomized.

She'd felt abject the whole afternoon, could hardly smile as Max put his head over the top of the hill, because of the confrontation of types. She never thought her friends would like one another and avoided mixing groups. She suspected Morgan too of cornering her, forcing reaction or agreement by asking Max along behind her back, instead of letting her be. And she was upset by the stories they told at lunch, and ran away to play with the boys because she couldn't bear to listen to their depressive talk, of sinking and death and poor Charles Rennie, a stranger in a strange land. That these tales had a common link of hostility and the ravages of neglect had passed them by. She shuddered, knowing she was becoming morbidly oversensitive again, the mollusc in the open, covering stripped.

Max, charmed as he was with the rest of the afternoon, his reception, the cottage he was taken back to for tea, was sad at Else's silence over his proofs. She was no more pleased than Marise at his galvanic efforts made on their behalf.

'I'm sorry,' Else said, catching the drift of his disappointment. 'It's so hard to see yourself in this perspective.'

A thousand people he might have laboured for who found a more gracious remark. The exquisite paper, the new typeface he minted on this run, the generous margins, these were the delicacies she normally appreciated.

He drove off into the evening landscape, cooling and shrinking like old stones. There was a special quality in the Suffolk light and in the flattened, taut landscape, which made him wonder if it could give rise to the epithetical Petersen country in time. But maybe it was its emptiness that was typical and tense, because you could attach any mood to it, like her. He recalled that the best life stories were those of the invisible people, where nothing substantial was known. Shakespeare, Bach, a man called Jesus Christ; the disappearing people were the best to write about because invention was the largest part of biography.

September

Salisbury was an easy drive from Windsor and Adrian savoured the rare expedition. A Sotheby's client had left six major works to the nation and he was carrying out a valuation on the spot, in a country house that was magnificent in disrepair, as well as putting together an inventory of lesser pieces prior to auction. This was the duke who the year before had got rid of his Goya in a hurry to Marise, which afterwards went out of the country, so one had to be grateful that death had forestalled more debt.

After lunch, he crossed to the south side of the city, dropping also in scale. Sheila Pennington lived in such hermit-like simplicity that her aura of *grande dame* was attributable to the internal, or the details of herself, strong grey hair tied in a knot, hands so elegant they could dig the vegetable garden and go on to deal a hand at bridge in the evening. One of the indomitables, he thought, set to see ninety.

'How good of you to come to see me, my dear boy.' She greeted him in the resonant tones of breeding. 'In or out?'

'Oh, out if you're half-way there.' But Adrian was glad he'd remembered to bring his overcoat with him and, although he didn't wear it, he spread it like a rug inside the wicker chair she offered him. She must live out here, he realised, in the suntrapped corner of a courtyard with a day-bed and a pile of gardening manuals, surrounded by trowel, trug and some improvised containers for her seedlings, and many Thermos flasks.

Sheila smiled to one side, assembling the tea things from among these outdoor supplies. 'You find it cold?'

'Only windy. One lives so much indoors, with air-conditioning – not healthy, I know.' It was February when he last called and full winter had exempted him from exposure to her hardy ways. 'Are you pleased with the house on better acquaintance? The town?'

'Splendid, both of them. The right size for getting into the corner of things, getting the detail. Belgrave Square, well, it was neither private nor public. Had a sort of waiting-room atmosphere. I'm glad to be shot of the responsibility. Here I descend into incorrigible dotage.'

'I think not.'

'Have you been busy all this while?'

She habitually tackled him on this front, of action, as if he ought to give a short account of himself as a preamble. At school, the only person who was remotely interested in his end-of-term report was his stepmother. She went through it word by word with him, scrutinizing his misdeeds as much as his successes, broadly uncritical. But *why* did the master tell you it wasn't quite the thing? He was her protégé. She felt responsible for him, and maybe was in fact. If she'd had children of her own, would Adrian have materialized at all? Ralph craved a son, but wasn't overly interested in the child when it did arrive, only the boy who yearned for a puppy whose daily routine care bored him. Martha Crane, meanwhile, was good-hearted but more concerned about her later marriage than her earlier child. It was Sheila who said he had to go to Eton, no argument, who insisted the boy was legally adopted at the age of consent and not left to drift outside official doors, uncertificated, who saw approaches were made at strategic moments to advance his career. And if he didn't know this, and gratitude went unexpressed, she harboured no grudges. IOUs were odious. It was her personal *noblesse oblige* to foster him.

'Well, yes I have,' he answered up, going minutely through his stocktake of progress in the last six months. The reading list which was planned to fill his commuting journeys had been her suggestion. She added to it periodically from whatever she herself enjoyed, for she was a prodigious library borrower, and they exchanged titles and critiques judiciously.

Sheila watched his face intensely as he ran this record through, not feigning her interest. She was genuinely fascinated by him, by Ralph's son and what was omitted from the replication. Thanks were negligible compared with the tangible reward of seeing the son and hearing the timbre of the voice. It was Ralph's form recast all right, but slighter, finer, plaster instead of bronze. There was a line too short about the jaw and, with his measured build and thinning blondness, Adrian lacked the father's scale. But this is all the kinship I have, she thought, realizing they were the modern parable of a family in sum, affectionate members of the same household group, but unrelated in blood. My husband's natural son; that was quite close as bonding went.

His successes. His tribulations. Who slighted him. How he knocked the kitchen and the dining room into one at Windsor. She would wait, knowing to the comma where he would hit the climax in his essay of self-exposition, and tell her why he had really come to visit her this afternoon. 'And I did go to see Allander and Furness last month.'

'Mr Allander is well, I hope?'

'Fighting fit. As brusque as ever. Else has sent me a copy of what pertains to be a hand-made will she says she found. I brought it with me to ascertain what you thought of it. It leaves the house to her, but I don't believe a word of it, not one!'

While he spread out a paper for her perusal, Sheila's eyes didn't waver from his face. Even if she were deaf, she'd have known his emphatic meaning by the disdain written in his features. 'Did *he*?'

'Allander? Oh, he advised me to give it up.'

'And will you heed his advice?'

'Absolutely not. But read it for yourself.'

She scanned a scant sheet. It was very painful, resurrecting old names and places when she had put them to rest. It passed her scrutiny, but barely. Several things made her sceptical: its too-perfect timing, its closeness to the phrasing of the official will that gave off a false echo, something in the hand not free or flowing. She doubted its authenticity, but not its truthfulness. 'Then will you take mine?'

'To give up? But why?'

'Because you don't want that difficult little house and neither do I. Down a dreary, dead-end road and such damp countryside. It wasn't included in the probate will so he must have had other plans for it.' Sheila noticed that they didn't talk of Ralph by name, their only connector. The same went for divorcees, who referred to a cast-off partner as the other side, himself, my ex, or you know who. Bizarre, that someone you had spent half your life with should be shuffled into the nameless incognito. Something like an incest taboo set in, to justify and reinforce distance with third-person names.

'That still doesn't make it right.'

'Right can be quite elusive, I've found. Anyway, I've no interest in pursuing this. I'm asking you to give it up, for my sake.'

It was the first time his stepmother had made a direct appeal or asked a favour, and he had no frame prepared for answering. On Else, she had been studiously neutral, so why intercede for her now?

'You're only aspiring to make life more difficult for her, and she makes life quite difficult enough for herself. What you resent is not that she should live on in a beastly, earth-floor cottage, but that he chose to live in it in preference to your house and to mine, although that wasn't at all her doing. I don't suppose for a minute she wanted him there. Blame anyone you like, if you must lay blame, but not on her. Blame heredity before inheritance.'

Sheila drove him wild when she went off into abstractions like this, with her herbal remedies and how he could grow them on a windowsill, probably useful to someone who wasn't in a hurry, but not to him.

'She never treated you badly, as I recall. You visited often. She made you welcome, made you tea. What is the difference between these two women connected with your father, Else and myself, that you discriminate between us? I see no difference. She didn't lure, my dear, he was not lurable, and didn't bind him, rather the reverse. But she gave him glamour and she gave him mischief. What more does a man want?'

Adrian was more bitter than she realized. What she took for loyalty, that he persisted with his mother's name, was more of a revenge against his father. Twenty-one was late in the day for changing names, when Ralph took it into his head to adopt him legally. He blamed Else for the delay, not his father. He felt she'd taken fifteen years of his father's attention, his near contemporary was promoted over him, unbalancing the apportionment of time. She'd harmed his professional standing, made him sell and retire prematurely. He saw no good in her.

'And a kind of unfairness was in his nature. He didn't mean to neglect. He prioritized on the urgent. Such is philanthropy. The greater the need, the greater the caring and the injustice. I think the parable of the good shepherd implies exactly that.'

She could see he was not convinced, the wrinkles on his long forehead no longer enquiring but rancorous. It was the postwar obsession, to be fair. She blamed it on the rise of the middle classes, afflicted with emotional thrift. What calamity would it take to make this young man large? She wanted to say that forgiveness was a measure of greatness, except that he wouldn't believe her any more than he would follow her advice. The limits to her authority were optional.

She underwent a brief crisis of choice, whether to tell him or not. Would Else's story, told baldly on a late afternoon, elicit his sympathy? The hurried student love affair, a mishap of conception, a tragedy in consequence that brought her to Ralph's attention and made him offer a house, out of the way, to convalesce in, as one sheltered stray cats. It might change Adrian's attitude, the better for his own register of compassion, but there were two other possible reactions: that he already knew and discounted pity, or that he would discount it anyway on hearing the outline from her lips. Besides, the metaphors of divorce held good. Sheila had learned the wisdom of never mediating or commenting with the benefit of hearsay. He'd have to hear it from someone other than her.

'The material is only a kind of flesh and passes. Look on the cottage as a repayment for nursing duties. And it was more kindly for him to be at home.' I've been spared all the inconveniences, she reflected, the child-bearing and the nursing, and can still call myself the wife.

'As you choose, Sheila. I can't gainsay you.' He rose and put on the overcoat gratefully, noticing that the tea in their cups had congealed to the consistency of cream.

'It's been lovely to see you,' she said with perfect sincerity. 'Don't leave it so long next time.' But she was left with an unpleasant sense of being used, because he'd come to enlist her support in a vendetta she found dishonourable, and wondered why it was he didn't have enough force of character to move against Else in person, if that was what he wanted, to hunt her down himself.

There was some less demanding business to attend to, a client of Harriet to whom Morgan was devoting a whole room in October, and they finished that first.

'I must say, you're looking very well,' Harriet conceded enviously. 'Very fit.'

Morgan looked at the brown hand underneath his cuff, admiring the new muscle and fibre of his growth. 'That was my fortnight on the farm. There wasn't much sun but there was a lot of compensatory exertion. I'd forgotten how good it feels to be fit. Although I'm terrified of those high-power executives who say they go to the gym at six and put in an hour on the machines. It gives them energy for the rest of the day. Never understood that, but it must be true.'

Harriet hung back, for Nick would have added viciously, Maybe the gym's the solution for all of us. After a moment she said, 'Laws of replenishment.'

'Are there such laws?'

'I suppose so. What else does it mean that nature abhors a vacuum? What empties must fill again. Use up your reserves of energy and more floods back. The pump-action theory of human endeavour.'

They laughed, then both paused anxiously. He'd taken her to La Marmite, flattered that people came out of their way to him, because his time was valued at a premium. The Dover sole was still reliable, but too many patrons came to eat it and he'd started to suggest lunch at one thirty to stagger the rush hour. It was still less than intimate, however, when he could read his neighbour's credit card number as he was signing his bill. Harriet waited tactfully until the next table was empty before she said, 'It isn't going well with Nick, Morgan. I don't know what to do any more.'

He groaned inwardly, sensing she didn't mean their turnover or Nick's sporadic work ethic. I'm no marriage guidance counsellor, he wanted to object. Look at my own record. Not even passing fair. But he restrained the brush-off. If people came to him, in either sense, it was a compliment, and he accepted those without attaching motives. Realizing he was the one person in the world Harriet would confide in, he made the leaps of assumption. 'Is there someone else? Someone I know?'

'Probably you do. Someone unimportant. That'll pass. But is she the first of a series, Morgan, and how can I stop it if she is?'

'Do you want to put a stop to it?'

'Yes, I'd like him to be faithful. Or isn't that the norm any more?'

'I really meant it the other way round. Do you want that kind of marriage, or still want to be with Nick even if you can't stop it?'

She shook her head, confused about whether the marriage was savable, not negative for its own sake.

'If you simply want companionship, he's the world's most companionable man. But reliability, fidelity, those are the sink-me words. How do you gauge them in the first place? Does Nick want out?'

'No.' It dawned on Harriet that one didn't receive advice or pardon at the confessional until one had told all, revealed the last weakness. 'I haven't said anything to him. Just hoped it would run its course.'

Her reticence pained him directly, making him wonder if he'd given Lorraine cause to do this to one of their mutual friends. Max perhaps? Said never a word to him, but complained about neglect behind his back.

'You must be feeling miserable,' he remembered to say.

Her eyes filled, as they always did when men were tender, making him regret the question because tears made her plain. He could recall when Harriet was thought a beauty, a luminary on the London scene, but even at the fading point, something splendid hung on in her. The eyes perhaps, like the shade of green she often wore that went with bronze hair, not in the least cold or cat-like. Rather restful, pensive eyes. He'd read that after thirty, you made up your own face, or were responsible for how it matured. Hers boded well. No bitterness. No pinched lines. The amplitude of her physique implied a generosity of spirit, after all. How much easier if they could have made a second match with each other, instead of the awkward partners they had chosen.

'We've been around for a long time, Harriet,' he said by way of compensation for the hurt and the intrusion. 'I've got the same options in reacting to this as you have. Are you expecting me to take Nick to one side and tick him off? I can't do that for you. It's none of my business, apart from not liking the grief it gives you. Or do I sit here quietly and listen and say it'll all be fine. Handing round placebos isn't one of the functions of friendship. So if you want to stop me, tell me now, and we may still be friends at the end of the afternoon.'

She smiled wanly. But Morgan didn't smile. The image of Lorraine persisted. The two women were equally mild-mannered, the docile creatures who attracted combative men, put up with them and finally bored them silly. He felt he was put in the position of advising his own wife on how she should have salvaged their relationship, long beyond mending. The basic exercise was flawed by the burden of his latter experience. Go out and find something better, for God's sake, find a stove that warms you and a mind that satisfies. However patchy or fraught the thing was with Else, he concluded, it was better than this.

He still regretted the advent of seconds, second chances, second time around. It would have been nice to get it right first time and he had a brief image of Else, fifteen years ago, playing catch round the orchard trees with his own boys but sighed and put it away, since it was not to be. The safe marriage might be unattainable for the egotist and loner in their walk of life. He'd shaped the quality of his own home, fifty-fifty, share alike, and had created exactly this unhappiness or a vacuum. There were too many away days in his calendar, too many lapses of attention. Weekends, parties, manuscripts; he gave them all priority over wife and son. Ralph in him and he in Ralph.

'What's your worst nightmare out of all this?'

'That he leaves anyway and it turns out we're bankrupt. That I lose everything. These are heady days in the art market. Everybody's making money faster than they can spend it, except us. We're struggling to meet the bills.'

Bought Greenwich at the peak, of course. Bad timing. But the comment was the key he needed. 'You'll have to take control of the money. Stop being so nice, Harriet, and thinking Nick's got a better nature you can appeal to. You'll have to bully. And you'll have to cheat. Do anything. Get your accountant to recommend a new contract that ties him down more, or make sure all the cheques require joint signatures. That sort of thing. Or separate your accounts again. He's probably got money stashed away as it is, and that's where your profit's going. Get the reins and pull. He may not like you any better for it, but he'll respect you. And give him more challenges. He's bored, and who wouldn't be, massaging fragile egos every day. Nick doesn't burn steady, he sparks, so make the most of it. Find him a big exhibition to organize. He's understretched. Let him go to Birmingham or Newcastle now and then. Let him go and he'll keep coming back.' The carrot and the stick. And heaven help them all.

She nodded, recognizing soundness when she met it. She could do all of that and became determined at least to gain control of their finances. But not one word had Morgan said about her emotional hold over her spouse, as if it were a negligible quantum, so that she was struck for the first time by her own folly in expecting the gadfly to settle.

Morgan knew it. He couldn't lie, or didn't think Nick was worth lying for. He'd been too direct, punchy with his own strength and sense of well-being. He was distracted, while he spoke to her, by the sense of corporation, or corporate responsibility one for the other. The group on the golden mile were interactive and interrelated in a way that was almost incestuous. He couldn't be more frank about Nick because next month he might have to work with him again, as indissolubly linked as man and wife.

The huntsmen gathered at Odham on the patch of grass beside the muddy duck pond which had earned the name of green only historically. It was the first of the autumn meets and, for several of the young foxhounds, their inaugural outing. The huntsmen were also a new and ragged band. The local hunt was trying to expand its membership with any farmer or weekender who could urge his mount over the dipping terrain, where the folds of ditches and hedges often disguised each other. The Hunt Master, bred out of Quorn stock, was particular about the finer details. Pink coats or black, no stray aberrations, the horse groomed to point, the saddle girths properly tightened. No laxness. All gleaming. He wanted a resurrected pack that would ride out in style.

The dogs were less obedient than the men, setting up an unruly yelping over which the Master's instructions were hard to give or follow. The animals chased each other in circles, churning up the green, which was sodden from a month's unbroken rain while Colonel Eversley, who'd been persuaded to take charge of the menagerie, despaired of getting them in order.

But they were a brave sight, the line of chestnuts and greys stepping out on to the higher and better-drained ridges of the hills, with the bright spots of red in the field as sharp as early set berries on the bough. The experienced lead dogs ran free, scenting out the favourite habitats of fox, knowing the kind of covert they preferred and the scent of badgers' and rabbits' burrows which the predatory animal might have adapted to its own use.

Clive, riding as one of the novices with the pack, felt no pangs of animal-rights sympathy for the quarry. Foxes had been allowed to overbreed in the neighbouring thickets over the years that the hunt was in decline. At a farm north of his, the whole battery of chickens had been wiped out and, even if it didn't maul, the fox could terrify a henhouse into not laying for a week. They were scavage-mongers. Just fencing and locking up against them was costly, time and money. He was glad to support this action. And there was something agreeable about the feel of mounted cavalry and trooping, gallop downhill, canter up. It was good cross-country, Suffolk, broadly flat with just enough gradient to keep the eye fixed and the stirrup mobile.

After the best part of an hour's aimless riding, the Hunt Master saw the hounds had picked up a scent and, with a tally-ho on the horn, he assembled the huntsmen behind him. They followed the cry, the riders converging in one small gulley like a stream rippling inevitably to its floor before rising again. A communal urgency gathered them. The horn sounded over the wide open sides of the valley and came back resonating from their constriction. The hounds ran on the scent, the bright enforcing morning provided a good, lung-bursting gallop after the dreary bouts of rain, the flash of countryside and colour merged too quickly to be distinguished other than as hazards imminent and overcome in seconds, like a test pilot's training video, virtual unreality.

But the fox, for all their flying, was cleverer, or more practised on the territory, than hunter and hound and rider, who moved clumsily over or through the wet hedges. Or he was the natural guerrilla fighter, more adaptable and quick-thinking in his native woods. He gave them the slip twice, the pack eddying like a whirlpool in frustration. And twice they picked the scent up again. The new dogs were hardly controllable. The younger bounced and tumbled over each other until the Colonel swore he'd never ride to hounds again in September, but wait until they'd learned a bit of formation discipline.

Finally, a long time into the afternoon, they lost the scent altogether. The countryside was laced with rivulets and the cunning animal would cross and recross these shallow irrigation channels until he baffled his pursuers. But it was a good ride none the less, and a good training exercise. The men were content to head back to the green by the short route across Clive's land, tracing the network of his concrete ridgeway paths, and con-templated the comforts of the inn ahead.

The pack was more independent. About five miles from Odham Green, blood up, they ran across a wild rabbit and gave chase in spite of the calling and transverse riding of the Master, to head them off. This scent they wouldn't lose.

At full speed, the hounds, followed by maybe half a dozen huntsmen who hadn't grasped that this was a paltry rabbit they had set their sights on, made across the woods. The whippers-in tried to control the runaway dogs but the lead hound wouldn't submit. The rabbit dodged and darted, and finally broke out of the wooded dell at the bottom of The Aviary garden, where, contrary to a basic rule of survival, it headed over the planked bridge into a walled enclosure from which there was no visible escape.

The dogs followed it, the Master, the whippers-in still trying to round up the pack, while Colonel Eversley and Clive and others of the village men reined their horses in the wood and stamped, watching the havoc grow from twenty dogs and a dozen hoofs in the confines of one small domestic garden.

Else heard the commotion from the studio and opened the glazed door to investigate. She walked into the middle of the kill, painless enough, the work of seconds as the dogs dismembered their living prey by tearing it apart. She saw this was a doe in the last day or two before littering. The young unborn spilled out on the lawn as she was ripped apart, and the dogs eagerly snapped up the kitlings.

She stood shock-still, surveying the instant devastation of her grounds, a trampled border, flowers rooted out, a long stain dragged up the lawn, terracotta planters overturned. The whole work of the summer was undone. Incensed, she seized the whip from the hand of one of the invasive riders and set about the pack, lashing them and kicking them in her soft shoes, without regard for her own safety. They would have turned on her, to bite and claw, if the Master hadn't ridden into the thick of them and ordered his own trained dogs to circle the runaway pack, and herd it back down to the woods.

'I'm sorry, Miss Petersen. You will accept the hunt's apologies.'

'Accept? I don't think I can find the words for now.'

'We'll naturally pay for any damage incurred.'

She raised her eyes to the mounted man, the crop still dangling by her side, her lower legs bloody where the dogs had brushed against them. She thought she might be sick at the sight of the half-chewed doe smeared on her grass. She had some pity for the creature's suffering, however brief, but couldn't see why her own peace of mind should be upset by this intrusion. It broke her concentration. It broke her space. There was something malign in the event, an impression she couldn't shake off, beyond simple seeing and reasoning.

When he saw the state of anguish she was in, the Colonel tethered his hunter in the copse and came across the open ground on foot. He sent the Master and the rest away and guided Else back into the house, shaken and trembling, for her to bathe while he himself cleared up the carnage from the lawn.

'It's a gentleman,' said Charlotte, 'who says he knows you.' Her outspread hands apologized that she hadn't been able to secure his name, but there had been a trail of these gentlemen in the last six months, all of whom did know Morgan, so that she didn't feel a need to shield him from his old friends.

He'd no qualms as he went downstairs to meet this caller, only noticing incidentally the patina the showrooms had picked up. He'd heard that others were calling it a club, but was sceptical about this term, being neither a joiner nor a belonger to those all-male institutions. It was one such who called on him today, the academic. From the top edge of the balustrade, he recognized Derek Hisslop's crinkly hair. 'What a rare treat. How long is it?'

'February,' the precise man replied.

'Is it so long?'

'I walked over from the Courtauld. I haven't come to buy anything,' said Hisslop briskly, 'but may I look?'

Still pleading poverty, the well-fee'd consultant!

Derek gave generously in praise, however, the informed praise that was worth double. 'You've done a rare thing here,' his visitor commended him. 'You've managed to extend the map. The golden mile is now redefined as the golden mile and a quarter. It's worth continuing past Bond Street these days. Keep going.' He stopped in front of the last of Else's paintings left on sale.

Hisslop recognized her hand without the benefit of labels and took an almost physical pleasure in seeing it written large again. 'Someone told me she's exhibiting in Cambridge next month. Funny place, but I would like to go.'

'St Martin's Anglican.'

'That's the best thing you've done, got her to show again.'

'Not my doing,' Morgan disclaimed the credit. 'But you're sure you're not interested in this? I'm surprised it hasn't gone already.'

Derek turned to look at a picture of a farmer whom he didn't know but recognized as real. 'No. It looks as though it's been planned as one of a series. I'd have bought the run, if they'd been complete. A broken hand, no. And I'm being cautious for the time being. Wait and see. Where have you got your money?' he asked without warning.

'Money? I don't invest in shares, if that's what you mean. I buy a frame once a month or so and put something in it.'

'Moderns?'

Morgan nodded. He remembered now that Derek used to play the stock market the way other men filled in crosswords or football coupons in the lunch-hour. He limited his spending strictly to one thousand pounds per annum, and shifted the profits into gilts. The theory of it might thrill, but it was the kind of numeracy that confounded Morgan, or bored him, chasing columns of figures to make them add up to something more.

'Maybe they'll hold their value. But if I were you, I'd shift them downstairs for sale and let somebody else bear the loss.'

'Loss?' Morgan asked. 'I'm fond of them.'

'Ah, fondness is loss, or the non-returnable.'

'I thought auctions were making record figures?'

'And the stock market. But did you notice there was a hiccup in August. Maybe you were on holiday. We've had our warning. It's turned into a seller's market. You should cash in while you can.'

Morgan was inclined to laugh off these sombre prophecies, not conversant with the jobbing terms that were written in allusion and double meanings as much as a soothsayer's. 'I'll take stock,' he replied, which was as emphatic an action as he could envisage.

Derek took a last turn about the hall. With its three recessed arches, the harmonies of that space gave great pleasure and Morgan noticed a lot of people hung about in the hallway, unconsciously absorbing the well-being it engendered. 'I was most annoyed last week. Sotheby's had a drawing queried that I'd authenticated in the spring.'

'Which was that?' asked Morgan, seized with apprehension.

'A little Gainsborough. Fetched an absurd price at Sotheby's. I think the Japanese buyer probably feels he paid too much and quibbles. They've developed a new infra-red camera in Japan which he had it scanned through, and it bleeped like fury. What does that prove? Machines haven't got eyes.'

'What was the subject?'

'Captain's boy, I think. We gave it a descriptive title because it was uncatalogued. Anyway, the buyer's made a formal complaint and Sotheby's are saying *caveat emptor* in their gentlemanly, coded way. It seems funny to start sniffing after all this time.'

'You mean somebody made the buyer suspicious? Dropped hints?'

'Oh, I didn't think of that. Why would anyone do that?'

'Small worlds shrink.'

'Irritating to have one's judgement called into question, all the same. I did a lot of work on that, a lot of reading round.'

Seeing him out, Morgan agreed. I thought it was genuine too and we are both discredited. Although he said affably at parting, 'I'm glad you dropped in', he wasn't happy with the outcome. Derek had had three motives in calling, to ascertain the where-abouts of Else's exhibition, to warn him of some financial calamity pending, to tell him the Gainsborough was disputed. A strange basket of currencies, those, and what had he to do ostensibly with any of them? Nick could have answered for Else's venue, Adrian was the man to consult about the head and, as for advising him to sell his modern greats, it was a bare-faced presumption. This was becoming too much of a club after all, members intimate and knowing, trading business cards and tips. Handshakes next.

What threads had led Derek back to him? Increasingly, he felt Else was right. London was a whispering gallery, rumour and intrigue circulating until they multiplied to malice. Alongside that ran a kind of protectionism which promoted certain notables beyond their level of ability and kept them there beyond common sense. The RA President was a case in point. Morgan had heard that Boris Fisk was resigning from his directorships and thought the man had commendable dignity, to pull out before he was voted off the board.

He couldn't help noticing that this encounter and the one with Harriet earlier in the month ran along the same course. Finance. Figures. Economic providence. Was that really what he was coming to, running a brokerage? Marriage and investment, all forms of business sought. He felt a spasm of disgust at himself, his very sleekness reflected in a glass door a reproach against the worn-down, hard-working man of principle he used to pride himself on being. In the middle of the city, he yearned for Odham and the unremarkable life; in sharp dealings he remembered the unblemished page on which he was able to control the very dot, and the zealotry of teaching, the wonderful slow-motion of self-improvement, like watching flowers grow. Should he do a MacPherson? Turn his back on this before he was ousted. Was there a village in the valleys with a university chair waiting for his incumbency? Open up a two-room cottage in Snowdonia and pump his own water and electricity? But maybe the purity of vision was in his own age, when he did those things, that he'd been lucky in hitting on the best era for television, as well as for universities. They might be more tarnished now. Producers would want to cut a regular ten minutes out of his schedules, to slot in the advertisements; and at academic boards, the talk was of price-cutting and streamlining, the unit cost per course which should be self-financing, and the expedient of taking on less experienced and less expensive staff, to hell with quality. That let him out. The taint of cynicism might be in himself as well as in the times.

Else had gone into a withdrawal that was almost complete. The appearance of Max's proofs, the incident with the foxhounds, were inward and outward pressures that collided. She had steel meshing put up at points through the bottom wood to keep more marauders out, not knowing if she had the right, although no one in the village disputed it.

Mentally she shut down. This happened anyway in winter, simply closing doors or coming inside out of a bitter wind, but hibernation started earlier this year or had a different feel. It was a grim, enclosing autumn. She loved it when the light stayed high until the end of October, ripe dropping days, but this was a sullen, rain-sodden year that made the months of retirement longer. A mean, shivering fog drifted inland from the North Sea and hung patchily in the thickets all day, the temperature never rising high enough at noon to burn it off.

Time of itself abbreviated. Five days instead of seven she could call her own. Two she shared. But the restoration of a normal balance, of week to weekend, increased other constraints. One bit of her mind was absent or had a secondary focus. Drawing in a face, she asked, How will he like this face? That process created a consultative, approval-seeking slow-down where she'd been quick and autonomous before.

Her work became compulsive and all-consuming. Ralph always encouraged her. It was he who suggested having the studio converted, but hitherto she'd achieved only the sporadic output of the amateur, the dreaded Sunday painter. There was no imperative discipline apart from seeking quality for its own sake, and no challenges. Now she felt like an athlete who had to regain his fitness to Olympic standards in six months. This was possible – nearly. She'd worked to a routine since the exhibition was confirmed and covered a vast amount of ground. She systematized the old canvases – they shocked, with her forgotten selves, just as Morgan admitted they shocked him on first sight – and went on painting to extend the range of work already exhibited. She committed herself to finish three extra canvases during the month and, to ensure she complied, had details of them printed in Max's catalogue.

Now, she crashed into self-made deadliness and would wake up in the night, frantic with a stray thought, a useful allusion, fretting that it wasn't feasible to go outside and add to the picture there and then. Or was it? She could get the torch out, light the paraffin stove, climb the stepladder, work till dawn. Ridiculous obsession. She switched the light on and jotted notes to herself instead, although it could be as frustrating as trying to catch clouds. This was brain-burn, and she had to admit that panic was not the best accompaniment to concentration. Beware, someone had said to Sylvia Plath, the lamp that burns too bright may shatter its glass.

She would have done anything rather than submit to the daily torment of what she was deemed best at, put in a month without remission at the hospice, work on Clive's bumper harvest crop of beet, chained to the combine if he asked it, any slavery apart from the one she'd chosen voluntarily. It was a continuous session of aerobics, the body high on oxygen of its own making, pump pump ideas like blood, until she wanted to scream stop to her own driving machinery, but couldn't.

Two letters fuelled this frenzy. Ralph's wife wrote a formal, colourless letter confirming her acceptance of the holograph, and stating that The Aviary plus contents was hers outright. Copy to the solicitor. In the same post, almost in evil coincidence, Adrian sent her a note in a private capacity but on Sotheby's paper, enclosing a complaint from a Japanese gentleman who disputed the authenticity of her old Gainsborough. Note? Well, that was too fulsome. He scrawled 'Any comment?' on a page.

The world gave her no peace, kept knocking at the door to break her concentration. She swung up and down on the two communications, relieved and terrified in bouts.

When Morgan arrived the next Friday evening, the house was standing empty and he pottered about clearing out the car and changing before he went down to join Else in the studio. It was growing dark. Concern that she would tire herself out by carrying on too late was muted by the pleasure of seeing her at work with this much dedication.

He meandered down the grass, taking in the new shades of the robinia. It had been, at best, a fitful summer although there had been enough light to endorse Else's first statement about the tree; it went on changing in the sun, a sap green into lime, then veered into the yellow associated with other plants, golden privet and a ripe quince. He'd thought, when he saw it for the first time in the winter, that it was like a fountain, the way it shot up out of the pool of the lawn, but in leaf the word was proved more apposite. Light fell from branch to branch like water splashing over tiers of ledges, and the wind made a spray. The whole of it rippled and moved like nothing botanical he'd ever seen. On bright days, it was tropical in the intensity of its colour, too yellow against too blue, and un-English.

'We're overdoing it,' Else said over her shoulder. 'I've been locked in here all week, sunrise to sunset. Not a word of a lie. Have you come to take me away from all of this?'

She was still painting, and hadn't started to clean up for the day. The pilgrims picture was completed, stacked in the corner ready for crating. Now she was at work on their open-air lunch the day they picked the egg plums, which she called 'Loaves and Fishes'. There was only some foreground work to finish.

He held her waist and leaned his head against her shoulder, feeling the muscles of her back work on. 'I'm pleased with how it looks. Are you?'

'Oh, still myopic. Next week I may have a better perspective.'

He stood further back to admire it, or give himself the distance she suggested, and collided with a small easel she'd set up. She often kept preparatory drawings and sketches to hand as a prompt to the current work. He moved it slightly out of his way – and came face to face once again with the Gainsborough midshipman.

Else listened to his surprise as she scraped her brushes clean.

He was going to tell her about Derek and the query later on, but she was several steps ahead of him again. 'How did you manage to get it back?' he asked, amazed. The frame had been removed, presumably by the man who bought it for seventeen and a half thousand pounds, and at that price you could afford to quibble with a frame. There was the head looking quizzically out at him again. It wrenched at Morgan a third time, because every feature was grafted out of his own. 'Did you buy it?'

'No, I did another one for you. This one you're to keep.'

Slowly the words gathered a definite meaning.

'You *did* another one? How could you memorize the original so well. Had you had it photographed?'

'No, I just remembered what I did first time.'

'First time? We're talking about the same thing? You're telling me that you drew the head that was sold at Sotheby's in March?'

'I certainly did. If you remember rightly, I was always adamant it wasn't a Gainsborough.'

His hands went limp with incomprehension. 'Then why did you try to get it back from Marise and from the auction room? You tried to persuade me to buy it too.'

She was methodical, working round about the sink and turned away from him, drying her hands. 'It hadn't picked up a tag by then which was unjustified, and which I knew would rebound in time.'

He began to recall the scene with Marise in pinpoint detail. Else had said, She will blame you for this ... say you were an accomplice. 'What was wrong with telling me there and then, Else? Why have you got to let things run until they're so involved you can't extricate yourself?'

'Because I didn't know you well enough at that point to explain, and thought I'd lose you if I did. Didn't know Sotheby's would validate it, wrongly. Didn't know Marise would sell at auction. Didn't know Adrian Crane would start to squeeze on it, and then on me. Didn't know a lot of things I know now.'

But she was unrepentant, walking ahead of him out of the studio and up the garden. She did this. Walked out and left him to close the doors, turn off lights and taps like a damned lackey.

'Picasso,' she said when he caught up with her in the hallway. 'Now that was one of Ralph's. He was quite proud of it because it was very tricky to imitate the blues. I know. I had to copy "The Blue Guitarist" as an exercise once. The mixing I had to do to get it right! After that he moved on to Chagall.' She went up a couple of steps to the half-landing and switched on an overhead light above the frame. Two lovers floating in space, he hatted, she sprouting flowers that fell off her dress and on to the background.

'So Ralph never knew the painters at all?'

'Oh, yes he did. I have letters from Picasso and Chagall and Dufy in the attic, a suitcase full of cuttings and things.'

The art historian gasped at the disclosure. 'But why didn't he sell those, or you sell them, instead of faking paintings?' He recalled now the earlier inconsistencies which he'd not followed through to a conclusion, a hoard of modern masters when she was declaring poverty, Adrian wresting the house back but ignoring her cache of priceless pictures in the meantime. Of course he wouldn't think to retrieve them; she was making them up as she went along, easier than turning out counterfeit banknotes. Morgan almost admired her audacity.

'Fake? But I didn't fake. Ralph didn't fake. And I wouldn't dream of selling his private letters to some tawdry little go-between like Nick or that awful American who was pumping you about Larkin. Would you do that, sell Larkin's letters if you had them?' She was outraged at the thought of betraying private messages and, in a more personal sense, that Morgan hadn't given the second Gainsborough boy's head its due. She'd drawn it for him to make up for the abortive auction sale but the loving gesture was lost among pedestrian recriminations. He'd wanted the head when it was masquerading as valuable, but it was worthless in itself. That little tilt was the fulcrum of an insincere regard for pictures which she pitted herself against.

Morgan was raw too. Every visit was the same: he drove for an hour to get out of London in the thickest of the traffic, hoping to share his working success with her, enjoy the peace of Odham, support what she was doing – pursue the elusive sanity of the everyday, just sit for one day in the sun – but had the ambition shattered by some new turmoil of Else's. It was as if she tried him to the limits, or deliberately produced an upset to thwart their normal progress.

He could smell something. Food. She'd broken off to come indoors and put a casserole in the oven during the afternoon. That was their trouble. They were hungry and overwrought with Friday strain.

'Shall I begin again?' He retraced his steps, and walked back to the door to make a second entry.

'It started when Ralph was ill. He couldn't do much else and became restive just sitting about here day after day. Of course, he knew what kind of paper or canvas they'd be using and how they mixed their colours. Little tricks he remembered. I told you he could have been a good painter if he'd tried but he didn't have his own style. He was a truly gifted mimic. I used to watch his hand movements and he'd hold the brush quite differently. Picasso had a quick dabbling style, staccato. Chagall was more fluid and slow, quite light. It was interesting to see how he'd sit in shape. Take on their physique, act it out. It was a compliment, and a way of thinking himself back, can't you see, to recall them, to be young again in Montmartre, in the heady days.

'Then one day, he looked at a portrait I was drawing and said, "You've got an English line here, eighteenth century. Bit of Hogarth. Bit of Reynolds." And I was away. It was a pictorial version of Charades that we were playing. We played the same game in Norfolk, remember, but with words. He'd choose my painting from one of the art books upstairs, I'd choose his and we had two days to make a companion piece for it. We didn't fake, I assure you, or sit with the thing in our hands to crib from. We made up new compositions given the style of the old. It was very academic, if you like. We didn't even try to copy, certainly not to sell. Why would Ralph want money? Selling the business to Max had made him a wealthy man. It was a completely innocent pastime, good-natured and rather stimulating. I went to the lengths of making a Gainsborough picture box for landscapes and used some model farm animals, cows and sheep and bits of moss to fill it, just the way he did himself. I learned a lot about lighting. It was sincere flattery.

'We found old frames in junk shops and old canvas to paint over. Ralph was ingenious about ageing them. He knew someone who smoked his own trout and used to add a century or two in the smoking rack. It was like a cabinetmaker who goes to the trouble of hunting down fixtures and fittings he can break up to put on his reproductions. Only the repros are so good, people come along and say, Ah, this was made in Dulwich in about 1810 by a well-known craftsman who specialized in bureaux. Odd his plate is missing, little metal plate he usually put on the back. I watched while you went through that yourself. Willing suspension of disbelief. People want to believe they've found something special. They want it so badly, they falsify the facts, or ignore them, like scientists with a pet theory they've got to make work, no matter how much they corrupt their evidence.

'I never offered them as the real thing, never pretended. I was appalled to hear you saying to Marise that the head was a Gainsborough. But that's greed, or glamour. I have the famous, I am famous. Vanity ownership. I deliberately didn't go to an auction or the big dealers because I thought they'd be scented pretty quickly. I mean, the paint was hardly dry on some of them. I was desperate. I needed the money after Ralph died. I've no income, no security. I didn't earn enough last year to pay income tax, or the year before come to that. I never thought about money with Ralph, so I suppose I was improvident. I felt, well, if I can't sell pictures under my own name, I can still use the skill to sell them under someone else's. Frank Keating thought it, van Meegeren, and why not? If the world is full of dunces, why should clever men not prosper? I knew it was a phoney enterprise, from beginning to end. Success spoils us, but failure spoils us more.

'I don't know why I went to your wife with them. She thought I might be hoping to meet you. But it was more devious than that. I felt if you spotted them, then it stopped there. But you didn't. You fell for artifice as well. The wagon kept rolling and I was trapped by it.'

He had promised himself after the Glasgow visit that he wouldn't quiz her again, although a battery of questions raged in his head. Just how many of these dissimulations had she launched on the market which might trace their way back to her in time? She'd retained Ralph's 'modern' paintings and sold only her own traditional ones. The Constable landscape which she said she'd offered to Lorraine was gratuitously good, the foliage, the tricks of composition would have taken in nine dealers out of ten. And all for a few hundred pounds. It was so unspectacular a profit that it was almost ludicrous. And it took up time that she could have put into work of her own choosing, that was the worst profligacy. But she was right in what she said after Marise whisked the head away – he was made an accomplice of sorts, and possibly so was Lorraine. How many people had been duped by the painting, whatever it was, that she'd given to Nick to defray her bill? Had she been encouraged by the mark-up on the Gainsborough at the Sotheby's auction to have another go at his style? Adrian suspicious, possibly tipping off the Japanese buyer himself, Marise always likely to round on them, how could you start to put this mess right? His instinct, to come clean, would precipitate a personal crisis for both of them with no positive outcome. It was a crime. It was a theft, but of what and against whom? It was a theft of make-believe.

At heart, he blamed Ralph. The mix-up over the house, the lack of foresight about providing Else with at least a minimal annuity, were the marks of a selfish or an unthinking man. He was a practical joker, the creature he most abhorred. Although, in the midst of his disapproval, something uncharitable gleamed. Ralph's standards were not unattainable after all, but left something still to do.

'Will you go now?' Else asked. They'd brought the hotpot through in front of the fire and ate off trays, Else cross-legged on the floor. It was a good meal, in her uncluttered, one-dish style. It mended the spirit as well as the body, whatever was in it. The room had many other buffers. In the rooms most women put together, these would take the form of worked cushions, favourite indoor plants or a flower display, something rather posy. Else's room was a matter of arrangement – that is, logic. Chairs were set under the window for you to read by daylight, see from in the evening. Logs were stacked in a trug that had doubled for picking the plum harvest on the farm and bore its stains. Most of her books and magazines had a piece of paper inserted, of words or sketches, and often both, to be stored later in the work files. The thing did. Sitting room? Only incidentally. By ranging round, his eye picked out half a dozen activities. No idle television or intrusive radio. It was her product, informal and unkempt. He simply came to rest in it. She was what she did. He couldn't better that.

So the question 'Will you go now?' disturbed him. Was it Else's polite form of an assertion. Will you please get back into your car and go away for good, inferred the first time she said it. 'Go where?' he asked.

'Leave me. I wouldn't really expect you to do anything else.' She was spent with the detail of her story, the final self-exegesis.

He lifted the hair on his side and let it trickle out of his hand, like sand or water measurement. Only so much time. 'Why would I go? We have things to do tomorrow and the day after that.'

'What if trouble comes?'

'I have a good drawbridge mentality. Nothing will happen. Sh.' He put a finger across her lip. She turned into his offered hand with a warmth that surprised him. She'd really thought that tonight she would be alone again and that brought home to her the sweetness of his company.

She knelt and undid his shirt to the navel. If anything, Else had struck him by a lack of passion, something not in the chord of the pictures at any rate, which he accepted might be locked into the imagination. She would obey, respond, be happy, even grateful, but these were the conditions of reactive sex. He was convinced she did want something from him, companionship and the view out of his eyes which she valued, but physical love, not wildly. She would never really let anyone in. The cool blonde, the woman who could be men's sex idol without doing more than wear old jeans, forever desired, never desiring. Else was not the cosy cuddle-up type; she was interested in lovemaking as the power of suggestion, where he offered her an idea and she thought about accepting it.

She undid her own shirt while he sat inert, just watching how the cloth moved against skin in firelight, yellow hair over blue denim. She kissed him roundly, drawing away and coming back firm again each time until he had to hold her still to press against him. Else had the wit to improvise on a sensual theme; this floor cushion she sat on cross-legged, now uncrossed, was many other things in the anatomy of one act, head, back, loin rest. This was her small style, intimate patches, clever composition.

October

Organizing the actual hanging was the best bit of an exhibition, a gravity-assisted swoop after the laborious job of getting to the top of the hill by herringboning. It was completely physical and Else, going outside caution with the last reserves of strength, threw herself into it with gusto. Bolted together in serial rectangles, the scaffolding stretched interior space, bare ribs waiting to be clothed, ladders reaching into trees. When he'd a practical job to do, Nick was decisive. He'd already worked out a scheme for the layout on paper, which he followed like a map.

Oh, I remember this one, he'd say. Good stuff, isn't it, good to see an old friend. He whistled softly at some of the nudes. Thank goodness we haven't got a church committee breathing down our necks. A bit seriously adult, aren't they, a bit skin-raw?

Hang them high enough, she answered, and nobody'll see the details. The two picture hangers, removal men to trade, edged and adjusted the frames until the three-dimensional jigsaw fell bit by bit into place.

Else couldn't disguise excitement at the mesh. The polished catalogues were piled up at the door in cartons, two room wardens were hired who dropped in and thought it was looking good. At each stage, her confidence rose, until the stress of the preceding weeks was subdued under the simple faith of a sentence Morgan often resorted to: Quality will out.

Driving up at the end of Friday, ready for Saturday's opening, Morgan himself was impressed by what Nick had achieved. He'd managed to borrow arc lights free of charge, like the scaffolding, in lieu of a fee for advertising, and angled them up into the vaulted roof so illumination was from above, or fell naturally like intense shafts of daylight. It was modern and hard and purely theatrical, but suited an internal paradox, or wasn't the polite, subfusc stuff of museums anyway. Nick had had a hundred long banners made up by silk-screen printing, stamped with the one word PETERSEN, and these furled and wafted in the rising heat, giving the illusion of movement. Sails, wall-hangings, flags creating a flutter like a ripple of excitement. He succeeded, did Nick. For once, he did well. Morgan conceded that in a thousand years he couldn't have made such a diverse blend of elements work.

'You're going to make a lot of money out of this,' Nick said to Else apart, as they locked up in the face of another damp autumn evening.

'I don't know that, Nick.'

'I'm telling you.'

He said this to reassure, but didn't. Else still shrank from his philanderer's techniques, undue praise, comparisons she found inept, the often-used phrase, 'It made me think of you...' He thought fondness was enough and didn't know the word still triggered folly in her mind.

Morgan took Else to stay for one night in Christ College, where the Master, a long-time friend, had an extensive run of guest rooms at his command. They went back to St Martin's after lunch, where things were already humming. The timing was right, students crowding into the colleges and backs again, fresher after the long vacation, lively, on the look-out for something new and sensational. They were the future taste-makers but, in the meantime, the *Granta* editor admired the collection and would say so. Steady, steady. The catalogues were going well, pictures more slowly. The wife of a former mayor had left a note to say she and her husband would be pleased to talk over a commission for a double portrait when Miss Petersen was free. After a last turn about the hall, they left. There was nothing more they could do.

It rained relentlessly all the way back to Odham and the wipers struggled to cope with the deluge, beating in the small space of the car like a third heartbeat out of synchronization with their own.

'You need to take a rest now, Else. We could go on holiday. Get out of this damp. I'm sure the sun's shining somewhere behind that cloud cover.'

'Maybe in November. I always hate it after the clocks change and it gets dark so early in the day.'

'What will you do till then? I'm going to Leeds some time soon.

Do you want to come? We'll find a country house hotel. Swim. Play tennis.'

'Leeds? No, thanks. I'll stay at Odham and try to get back into a routine. I'll give Clive a hand. I've been pretty self-indulgent with my time of late. Haven't been near the hospice for two months.'

'Don't you think you should give that up?'

'Why?'

'It's a bit draining. A bit like permanent November, getting dark too soon. You've done it for more than two years. Time to move on.'

Morgan went as gently as he could. A lot of things worried him. Else was sleeping badly. She hardly ever slept out the night with him but got up and moved elsewhere. Too hot, she said, but these were the cooler months. In the morning, he'd find her surrounded by the debris of a broken night, empty teacups, newspapers, the wool-shedding sweater she draped round her shoulders like a shawl, propped up on the pillows like an old lady. Except she wasn't old. Oh, Else, love, what are you doing with yourself? She looked tired to death, worn out with the nervous strain he'd begun to feel guilty for imposing on her. Her hair had gone flat and lustreless, and nearly dark from lack of sun. He kept finding cuts on her hand, exacerbated into weals by the long hours of contact with pigment and chemicals. She cut herself on everything, a tin or a tin-opener and sometimes both at once, the knife as she sliced a loaf of bread, or she burned her arm on the hot stove because she wasn't even looking at what she was doing. The examples of neglect were legion and he was alarmed at the harmful trance she was falling into, because she didn't even register the wounds, leprosied by indifference to herself. She'd turned the precepts of the casual into self-abuse. The mad dash round the kitchen was all very well under supervision, but how could he imply she was in danger of becoming the one in need of care when she'd no time for cosseting, and brushed his tender considerations aside.

The wipers beat on the windscreen with the noise of birds' wings when they were trapped indoors, thresh and clatter against the glass, in a horrible rhythm. 'I'm all right. I'm just tired out. I'll have a few days away. Sybil Edelman invited me to Southwold. I might go there.'

Morgan stared at her in dismay. 'But Max and Sybil went back to

London at the end of August. Holding court in Portman Square again.'

'Oh, are they?' She shook her head to clear it of a buzz. 'Yes, I remember now. Well, no great loss, is it, walking on the beach in this?'

It lashed throughout that night, with noisy bangs and crashes keeping them both awake. The wind swept into the garden and, finding no escape, blew round and round, upending tubs Else had thought secure and tearing down a high-grown honeysuckle. Normally, she had a ready supply of energy for these jobs, flick and it was done. This morning, she stood dispirited and limp. The rain hadn't stopped, only abated slightly into drizzle. Year of years, this was, with every imaginable extremity.

'Come back to London with me. I'll take time off. We'll go to the theatre every evening.'

'*Every* evening? It's not that good a season.'

'Every second evening. You shouldn't be by yourself. Come and celebrate and spend some money.'

She laughed. 'What on?'

'The non-essential.'

'Soon. I need a day or two to—' but she trailed off, opening the back door and walking out barefooted and bareheaded into the rain to examine her honeysuckle, while he looked on, powerless to redirect her.

After Morgan left, the rain puddled endlessly across the land. Clive gave hourly thanks for his solid, foot-hard paths and the massive clearance he'd carried out early in the season that left him slack in hand for wretched weather, and turned his attention to the rewiring of the house at last. Round the farm, the ditches filled up with hardly an hour's respite for the water to drain off into the sodden fields. The stream at the bottom of Else's garden rose and broke its banks, reaching over into the wooded enclosure, and lying two or three feet deep in places on the lawn. She needed high boots to wade, and even then couldn't ford the stream entirely. It was dark and muddy water that swirled by. She watched it listlessly in the vacuum left after massive expenditure, not able to switch to the next job easily.

One night, she went to bed and slept in fits and starts through the same noisy buffets that had been blowing all week. About four in the morning, she woke up cold, with a creeping sense of eeriness. Round the eaves, the consistency of the wind force had changed. It wasn't blowing in gusts any more but in one long, continuous roar, like the velocity of helicopter blades, or a railway tunnel rocked by high vibration so strong the sound achieved its own stillness. She judged, from a contraction of her skin, a shrinking apprehension along the scalp, that this wind was unusually high. She pulled the curtains open on the garden but it was hardly light enough to see more than a grey, toppled scene outdoors. Her main concern was that the water might have flooded further up into the garden, although it was never likely to threaten the house.

But as she peered into the thinning half-dawn, she saw the impossible had happened. The robinia had been blown down in the night, completely keeled over. It hadn't lost any of the brittle branches the way it had in other storms, or snapped in half. The whole trunk of the tree lay sideways on the ground, held aloft by the strongest bough like a human figure reclining on one poised elbow. It had gone tactfully, falling in the most convenient position in the centre of the lawn, and so had breached neither the boundary wall nor the studio nor any other living plant. She pulled some clothes on and, at daylight, went outside to inspect the full damage. It almost made her laugh to see the thing prostrate, because it was the unlikeliest mishap. The tree fell fully leaved, brought down by its own rain-saturated weight. The root ball was like a head, lifted enquiringly from the ground, while the pale yellow leaves streamed behind it, still tossing in the wind.

She tidied what she could in the garden, on a morning that relapsed into wilful calm. The sun came up and made her blink at what mischief was done in the space of one night. She'd no inkling of the scale of a major, national calamity until the Colonel and Clive arrived at midday, to check she was all right. They told her she'd been lucky, secluded behind her stone walls. Higher and more exposed houses had lost their roof tiles. Trees had fallen in on others, or crushed parked cars. Everyone had woken up about four with the same sense of cyclonic roar that she'd experienced. The electricity lines were down in parts of Suffolk, the telephone was out of order, while Odham itself was cut off in all directions by trees that blocked the side-roads. It was a disaster more widespread than the immobilizing January snows, and people were calling it the hurricane. Her one tree was a token of millions that had fallen all over the south-east. Only one stretch of land, from the English Channel to the Wash, was affected, they told her, as they went off with their chain saws and snare-proof jackets to help some council workmen who'd turned up to cut the village free. They were jaunty and exhilarated at the adventure of it, because no real harm was done.

The next day, Clive came back again with a couple of villagers to clear the debris from the robinia. Else had thoroughly warmed herself by taking off the smaller branches with a handsaw. Hard work, that was, going into sap-green wood. The men lopped the larger branches in no time but left the trunk intact for Clive to attach a hawser line to it from his winch.

The shallow, giving root was stubborn at the end. The team cranked the winch up to straining point and hacked underneath, until they found the tap root, winched and hacked again. It was a grim sort of dentistry or amputation, as the roots came resisting to the last fibre from the soil bed. In normal times, Else would have got out her pencil to record an exceptional series of events, but she was too flat and dispirited to take part in what felt like a celebration – or the celebration of a demise.

The chain saw ground into the pulp, churning sawdust, until it fell in neat pieces. 'Do you want to keep the logs for your stove? It ought to burn pretty well if you keep it dry till next winter.'

'Oh, stack it then. What about the root?'

'It's not burnable. I'll try and grind that down. We'll put it on the back of the lorry, if you like, and get it out of your way.'

Thoughtfully, Clive had also put a pile of turves on the back of the truck and afterwards he filled and neatened the gaping hole, and tamped it over. In no time, the space would be invisible. But her focal point had gone and Else wandered abstractedly up and down the garden for the rest of the day, tidying twigs and feeling the exact size of the new emptiness, like the gap left by an extracted tooth.

Clive brought a bundle of the weekend newspapers with him, knowing none had been delivered into Odham since the storm. 'You're in them,' he said, pleased at seeing a familiar name in print.

After supper, she unfolded the sheets with some curiosity. Three major dailies covered her Cambridge exhibition in the weekend Arts section. That was flattering on the surface. As she read through the reports in turn, however, her heart began to sink.

No, something more trenchant invaded her. Disbelief. Hurt. She hadn't expected the eulogy of congratulations. No rave reports, See this and die, but she'd anticipated an assessment that was objective and useful. Could anybody honestly say of her style: Pastiche of good painting is always bad, and this is very bad. Surely it was gratuitously unkind to say her work seldom rose above the formulaic in composition? Fifteen years of work reduced to a throwaway phrase? Had they been looking objectively, these critics, seeing out of open eyes? Even the shreddings of praise were damnably faint: Patchily imagined. Too various for consistency. Her drawings are accurate, but experience will teach her how to centre her work better. Will it indeed? Who was this man who was so needlessly insolent? Who were these people? Morgan had told her professional picture people weren't to be trusted; they'd stopped seeing normally, gone blind with too much analysis. But that wasn't much consolation.

She got up from her armchair by the stove and went outside, nursing several kinds of murder in her heart. Against these faceless names, to each of whom she vindictively attached a pin-stuck body. She carried out death by infinitely slow degrees of torture. An unskilled acupuncture of the brain, preferably with meat skewers, that was what it felt like. Against Morgan because he'd done this to her forcibly, none of her wanting, and against Nick, who said with a smoothness so round but inexperienced that you couldn't hang an answer on it, There's no such thing as bad publicity. It all counts. Get yourself talked about, no matter how. Glib and insincere.

She closed the gate and climbed part of the hill to the farm. Better company than her own called her, and a ribbon of lights in the distance. The sky was unnaturally bright. All over the valley, they were burning their casualty wood, in bonfire after bonfire like Hallowe'en or Guy Fawkes Night come early. But this was a charnel smell in the air because the tinder and brushwood were too green for burning. It cindered in the nostril with a sulphurous aroma. As far as darkness reached, a smoke pall hung over the valley like medieval plague fires lit to burn corpses. She felt a surge of grief for the waste and devastation of the storm, demonstrable even in the dark. She knew these woods intimately, every foothold, every intersecting angle of the view. They were laid low, and became unrecognizable. The outline of the forlorn trunks was scarred and skeletal as she walked through them, completely stripped of their foliage down one side, like fire victims, the damage more shocking when it was selective and illogical.

She sobbed aloud in a bizarre transference of sorrow at seeing her natural environment turn hostile, didn't shed tears but gasped out of control, and stood for some seconds with her face in her hands while two contradictory impulses raged. Go on up the hill and do some work to pay Clive back for his kindness, hold the torch or the screwdriver for him but do something to make you forget about yourself. No, go home, the quieter voice said. You can't inflict yourself on other people like this.

And the insults that they hurled at her were so personal! Vague, her biography had allowed of every misinterpretation. To one critic, she was a newcomer, to another was of retrospective meagreness. Under which bushel had she been hiding her light? What did these phrases signify except a torment to which she had no right of reply. This critic had probably stopped off in Cambridge on the way to somewhere better, tore round the gallery in half an hour to snatch an impression, glad he could fill the wordage of his column requirement while eating lunch, or even made do with buying the catalogue, deductable as an expense. So journalists wrote up the delights of Sri Lanka without setting foot on a plane, or reviewed five hundred pages of a researched book from press handouts and the blurb. But fifty people who knew her would read the account with the glee of satisfaction that she had so ardently wasted her life's effort.

Stumbling back over the shifted ground, she thought, I've got to get out of here before I go mad. On Sunday, she telephoned Morgan from the station to say she was coming up to London after all, and was mindful to take Adrian's letter with her as well as Sheila Pennington's.

Morgan came to Liverpool Street to meet her and waited on the platform, pacing up and down fretfully, his raincoat flaps flying. From the open door of the carriage, she saw him newly and with shock. How completely their situation had turned round from the first lunch in January, when she'd escaped to town out of the snowbound landscape and found him a little worn, a little despondent with himself. She emerged from another storm but this time she was the one who was bedraggled. Else realized she hadn't been inside a dress shop for the whole year, that most of her clothes were five if not ten years out of date, and that she looked rather dowdy beside his citification. Not flashy. He was a mile from Boris's blue gloss or Nick's aggressive, ageing trendiness, always solid and understated, but Morgan now looked a man of substance and proven ideas. He had arrived at the pinnacle of the person he had always wanted to be, the man with infinite and unencumbered choice.

So far she did envy him, or the relative ease with which he'd sloughed the old life and grew another. Not so easy for women to replace the moving parts. Through the turmoil of their middle ground, she could go on admiring the raw solidity of him that attracted fifteen years ago. She still believed in class, or classification, that breeding stood for something whereby the gentleman looked more aristocratic with advancing years, as if age were a transparency, while the miner's son reverted to type, like Richard Burton, more pockmarked and louche with time. Not so here. A stray gene was at work. This man was endowed, but with a quality she couldn't trace back to source. He was one of the modern people who came from nowhere, like herself, but who picked up impeccable manners and flawless speech, not cynically, but to be neutral or give their talents the best showcase. They were quick learners.

'You're frowning,' she said in the car. 'Did I put that frown there? Have you got other things to do today?'

'Nothing better. I was worried how you'd be.'

'Oh, not completely blown away by so much wind.'

He glanced at her. So she had read the worst. That spared him bringing up the subject. Funny how bad news could travel against time and flood into the backwoods. 'I had three phone calls yesterday, if it's any comfort, from people whose opinion I respect, saying your notices were barbarous and asking what they could do about it.'

'Nothing,' she said. 'Grin and bear it. Who were they, anyway?'

'Derek's the only one you'd know. He went up specially to see it midweek. He's dropped off a note for you. And Nick phoned to ask if I'd seen the piece in *Apollo*, which I hadn't. It's a very handsome credit, and at least their correspondent knows his stuff. Nick rang him up to thank him personally because he thought he'd got it exactly right. He says it's always worth doing that, thanking the perceptive critic.'

He imagined this would mollify her but she only said, 'Obnoxious little toad. That's just the sort of licking thing he would do.'

Adrian choked involuntarily on Monday afternoon when he came back from lunch to find that Else was sitting waiting for him in his office, arms folded, looking out of the window at the passage of shoppers down New Bond Street.

'Did my secretary let you in? You didn't make an appointment.' He rifled for confirmation in his desk diary.

'No. I just came through the main entrance and walked up here.' Adrian calculated the gross breach of Sotheby's security system. He'd always said the door from the public showrooms to the directors' staircase ought to be kept locked. Guard on duty snoozing as usual.

'You did invite me,' she reminded him. 'Or you invited me to comment about your disputed Gainsborough, if that isn't the same thing.'

Adrian subdued his loftiness, and contented himself with shutting the folders on his desk and assembling them in a neat stack, as if she might have spent the time alone perusing his professional secrets. All the same, he recognized a courage he didn't have in coming here in person. He preferred an epistolary distance. 'And can you comment?'

She'd known Adrian for fifteen years, schoolboy, student, man, and through corresponding phases of closeness. They'd been good friends at one time, exchanging confidences. After all, the age difference wasn't wide and, if anything, she thought of him in brotherly terms, confronting the same problems at the same time as herself and often equally irate with Ralph. That was before the onset of coolness and a final alienation. Why he went through these transitions was likely to be hormonal as much as for any other reason, and was as puzzling to Else as total strangers writing about her in the papers with a knowing virulence. She couldn't fathom it, or why others had such an extreme reaction to her, even to the same person's love and hate. But she was still fond of him, or hadn't reached the point of hopelessness about changing him back.

'Why should you think so?'

'I've been able to trace two pictures back to you, or find that you presented them for the first time publicly. They're both now in doubt and doubt is a thing the auction houses seek to clarify when it undermines their reputation.'

Maybe at the outset Else had thought she would make the same confession she had to Morgan, to disembroil herself, or warn him. But the light-hearted, or the joke at his expense, would be lost on Adrian. 'The house was full of oddments. I just got rid of the least interesting bits. I never put a name to them. Other people did that.'

His annoyance with her gathered. 'I came to Odham one day last year when you were out. Ralph showed me round the studio, very proud he was, and he told me you were doing an exercise to train your eye, copying a Constable. He let me see it on the easel. It was very good. A very good copy.'

'Dozens of them,' she said as she got up and walked about his spartan office. 'Remember, that's standard art school stuff. How many students are sitting in the National Gallery making copies at this moment?'

'I forgot all about it,' he carried on, ignoring her. 'I could have stopped the thing from snowballing. But when Morgan brought that drawing of a head for us to authenticate, I simply never made the connection.'

Else wasn't deeply afraid of him. Like a bank clerk altering a figure, she thought, it isn't embezzlement or major fraud. 'Does it matter, Adrian? In the scale of things, it's fairly unimportant. We should keep some perspective about what we're doing. You're only guarding bank vaults here. If Sotheby's went up in smoke tomorrow, it wouldn't even rock the Bank of England. Someone said to me a while back, It's only a ruddy piece of paper. A banknote or a picture, all the same.'

Adrian was offended by the dismissive tone. She and Sheila had that in common, a queenly nonchalance about the material which made his insistence on apportionment and exact dues look pedantic. Else undermined the academic purity which he strove every day to uphold. It did matter. Provenance was proof. He felt he was a simple man bedevilled by the complex, the honest by the false. This woman had such loose standards and was all of a piece in her haphazard rush on life, now manic, now depressive, never reliable. She didn't see the flaws in her own logic, that the piece of paper she scoffed at did have a fixed value, and to lower it artificially by issuing the counterfeit was indeed to rock a nation's credibility. Dealers did not aspire to be swindlers.

Else walked about the room, intrigued by its selective sparseness. There was no pattern, no break, no intrusive colour in Adrian's choice. Only a fall of slub linen curtains and a Berber carpet, the absolute reductionism of the ascetic. This might be why she didn't succeed with him. Other men she could charm, or win over with an allure that suggested the magnitude of diversity. Adrian was able to resist the eclectic. He should have been an oriental, living in a paper house, surrounded by one single element, his clothes spun from fibres of bamboo, even his stylus cut from the reed. His single luxury was books and she strayed towards the bookcase, magnetized by what he did escape into frivolously. She recognized several of them, familiar texts, gifts from Ralph's collection at Odham which he used to press on visitors as they left. One or two of them ... she picked out a volume of Joshua Reynolds's *Discourses* which was inscribed, 'To my dearest Else, and all other anagrams of joy'. She smiled at the memory of when he'd given it to her. A birthday present. It probably did grate on the son every time he looked at that. She flipped the book back in place without comment.

'Sheila sent me a letter,' she said, coming down to business. 'She wanted me to know the house was mine, free and clear, with all the contents.'

'Sheila? Do you correspond with her then?'

'Do I write to her, you mean? Only this once.'

He was irritated again that Else had undercut their joint position of solidarity. 'That was too good of her. I had that scrappy will you sent to Allander and Furness examined by a graphologist who said it was emphatically not Ralph's handwriting.'

Now she did pay attention. So, he accused her of forging a will as well as faking the paintings. She drew a deeper breath, only partially relieved that Sheila's intervention had made the document irrelevant. She'd had her own doubts about the page, turning up in a spot where she'd looked a dozen times. And if she hadn't put it there, who had? Anybody who had access to her house in the hours she left the door ajar, and wished her well, which included several.

'I don't suppose for a minute it did match old samples of his handwriting. He was hardly the same man. Cancer, chemotherapy, a long course of painkillers, what do you expect was the result of all that, Adrian?' She wanted to add that the son had spared himself the closing details of that reaping illness, but held back from being acrimonious. 'I absolutely didn't tamper with anything like that, though I don't expect you to believe me.'

But she saw several things with unsurpassed clarity. Adrian wanted her to get down on her knees and beg, wanted to set his foot upon her neck. He would never have gone all the way to evicting her, or harrying her into court, because that was too public and threatened his tidy in-ness. He wanted only that she submit herself to his authority, and that gave her a signal clue about her own character. She could attract, or magnetize, but the converse of her drawing power was that some were repelled by it. She saw herself reflected in his eyes, moody and changeable and just an irritating person who didn't simplify enough. She wasn't open or self-explanatory, and, like the minimal biography she put out, allowed of several false interpretations. Too late. She'd gone to print.

'What I came to say,' she went on quickly, 'was that Ralph left a box of papers in the house, old letters and personal things. Did you know he'd kept them? Morgan tells me they may be worth something, but I don't want them. I don't rightly know who they belong to. You can sort that out. They're not the kind of thing you want to trust to the letter box, so I decided to deliver them in person.'

He hadn't noticed a small suitcase tucked alongside his desk, camouflaged in brown leather against the wood. He knew this valise of old, with its reinforced corners, the lid stamped with initials. He used to borrow it when it was battered rather than fashionable. Snapping open its clasps let out a hundred other memories. The smell, the stains on the cotton lining, redolent of old journeys, a label stuck on for redirection. The case was heavy, densely packed with memorabilia. It contained four large diary folios, a decade to each, and hundreds of letters which were bundled up by author. Adrian couldn't believe the prestige of the signature names, which unrolled the history of the twentieth century in pictures and in books. The letters were interleaved with Ralph's meticulous replies, tissue transcriptions he'd made, not for his own posterity, but because he didn't want to repeat himself next time round.

He glanced at Else, who was impatient to be off. Did she have any idea what this treasure trove signified? Apparently so. 'I've only one proviso and I'll write to Sheila to that effect when I reply. I don't want them sold. They should go to a public library afterwards, the Courtauld. I don't know, wherever they'd be most accessible to others.'

They were in French, German, Italian – some translating to be done. A long account of a meeting with Modigliani, conveyed fifty years ago by Chagall. The history books would have to be rewritten. Else was handing him access to instant fame, or the opportunity ready-made. In minutes, Adrian had envisaged how the material could be adapted into three volumes, a selection of letters intercut with diary extracts, as Nigel Nicolson had carried it out for his politician father. Ralph lived through illustrious times and knew everybody in Europe who bought above a certain price. Burrell, yes, a small package lay here. And Else had walked through the mugging streets of London carrying this, unshackled. The absolutely irreplaceable.

She waited for him to utter thanks, or even a simple acknowledgement, but Adrian was struggling to find a salve for his conscience. He thought the papers were a bribe, to get her off the hook. His evidence against her was accumulating; very soon, he could have her completely discredited. No one would touch her. He balanced the two: his personal gain and recognition in the world of letters; private triumph over her.

'You must want something for them?' Royalties. A mention as finder, helper, co-editor, some glory.

'Nothing. I'd enjoy seeing Ralph's letters published at last. He was a good writer. He spent enough time on it. I'll mention it to Max. I'd like him to have the first refusal about publishing them.'

Adrian repacked the case, solid edge to edge as with bundles of banknotes. He didn't weaken towards her, only delayed a decision, although some hinter cell in his brain reminded him that if the contents of the house really had been signed over to her, so prematurely by the widow, then the copyright on them was Else's.

Outside in New Bond Street, Else recollected herself. She knew most of the people who passed her on the pavement would say she was a fool to have relinquished her bargaining counter that readily. They were pushers and drivers, by the look of them, bustling to some purpose. She had no push power. Should she have made Adrian sign a receipt for the documents, or a publishing contract, breezed in with a lawyer at her elbow. What an appalling thought. But every single person she could think of would call her inadvertent. She made a reconciliation with her own debts, however, and was accountable to no one.

In the Fisk Gallery, the lights were bright, blazing into the halogens of the enclosure with a neon glare. Good times, fat times. She added up the months, and thought Boris had overlooked her cheque this quarter. Another absurd relationship, that filial dependency. What was the matter with her that she couldn't settle for the one-to-one?

At the corner of Piccadilly, the newsboy stood with the tag end of the daily papers, and a fresh supply of the *Evening Standard*. Its banner headline was repeated on the pavement hoarding in flurried letters, with the vendor's voice reinforcing the message across the hurrying pavements: Stock market falls.

So disoriented was she by the city bustle and the hectic pressures of the last few days that Else misheard or misunderstood. She thought it meant Stowmarket, or another beleaguered, storm-swept village in the south, and put her money down for better clarification.

She read that there had been a huge collapse of monetary confidence, New York, Tokyo, London in domino. The phenomenal market gains of the last couple of years were wiped out in a single day. Private investors were ruined, while the new breed of small shareholders woke up to find their profits were in suspension. It made no difference to her, but there was something uncanny about the timing. Looking again at the faces of the pavement pushers, she thought they were furrowed to meet a world in turbulence. It was strange that she'd mentioned a Bank of England collapse to Adrian, out of the normal run of her concerns, and she wondered if stress endowed her with the power of evil prescience.

It was Lorraine who caught the first rumblings of an organized opposition and, in fact, she was present at the start of it. She'd been asked to lunch in Cambridge by a man she'd introduced to Morgan at her gathering in May, Councillor Adam Robarts, but suspected they hadn't hit it off. He was a useful man to know, one of the small powerful: a former accountant, the man retired early and diversified. A Methodist lay minister, a committee sitter, a phenomenal rememberer, so that Lorraine had only to mention a concert they'd attended and he'd effortlessly add the date. She found he was the opposite of Morgan, eschewing questions because he already had the answer. She was drawn to him and the affirmative. His prime asset was that he did things, got out and met and spoke and connected people to other people, a flood tide of socializing on which she let herself be carried. He was a widower with grown-up, married daughters, older yes, but also richer. Adam was the best of escorts, the more so for being readily available.

And she availed herself. Over the summer, she'd seen him very often. He lightened her, or gave her a new looking glass. She noticed herself again, that her hair and her clothes were turning very ashen, and she changed them. That she spent too long tied to shop-opening hours, pretending she might be busy, and she curtailed them. She closed on Mondays and Tuesdays, and discovered that time could be infinitely adapted, or the concept of the weekend was pliable, stretching from two days to three. Always tidy, she found this could be seen as pretty by someone who was himself neat-minded, just as hard work might be the complement to leisure.

They were twelve at Adam's house outside Cambridge that Sunday, a number which the host juggled skilfully around the table, making the gentlemen move on two places between each course. The relay had its merits, but Lorraine found the conversation never became general across the room or that, occupied every half-hour with a new set of immediate neighbours, she didn't have a chance to talk to the other women present. At the far corner sat the wife of a former mayor, an amusing and talkative lady who, at the end of the meal, proposed something to the whole company which she didn't quite catch. But Adam did, and said, 'Why not? If it's very good, we ought to be in on it.'

Lorraine would second that, happy to drift along a guided path when her powers of resistance were hazed with Croft Original and an excellent Vouvray. This veil thinned a little when the group descended from their fleet of cars outside a church, on the façade of which were hung long floating banners. Beside her, Adam tutted at a small profanity. He was absolutely against such church conversions and always voted down planning consent in council, although he supposed change of use to a gallery or a concert hall was better than to housing.

It was the name that caught Lorraine's attention: PETERSEN. She hesitated at the porch, wondering if she would have come if she'd known who and what they were going to see. 'Do you know this painter?'

'Can't say I do. But Beaty thinks highly of her. A Suffolk painter with a decent pedigree. I'm looking for something modern. This may be it.' The councillor thought he might risk a modest purchase. He had a small collection of English landscapes, with a representative from every decade since 1700, apart from the present one. A waiting space.

Lorraine was intrigued in spite of her reticence. She knew Else well under several secondary personalities, the woman who called intermittently at Bury, the rain-soaked, depressive Garbo look-alike, I want to be let alone, the woman in whom her husband ended his searching, or the woman Derek spoke about with a pained frustration. But still there was a throbbing vacuum at the centre which this set of images might fill. She walked on, ready to be convinced of something primary.

She was constantly interrupted. The room was busy. It was hard to see. Walking companionably beside her, Adam was often heard to tut, which broke her concentration. Methodically, he'd bought the catalogue and sometimes held up their progress while he checked data in this, or rerouted them to see an illustrated picture in its true dimensions.

Lorraine tried to focus honestly on the two-sexed mask, the overlit tree, but they were too strange to take in at once. The sad fact was, as Morgan had instilled in her, she had no creative sense. She thought them clever and heartless. But within earshot, the mayor's wife went on enthusing aloud and several onlookers gathered in a clique of agreement.

'What do you think of it?' Adam asked her in one of the smaller, banner-hung spaces.

'I wouldn't buy one,' she said negatively, 'or maybe I mean I couldn't sell one.'

'They are technically very fine,' he told her. 'But the imbalance is regrettable. Poor choosing. How often you see this, talents out of harmony, or misapplied.' He looked up into the rafters. He had long vision. No matter how high they were hung, he could pick out the obtrusive detail. In his view, those pictures veered towards blatant pornography. The material really was outrageous. He didn't think he was prudish, or pictorially illiterate. He wasn't averse to the anatomical, or even to the depiction of the act of love, tastefully done. But anatomical lovemaking was a different matter, or, as a fellow office-holder put it ten yards away, the subtle difference was between the erect and the inert. Adam applied the standards of obscenity as they pertained to television and publishing. It wouldn't do. This was the stuff that was still locked away in the reading rooms of the British Museum as unsuitable for public display.

Lorraine too averted her eyes from the shape of their sex. No, it wasn't learnable after all, or not by her. At this moment, it was embarrassing because of her escort, or it challenged the modesty of their current address. Unseemly. Indecorous. At the same time, she felt she ought to say something in their defence, that the bold statement always risked offending or that they themselves might be rather staid in outlook. She wasn't impelled to make their passage any easier, Else and her husband, but in the interests of fairness, she should say something.

'I wonder who approved this. I wonder how it ever got past the—'

'Censor? I thought the days of censorship were over.'

'Standards of public decency. This contravenes them.'

'Don't you think we can take it or leave it, as we choose?'

Adam looked around the hall, which was packed mid-afternoon. 'These students. Impressionable.'

She laughed in spite of herself. 'Come now. They've probably seen more life than we have.'

'That hardly condones it.'

Lorraine didn't want to fall out with this man, and sensed how her argument for would only harden his against. She thought of all the other jaunts they could have made, and wished the afternoon had taken a different turn. A walk through the college gardens she always held dear, walking closer to her son with a regret that had its sweetness, for she had loved him perfectly, without reserve, and was not tormented with the idea that she had even once been unkind to him; a small recital where students made a quartet in a room with flawed acoustics; or even stumbling on an organist who was putting in an hour's practice for Sunday Matins or a wedding, filling the wood-panelled chapel so tight with sound that it resonated like a drum. Now that was entertainment. She didn't want to confront the awkward at this moment. Another day.

But Adam had already made up his mind, and wouldn't have been dissuaded whatever she said. He thought the council as a body should re-examine the contents of this exhibition, and in chambers attacked it on several fronts. He asked the Sport and Leisure Department to monitor the application made originally for opening the building to the public. Entertainment. No gambling. No licence for alcohol consumption. Adequate fire access. There were no infringements there. But maybe there was a loophole in the fact that St Martin's, technically designated for domestic redevelopment, was a church and was still referred to by its parish name. At what point did a church cease to be a church? He telephoned the diocesan office of the Bishop of Norwich, in whose see it fell, and ascertained that by a quirk the church had not been deregistered. It was still sacred ground.

In the view of the Councillor, that might alter the charge against the exhibition organizers into one of blasphemy, an ancient offence but revived quite recently when a case was brought against a magazine for depicting Christ as a practising homosexual. He had lauded that attempt, and applied himself more diligently to this.

Nick panicked. As the agent, his name appeared as promoter on all the printed literature, and he was the first contact. Unable to get hold of Else at Odham, he rang Morgan and found that she too was at Covent Garden.

'Trouble. Big trouble.'

'You'd better come round then, Nick.' Calm, together with Else, talking the futures market, the last person he wanted to see was Nick.

They poured him several whiskies before he was coherent, and even then he spoke in syncopated phrases for half an hour before they teased the story out of him.

'But blasphemy's written, not visual. You can't have a blasphemous picture any more than you can have a defamatory one, however grotesque.'

'I'm only quoting. I'm only the messenger in this. Incorrect use of the property. Blasphemy, and the catalogues are to be impounded as pornographic material.'

'Preposterous. The man's a crank.' Morgan was moved to laugh. 'What's his name?'

'Councillor Adam Robarts.'

That dull friend of Lorraine, Morgan recalled. Get her to ask him to cry off? Then he dismissed asking favours.

'We fight it, that's all. If he wants a battle, he can have one.' Else sounded resolute enough. This was the woman who dismissed legal action when she thought she'd lose her house. The only principle she'd go to court for was freedom of expression.

Nick swallowed. 'I'm not sure about that. I'm married to a wife who'll say she doesn't want me to get mixed up in legal wrangles.'

'Surely bad publicity's the best kind, Nick. If we hang on, we could make even more money out of this.' She watched his face closely, but there wasn't even a flicker of recognition for his own premise. Yes, he's a fool, she thought. I knew he'd rescind that opinion in front of a third party, or forget he said it. Forget that I'd remember. How can you talk to a man who's got no memory? She recalled that Clive, talking about the reaction of the villagers to him, pinpointed something that had baffled her from the start about Nick: he did want her work to succeed, if that meant glory reflected on to him, but he wanted her to fail personally, in revenge because she couldn't be impressed by his talents to any reciprocal degree.

'It's a matter of indemnification,' he blustered. 'It's what you stand to lose. The local firms who lent us props, they've got wind of this. I suppose our councillor friend has been leaning on them. They could lose a lot of council contracts. Goodwill. They can't afford it.'

'You mean they want the lights and the scaffolding back?'

'I'm afraid so.'

'So we'd have to dismantle the whole thing anyway?' Folly was turning into farce.

Morgan felt the pulse of rising hysteria and moved in to separate them. 'Damage limitation. How long have we actually been open? Two weeks today. We could close on Monday and say the exhibition was transferring to London.' He hadn't cleared his original idea with Marise, but she'd gone along with stocking Petersens on a larger scale, and he'd make it a resigning issue should she refuse. If space was a problem downstairs, he thought, pacing the subdued arena of his living room, he'd open up his own quarters to the public. They wouldn't make a bad showroom. The height of the stairs would accommodate the biggest of her pictures.

He wasn't going to be downed by a reactionary public servant with overactive scruple.

'But that's still backing down, or giving in,' Else objected. 'I won't agree to it. Crumbling at the first opposition. His complaints are thin, and we ought to take legal advice before we decide anything. Surely we can hold off on the props. We've got contracts, a loan in lieu of advertising costs.'

Nick sucked his cheeks in. 'No. Gentleman's agreement and, anyway, if the catalogues are tied up, there's no reciprocation on our side. We're not doing any advertising.'

'We mustn't waver,' she insisted.

The three attitudes, capitulation, compromise and Else's dogged insistence, seemed impossible to fuse into one plan of action.

'Let's backtrack,' suggested Morgan. 'What are the terms of our insurance policy, if we decide to stick with it?'

'I didn't take one out,' Nick admitted quickly, dodging a display of Celtic wrath. 'It hardly seemed worth it.'

'You didn't insure? But you always insure. What if they'd been stolen, or the whole lot went up in flames?'

'They're too big to steal,' Nick interjected. 'Half of them are bolted in place. They'd kill you if you tried to get them down. The caretaker's living twenty yards away, and no heat in the place. Low-risk venture.'

'You didn't insure. We're not covered.'

Else had kept up a degree of mental attack which the two men could hardly measure. It seemed at last that there was a malevolence at work which she fell silent contemplating. Another abortive exercise. Nothing she turned her hand to would succeed. Luck, or the tenacity that makes luck work, eluded her. She'd had more than her share of misfortune. Ah, was that true? Was that what second-raters said? She heard the men plan the details of a strategic retreat, until Nick got up to leave. He swayed as he walked across the floor, briefcase in one hand, raincoat in the other, with the rapt concentration of a man on a tightrope. He knew he could fall down. He looked old because the attempts at aggression, or even resolution, robbed his features of the character to make such threats stick, or only reinforced his weakness. He would go that way very quickly, from looking young to looking old, pale and puffy, like a watery legume.

They'd talked of every issue except the central one, that there was no reasonable cause for crying obscenity, and that what this stranger hated was the image in his own brain, but not in hers.

She was prostrate again, and terrified of the recurring symptoms of her own malaise. Some diseases hung on in the blood, the tropical ones, fly-borne, water-borne, a strain of endemic sickness which travellers picked up like amoebic dysentery or quartan fever that came back time after time in bouts to weaken and sicken, swell the joints, paralyse the will-power with malarial sweats.

Madness was her recurring nightmare, or the fear of a lapse into a mental blackness and depression so total it was the next worst thing to insanity: the recurring fear that took Virginia Woolf one blameless day to the banks of the Ouse, and set her adrift in it. Else had pulled herself back from the waters of that oblivion many times. She knew it intimately. Even the dearest that I love are strange. Loss of energy, loss of appetite, whole days spent lying down when the fire in her brain and the weight of her eye sockets prevented any constructive movement. What made the spells so acute was an equivalent determination not to accept them, not to be ill, not to make the smallest excuse for her own feebleness. The active part looked down on the inactive with utter disgust at being impeded by what was no more debilitating than a paralysis of will. Get up and walk, one half of the cranium shouted, but the other just wouldn't, and so her limbs failed to function and she fell down again.

November

Nick got back to Greenwich after midnight to find the flat was empty. He'd overlapped with Harriet, who'd spent the day at a trade fair in Birmingham; she'd come in after he went to Covent Garden, changed and gone out again. It wasn't disagreeable to have the place to himself for once, although the question of where she might have gone kept re-presenting itself. Wherever, she hadn't told him, so that the vacant space had an anxious, unaccustomed edge to it. When he said to Morgan and Else, I'm married to a wife ... he'd surprised himself as much as them, in making Harriet an excuse for his own actions. He hadn't consulted her beforehand, so the saving lie came unrehearsed.

He was facing stark ruin. What if it really did come to an obscenity case? It had happened before, if not to him personally. A trial, with no backer, Max, Else and himself meeting the costs out of their own limited pockets. There was nothing so threadbare in the flat that the threat of loss didn't enhance. A sofa from his father's house, whose handsome bulkiness he'd often cursed, became immensely sentimental when he imagined it being bumped downstairs to meet the bailiff's demands.

He didn't think for a minute that he was to blame for Else's débâcle. What could he have done differently, or to change the outcome? Even with blessed hindsight, he was satisfied that what he'd done was good. The thing was impressively mounted and put together. If a madman came along and shouted "Foul!" well, that was the million to one chance that any publicist took, and was uninsurable against. He felt hard done by that Morgan and Else set about accusing him of negligence. Run himself ragged, hadn't he? This was the game without rules or even a code of gentlemanly conduct, so he'd been doubly honourable.

The clock moved to two. The room echoed with its empty chime. Where was she? Just at this moment, Harriet was the one person he wanted to talk things through with. Pretty inconsiderate of her, really.

The room was half dark. He'd lit the lamp over the drinks cabinet and sat nursing a last whisky, which turned into the penultimate. It seemed to clear his vision. He noticed, after an hour of this morose mulling, that Harriet had left a pile of papers on the coffee table, unusually for her, as if she'd gone out in a hurry. He got up to look at them, mostly in case they left a clue to her whereabouts.

On closer viewing, he saw the papers weren't in a mess at all. They were arranged with a clinical regard to system and left conspicuously, so that in the course of Sunday he must read them. She'd typed out an agenda, referring to several supportive documents which she laid out radially round the low table. It ran:

Agenda for meeting 9.30 a.m., Monday, 2 November
Offices of Wylie Associates, Piccadilly
1. Necessary cuts – dismissal of one secretary
2. Lindsay guest at Arts Club, 20 August, purported to be at theatre – JC – inconsistent dates
3. N. Wylie operating separate and undisclosed bank account, review of payments on cheque stubs, e.g. Phillips cheque, July
4. Accountant's report on trading loss – see attached
5. Recommendations – division of business interests – N. Wylie to take paid employment out of London, append file of suitable posts

Not the most logical order, but it would do.

Nick flicked over her supplementary material bit by bit. Thorough, she'd been that. He'd heard of people at the same address who sent letters to each other, not always as lovingly as Proust and his Mama, but this really beat it all. He thought it was horrible and cold-blooded of her, horrible to sit and stoke a volcanic anger since August, horrible to rifle through his private papers for evidence, and positively odd to present him with it in this roundabout way. She couldn't sit down and argue her point of view, because she'd dissolve. Her paper accusations were so weak, they were despicable. Who else was going to be at this projected meeting on Monday morning? The accountant, their solicitor? Was this preparatory work for a divorce? Submissions only, no proof.

His wrath subsided slowly into fear. Hit twice in one day, it was too much for anybody. He didn't think he'd deserved it, or was no worse than many others. Maybe this was a broad salvo, from which Harriet intended to narrow her range. Loss of home, of status and of earnings. Surely she wouldn't penalize him that heavily, although it was gradually dawning on him that his credit rating was intimately bound up with the senior partner and, on his own, he was regarded as a bad investment.

He read through the job specs that she'd cut out for him. Norwich, Oxford, Cardiff. Off the map of the known world as far as he was concerned. He'd never consent to moving off the mile and wasn't going to be pushed. He foresaw a nasty fight ahead, only consoling himself grimly that she hadn't done what many wronged wives were reputed to, slashed his suits or, worse still, slashed his pictures.

True to his promise to take Else to the theatre, Morgan got hold of four tickets for the National, ruthlessly wielding privilege, and asked Max and Sybil to join them for a drink beforehand, and come back to Covent Garden after the performance.

Max bustled round Else fondly. He'd heard of the fiasco over her showing from Adrian Crane, who lost no time in bringing him a sample bundle of his father's letters, one of the journal folios, together with a rough out of how he proposed to integrate the two. Forewarned by Else that this was coming his way, Max had his reaction prepared, but was overwhelmed by an almost sacral reverence. Beginning at an apex, Adrian brought the Picasso letters, a fifty-item addition to scholarship that slotted in before the famous, post-Guernica years. They might trigger a critical reassessment for both of the correspondents. Adrian was well suited to the task of editor: painstaking and academic, he could bring a personal feel to the thankless task of preparing a manuscript. Some books were a matter of destiny. Adrian's major calling might be to promote his father in this way and, as he fingered the deeply creased sheets in awe, Max felt that Ralph's own hour had arrived. After the dead, their letters. The man hadn't received his proper dues, with printing as a profession so ephemeral, or instrumental to the word portrayed. But he'd carried out good work, publishing meticulously scaled books that were still a pleasure to handle, objects in themselves, and some high quality reproductions for the museums and galleries. One copy of drawings for the V and A, with the originals then time-sealed in cabinets for ever, impervious to light. Ralph's life was tantamount to a history of printing in the twentieth century. Time it was told.

Yes, he said unhesitatingly that he would take it on, thinking at the same time he could guide Adrian with paternalistic tact to achieve something close to perfection. The perfect book, it always did elude.

And as for Else, as she came down the majestic curve of staircase at Covent Garden to greet them, he knew he hadn't arrived at knowing her or being unsurprised at what she prompted. She still was a mystery to him. He couldn't analyse her motives in handing over the case of papers to a man who wasn't her friend, because the impulse was so far removed from his own. He couldn't physically have parted with the pages, which made him wonder more. Remote and elliptical, she had a meteoric quality, or the fitful radiance of passing lights. The closure of her show? The canvases packed back into their crates in a warehouse off the M11, that was neither here nor there. A remote author of his childhood, who'd never been successfully translated into English, gave it as his theory of human dynamics that success consisted of going on and on, in the face of failure, until you did something good, and that good would be what others remembered about you, for it eclipsed the bad. The power of reaction which Else elicited was a measure of her dynamism. Such extraordinary things did not befall ordinary people. All she needed was the staying power to convert minus to plus, only compensatory energies on either side of indifference.

Walking quietly at their side, Sybil was wiser. She saw the signs of strain, the waxiness of skin, the distraction in Else's manner and her slow facial responses, quite unlike her usual self, someone drugged on pain. Where was the stamina for any attack to be found in the consciousness of zero?

The play did start out as a diversion for them all. Morgan sat at the end of the row for maximum leg room, Else next to him. By good luck, it was the front row and so they abutted on a semi-apron stage without obstruction, making them intimate to the drama. This was good and bad. It was almost a private performance, if they shut out the open space of the auditorium behind them, reducing it to their row and the players, like a masque at the court of St James for their sole benefit. The actors were so close by, you could see them breathing. It did involve.

Morgan wasn't sure which of the cycle was playing that evening. It wasn't important to his escapist aim. It might as well be *Antony and Cleopatra* as *Julius Caesar*, and better than either of the other two Roman plays, which were best left in book-bound obscurity. He'd heard they'd been produced in modern dress, which he thought was going to be dubious with swords about the place, but it wasn't an absolutely contemporary format. Setting it in the First World War meant that the military uniforms, and the collision of imperialism against more democratic forms of power, had a relevance that managed to achieve the object of intrusive, tinkering devices – it added another layer.

However, he couldn't have guessed the special place this play had in Else's canon. When she was in her teens, she was an ardent Egyptologist, passionate about the alabaster art and water-fertile culture, object- not word-based, unlike the other civilizations round the Mediterranean which stressed the recording of events. The lives of the children of the sun god had passed almost without comment. No poetry. No surviving theatre. Else knew this play intimately from studying it, loved it largely with forgiveness, the idle density, the careless and bitty construction that both moved and impeded the flow, where every word was as familiar as her own response. But she'd never seen it staged till now, seldom going to the theatre, when she preferred *cinéma vérité*.

The ancient language, with biblical rhythm and intensity, quickly took a hold of her, more forcibly because it was known and then forgotten again, and hit her ear like powerful music in which she was attuned to hearing the connective chords rather than single notes. The words agitated her as they built and crashed, setting off ripples of sound and association like echoes coming back to her, describing an intervening span of vacant time.

Morgan could sense that she was balancing on a knife edge. Her attention on the stage was rapt. She followed the minute details of the setting, movement, dress, the *tableaux vivants* by which a knowing director took time to remind the onlooker about a dozen sources he'd woven in, Veronese's 'Banquet', Helen of Troy and the long war of attrition she unleashed, down to the modern version of a culture clash also triggered by religious intolerance. What was this piece but a war of theologies? Else read it all and

251

reflected the sway in her face, while Morgan sat intense through her reactions.

The last act came round, in which she dreaded the climax of recall. The soldiers had gone out of the drama, Antony and Enobarbus, the men of action leaving the men of political manoeuvre to outthink the queen, who, wayward and tempestuous, was ill-equipped to match them. Cleopatra was played this evening by a controversial actress, in that some critics said she was too old for the part, others too heavy, or too serious for the fickle changes of mood demanded of her. She'd worked hard to confound them, and succeeded. She'd a seductive voice, warm over its whole range, so that even when she was angry, it was a laughing angry which made her very appealing in among the grey Fascisti uniforms of Rome, and the shifting-sand idleness of Egypt. She was lustrous. A golden voice and a golden presence, lifted and light against impending darkness. Else was concentrated and had temporarily lost any awareness of herself, fused into one character in the spotlight.

Caesar had been translated into the period Kaiser, keen to take his plunder home to prove and enhance the scale of his foreign victories. The queen's person was simply another piece of booty to parade in his triumphal re-entry to the imperial city.

> Mechanical slaves
> With greasy aprons, rules, and hammers shall
> Uplift us to the view ... saucy lictors
> Will catch at us like strumpets, and scald rhymers
> Ballad us out o' tune.

For Else, this image was particularly grating. She recoiled from physical indignity and the mimicry of the once-noble woman, down to street levels of comprehension, the gold dulled and the lustre gone.

But the poignant messages, like low light, carried further with the flickers of a superior mortality on the wane.

> Finish, good lady, the bright day is done,
> And we are for the dark.
> I am marble-constant: now the fleeting moon
> No planet is of mine.

They got very little further. Else was overstrung by her own internal anxieties and excited by the extravagant bursting emotions on the stage that evoked an old persona in herself, someone who'd read words like these but mislaid an intensity that came back with passionate and redoubled force. Towards the end of the last act, she got to her feet before Morgan could realize what she was about and stop her, and cried out with the spasm of involuntary reflex, 'No! No!'

She said it in rending tones the actor couldn't learn to simulate, a moment never repeated. A hush went round the auditorium, a polite suspension where the audience refrained from reacting, as if they were loath to break the mass concentration, or their own version of empathy. Fortunately, Else's outcry coincided with an end-of-scene change, and the response on stage was stiffness, of holding positions a moment longer than normal, as if they were on camera and waited for a cue.

The sound went ripping through Morgan. She'd gone. Gone over the edge. He felt he was looking down a chasm of the abnormal and couldn't see to the end of it. Somewhere he'd read about such a thing before, someone standing on his chair to berate Shylock when the line of actuality and invention became blurred. It was a foolish oversight on his part, not to anticipate how she'd be moved by the coming suicide. Else was standing completely rigid, her arms clamped in a trance. He touched her and she relaxed. 'I'll take her home,' he said almost inaudibly to Max and Sybil, and motioned them to stay behind to the end. He guided her, practically sleepwalking, towards the exit and got her back to Covent Garden by taxi without another word being spoken.

Morgan gave her a sedative, but paced anxiously throughout the night. He was out of his depth with this. The collapse of the exhibition, on which they'd pinned all their hopes, he could probably turn around, but Else's prostration wasn't so easy. He didn't know the specific cause, or the prognosis. Was she really ill, or mad, or manic? What was madness anyway, apart from a greater localization of heat and feeling than other people experienced?

He watched her while she was sleeping, which felt a particular sort of intimacy, she trusting and vulnerable and childlike, he guarding her through the vigil hours. But there was a voyeuristic tinge to it as well, invasion of privacy where she couldn't hide the involuntary reflexes, the groan, the murmur. This was the room where she wept so oddly about that wretched boy's head, where they made love after its auction back in March, where they'd arrived at a semi-accord with London as the framework, their countryside life the filling, the reality. A long, long way they'd come in half a year.

He thought about her as she was at the beginning, while he smoothed the inert hand, calloused and only partly healed of its neglectful cuts. Cool and composed she'd seemed to him on meeting, although there was a seethe and frenzy going on below the surface he'd not remotely guessed at. Had he pushed her over the edge? There were a lot of contributory factors if this was a breakdown, the threat of losing her house, the actual penury that made her sell those pastiches, as well as the failure of the show, but Morgan couldn't help condemning himself for urging her into that exposure. He did what men did, made her want what he wanted, leading to the unsettling conclusion that he'd used her for his own ends. Yes, she looked frayed while he was mended. Parasitically, he had sapped her. She boosted his ego; she provided the second home, and the second line of success, a sexual relationship with a beautiful and aloof woman which others envied him for. One could read it that cynically. The ultimate irony for Morgan was that she'd boosted him professionally as well. There came these careful, mending women putting him back together, and being discarded in turn when he was whole. Else's had epitomized the kind of work he wanted to promote and be associated with. Who was to say she wasn't the core of his collection at the Green Gallery, attracting likes around a nucleus. Maybe when he seized on her work so feverishly last December it was in unerring recognition of his own need. He was the vacuum. She would fill it.

In the power of the impact, he'd overlooked her needs or the warning signals she'd put out about losing her anonymity. These were pathological fears, although he didn't know what had put them there and maybe never would. The reasons were immaterial. Did he know her any better than a year ago, any better than Max? He knew more of the foreground range, the things she felt passion for and against, but in depth, the background, no. She was still a blank.

Her forehead was moist as she slept, her hair damp. He stroked it in awe and fear and a wave of devotion. He knew this. He'd been here once before, with the same tiptoeing anxiety. But it was a child he loved out of his mind that time, and his apprehension at the brain fever was commensurate. She was too blue, too veined, and familiarly frail.

In the morning, however, she woke up refreshed, torment burned out. 'I'm dreadfully sorry,' she said. 'I misbehaved at the theatre and must have embarrassed you all. I was overwrought. I'll have to ring Max and apologize, and then I'm going home.'

Her charm and good sense were apparently restored. Morgan said, 'I've got to go and see Marise this afternoon, in Chelmsford. My palace summons. I'll drive you back and go in to see her on the way down.'

Morgan knew Marise was brewing something because she'd been silent of late, when her natural style was discursive, challenging but chatty. His contract must be on her mind, as it came round for renewal, but he suspected that she was rewriting the terms in a way that disadvantaged him. There were quite a lot of lapses on his conscience, as it came to signing. He'd left John alone too often, missing too many Saturdays when he preferred to be at Odham, although Saturday wasn't a busy day in the heart of working London. She might niggle at such omissions and he found himself running through a long series of self-justifications that made him cringe.

For once, the room to which the housekeeper admitted him was in a state of mild upheaval. While he waited for somebody to join him, he was surprised at the disarray, of packing boxes and a trunk half-filled with books, and even more so that Marise and Boris came into the room together. This didn't signal the importance of the meeting, as much as their wish to get it over with quickly and back to the packing.

'You're not moving house?' Morgan joked, thinking that to ignore the disorder would be positively bizarre.

'Oh, Boris is having a trip. A walkabout. I think those are very modern terms. Very emancipated.' The woman smiled disarmingly as she settled into her favourite armchair, the position that was promontory more than comfortable. Boris didn't smile back.

'Pleasure?'

'Not business anyway.'

So movements were made off. 'You wanted to see me about my

contract, I presume.' Morgan hurried them along. He'd no time to dawdle either, anxious to get back to London before nightfall and put half a dozen things in hand that he'd delayed while Else was at Covent Garden. There were some imperatives pending.

But Marise had taken to analysis. The three-way meeting took on a valediction for her, which she wanted to prolong in savouring her own past. 'When you came last year, you gave us a breakdown of what you foresaw as the problems you'd be facing. I was impressed. Have you given any thought to the solution of those areas, or future progress?'

No, he hadn't. She'd caught him out. He'd expected a yes or no choice on her dictated terms, or hadn't expected the chess play of moving pieces over positional squares. Frankly, he couldn't be bothered, or had nothing to win. He'd become mentally preoccupied with the doing, or didn't have the redundant man's time to spare. 'Not beyond restating that I've done what I set out to do a year ago. I promised I'd make a profit, and I have, in multiples. I promised I wouldn't be tawdry or embarrassing. You thought cutting the deficit might be enough, but we started to move into the black in February.'

'And the year ahead?'

'Foreseeably, we're tied to the general economy. We're still a luxury commodity dealer. If this down trend goes on, we'll be hard hit. The market hasn't recovered in a month. That's bad. But you could also argue we've pitched ourselves at a level that won't be unduly affected.'

'And for yourself? What will your own progression be from here?'

'Who knows? That's not prediction but prophecy.' He didn't want her prying.

She meant the question kindly and for a few seconds went on assembling her papers like prompts on the side table. She was disappointed in the lack of energy in his reply, and saw him anew as a man more adapted to the management of failure than the capture of success. Boris meantime hadn't settled but paced in front of the garden window, quiet as a panther, impatient at being caged indoors. 'For ourselves, we're on the verge of a transition. Boris has other interests he wants to develop. I don't disagree with those priorities. Time dictates our actions less than crisis but is still the key that winds us. We must plan ahead, Boris and I.'

Morgan saw that she disliked some aspects of the self-review. She didn't look tired but set, as if forbidding herself to run down. 'It always was our intention to offer you a seat on the board. So much you'll have inferred. But it comes increasingly obvious that we have no natural heirs. Who will inherit? Our business has been our life's work. We're proud of it, of the elusive quantity called a good name, and we want to pass it on to someone who will guard it. Do you see? We'd want to offer you a director's chair under some conditions. Part of the package is a block of shares. Profit-sharing is still the best incentive. In time, say ten years, you would own fifty per cent of the company while Boris and I would retain joint share of the other half and look on it as our pension plan. I can't imagine that in ten years' time, we'd be motivated to be active in the running of the business. That's why I asked about your long-term projections. We think you should be writing, being higher-profile, and we look on our offer as a resident consultancy, say three days a week, leaving you scope to follow the other channels. It would be beneficial. What we want to secure is tone. Good taste. The ineffable.'

She drew to a close. Her chair was a tall wing-back, and throne-like, her hair a tiara of blended highlights, while she waited for obeisance.

'I'm flattered,' Morgan said, 'and grateful for the opportunity. The truth is, I've been too busy to give much thought to the way ahead. This is an attractive proposition, but it raises as many questions as it answers. Would I be based at Covent Garden or in New Bond Street? If I'm to have this wide freedom of movement, who's going to do the chairing, the solid commercial and com- mittee stuff that bores me? This is a good outline, one I'd like to work on, but there's a mass of detail missing.'

The unanswered questions mounted. Was it really in her nature not to meddle, however nominally retired? He saw the faxes from Chelmsford proliferating, the phone calls ever more waspish as release from the chores of management added to her potential for interference with the theory. To justify – to argue every point – to be her heir: grim thought. He'd test her genuine liberality.

'I'm a modernist. I'm not sure I want to be tied to old masters every day of the week. I'd want more flexibility to catch the pulse.

For example, I want to transfer Else Petersen's exhibition whole-sale to Covent Garden, make the place less of a shop and more of a true gallery. Use the staircase. Perhaps I ought to move out altogether and release the wall space upstairs. It's that good a venue. Shame to waste an inch.'

Marise didn't look to Boris, although she heard him stop his pacing somewhere in the room behind her. 'What do you mean, wholesale? At reduced prices? I never take remainders.'

'I mean in their entirety. Her complete output.'

'From that abortive exhibition? To Covent Garden. I think not.'

'Why not?'

'Her work has become tainted.'

'What with?'

'With self. We can't take that sort of risk. It's as well you mentioned this. Last year, if you recall, I said we reserved the right, Boris and I, to veto certain artists whose motives we felt were not in accord with ours. Sensationalism we have never courted. I would prefer not to carry Else any longer.'

Yes, he did remember the warning, on which she served her first exclusion order. 'You recapitulate, Marise, and so must I. I can't work with you looking over my shoulder. I haven't moved position either and you won't curb my choice. I think your reaction is personal and so I'll be personal too. Love me, love my dog is a primitive code of loyalty but it serves. If you can't respect my judgement on this, you respect it on nothing.'

Marise breathed heavily with indignation. She hadn't meant to confront him at all. He'd pushed the issue on her and she floundered with an argument for which her papers and profit graphs hadn't prepared her. It wasn't a straight swap bribe, Give up Else or go. He'd overreacted but she was so taken aback, she had no reserve position. He had snubbed her, in the very heart of priceless giving, he turned her away. Morgan was a man you couldn't bribe or threaten because he was his own resource. He wouldn't be her protégé, or placeman. She could throw him over if she liked but knew that in the past year, under her tutelage, he'd gained an advance of reputation which others would take up.

This he knew.

'You've made me an offer, Marise, which broadly I reject, but I'm prepared to make you one in return. I offer to buy Covent Garden and its stock at current market prices. I did have it valued. The building is not hugely saleable. You had problems with it before and will again. What I am selling there is me, and nothing else will work.'

'You buy it?' she cried in disbelief. 'What with?'

'My investments. Proceeds from purchases and sales. The same formula that other people use. Half cash, on Monday if you like. The other half I can raise a bank loan on without difficulty.' Prompted partly by MacPherson's state of floundering dependency on her goodwill, partly by Derek Hisslop's hint, he'd sold his entire collection into which he'd sunk his annual salary. He didn't like selling, when it felt like cashing in his life insurance policies early, ahead of the final bonus, although he recognized there was a freak variable he'd harnessed. They were private sales from his private apartments, hung along the landing and the drawing room, no need for entry into the stockbooks. The profit on his initial investment was fourfold. He set his own agenda and was a freeman.

'Do it,' said Boris.

'Never.' She needed no sideways suggestion from a man intent on exhuming his ancestors. But the word was an escaped wish. She knew that was the way it would go. She'd hung on to her offer of preferment too long, until Morgan didn't need it, and was left with an embittering sense of having nested the cuckoo.

Boris stepped in to salvage what he could of mutual wreckage. 'We've tried to go too far in one session. A step at a time. We agreed the first premise. It's still on the table. Let's hold on that and reconsider your plan in the light of it. There may be another formula. We'll come back to this another day. There's a little time in hand before the start of the New Year.'

The two men rose and Boris offered him a hand as they reached the outer porch, although Marise neither spoke nor moved to acknowledge their shifted positions.

November

Dear Boris

I've come back after a long absence and go through a bit of ritual nest-turning. I pass a good, settling-in sort of afternoon. I've never felt so be-longing before. I walk into one room after another, where my eye falls on a set of sun- and wash-pale linen covers, or the time-rubbed carpets, and it's all as worn and comfortable as my own skin. I slip back into it with sheer repose and wonder why I ever go away.

The storm blew through here, uprooting one of my best props and I thought I'd never recover from the loss of it, but, gratifyingly, I do. Confronting the empty space, I find I prefer it, for it creates openings and views I can take solace from, like chinks of perception in the mind. One may lose innocence, but experience is a more open and beneficial vantage point.

Later, I took a few presents up to the farm for the boys, motor cars you build out of a kit. I'm looking forward to having a lengthy play with those myself. I haven't told you much about the Ramages, because I take them for granted, like the house. They're intrinsic to my daily life. I see them every day. I like each one of the four in a special sense but my favourite is their joint persona, the family. Their welcome was so hearty, I was touched by it. A cushion with the offer of the fireside chair, a cup of tea, come and see the pigs, this is my new football, I came first last week – as if I was needed and wanted, and the whole fascinating ordinariness of their news had to be reviewed through me to be complete. It gives me more pleasure to be their honorary relative than I can easily say because it defines gentle acceptance. They ask no questions, which exempts me from telling lies. Or maybe I mean they gloss with the understanding of families, but have the supreme advantage that I was able to choose them in the first place.

I do attach myself laterally to things. I had some schooling, but I wouldn't call it an education. Had some people, but not what you'd call a family. I don't like those big, big words like art and literature. I'll settle for plain pictures and books and one-off people. I don't expect any more than that.

I potter. I go back into the studio which is a place I'd frankly been afraid of, and kept till last. It stands empty, cold, chill, bare. All my finished pictures are stored elsewhere in limbo, but, you know, that's no bad thing, a bit of artistic amnesia. To be temporarily robbed of your past cleanses the palate in both senses, as astringent as salt or lemon – oh, bitter if you're expecting anything pleasant to come your way, but strong and tasting and more durable than saccharine success.

So I begin again. This is called picking up the pieces and

people do it every day in humble walks of life. The livestock gets foot and mouth disease and is put down. The land fails to produce in a season of abominable rain. Your marriage crumbles, your business goes into liquidation although you put your best into the endeavour, and you just can't trace what went wrong. Not knowing is the most frustrating aspect because, if you did know, you'd eliminate a repetition of disaster. I used to think those Shakespearian metaphors were overdone,

> As flies to wanton boys
> Are we to the gods. They kill us for their sport—

and unacceptably cynical. But, if you accept the despair of it as a precondition, not a bar, you can move forward. Fighting the pain is pointless. You have to learn to control it by absorption and turn it into energy.

I am hurting, bruised and tender all over, in every part of me. I am mystified about its source or resort to the useless imprecation, Why me? I tried my damnedest, why can't I succeed? The only remedy I know is to get out the stepladder, covered with the spatter of a hundred earlier efforts, light the paraffin stove and note my own excellent order in the arrangement of the hardware, with the brushes clean, the canvas ready. There are no excuses there. The ideas wait for my input of a system, and I feel the old thrill about how to do it stirring in me. I've a commission to fulfil. Man and wife want me to paint them. It's the drudge work but it comes with payment secured and, who knows, I may like them and do something worthwhile. I've no notion what will happen next, that is next week, can only try to keep as positive and cheerful as I would do for others in my predicament.

> We two alone will sing like birds i' the cage;
> When thou dost ask me blessing, I'll kneel down,
> And ask of thee forgiveness; so we'll live,
> And pray, and sing, and tell old tales, and laugh
> At gilded butterflies, and hear poor rogues
> Talk of court news; and we'll talk with them too,
> Who loses and who wins; who's in, who's out;

> And take upon 's the mystery of things,
> As if we were God's spies.

Pity. The old words are the best.

The mail has piled up in my absence. I sift it half expectantly. Bills. Junk. For deeper consideration. There's precious little of the last. I come to the end of the envelopes and my fears are confirmed. There is nothing from you and never will be again. I am very demoralized about that, not because I miss the money, which I frankly will, but because it was one of the few continuums in my life. Every three months for nearly fifteen years. That's longer than most things for most people. The strokes falling at regular intervals lead us to expect the next chime at the quarter. I begin to mark time.

Why have you gone away? is the simplest question to ask, and the hardest to answer. You probably don't know why you've cast me off, or there's a complex mesh of reasons that's impossible to unravel. You're not the first to do it. A lot of people take against me unaccountably. My friends forsake me like a memory lost, said the man who knew. And I've done the same thing myself, walked out of relationships or discarded them, like an object one is suddenly tired of dusting and throws out. But will you miss it in afterdays and wish you hadn't been so hasty? I hope so. There was something there. I don't know what it was on your side but on mine it was the source of confidence, that you liked and supported me for nothing I could tangibly give but out of an absolute and pure impulse towards patronage; buyer, father, friend in one.

But maybe it was all wrong, the whole thing slewed like almost everything I've done, because it was marked in secrecy and false assumptions. I face a rather hard fact about myself, that I'm a cheat for having encouraged a good half-dozen people to tolerate me for the sake of a potential which I may not realize. Mistaken identity: that's mine. The letters I've written to you over the years are an analogue of the best in me, and the worst. I've put everything into them, spared nothing and hidden nothing. Nobody in the world has been a party to my thoughts as intimately as you. And yet we're strangers when we meet. We don't celebrate any of the anniversaries or the conventions. We don't commune. Like much else, it's been a passionate effort and outpouring to no avail. I find I am speaking into silence. The echo is rejection.

Goodbye. Goodnight. I feel exempt from any form of obligation, and you are from yours. I do thank you nevertheless for what we had. The envoi is without bitterness or complaint.

Else finished the letter but held the pen poised for her closing signature. The landing where she always wrote had shrunk down with the onset of evening, and she was writing without artificial light, the words outlined by a glow given off by the white page. She therefore jumped when, out of this silent gloom, a head appeared up the well of the staircase, indecipherable in its features except that only Morgan would walk into the house without knocking, or an intruder. Morgan it was. Leaving Chelmsford, he'd wheeled about and driven the twenty miles back north again. To hang with the Fisks and servicing their priorities. They'd have to wait for another day.

'What has she done?' Else cried, seeing the wrath twist in his face. 'Refused to renew your contract? Or is it me?'

The swift deduction caught him off guard because, in the seethe of his thoughts on the road, he'd not worked out what to say to her. The moment he saw her, sitting alone in the dark space, he knew he'd been mistaken to follow the returning impulse. His troubles were his own. However implicated, Else didn't have the mental resource to share them at this moment, couldn't be baldly told, Marise wants to wipe you off the list. He took off the constrictive jacket, which he hadn't noticed was irritating him in the driving seat, and threw it into the doorway of the bedroom, where, missing any supportive piece of furniture, it heaped on the floor.

'She sacked you?'

'Oh no. Quite the reverse. They wanted to adopt me. Their heir. Did you ever hear anything so unnatural?'

'Tell me what she said. She said she's going to leave you the business? Or is she offering you advantageous terms for sale, as long as she can have a trade-in on your soul?'

'A bit of both. Yes, the Faustian contract would appeal to her. I should have said that.' Sitting down opposite her, he steadied, and switched on the Anglepoise that lit them too sharply. 'It was meant as a compliment. I did manage to acknowledge that. Company shares were on offer. Considerable freedom to do what I wanted, or construct my own job specification, it seemed.'

'Then why?' The interrogative light pulled them together, so that Else could feel his confused emotions firsthand, she prompt, he feel.

'Because she means to own me and, whatever happens, I'm afraid I've made an enemy I'll never get clear of.' In some mental warmth, he ran through what he could spell out to her, although he was loath to talk about plans ahead of finalization. In the concentric focus of the spotlight, he became aware of what she'd been doing, and how she'd spent part of her afternoon while he was with the Fisks. She'd been writing a letter. Three pages of amplitude impressed themselves on his retina where, even upside-down, he could read the opening salutation. Dear Boris. Else followed his downward eye but didn't make a move to cover the sheets or any part of her writing, remembering how Adrian had shuffled up his papers like a clerk to prevent her peeking. She valued privacy, not secrets.

Morgan was susceptible to jealousy and to anger, an inflammatory mix. He remembered that over the last year, he'd been exemplary in granting Else considerable licence, hadn't asked or probed or followed up, which left him in an agonizing state of doubt for a man who had to know everything. Nick said she had a rich sugar daddy and Nick's gossip usually had one grain of fact, albeit misapplied. Boris, it transpired, was intent on travelling. Did he have a companion designate? The skiing trip resurfaced. Slowly, to put his mind at rest, to see if she'd resist, Morgan turned the pages around while she reproved him only with a wordless dignity, refusing to protest or snatch her letter back from his insolent perusal.

In a warm mood, he wasn't able to make sense of what was written there. He only knew that the imaginative score wasn't composed for him but for some other man. Its real emotion was directed elsewhere. He thought there was a profound dishonesty in her screed, more lying than she knew. She never did clear the air or talk things out with him. He looked back at the vastness of omission in their dealings, the worn-out passions they'd avoided, which most men and women reprocessed into energizing strength, and felt the reason they hadn't made real, cementing, normal progress was that Else had put her past into a vacuum, and capped it with its own enclosure until it went bad. What was he to make of the tone of this letter? Its pleas, its heartache were perturbing, having no actual cause. A plain man might reason that he'd risked a major sacrifice for her, exclusion from his own circle by tying his fate to hers – although there was a balm to his guilt that this was on the downward as well as the upward curve – while she went slyly plotting and hatching behind his back and, because of her strangeness, was unlikely to discover what it was he'd gambled on her behalf.

'Pshaw,' he said, pushing the sheets back across the expanse of the library table. 'You've got too much black on to your brush. You need to lighten up.'

She quietly tidied the corners into symmetry. She was good to hurt because she felt so much or had no flip answers. His own pain eased as, languid and passive, she turned away, exposing the broader reach where he might land a blow. She'd changed out of her city-smart clothes and was back in the big cotton wraps she liked, a beaten blue jacket, a white collar turned up inside it, her hair in one long, simple tail. She'd regained her composure in her own setting, isolationist and withdrawn.

'I mean, can't you stop being so bloody weird?'

'Is that your definition of someone who won't feed tittle-tattle?'

'You need to learn to make distinctions of degree.' He should have said this a long time ago, when she smashed the plates on to the floor, but he was afraid of a more stormy outburst. 'Confidence in the human race isn't always abused. I'm not an abuser. I just get abnormally frustrated when you don't let me in. Don't talk, explain. Other people speak to each other. Do you know that? They go in at the negotiating stage and talk things through.'

'Ah, you have the advantage of me there. You got things abundantly right the first time. I never acquired the habit of tell all.'

Her rare sarcasm silenced them both while her eyes fell back to the unfinished note.

'Boris? Is this about poor Boris? He's a man to be pitied, you know, someone who missed his aim. I wonder what you're thinking with that feverish need you have to be presented with reasons. I won't tell you all, but I will tell you something. For a while, Boris thought he was my father, or he wanted to be. The adoptive tendency can be quite strong in some people, or quite misplaced. I wasn't fostering material any more than you. By a bizarre coincidence, I'd changed my name, yes, I changed it consciously. Not by deed poll. I didn't have to be so formal since nobody important knew about my previous existence. Anyway, I like colours that shimmer a little. It was this invention Boris was drawn to. By accident, I'd fabricated something that fitted with what he was looking for. What's that anyway but a definition of love?

'When that fell through, he thought he might want to be my lover. I did meet him between men. And it would have been not impractical from either side. There's a strong affinity. I found his silences companionable, or compatible with mine. He is a silent man. Some men you can breathe in harmony with. But I already knew Ralph, was indebted to Ralph, and his talkativeness was more compelling. It's true, I'm a woman who lives on men. Not cynically, or in the slightest way grasping. I don't want their money. I want their—'

She hesitated in this long preamble, searching for the apt word. In the end she tapped her head, while a current passed between the hand that did and the brain that thought. 'Expertise. Experience. The rest, well, one has to put up with that as the standard coinage. You have to consent to be imaged. Live up to the image.'

Ever a reluctant speaker, she changed in the act of talking. It was a great effort in which the features, mostly somnolent because she relied on being seen, not heard, turned unexpectedly mobile. As her tongue loosened, her face relaxed. Not happy or smiling, but relaxed in the sense that the muscles became elastic and expressive. The thing convinced, in the same way that the provoked 'No! No!' at Cleopatra's end stood in his recollection as an absolute of despair, that life and light were imminently ending.

'This image, what is it? Other people attach to me something which I'm not. Being touched by Nick in the corners of his mind, the amorous phone calls at midnight when Harriet's elsewhere, I didn't want that. The real horror in being molested isn't the men you don't know, but the men you do. I can see the same sort of tendency in you, wanting me to be profligate, willing me on. But I'm not. I'm completely simple, or innocent. I've slept with two men before you. One so young and one so old, they hardly counted as men. There wasn't any real pleasure in it either, I never had much pleasure from them. Can you match that for virtue? Well, I wouldn't ask you.' She shook her head. 'It's disgraceful that you're forcing me to say this, because it's my absolute self. Why must you know me so much? When you know me, you destroy me. I am illusion. When have I ever asked you an intrusive question? You're sacrosanct to me. Everyone is. If I'm not told, I don't ask. But for some reason, my silence begs questions. I don't know why. Sex, aura, even my hair, something I can't help having.'

Before he could intervene, Else moved ahead of him again. The library table held a wide tray of stationery items, from which she picked up a pair of scissors. With one savage snip, she cut the long yellow pony tail that was hanging on one side of her shoulder and, with a gesture of complete disgust, she threw the misleading ornament on to the floor behind her. Fifteen years' growth she discarded. Without it, the rest looked ridiculous, partly because it was six inches longer under the right ear than the left.

As he watched her do this, two parallel sequences unrolled in Morgan's head. He could take the scissors and even up her lopsided cut. Smoothing and equalizing were talents he was wearing thin, however, compared with the impulse to say it simply hadn't worked, and leave. They'd brought each other more trouble than compensating ease. He thought that, at this moment in his own crisis, she might have given him the sum of her attention. It was true she didn't harass with questions – but sometimes he wanted them, wanted to feel the butt of her enquiry and her curiosity, expressing warmth. Between their respective positions of total introspection and total openness, there was still no common ground.

He got up. It was pitch dark. The curtains were open, the window on the latch as usual, the cone of light hard on her slant-away face and hair. He shivered and went to retrieve his jacket, from which half-way position it was easier to go downstairs and out of the door and into the car, which had barely had time for the engine to grow cold, and drive off down the wooded lane, because at no point would she call him back. Again and again and again.

Else waited motionlessly, guessing by the soft fade of sounds where he'd got to on the outward path, reached the notice, then the B road before the car roared off into the darkness. She shivered in turn, feeling an unaccustomed draught cool on her exposed neck.

She'd been justified. He compelled her to part with something of her own, a truth or a memory, and sure enough he despised it. She dragged a fact shy and palpitating into the light of scrutiny, and watched it being trodden on. Men only wanted their dreams safeguarded. Truths and memories were utterly personal and unsharable, so that, giving them away, she felt diminished. And it was that as much as the expurgated hair and the certainty that there would be no renewal between them which made her put her head down on the blame-inducing sheets and cry, bleak and unhappy, for the first time in months.

The dream came back. She dreamed it when she was alone at nights. She was alone in a hospital bed, naked and vulnerable to view, lying with her legs through the obstetric hoops while a doctor was at work painting her insides. He painted her with a set of very long-handled brushes and in several colours. Black and blue. And shades of red, tincture of iodine, and the mauve of meths. The smell of the compounds wafted back to her, nauseating her, while he went on grinding and mixing at the operating table for hours. The process was an endless ordeal. He touched her somewhere deep. He touched her where it hurt.

That was the first pregnancy, at nineteen years of age, gestation sixteen weeks. She terminated it unwillingly or unknowingly – that is, without realizing the consequences. In another sequence, a woman sat at a kitchen table, draining tea, rubbing a cigarette out in a pool of dirty liquid, and said, 'The only way I'll help you is to pay for the abortion.' Those words echoed over and over again down the years, across space; she had stitched them into a personal sampler of mother love. Then the woman turned round and picked the green notes off the wall behind to pay for her handiwork, evil indoors. Consulted and confided in, that was her best offering, a wad of bank notes. It was the sum of Else's value and her child's value, at nineteen, while she was still so naïve that it would have made the most hardened person weep for pity. She'd no resource to put against experience and the brutal wisdom of the cynic.

Wrong to do it? Yes, she was wrong. But she was also very sick, frightened, single and had other potentials that were more immediate. Time enough for the baby business later. She listened to the rationales of talent and was persuaded against a deeper judgement.

While they were at it, they had stitched another sentence under her skin. We have introduced a small infection, small infection, small infection. Did it scan? Did it rhyme in some way that made it so very memorable in the middle of the lonely nights? There were no more pregnancies. The first was the last. People don't die of abortion, if they're done properly, they told her, it's quite safe now, no danger whatsoever. No, but women can die through them or after them, can kill themselves and kill others. Her latent potential receded as this one talent became the most important thing she could have achieved, negating the rest.

She'd had the dream visited on her for years afterwards – who would wish it on themselves? – the doctor, matron, mother couple, at one, and indistinguishable from each other, left hand right hand hauling out her innards on a trolley. The ritual disembowelment.

I was mad, she often thought, I went mad for a while, and wept without control at trigger words.

Nick came along in time and joined in the hallucination, while sometimes Marise swung into view, passing the same soiled wad of notes between them. Abort, they said. Abort, girl. We want whatever it is you've got inside yourself. Abortion on demand. They sold this fine-spun tissue of hers, replacing the notes that spilled out of their other fist, while they went on prodding and prodding her, goading her to miscarry to better purpose next time. You will do very well to reach that pitch again.

It is the unfinished work.

She thought how often she'd come close to confiding all of this to Morgan, and now was glad she hadn't. He wanted his own reassurance. He was warm and clean and comforting, and she didn't take that small normality for granted. But how could you say to such a man, I haven't got the aptitude for sharing? She didn't know how to put her trauma in his context. What would he make of the savage images that erupted in her head, and in which any lover was implicit – her body violated, her self-esteem nil – apart from think her savage and strange as well? Why me? Why is this injustice served on me that makes suffering such a close companion, and drives away other friendships, puts out the fire in rooms, draws blinds on light? I have a hole in my heart where happiness used to be. Say that out loud? Impossible.

The most erudite utterance ended up belittling what it tried to say. She'd already discovered that the words she might have chosen to mould her experience were unreliable, more likely to be misquoted, repeated in brief or out of context, and tended to portray in burlesque or one-liners what in full expression might have been a noble and sombre play – not the stuff of men's plays but the stuff of women's, and forever unwritten.

December

Darkness fell in London. Day work was a prelude to night work. There wasn't any final switching off. He moved desks, moved rooms. Lights burned late.

A year later, almost to the day, Morgan signed his second contract with the Fisks. That was how it looked on the surface. In fact, Boris did the deed in a formal meeting at Allander and Furness; Marise wouldn't come to table. The man always had been the signer but Morgan sensed that this way, when he was gearing himself for off, she could blame him for the transaction in his absence, saying it was all his idea. *A foible I indulged and maybe it's sensible to tidy up and shift the back stock of one's life. Of course, Morgan made us a fabulous offer ... why refuse it?*

The two men stayed amicable through the negotiations, or left big open spaces where the questions hung unasked. It went smoothly, a formal written offer, a speedy acceptance. The intrigue was in the details. Morgan wanted to take over the stock of pictures – they were his mission statement, after all. No point in sending them back to their owners and then having to negotiate replacements. Better all round if the transition was invisible.

He'd thought Marise would haggle to the end, but she passed over the contents indifferently. What she seized on was the decorative fittings she'd supplied and, when he read her inventory, he was dismayed that it ran to bedlinen, the lantern in the hallway, the carpeting, for which she asked five-sevenths' cost, the amount left over from what she'd claimed against tax relief in setting up the gallery. In his head, he heard an old echo, *Else in this same room sending notes around the walls* to haunt him. *Marise doesn't care about paintings, that or any other.* And so it proved. Marise would fight him on brass taps and so many yards of muslin, but the glorious concept passed her by. He regretted that the woman with the power had no vision and no loyalty. So be it. They were done.

By mid-month, he was the new owner of the Green Gallery. The thrill of handing over keys hadn't faded, although it was twenty-five years since he'd last bought bricks and mortar, in the square at Bury. He came back from the final exchange of contracts late one afternoon, put on all the lights and walked round every foot of wall, feeling jubilantly buoyed. The position he'd arrived at consolidated the value judgements of his working life, as if nothing he'd done so far had turned out to be a side issue but bore towards a climax, which formed itself in praise. He can't go wrong, he can turn his hand to anything, were plaudits others had given to his career. He started to believe them, brushing up the nap of his confidence.

By day he worked hard at this social asset, whatever it was, selling, representing, talking up. By night he wrote in solitude. He burrowed himself in the thick mantle of mid-city darkness, apportioning his schedule and his energy strictly. Two hours and a break of one. Two hours and a break of one. Morse code for slog. The young Dickens worked around his paid schedule that way, probing into the early morning time, the older William Morris. He exploited the silent, concentrative hush when the traffic stopped, and the Strand reverted to the natural line between sea and land, and was a quiet bay.

He'd started to write systematically again when he was on trips away, prompted partly by Max's assumption that he'd never stopped and partly by Else's that the time was right for a reappraisal. The New Revisited? He overhauled his old notebooks that had lain about for years, and felt he could requarry what had been worked-out seams. So the outline of his diary engagements and transactions merged into an alternative current; or became a second yield from the same source. Doing and then writing. Forming an opinion and broadcasting it. He didn't esteem one over the other but, as he'd perennially done, found the balance of an active life and reflective penmanship close to his ideal.

He had Max's ear. They discussed dates and deadlines, which gave Morgan the old sensation of being driven, for good or ill, into a narrow pen or over a waterfall, hazardous, painful, blood-pumping, but the real current of energy. He gathered stray references, hunted better words, banged them down on the page with the frenzy inculcated by definition and time. He'd have to put in the last word by the New Year.

Head down, he was frequently distracted by something that cut across his line of vision, a speck in his eye he couldn't remove, more of an irritant the more he blinked and poked and drove it further in. Maybe it was only a space or a tiredness or that flaw they called the blind spot, except that it didn't feel like vacancy. It felt like plenitude and sometimes he was so distracted by the speck or spectre or spectrum that he was forced to put his pen down and attend to it.

What did he miss about her? Everything. The weight on his arm, the buzz in his head. It was as well his energy was subsumed in print because sexually he was going quietly out of his mind. Her exquisite finishing gestures came back to him, like endpieces that close a theme. The only woman whose last touches didn't make him squirm, just shifts of weight or balance. He was curious about what she'd taken out of him and what those sounds meant, despair, joy, a birthing of some sort. What was she thinking about him? What was she doing?

His anger cooled more slowly this time, partly because he was more ashamed of himself. He hated the fiery ball that raged around his brain with her fanning, when it impeded logic and proper concentration. The sheep pen and the waterfall looked like leisure pursuits compared with the stress of sorting out his reactions to Else, and he resented how she took up residence in one room of his brain, driving out his whole occupancy of himself.

He re-tread their events. He thought she'd never told him a barefaced lie, just hadn't been forthcoming with the truth, a significant distinction. So when she finally said, two men before you, one so young and one so old they hardly counted as men, that took hold of him all right. He thought she wasn't somebody hiding secrets, as much as hiding the fact that there weren't any. That was a basic mistake to make about anyone. Translating the text of their lives with her sentence as the key, he deciphered that after the catatonic meeting with him at the Slade, he blithely unaware of her fixation, she went to live with MacPherson over the summer months. Why that relationship broke down, he'd probably never know for sure but he slotted other phrases into place to see how they would read. Free love? I'd like to see it. Nothing's free for me. Did that fit with a pregnancy that was unwanted and terminated, whether by accidental means or induced, leaving her mentally scarred? The suicide attempt afterwards. A philanthropist who came along and fell in love, not with her, but with what she could do. Clever fun. He wouldn't disagree. She'd put in fifteen years at charitable repayment of Ralph's kindness. Some price she paid for her restorative peace.

Would that fit, superimposed on the missing sections, to form a whole? It passed for one, in an unsatisfactory way, like a long run of canvas someone had seen fit to cut down to fit into small rooms, or suit diminishing fashions. Even when they were reassembled, the parts defined most clearly were the missing ones.

This time, Lorraine didn't include him. She held a small drinks party before Christmas, placed to lead into the general festivities but be distinct from them.

Since the summer, she'd overhauled the house as well as ending her personal, dust-settled greyness. Else Petersen's visit in July propelled her into facing several upheavals, the principal being that Morgan wasn't coming back. She'd half hoped he would, keeping a mental door ajar, but watched it close imperceptibly when the young woman took up her umbrella and set out in the downpour across the square in Bury.

Dozens of them there had been, adoring muscled intellect. Some bought, some browsed, some probably stole pathetic little things to cherish in lieu of the man himself, but none of his fans had materialized into a lover before, or none that she knew of. The wife rather resented being housekeeper to Morgan's reputation, when it included being stared at and dismissed in turn. A very insipid woman, she could hear them think, how disappointing. Would they have been more fascinating additions? Her door-holding was over, and when it finally shut, she found she warmed up after losing so much of her surface energy through him. The invitation cards thickened and the thank-you notes along the kitchen mantelpiece. A phrase she cherished was, I'd love to come to dinner but I'm terribly busy for the next few weeks ... although the cynical man lingered in one cell of the receiver, saying, Busy with what, Lorraine?

Adam busied too, active and propelling. At the far end of the upper sitting room, he lined up bottles more methodically than Morgan, who drifted into talk and forgot his duties as a host. Adam

274

had come up with a brilliant little system of different glasses for different drinks, so that he could replenish without interrupting the conversation. White in the tall stem, red short, punch round goblets. She liked this neat-minded man. She liked his close range, his love of detail, his reference to the scale of the provincial town, neither term a denigration. Morgan's cleverness made her fretful, because it tended to suggest some core work she hadn't read, or a name she muddled up which invalidated her comment. Books are only ideas that have been printed, she once objected tentatively, and I have plenty of ideas of my own. He howled.

Part of her clearance was his books. She'd emptied the shelves, sent her once-read novels off to charity shops, and put his own volumes to the side, for sending on. She sifted after all into bundles of his and hers and, no matter how much common sense prevailed, it was an awful wrenching separation. They were propped up against a far wall, laid sideways like uncemented bricks.

Her guests were bright. Someone was planning a summer fête next year on a date she mentally circled. The prospect pleased because they juggled round Ascot, the Wimbledon final and Henley, bringing these luscious, sun-laden days nearer. Unwillingly, she heard a sentence spoken over in Adam's group that made her wince. 'Have you heard that Morgan and that Petersen girl split up? The painter. Sudbury way.'

The tones dipped. An empty glass asked for refilling and she lost the rest of it.

The wince was manifold. She didn't want a rift because it made her responsible for Morgan again, burdening her conscience. She dodged admitting to herself that she'd formed her own connection with that strange young woman. She didn't want Adam in on any untidy postscripts and was thoroughly displeased when he said, the moment everyone left, 'You didn't tell me there was a link between your husband and that painter whose exhibition was closed.'

'*Was* it closed?' She hadn't asked for details.

'There was no acrimony. Her team just folded. No staying power.'

'And the pictures?'

'They're still in crates in one of our warehouses.' Adam concentrated on tidying glasses on to trays by size. 'Nobody is claiming them.'

'What do you mean, claiming?'

'The council wrote to an agent in November about removing them but they've had no reply.'

'And what will happen to them if they're not claimed?'

'After six months, all unclaimed property is destroyed. Incinerated.'

She cried out in spite of herself. 'No, that's not right. There's been some mistake. I can't let that happen.'

'Those are the rules,' he said. 'All the lost property, buses, libraries, you can't hang on to it for ever. People don't even know what it is they've mislaid.'

'I'll tell Morgan. I don't think he can know.' She hadn't cared for those effulgences at Cambridge, but knew her own opinion was subjective and that she was a dull judge. Several things she was able to discount in the scale of her reckoning, the putative worth of them, and the fact that she'd been supplanted by what she didn't understand. Else the painter; Else the lover – they were nobodies to her. But Else the pale, the courteous, the damp presence, she'd started to look forward to the slight apparitions and respected a quality the more for not being able to define it. 'If no one else claims them after six months, I'll make myself responsible for what happens to them.'

'You'll have to sign.'

'OK. If the worst comes to the worst, I'll sign for them.'

Adam took a short turn about the room, drawing the curtain as if it were his own. 'Not quite above board, this. I'm disappointed by what you say. I still feel my own behaviour is completely vindicated.'

'Cousin to vindictive.'

He bridled at that. 'Nothing of the sort. By not telling me that she was anything to Morgan, you've given it that complexion, as if I acted knowingly. I was quite impartial. I don't like moral equivocation. Those things were unhealthy and unfit to be shown in public. End of story.'

Lorraine blanched. For half of her life she'd been pulled in the other direction by a man of Zionist liberality, to whom the fact that a thing existed was its justification. Intolerance was a philosophy she'd given up on. She could find one good word to say for everything and that made her feel old. Adam's closing arguments sounded easier because they didn't harbour opposites but, in truth, all she wanted to do was wash the glasses and then go out for dinner at the Angel Hotel.

A week before Christmas, Morgan stopped pretending. He knew Else didn't have it in her to apologize, while he couldn't sustain a feud with anybody long-term. Lorraine's phone call about the impounded pictures, still crated off the M11, made him nervous, so he personally arranged for their insurance and transportation. He thanked her for calling, knowing she'd had to go against several tendencies in herself to ring him. He remembered that when his mother met Lorraine for the first time, she'd approved with the phrase, She'll be as good as her word. Slight, the commendation swelled in time because her plain-dealing turned out to have rarity value.

Thinking he'd pocketed the best present of the season for Else, the safeguarding of the pictures, while securing a new and permanent home for them at Covent Garden, he went to see her again. Maybe for the last time. He faced head on that they couldn't make the final pact. Nine-tenths in common, so many years locked in to an identical process, missing each other by a hair's breadth, but still they couldn't make it work. He didn't want to go on in enmity, however, or harbouring this much resentment. He ought to reinstate friendship, or at least contact, and so he set out semi-hopefully early on Sunday morning.

Clive set out too, on the shorter journey down the hill. He thought he hadn't seen Else around for a day or two, but left it, knowing she'd be immersed in her double portrait, and then he realized, when the chimney wasn't smoking from the stove, that she must have gone away to London or gone skiing without telling them. When he had his first free time, after church on Sunday, he went along the lane to check that the house was securely barred. Burglars were becoming more adventurous up the motorway, and one or two empty properties had been looted.

The house wasn't locked. The door stood on the latch and for some minutes he went about the rooms calling for her, confirming that the fire was really cold, before he thought about the studio and headed down the garden in search of her.

It was on the returning path that Morgan spotted him, cutting up the hill white-faced. He wound down the car window and called him over. Clive leant on the sill, cold perspiration lying in a ring under his winter hat. 'I think you should turn round. You don't want to go down there.'

'What's the matter?'

'I'll have to telephone from my house. Will you come with me?'

'No. I'm going on down. I'll come up to the farm when I've seen Else.'

The farmer debated. A swift choice. He opened the door and got into the passenger seat. When they drew inside the shelter of the wall and Morgan turned the engine off, Clive said, 'I've got to prepare you for the worst. Else's dead. I've just been into the studio. I don't want you to go in there alone. I don't want you to go in at all, but I suppose you'll have to do it. See it for yourself.'

Morgan looked at the face of the virtual stranger, a man he saw rarely and in passing, but noticed with exaggerated point the pallor of his skin, a startled rim around the eye, a chipped shirt button, and knew he'd not forget the curve of it in shock, strictly held in place. He didn't know this man, but he was locked into him for good. Straight away he knew what he meant. She'd made another attempt on her own life but successfully this time. He was shocked too, getting out of the vehicle by sheer instinct, walking down the spongy lawn, but angry that she could do such a thing to herself and to him. Nothing was worth that. How could she inflict the sight of her death on whoever had the task of finding her, Clive, Jack Eversley coming up the hill to ask if she'd got heat and light, even one of the Ramage boys carrying eggs? The selfishness of it was a separate pain. He dreaded her disfigurement.

He misprized her for the last time. There had been a senseless and completely avoidable accident. As they came up to the studio, Morgan saw the windows were black with smoke and some of the panes had shattered from intense heat.

'Are you sure you want to?' Clive asked again.

No, he wasn't at all sure, but it was like the formal process of identification by the next of kin, something manhood didn't shirk. They stepped inside together. Else was lying to one side of the room, anybody would have said asleep, virtually unmarked, just curled up and resting. Morgan stepped over and pulled back the cropped hair. It had happened yesterday maybe, or the day before. Quite recently. Instinctively, he took her hand and chaffed it, as if that might start the circulation going again and bring her back.

Looking in more detail round the room, Clive was able to reconstruct what had happened. Working out here alone, too late at night without proper lights, too tired, she'd toppled off her ladder and, in falling, knocked herself out. The paraffin heater was pushed over by her fall, and the fuel spilled out, caught fire, with the flames spreading through the highly inflammable materials of the studio like a reapwind. Turps, thinners, new canvas, stretchers, the lot was tinder to charnel. She must have died from inhaling toxic fumes while unconscious. But, strangely, only one half of the room had burned out. A change of wind direction, a sudden shower had doused the fire. Where she was lying was pristine, nothing touched. The high-hung portrait had been finished, man and wife smiling down at them, complete after six sittings. It was some new piece of work that she'd been stretching up to see.

The farmer watched Morgan in dumb show, as he knelt rubbing the cold and unresponsive hand, chilled with some recollections of his own. The pack running riot in the garden, tearing the doe rabbit limb from limb, the felling of the golden tree, hacking it down to burnable pieces. Shudders went through Clive as he remembered invasions that had felt natural enough at the time, to him natural manifestations of dog and wind, the laws of the countryside which turned into disasters at The Aviary only because the big had been confined inside the little space, and she had taken them badly, as portents. She made them happen too seriously, with the gravitational force of her own fate.

Death wasn't new to either of them but it was always unique. Uniform had given Clive some objectivity. He could subordinate his feelings, even over a good friend blown up needlessly by a landmine, into the practical, however much he screamed inside. He knew he'd suffer in delay. Morgan had enough preparation too, his grandfather, two parents and a son. Sufficient for one adult life. With each of them the regrets had been long-term and focused on a repetitive theme, Why wasn't I a better son, why wasn't I a better father? With Else, the regrets and self-recrimination for both of them set in at once. Why did I go away? Why did I leave it so long? On Friday night, I could have walked in here and saved her. He'd had the warnings about her self-neglect, but not acted on them. The sorrow wormed away at him.

'You couldn't help it, you know,' said Clive, reading the stun. He made his own accusations. When he'd finished his wiring at the farm, he'd offered to electrify Else's studio. There would have been no need for lamp, or candles or antiquated paraffin heaters then. Distracted by his livestock, he just hadn't put it in hand. 'Let's go.' He held the other man's shoulder and propelled him away.

Although its spaciousness was hardly called for, Jack Eversley offered the use of his house, close to Odham crossroads and adjacent to the church. The minister had doubts about the form of the service he should use, not knowing her denomination. Was she Church of England? Was she anything? As simple as you can make it, said Morgan, the plainer hymns.

They came. Mostly men, heads bared and numbed into a non-communicative coma. Unlike Michael's funeral, it was disorganized, long spells of waiting passed uncertainly in cold corners. There was that embarrassed hush when people couldn't speak without sounding either forced or irreverent.

It was an odd collection. She'd attracted odd people. The villagers came, the faces looming out of old pictures and half-familiar; the Ramages brought their boys, who stood candle-pale and very stiff. They're too young for this, thought Morgan, not knowing that the boys had insisted on coming. Well, she'd have been pleased to see them after all.

They sang 'All things bright and beautiful', which was more childish than plain, and more childish than he'd have wanted. He tried to sideline such distractions to focus on the cross which she hadn't believed in, and the church building which she had. This wasn't Binham Priory, the music wasn't Bartók, but he had those memories put by. He felt he wasn't much of a chief mourner, a man who'd walked out on her time and again. Now he reduced the question he had used to reprove himself before, until it became simply, Why wasn't I good?

The colleagues came. Nick without Harriet. Boris without Marise. Else made those separations. Boris, a pew away, dark-raincoated with a belt, looked a man within himself. But he was heaving with the palpable knowledge that the journey he was launching himself on in the New Year was futile. There was nobody waiting for him. He carried Else's last letter in his inside pocket, as a sharp reminder of how he'd cast her off. What can I do? he thought. Nothing. The spark has gone and the rest I will complete, but with an infinite sense of labour. He squeaked audibly. His body, wrapped in layers, moved against itself and sent out a noise like shrinking rafters.

Max, MacPherson, even Hisslop; every glimpsed face reminded Morgan of the bank of their mutual experience and its pointless waste. A holed life, his and hers, or a patched one with areas disastrously thin even in overlay.

Lorraine walked into a side pew, ever quiet, ever seemly. She'd gone through a good deal of dissuasion about interposing herself, anticipating that the turnout would be ragged, the arrangements weak, neither church nor music in any sense remarkable. Then why expose herself? The same instinct that led her to take those unwanted frames on board, if nobody else came forward. She'd done nothing dishonourable in relation to the dead, and stood by that. She came finally to support Morgan, although when he turned back along the central aisle and saw her stalwart, he broke down completely that she could always be relied on to display the steady decency which he hadn't managed. Neither of them was proof against the raking spasm that shook him, until she caught it too and shook in her own bones, as they revisited their mutual but unshared grief again.

Nick hovered, ready for the off, smoking hurriedly in the churchyard with quick puffs. 'Terribly sorry, I've got to rush. Going on to Norwich. Arts administration job. Wonderful brief. Unlimited scope.' He paused as Morgan turned to go. 'She didn't sign any of those catalogues, did she, by any chance? Pity. Worth a lot more signed.'

Moving away, Morgan didn't blame him. The process of salvage had started, which was good, and he himself had had a parallel thought quite early on, grateful that the pictures in their storage crates hadn't been delivered back to Odham, to add to the incendiary pile in the studio. The greater part was saved.

He realized already that he had no image of her. Her wish never to be photographed meant there was no recent record. No self-portrait. No album of mementoes.

She'd left him something, however, turning meticulous after her own experience in almost losing the house. She'd made a legal will in Sudbury, dated September, as soon as her personal ownership was assured, leaving him the pictures and the books which he'd loved, the rest to be sold and donated to the hospice for its third scanner. By a quirk, this legacy was deemed to include

Magda Sweetland

Ralph's letters, so part of the copyright of Adrian's book fell to him. In the latter days of the year, he closed his own script and thought he would add a dedication, against the grain of his previous tendency, and put in, To EP, above all else.